I0594182

# HO′KWAT

*An Englishman's Adventures
on the North-West Coast of America*

His Encounters with Whales,
Russians & Wild Indians

A NOVEL BY

# DAVID HOOPER

Epicenter Press

Kenmore, WA

**ᴡᴡᴡ Epicenter Press**

6524 NE 181st St., Suite 2, Kenmore, WA 98028

Epicenter Press is a regional press publishing nonfiction books about the arts, history, environment, and diverse cultures and lifestyles of Alaska and the Pacific Northwest. For more information, visit www.EpicenterPress.com

*Ho'kwat*
Copyright © 2023 by David Hooper

All rights reserved. No part of this publication may be reproduced, stored in a retrieval system, or transmitted in any form by any means, electronic, mechanical, photocopying, recording, or otherwise, without the prior written permission of the publisher. Permission is given for brief excerpts to be published with book reviews in newspaper, magazines, newsletters, catalogs, and online publications.

*Cover design: Scott Book*
*Interior design: Melissa Vail Coffman*

ISBN: 978-1-684920-69-3 (Trade Paperback)
ISBN: 978-1-684920-70-9 (Ebook)

Produced in the United States of America

*For Candace*

# Contents

# 1 | Greetings from Lovely Neah Bay

MEN WITH GUNS USED TO COME here looking for me, but that was ages ago. The coast is clear now. Time to come in from the cold, as we say in the trade. British secret agent John Williams at your service.

Annie, my amanuensis, insists on inserting comments, which I will delete, later, if I remember. She presses her palm to her forehead and mutters. She doesn't like my old laptop, and when she's angry, she writes in italics. *I do not mutter. Don't tell people you were a secret agent. They think you have old-timers'.* She wishes I'd forget about writing my memoir just as I do everything else, but she knows I really was a secret agent, back in the day, starting on the day in 1806 (sorry, I know this is confusing. Please bear with me) when my chum in the Admiralty put me on a Dutch merchantman bound for New York with orders to sink the *Emily*, an elderly trade brig owned by John Jacob Astor, the American fur tycoon. The Admiralty believed *Emily* was loading cargo for a voyage around the Horn to the Columbia River, where Astor intended to build a fort to control the Pacific fur trade. England had similar plans and would have waylaid *Emily* with a swift frigate, but the Royal Navy was busy with Napoleon. I was on the outs with the Navy (spot of bother about cowardice under fire), but my friend said this would put me right again.

"Bit of a rush, old boy. *Emily's* due to sail on Christmas Day. Tons of gunpowder aboard, we're told. You know about powder

& fuses. Blow her up in harbour and come home for your reward. Otherwise, get aboard somehow and sink her at sea. If you can't escape without compromising the mission, go down with the ship. Chin above the waves, think of England, that sort of thing. *Emily* must not reach her destination. And don't get caught. Shouldn't want another tiff with the colonies just now. So. Best of luck, off you go, there's a good chap."

After seven stormy weeks at sea made bearable only by opium *(delete)*, I set foot on the wild docks of Manhattan (85,000 restless natives) just before Christmas, introducing myself as a runaway British naval officer, wound'd in action with scars to prove it, disillusioned with the glories of war, seeking a fresh start in American merchant shipping. I fear'd that *Emily* would've already sailed, but my contact said I'd find her still wallowing at wharfside, loaded to the gunwales, guard'd jealously by a company of uncouth but vigilant plainclothes mercenaries sporting new army muskets. They planned to sail the day after Christmas, all berths were filled, and they weren't letting anyone near the brig. Fortunately, her captain perish'd *(apostrophes irritating and pretentious. Normal punctuation please)* suddenly, an experienced navigator was required and I was available, but Astor's men, hateful of the English, watched me constantly thereafter, leaving me no opportunity to accomplish my mission until we'd reached our destination.

Proof, you ask? If official documents ever recorded *Emily's* passage, Astor erased them just as I erased his ship & all souls aboard *(DELETE)*, save for one. As for me, the Royal Navy's Sick & Wound'd Board says a midshipman named John Williams was released from duty after Trafalgar (*Bellerophon*, 74 guns) for unspecified medical reasons, but mine's a common name, and the Admiralty denies knowledge of me or the operation against Astor. Thanks a bunch, mates.

My sojourn with the Russians came about by chance and was not part of my brief. England was friendly with Russia, allies against Napoleon, but Tsar Alexander, who already had several small Alaskan fur colonies, also wanted posts at the Columbia River and on the northern California coast, and he hadn't discussed his plans with King George. I discover'd the Russians' intentions when I reached their fort on Sitka Sound, and I sabotaged the Tsar's plans just as I had Astor's, for I was at the helm of the Russian ship that wreck'd just down the coast from here in 1808, carrying Russians intent on colonizing America.

For that, I have evidence. I am mentioned in a Russian account of this voyage published in 1822, and an English translation may be found in *The Wreck of the Sv. Nikolai*, by Kenneth N. Owens and Alton S. Donnelly, 1985. However, the Russian version of events, a Tsarist whitewash of the survivors' accounts, fails to mention such details as the massacre of the Quileutes at the above shipwreck (the Tsar considered himself a benefactor of indigenous peoples), but I was an eyewitness, and I say the Russian version is Propaganda wrongfully labeled History. My memoir is the Truth. *Hysterical laughter in background.*

Codswallop, you're thinking. If I was telling the truth, I would have died a long time ago. So it would seem. Yet, here I am, alive & well *(delete annoying ampersands. When are you going to explain how you lived so long?)*, sitting by the sea with darling Annie, whose father has given her the day off from the family fishing boat, at the beach where we stash the Tsar's silver *(Delete silver. Awkward sentence)*, where she was born and her mother died, where we tell stories and wait for the whales. I am, yes, old, but Annie helps me remember. *Remember where you left hearing aid. Title this "Introduction" so people can skip over it.*

# 2 | Columbia River, July the Fourth, 1807

I REMEMBER THAT WHALES FLEW FROM THE SEA AT DAWN, dancing on wing'd tails. They blew stinky clouds at *Emily* and with their great snouts they nudged us toward the river's mouth. *OK better. Delete boring/confusing Introduction and start with this.*

Astor's mercenaries cheer'd the whales, wanting women & solid ground, but we required a strong westerly to push us into the river, not just vagarious & vicissitudinous breezes, so *Emily* sulk'd in doldrums with both masts bare of sail, creaking & groaning, as tired of the sea as we. She'd earn'd the right to grumble. She'd rounded Cape Horn in weather that would have sunk a swifter sister, and I'd grown fond of her deep copper-plated keel and the ponderous tonnage in her belly, a ballast of iron cannons and ten-pound balls. She'd stood up to wind & waves, but if her hull was breach'd by rock or cannonball she'd sink fast. Atop the ordnance lay a protective cocoon of crates (tools, cheap jewelry), food barrels (beans & hardtack, what was left of it), all packed tight around our precious core: ten tons of gunpowder, more than many men o' war carried into battle.

Astor wanted big guns for his fort, but not to shoot at the Indians. Astor liked the Indians. He gave them whisky & muskets, they gave him fur, and they made him the richest man in the world. No, the cannons were for the British. Astor knew England had got wind of his plan, and fear'd his fort would fall to Royal marines. They sent me instead.

*Emily* had cannons in her belly, but none mounted on deck, the better to appear an innocent merchantman, and save for our muskets we were defenseless. We were a bit north to worry about Spanish frigates, but we anxiously scanned the horizon nonetheless and prayed we wouldn't be preyed upon.

For a week we'd loiter'd on fair Columbia's doorstep, nervous suitors seeking favour but afraid to touch, hoping America might awake from her foggy slumbers and yield us entry to her most notorious portal. We glimpsed gentle green breasts behind wispy veils, but we couldn't see the mouth, just fog, and after a brief flirt we'd lose our nerve and run back to the sheltering sea.

The sea has many voices *(You can't steal quotes and pretend they're yours. Delete or cite reference)*, but the river remained demure. We could sense it, felt drawn to it like iron to magnet. We were children of the earth, returning to womb, seeking sanctuary, but the price of safety might be death.

America's siren call was soft but sobering: unseen waves crashed in fog on rough coast, booming like muffled drums. We could hear & smell her. Some coasts greet the arriving mariner with a whiff of new-mown hay before revealing seaside pastures, and sailors say that long before they glimpse Oahu's landmark volcano, the trade winds carry the scent of rotting fruit & wanton women. The Columbia River smelled fishy, and this morning she was flushing herself, staining the sea brown. Red, our colour'd boatswain, tied his tin cup to a line, dipped, sipped, and spat.

His report: "Ain't so salty now. Tasting dirty."

He listened fretfully to the booming surf, cupping a ruby-studded ear, judging the distance to destruction. We nipped from his flask as we harken'd to the pounding death knell, whisky & drizzle dribbling down our chins. Goosebumps blossom'd.

At noon, I read a pale sun with my sextant: forty-six degrees & perhaps fifteen minutes north latitude, give or take. The accuracy of my reading might have been affected by the rolling quarterdeck, the obscure horizon and Red's whisky, but if the charts my countryman George Vancouver had drawn in 1792 were to be believed, the river was nigh. *"Nigh"? This is America, Your Grace. Speak English.*

Its mouth was a mythical monster awaiting prey. White men had no settlements on the Columbia, and no one knew how many fur-trade ships had been lost trying to enter. The river promised riches to traders who survived their arrival, but those who could describe the maelstrom at the mouth remained silent on orders of their employers. Astor's orders were to build Fort Astoria or die trying.

We peer'd through drifting mist for a glimpse of our landmark, a headland overlooking the north side of the mouth, a forested promontory several hundred feet high named Cape Disappointment by John Meares, an English fur trader, twenty years ago.

Red, a wary query: "Why he disappointed?"

"Couldn't find the mouth. Spanish saw it in '75, or said they did, but they couldn't enter. An American named Gray claimed he was first, in '92. Few have done it since. 'Tis a bottleneck, half-a-mile wide, hidden sand bars. Bear to the north side, they say, come in under the cliffs. July's said to be the strongest outflow, so we'll have to hit the tide just right, pray for a good wind aft."

I do not pray. I fear that God might hear and come looking for me. Red prayed fervently, enough for us both, and his whisky numb'd my fear, but I fancied a wee puff of opium. One reclines on one's side to smoke, and British naval officers may not lie down on deck, and belowdecks was a descent into hell.

Indeed, sulfurous smoke had been drifting up from the hatches all morning. Astor's men were fashioning fine-grain musket powder into miniature rockets, and the waves' distant booms were punctuated by small nearby explosions from these "firecrackers" being tossed about or mischievously inserted into the bodily orifices of the somnolent. My order, to the effect that all such devices must be surrender'd, as they presented a threat to our safety, was met with jeers, and was not supported by Mr. Peabody, the appointed commander of the future Fort Astoria. Our employer had forbade tampering with the munitions, but Peabody, under pressure, had authorized the release of musket powder in recognition of the holiday. Firecrackers were necessary to the occasion, he informed me, that being the twenty-first anniversary of the colonies' impetuous leap from the Empire's maternal embrace. Suffice to note that

Americans had so far proved inept at both independence & gunpowder, squabbling amongst themselves when allowed the former, blowing off their fingers if provided the latter.

No matter: the three dozen souls aboard, both mercenaries and a dozen alleged sailors, would soon be relieved of their misery. 'Til then they would drink whisky, quarrel, and hibernate in embryonic hammocks. Diseases of the bowel wreak'd havoc, sanitation was a distant memory, and our water barrels were almost empty. We'd stayed well off California, fearing the frigates, afraid to send the boat ashore for water lest it be captured by Spanish cavalry, but in recent days we'd had tantalizing glimpses of sparkling creeks pouring from cedar forests. Peabody had called for volunteer oarsmen to brave the surf, with no response.

We did have plenty of food. We'd consumed the voyage's rations and started in on Fort Astoria's first-year provisions, which were intended to last until a supply ship arrived the following summer. If a deficit occurred, the mercenaries planned to hunt & fish. Indeed, even as our larders shrank, the ship's company grew pudgy.

Hearing that we would try for the mouth again, Astor's men swarm'd up from their netherworld nest like fat squirming larvae, crowding about the deck. Their fragrance followed.

Red fanned his nose: "Be back in jail, had my druthers. Food's better, more room, and there ain't as much chance of drowning." *You stole that. Cite reference.*

"True," I said. "But look, nobody's trying to escape. Sure sign of a happy ship."

ACTUALLY, WE'D BEEN ON THE VERGE OF MUTINY FOR MONTHS, ever since Astor's men had learned that, due to a late start, we would not be stopping by the tropical paradise of Oahu as had been their understanding, but would, after rounding the Horn, instead proceed directly to the Columbia River. Violence threaten'd off Patagonia as we cruised north past a backdrop of glacier'd Andean crags. The mercenaries said I would swim for shore unless I agreed to set a new course for Oahu, and I was forced to place my hand upon my sword.

Peabody was not so fortunate. His men confiscated his sword and dangled him over the rail by his heels until he announced that we carried a hidden chest containing a thousand silver souvenir coins, funds Astor had entrusted to us for securing waterfront property. Pandemonium ensued.

Eventually the mercenaries consented to forego the Sandwich Islands visit and continue instead to the Columbia River as ordered, provided that Astor's treasure would not be squander'd on the natives there, but rather be distributed amongst themselves, that they might thereby acquire female companionship, that commodity having been wrongfully denied, and that the fort's site might instead be secured through direct acquisition, albeit in a dignified manner.

While the mercenaries wouldn't part with their newfound booty, neither could they distribute the coins satisfactorily amongst themselves, thereby falling into dispute. Factions emerged & splinter'd, each group advocating a different formula for dividing the loot. War veterans demanded that wounds count extra, and thus questions were raised, flesh exposed, scars display'd, honours challenged, and duels conducted, with the losers consuming vast quantities of medical supplies. The colour'd contingent (Red & five others all told, sailors & mercenaries combined, runaway slaves & freeborn blacks) argued for equal shares, thereby provoking emotional discussion on the subtle nuances of the Declaration of Independence's "all Men" phrase, at which point this group withdrew sullenly to the forecastle, where a split occurred even in the black caucus. I queried Red, to no avail. Shouts of "Uncle Tom" rose from the open hatch, references, I assumed, to President Thomas Jefferson's colour'd progeny. Meanwhile, the Fair & Square Distribution Committee conducted a fractious grievance-resolution meeting in the ship's mess, a term applicable both to our dining area and general conditions below decks. Red & I gazed pensively toward America.

The wind was shifting to the southwest.

A plaintive voice: "Well, Mr. Williams?"

From the companionway hatch a pale skull protruded, beady eyes squinting through thick spectacles. 'Twas (*'Twas? Really?*) my counterpart Mr. Peabody, the scion of a prominent Boston family; like me, dishonourable but unspecified circumstance had brought this gaunt scrooge to Astor's employ. He reached the rolling quarterdeck, his cadaverous figure clad in a soiled colonial army overcoat from which the shoulder epaulets had been ripped by an angry hand. He stumbled to the rail, where he launch'd partially-digested oatmeal into the wind, losing his tricorner in the process. His men had not returned his sword.

Mine remains mine, and it's a beauty: forty inches from stem to stern, ivory grip, gold-plated hilt. Just like Nelson's. *(Who?)* Slender & sharp. Slides right through a man's chest. *Psycho killer, qu'est-ce que c'est?*

"Water's brownish," I said. "Leaves & twigs. We think we're off the mouth. The tide's behind us, and the wind is finally coming around."

Red rolled his eyes dramatically: "Big mother of a river 'round here somewheres, Massa Peabody." *Nigh, Red. The river is nigh.*

Peabody wiped his mouth with his coat sleeve: "Hurry up and find it if you please. We must disembark from this wretched vessel soon, or I shall no longer be able to control the men."

Onlookers guffaw'd. Peabody, flushed, fists on hips: "This is the Fourth, captain, which, for Americans, captain, is a historic occasion. Might I suggest, captain, that today might be an auspicious . . ."

A jovial musketeer fired his weapon into the rigging, nicking a yardarm. Peabody jumped. The shooter lurch'd across the deck to offer me his bottle: "Happy Fourth, limey. Here's to our new fort or trading post or whatever. God save King Astor. Let's get this over with. Ain't skeered, are ye?"

Indeed, I was constantly skeer'd, but I adopted a confident air: "Red, if the wind continues to improve, we shall try again today."

The rabble clamour'd: "Hooray! Fort Fourth!"

From the forward hatch, a rocket's red glare. A firecracker burst in the air, terrifying a flock of tuft'd puffins who'd been loitering off our starboard bow, and it died sizzling in the swells, which were now folding against their forward slopes before a west-southwest wind blowing ten to fifteen knots.

Our deck watch, six weary tars, huddled like shivering puppies under a shroud'd jib. Red roust'd them and sent them aloft to unfurl all sail; *Emily* would need her best speed against the river's current. I ordered hatches batten'd, informing those on deck that we were about to experience some turbulence.

"Best go below," I said. "If you fall overboard, don't expect rescue. If the ship should come to grief, hang on, for she may float long enough for the waves to push us ashore."

Most disappeared down the hatches, with a few volunteering to assist the deck watch. Enthusiasm for Fort Fourth ebb'd, but our following sea and westerly breeze held firm. *Emily* made five knots into dense fog with good humour. A whale led us, tail wagging.

The maintop watch pointed: "A cliff!"

There: a glimpse of black precipice towering o'er crashing breakers, of wind-blast'd evergreens wreath'd in swirling diaphanous vapours. I took a compass bearing: due east. We were here. Red gulped from the flask. We plowed on through increasingly tumultuous seas, feeling now the river's force against us.

The fog thinned. We froze. Before us rose a green wall of water. The briny tide and the still-unseen river crash'd against each other over a submerged sandbar, rising to create a white-crested ridge high as a church steeple. *Emily* shudder'd & groan'd.

Peabody screamed and threw his skeletal frame against the helm, knocking Red off-balance. Our stern swung through the wind with the sails flopping, leaving us becalm'd in a deep green canyon. Red & I separated Peabody from the helm and endeavour'd to bring the rudder amidships. Green sea collapsed thund'rously on the deck, ripping away the starboard rail. At least one man overboard. Men hugged the rails & masts. *Emily's* heavy bottom saved us from capsizing, but the deck was flooded, the mangled rail under water. Sea filled our boots. Off to port, a man flounder'd, waving his cap.

A gust, and our canvas strain'd at its tethers. We gathered momentum, crest'd, plunged into another green abyss. A soft thump. The brig trembled. We'd hit bottom. Was the hull breach'd?

Then up, up, high into fog. Peabody curl'd around the binnacle-post, mumbling, palms pressed.

Red, a report: "Rudder feels funny."

Our wind faded just when we needed it most. Another wave bore down on us. The canvas hung limp. The rudder had been damaged in its encounter with the bottom, yet still seemed intact & operable.

A gust, full sail again. The bowsprits disappeared into the wave. The brig rolled, fought for her balance. We braced for the next wave.

No more waves. A strong current pressed against us, trying to push us back to sea, but a promising breeze aft filled our sails and blew the fog away. Batter'd & soak'd, we stared at the black cliffs of Cape Disappointment looming off to port. Seabirds & sea lions stared at us. A tranquil inner bay, four miles wide, beckon'd. A white-capped volcano, close by to the north. Another on the southern shore, cloudy, distant.

Smoke plumes rose from the forest.

A cheer. Hatches & bottles, unbatten'd. Boots, drain'd. Heads, count'd.

A conscientious soldier spoke up: "Should we send the boat back out, to look for . . .?"

I say: "Quite so. Volunteers?"

The crew declined: "Pockets full of souvenir coins, rest their souls. Straight to the bottom."

The wind held steady aft and gave us purchase against the river's current. We passed beneath the cliffs and crossed commodious Baker's Bay, named after the Englishman who, 'twas (*in this country we say "it was"*) rumour'd, had actually entered the river shortly before Captain Robert Gray, the American trader given credit for the premier arrival. On the fogbound north shore, the longhouses of the Chinook village began to emerge, the realm of a peaceful (at last report) chieftain named Comcomly.

The bow watch pointed: "Is that a ship?"

A league up the river, just off the village, a bare-mast'd brig lay at anchor.

Peabody peer'd through his telescope: "American. *Guatimozin.* Lyman Company. Sailed from Boston spring of '06, memory serves. They see us. They're on deck, roasting meat. Deer. Dear me. Native women. In a state of, ahem, nature."

Scuffles. A clamour for a look through the glass. The crew demanded that we anchor near the Bostonians. Peabody rejected that proposal.

"We'll cross the river without delay," he said. "The *Guatimozin's* obviously abandoned herself to sin and depravity. No point in inviting mishap. The fort comes first."

An aggrieved moan from his men. Aromas of sizzling venison escaped from the *Guatimozin's* deck, as did a dozen copper-skinned Loreleis who, when they saw the glint of our souvenir coins, donned cotton frocks, departed the Boston ship and set off in pursuit of us, in canoes.

The *Guatimozin's* capstans creak'd. She was weighing anchor. Her crew gestured rudely, but they were leery of us, and their comments weren't loud enough to reach our ears. We would forego the customary greetings and exchange of news required by maritime protocol. Our lads jeer'd. Caught by the river, the *Guatimozin* drifted sullenly oceanward, trailing venison smoke.

We changed course, setting sail for the south bank, cutting at an angle into the river's flow. Red struggled with our damaged rudder.

"We'll careen her and fix it," I said. "First chance we get."

The Chinook village, three dozen longhouses, fell away in our lee. A canoe came abeam. A bent & wrinkled crone stood astern, shrieking commands at a crew of female paddlers in prim dresses. This would be the infamous Bawd and her retinue of slave girls. Enticed by our coins, the Bawd chose to hasten in our wake, a decision she would regret, 'ere the day was o'er. *Before the day was over please.*

A PRETTY POINT BECKON'D ON THE SOUTH BANK, a protuberance Astor favour'd as the future site of Fort Astoria. It embraced a tranquil forest'd bay offering a tidal harbour ten miles upriver from the mouth wherein a dozen ships might swing on their anchors under the protection of Astor's cannons.

Glossy seals blinked brown eyes. Scents of seaweed, mudflats, evergreen forest.

No forts, no flags. Native longhouses. Nobody here but the natives.

The Bawd's canoe beat us across. More canoes came off the beach, bearing more rouge-cheeked females, and as we anchor'd a flock of watercraft gathered on the starboard beam. The occupants climbed our cargo net and huddled on deck apprehensively. Pushing & shoving amongst Astor's men.

The Bawd squint'd at a souvenir coin: "Not so fast. Drop pants first."

A soldier, suspicious: "Ye speaks good English, crone."

"No such thing as good English," quoth The Bawd. "Yankee bad too. Scrub-a-dub. Got clean girls here."

The men grumbled. The Bawd insisted, also demanding that we smoke out the reeking hold. Dutifully we prepared pine-tar torches and our blacksmith warmed a barrel of green water on his forge. A lass with 'J. Bowman' tattoo'd on her shoulder offered to soap a sergeant. Her sisters continued to huddle. The Bawd haggled in a screechy tone.

Red nudged me: "Canoe coming alongside. Looks like a chief."

A barefoot but dignified elder with long white hair heaved himself over the shatter'd rail. He wore a fur robe and satin gentleman's breeches owned previously, I would later learn, by Meriwether Lewis of the Lewis & Clark expedition. His ascent of our net caused him to perspire profusely, raising havoc with the hastily-applied red & black cosmetics adorning his visage. His forehead was flattened in the tradition of the coastal nobility, one eye was gone, and a brass ring pierced his nose.

An attendant cloak'd in elk-hide thump'd the butt of his spear on the deck, and, addressing us in the trade jargon, announced his patron: "Comcomly of the Chinook, highest-up *tyee* (tribal leader) on the river."

Peabody introduced himself, extended Astor's regards, and gift'd (*not a verb*) the tyee with a souvenir coin, one of the few not confiscated by the ship's company. Concomly studied it with his good eye and seemed impressed. I introduced myself.

The tyee noted my accent: "King George man is tyee of Boston ship? No more enemies?"

Peabody explained: "Me tyee of ship, chief. Williams just make ship go. Him run away from King George. King still bad man. Our first captain, him robbed and stabbed to death right before we sail, no doubt by opium fiends. We need good captain on short notice. Williams best we can do."

A moment of silence for my predecessor, rest his soul. Yes, we may indeed attribute the above skullduggery at least in part to the seductive charms of Lady O, whose vapours kissed the unfortunate captain's lips just prior to his demise, thereby obscuring what remained of his awareness. He'd been drinking in a dockside alehouse on the eve of his departure and, on the promise of a puff of quality opium, had ventured into a back room with a fellow seafarer, an affable young expatriate English officer who shared the captain's hatred of the Royal Navy. The Englishman sport'd an exquisite Chinese lamp & pipe set, one fashioned of brass and trimmed with gold & jade, and the captain hadn't had a taste in months. We hasten to note that he was not "robbed and stabbed to death." He had already emptied his purse in the manner departing mariners are wont to do (scavenged by whores & pickpockets, he'd tossed his last penny to a chorus of ragged waifs singing Christmas carols), was grateful for the drink supplied by the generous new acquaintance who listened so politely to his detailed description of *Emily's* forthcoming secret voyage, and was pierced by a single sword thrust through his heart & lungs, surgically severing several essentials. Thus, thanks to our Mistress of Mercy, the departed departed without undue suffering: a wide-eyed gasp, a throaty gurgle, a hint of bloody spittle on the lips, but nothing more. *You just confessed to murder. Delete.*

Preliminary protocol concluded, I indicated the gulls swirling around the mouth of a small tributary on the bay's wooded southern shore. Lewis & Clark had dubbed it the Netul River, after the predatory shrubs they'd found lining its banks, and the expedition had fortified itself three miles upstream the previous winter to await Astor's supply ship, which mysteriously vanish'd en route. In spring, the Americans had abandoned their fort and returned home overland. Astor wanted a report on the fort's current status. I asked Comcomly if I might visit the site.

Comcomly: "Why? Just pile of rotten logs. Don't fancy Bawd's girls?"

Peabody voiced righteous concern: "Chief, as your Christian benefactor I must express sentiments of disgust and revulsion, that you kidnap innocent girls and cast them into . . ."

The Bawd screamed a curse. We turned to glimpse unauthorized departures from the bath line down the hatches, from which smoke billow'd. Discipline crumbled. Comcomly looked worried, and readily agreed to my request for transport to the site of the abandon'd fort, noting that it lay within the territory of the Clatsops, a friendly tribe. I went below to fetch my gear, finding lewd conduct in progress. Mercenaries & women crowded my tiny cabin, and a breeze wafted torch-smoke through open salt-caked portholes, ruffling the hair of a girl who scrutinized my journal by the dying sunlight, her raven tresses spilling across the pages. I informed her I should like to have my journal returned.

The soldiers laughed: "Let her keep it, Captain Willie. She's the pick o' the litter. Or would you rather snuggle up with your black bo'sun?"

We should not dignify such comments with response. I would have thought the ship's company would first want solid ground under their feet before seeking the company of women, but that proved not to be the case. Cupid *(try "lust", Romeo)* won out, and the list of complicating factors included whisky, souvenir coins, firecrackers and soap-suds. I left my journal in the girl's custody and proceeded forward through the galley, where a swinging lantern eerily lit the lingering torch smoke. Flesh writh'd, moaning, on the plank table. The clink of silver. Threats & scuffles.

I did not tarry. Light-headed from the smoke, I descended to the cargo hold, squeezing between crates & barrels. My lantern illuminated dank recesses. Above, thumping on the overhead planks. Shouts & curses.

The hidden fuse sizzled to life at the lantern's first kiss. A rat scamper'd up my arm. Startled, I spilled lantern oil on my hand.

Flames raced up my sleeve, and the fuse's sputtering flame slither'd off in search of gunpowder.

Time to go.

I scrambled up into the forecastle, stumbling through the galley. The Bawd hobbled by, a smouldering torch held aloft. Cackling, she showed me a handful of soapy silver. Dirty money, launder'd. I plunged my throbbing red hand into a water barrel. Empty. I hurried aft.

The girl was at the cabin door with my journal, black hair flooding down over bare shoulders, and with my good hand I snatch'd the book from her grasp. Mischievously, she held on and pages tore away, took flight in the breeze from the porthole, like birds disappearing into the sunset.

I won the tug o' war, stuffed my journal into my bag, went topside, where lust *(what happened to Cupid?)* & inebriation prevail'd. Firecrackers popped. I hid my throbbing hand in my coat and informed Red that I would disembark with the tyee. With the ship at anchor in our destination's harbour, Peabody was technically in charge, but I didn't ask permission to go ashore.

Red eyed my smoking sleeve and sensed something amiss: "Be dark soon. Ain't safe."

I indicated the Bawd's fumigations billowing from the hatches: "Safer than here, dare say. Back in a flash."

The sun flash'd green as it touched the sea. To the north, the white volcano floated in clouds above forest'd hills, glowing. Shaggy eagles hunted salmon, circling, suspend'd on updrafts.

Our canoe glided under *Emily*'s stern. The brig seemed strange viewed from this perspective, even though she'd been my home for half a year.

Scuffling on the deck above. Drunken guffaws from the cabin. The girl appeared at the portal, framed in tarnish'd brass and her own black tresses. She regarded me with a sad, berry-stained smile.

I sat in the bow, sword & bag stuff'd under the thwarts. The cool ripple of our wake caress'd my throbbing hand. The tyee lounged amidships. His attendant propelled us from the stern. The canoe was a sleek little thing, an eighteen-footer with delicate carvings adorning the polished gunwales.

Large fish, just below the surface. I commented on their size.

Comcomly: "We got salmon that will walk up on shore and kick your dog. Why, I . . ."

I was sinking, plunging into the depths with great force. Body like a rock. Arms & legs weighed tons. Light-head'd. Air gone from my lungs. Dark shapes the size of whales.

The depths were lit softly as though by a cathedral's stained-glass windows. Strings of bubbles like prayer beads. I imagined eerie musical sounds, that I was surrounded by a choir of whales. Far above, the canoe silhouetted against a distant sky. Silver coins appeared, sinking into darkness.

So this be death, I thought. Try not to succumb. Swim to the surface, get back in the canoe. I stroked mightily, but my efforts were for naught. As my descent continued, I sensed something huge nearby. Fleshy cetacean lips pulled away my boots & clothes, and I was caught. Resistance was futile. I remembered stories of dead whales cut open, revealing drown'd sailors inside. I imagined that a large soft mouth slurp'd me in, holding me tight. I was transported down a tunnel of rippling moist tissue. I suffocated, swooning, in an awful stink.

I dream'd, while drowning, of serenity, forgiveness. Of being in a place where all life was one.

With a great blast I was propelled out into the cold depths, set spinning with a flip of a tail. The sunset beckon'd from above. I told myself to go to the light, but I was oddly reluctant, longing for the womb from which I'd been so rudely birth'd. A massive push from below and I was splashing in air, gasping.

Concomly bobbed nearby, dumbfound'd. Above us a cloud of black smoke scudded inland. Wreckage splashed around us, hissing & smoking.

Mission accomplished. I had reduced Astor's ship to debris, just body parts & splinters, the lot floating off to the ocean. What had just happened down below? Hallucinations. Shock of the blast. Oxygen deprivation. Never mind. Now for my triumphant return to England.

The tyee & I threw a leg over opposite sides of the canoe. His slave lay face-down in the bilge, gurgling, a foot-long splinter of white oak protruding from the back of his neck. I was starkers, and covered with foul slime. Concomly, gasping, climbed in, fell back on his posterior, slapped his port-side ear.

"Can't hear nothing," he said. "Where's your clothes? Where's your ship?"

The slave: "Gack?"

I felt the strangest urge to slip below the surface again, to be draw once more into . . .

Comcomly yanked me back into the canoe. He smelled his fingers, wrinkled his nose: "Whale poop?" He wiped his hand on his dying slave and peer'd at me incredulously. Something had changed.

*There is no statute of limitations on murder and you are not wasting my money on attorneys so delete everything about killing people. Also, readers may find tale of whale a little hard to swallow so to speak. Delete please thank you.*

I WALKED THE RIVER'S NORTH BANK BELOW the Chinook village clad only in a fray'd blanket, the tip of my scabbard dragging in mud & seaweed. Bit fogged in. Concuss'd by the explosion, no doubt. Mental mists linger'd like the ancient fogs covering these riverbanks, leaving wisps snagged on storm-tattered cedars. I was caught too, strand'd on strange shores, but I wasn't all there. 'Twas as tho' I'd slept, and dream'd, and couldn't quite awaken.

No matter. I wasn't about to go anywhere. The canoe fleet hauled up below the village represented the only method of transport available, and some were for sale, but I was destitute. They averaged perhaps thirty-five feet from stem to stern, and a few were seagoing fifty-footers. High prows were typically crown'd with a wolf's head, and the hull, carved from a single cedar log, flowed back to a raised sternpost shaped like a whale's tail. Some, expensive imports from Vancouver's Island & Cape Flattery, sport'd oornementation, delicate carvings of animal & bird spirits, as well as glossy white inlaid snail shells. Prospective buyers with trade-slaves in tow toed polish'd hulls.

I hunted & gathered on the beach, fancying myself a modern Crusoe. I skipped stones with ruffians as the ocean's distant roar rose & fell with the wind. I stuck sticks in the muck, gauging the water's rise. Vancouver had noted the tides climbed eight feet up the river's banks and surged upriver for another hundred miles, whilst *(?)* distant storms flood'd the Columbia's tributaries. Vast herds of wild-eyed salmon stampeded upriver against this mighty flow, rushing to mate & die in ancestral spawning streams. My mates informed me that they could walk across the river on the salmons' backs.

Preposterous? No matter. My mind remained altogether disconnected from my situation, yet I wasn't worried. I felt at peace, sanguine. I'd completed my assignment. Assuming safe return to England, my future was assured. After Comcomly directed the village's four remaining slave women to scrub my stinking flesh, I found that my twice-burned hand, though still tender, had almost healed.

How had that happened? How long had I been here? Was I in shock? What was the source of this detachment, this holiday from anxiety & concern?

Scavengers returned bearing but scant salvage: a shatter'd yard-arm, scraps of burned sailcloth. Women dragged the foretopsail up to the village, draping the blacken'd canvas over a rack used for drying salmon.

No survivors of the explosion yet reported, except the Bawd, who'd been blown from the ship but rescued, her hair & clothing burned from her wrinkled flesh. Bright pink and in bad spirits but otherwise unscath'd, she issued a statement from her sickbed to the effect that she'd seen me emerging from the hold just before the explosion, and that I was therefore to blame for her ruination. I suggested to Comcomly that the Bawd's torches might have sparked the blast. *Good idea. Blame it on the old lady. Reasonable doubt.*

He agreed & protected me, and even though my status remained that of a common slave, conditions could have been worse. My apparent change in age fascinated the villagers: as Concomly had noted previously and as a looking glass confirmed, I'd inexplicably aged years in the blink of an eye, thereby lending myself a small degree of celebrity. The Chinook displayed an avid interest in the supernatural, believing that living beings can shift their shapes, be transformed like Proteus into monsters and back again, that man can take on the appearance of a beast, that, for example, the ubiquitous raven can change itself into a human scalawag. Apparently shape-shifting was commonplace, but age-shifting, while not unknown, was rare.

I JOINED COMCOMLY IN HIS MEANDERINGS about this village of a thousand souls, taking care to remain a step in his lee as befitted my status. We conversed as best we could, given the constraints of the trade jargon, a polyglot collection of necessary words & phrases drawn from native tongues and European languages, a commercial *linqua franca* employed by both native & white traders. The jargon was called Chinook, after Comcomly's tribe, which, I learned, had played a pivotal role in coastal trade since The First Light.

The Chinook jargon was much simpler than the Chinook tribal language, which contained, for example, a hundred different words for rain, a subject discussed by the Chinook with precision. My hosts could therefore communicate with me as they chose, but they would also discuss me in my presence as though I were but a dog, leaving me to listen for subtle clues in the tone of their voices.

Nonetheless, with my age stabilized, my novelty faded. Fine with me: I preferred to amuse myself at any rate, but Comcomly felt that my time would be better spent carving out his new canoe, which at present was a horizontal cedar log stripped bare of bark, still sticky with sap, forty feet long.

Commonly ordered me to turn to. "Your job is chop out insides," he said, handing me a dull chisel. "Let chips fall where they may. (*Cliché, delete*) Has to be done before daughter's wedding *potlatch*."

He explained that the potlatch was a wealth-sharing rite sponsored by tyees on auspicious occasions for the purpose of lavish gift-giving (furs, slaves, canoes, guns, copper plate, blankets, whale oil) to invited dignitaries from near & afar. It sounded rather like Christmas: the more ostentatious the gifts, the more honour accrued to the generous giver. At potlatches, however, only the host gave. The recipient guests were enrich'd, but also socially diminish'd.

My host acknowledged that he was the most influential tyee on the river, but said he owned only his canoes & slaves (about a dozen of each), his summer house here on the river and a winter lodge inland. He dedicated all trading profits to the maintenance of a strategic stockpile of potlatch gifts, an arsenal he employed at leisure. Neighboring tyees trembled at the approach of Comcomly's messengers, fearing invitations to potlatches that would inflict upon them wealth & disgrace.

Boys dragged ashore a shatter'd plank from *Emily's* hull. Comcomly laughed. "First time we see a ship, we say, 'Look at that. *Illahee* (house) that floats. Big medicine.' But, by and by, we find out sailors are men like us, and ships are wood, like canoes."

I say: "Quite. So when's the next trade ship due?"

"Maybe no ship until spring."

I groan'd. I couldn't bear a winter here.

Comcomly noted my distress. "I better send word to Yutramaki," he said, noting that Yutramaki was a famous Cape Flattery tyee as well as a shaman, a medicine man. Like me, the tyee noted, he experienced sudden changes in his age.

Also, he said, "Yutramaki is part white. Speaks English good as me. Learned from traders. Trader shot him in the leg once, but he still fancies fishbellies. He helped that young Englishman find a way home, fellow named Jewitt. You too maybe. 'Til then, stay on this side of river. Clatsops angry. Lewis & Clark steal their canoe. Thomas Jefferson sends souvenir coins, but now silver sleeps with salmon. Better you get into woodworking."

My protests were to no avail. I pounded on the log until Comcomly departed, then wandered down to the riverbank and found another log, one upon which I could rest my weary head. When I awoke, eventide had drawn nigh. *Just like the river.* Hunger bade me seek hospitality.

Fragrant smoke drifted from the tiers of longhouses, which were, like the canoes, of a type: pitch'd roofs & wide eaves, all fashion'd from thick planks split from the massive cedars which infest'd the hillsides. The domiciles varied in length, as they'd been supplemented at both ends as the resident families had likewise extended themselves. *Is this a textbook? Pep it up, geezer.*

There was an extended line for dinner at Comcomly's, fifty hungry souls. The cooks, all men, served the upper crust an entrée of boiled seal flippers. When they'd finished, the household's commoners, the village's majority, dug in. Finally, a dozen slaves snatched up greasy wooden bowls and queued. I served myself salmon and a *wappato* root, a small potato. From a woven basket I obtained a handful of ripe red berries. Sticky yellow whale oil served as a condiment. The flavour & odor were loathsome. The Chinook considered it a delicacy.

They squatted while they ate. I sat on my rump, dining without benefit of utensil. I'd scarcely wiped my chin when Story-Hour began, with various uncles singing mythic tales. Children cluster'd at their knees, transfix'd. A slave at my elbow translated: once upon a time, a giant bird appeared from a thundercloud, with bolts of lightning shooting from its claws as it snatched up and flew away with a whale as big as this house. A chorus added harmonious vocals at appropriate intervals, and a drummer beat a rhythm with whalebones on a hollow log, pounding ominously when the bird-monster swoop'd.

Eventually, the household turned in. I curled up with the slaves near the oval doorway, well beyond the fire's fading warmth. If predators intruded, they would stumble on us before they reached our masters. Holding a stone whale-oil lamp aloft, Comcomly retired with his five wives to his sleeping-platform in a far corner, to berths of fragrant cedar, bearskins, and English wool. Other branches of the family cluster'd in assigned corners. I winked at nubile lasses with sloping foreheads (as previously noted, the tyees flatten their children's heads in infancy with cradleboards, much as Chinese nobles bind their daughters' feet), but was ignored. Nobody wanted to talk to the age-shifting stranger. I gripped my meager blanket about my shoulders, my bed a smooth earthen floor ruled by voracious fleas. A tag on my blanket's hem flicker'd in the fireglow. Made in England. When I awoke, there'd be tea & crumpets.

I awoke in the night. Not a soul stirred. Even the fleas slept, satiated. Gentle snoring echoed in the dark interiour. Orange embers popped.

As I drift'd off I imagined I heard the eerie moan of a whale's song. Something huge swam past the entrance. An eye appeared and moved on. A girl swam through the door, the lass from the ship, unharmed, her hair sweeping in waves of black liquid. She took me by my tender hand and we drifted out into the moonlight. Whales frolick'd above us, and Astor's men danced with slave girls.

AT FIRST LIGHT, A STIR IN THE VILLAGE. After a fortnight of moist & foggy mornings, a clear dawn swept over the longhouses, bearing rumours of a ship.

Comcomly's slave prodded me awake: "Lookouts say ship tries to enter the river, but becomes afraid, runs back to the ocean. Tyee says we go to top of *Kah-eese* (Cape Disappointment) and look."

The river slept under foggy blankets. I strapped on my sword, pocket'd my journal, and joined Comcomly at riverside; the current carried our canoe seaward and we soon beach'd below the cape, ascending a path to the summit. The sea froth'd & churn'd below the cliffs, with freshwater's brave phalanxes rushing out upon a vast gray battlefield to oppose the invading army of the brine. We were ruffled by a breeze from seaward, but it failed to stir the sedentary fog. No ships in sight. I seated myself on a rock, opened my journal, and, with the aid of my pocket-compass, continued my cartographical depiction of the river's booming embrace with the sea.

I queried my host on the local geography: "Help me get my bearings, tyee. This snowy peak, that's the mountain Vancouver named St. Helens?"

"Already has name: Loowit. Don't make her angry or she blows her top. Last time was five summers ago, before Meriwether comes. The ground shakes, Loowit roars, throws dark clouds into sky. Day becomes night. Loowit is *sollecks* (angry), ever since Wyeast hits Pahto."

Comcomly indicated a white hump rising behind Loowit, a landmark described by Clark as "a Sugar lofe." Pahto, the tyee called it. He pointed southeast, explaining that Pahto's brother Wyeast was hiding across the river in the clouds, a reference, no doubt, to the volcano Vancouver dubbed Mt. Hood, after a Royal Navy chum.

"Pahto and Wyeast are the original twin peaks, both tall and handsome, but they are both hot for pretty Loowit, and they fight all the time. So Loowit chooses Pahto to be her sweetie, because he lives close by."

Dramatically, the tyee shook his fists in the air: "Wyeast is jealous, goes on the war path, hits Pahto so hard his head gets flat. Makes the Great Spirit sad, so he creates a river to flow between Pahto and Wyeast, so they don't fight no more. Pahto is stupid from getting hit on the head, and poor Loowit is stuck with him."

"A charming tale, tyee; I shall note it in my journal. Our scientists claim that a volcano's smoke & fire come from coal burning inside the earth, but the religious insist it's Lucifer's brimstone, that volcanoes are portals to the nether . . ."

The tyee's attendant exclaimed, pointing seaward. I focus'd my telescope.

A little brig or schooner, all sail up, headed for the mouth. Sleek, two masts, distinctive English lines. She sport'd a schooner rig, headsails & gaff sails set fore & aft lengthwise, enabling her to sail into the wind much better than a square-rigged brig, better for island-hopping or coastal waters. The sails were carelessly trimmed. Not British, obviously.

Enshroud'd in fog, the ship plunged ahead bravely just as *Emily* had. A sandbar lurk'd, but she jibed and set her sails for a desperate reach toward the cliffs beneath us, only to be trapped in a whirlpool created by the opposing currents. She spun like a child's toy. We feared she was lost, but at the last moment her sails filled and she was free, slipping into the river's mouth. Wisps of music reach'd our ears, the wail of a fiddle.

The servant squint'd: "Strange flag, master. Thunderbird with two heads."

Russians. From the little ship's mizzen, Tsar Alexander's double-headed eagle spread its proud wings across an undulating tricolour of red, green, and white. We descend'd from the summit, watching our visitor maneuver inside the mouth in vagarious breezes, narrowly avoiding another sand bar. The crew, aloft in the rigging, struggled to gather their sails like laundry maids with storm-blown clotheslines.

What were Russians doing here? My mind raced as we hurried down the path to the canoe. Were they traders, seeking fur? When they depart, where might they be bound?

THE RUSSIANS' ANCHOR DROPPED AS WE APPROACH'D. She was about 170 tons, sixty feet at the waterline, teak hull, soaring bowsprits, graceful lines. Built by Englishmen, wager anything. The helmsman, bulky & beard'd, hurled threats into the rigging, then turned to view our approach. A crew of twenty crowded to the rail, whites, and copper-hued natives.

The helmsman responded to my greeting with a serviceable mixture of English & Chinook. "Sysoi Slobodchikov," he said, "elected by my heroic crew to be supervisor of this, the Tsar's ship *Tamana*. We voyage for a year and now we return to New Archangel, our fort on Sitka Sound, if the saints are merciful."

"This is Comcomly," I said. "The eminent tyee. I'm John Williams, a strand'd Englishman."

Slobodchikov's furry brows crowded together: "Your ship, she leaves you behind?"

Comcomly snort'd. I nodded. "More or less. *Tamana*? Is that Russian?"

"Language of Oahu. Means 'shipbuilder.' Made there by an Englishman. One hundred and fifty pelts we trade for her down in California, after we argue with the thieves from Boston. Our beloved leader Aleksandr Baranov sends us with the Bostons to California to hunt the sea otter. We learn to speak the English, but still they cheat us, so, we depart from the Boston ship, we buy this one, and we sail to Oahu, where we cavort and are asked to leave. Now we return to our proud fort New Archangel, on Sitka

Sound, or in that direction, perhaps. When we return, God willing, Baranov bestows upon our ship the good Russian name. Speaking of which, what is the name of this river?"

Comcomly stood in the canoe, spreading his arms wide: "Behold, *Nch'i-Wana*, the Great River. Also known as *Yakaitl-Wimahl*. Brits and Bostons call it Columbia. You first Russians come here."

From the deck, a roar of jubilation: "Praise the saints."

Slobodchikov: "Now we celebrate. Join us, new friends."

Comcomly: "Ugh."

I translated: "The tyee expresses regrets. I'll come aboard, though. You're bound for Sitka? Do trade ships visit there?"

Slobodchikov nodded: "Too much they visit. English, Americans. They trade guns and whisky to the *kolosh* (native Americans), then they take our fur to China and become wealthy. Come aboard. We welcome you to our voyage. First we go ashore for water and to bury this beautiful plaque in a secret location, for Mother Russia, to prove that we are here. See? It says, 'This Land is Property of the Tsar.'"

Comcomly: "Here, hand it down. I will hide it for you."

Slobodchikov: "Are you sure? Careful. Heavy. Solid brass."

Comcomly assured him and departed with the plaque, leaving me to climb the Russians' cargo net in my blanket, bag & sword swinging. A boat laden with water barrels set off in search of a creek. My hosts offered a traditional welcoming crust of salted bread, followed by a swig of vodka, a clear, fiery liquor, from a spit-caked jug. Amused by my threadbare blanket, they escorted me below to the dim confines of the reeking hold, where they forced upon me garments that made up for in diversity what they lacked in cleanliness, and I became sartorially indistinguishable from my newfound benefactors. Some crew members with native blood favour'd *kamleias*, hooded rain jackets tailored from the intestines of sea mammals, waterproof'd with grease. The white men sported *rubashkas*, thigh-length linen shirts belted by festive sashes from which knives & pistols protruded rakishly. Baggy pants drooped over sealskin boots. They all smoked pipes stuff'd with twists of wretch'd Circassian tobacco, and their exhalations cloud'd the hold.

THE RUSSIANS CALLED THEMSELVES *PROMYSHLENNIKS*, fur hunters, although they acknowledged that the Aleut & Kodiak crew members did the actual hunting, under Russian supervision. All available space below was filled with suspend'd sea otter pelts and Sandwich Islands pineapples & yams decomposing faster than they could be consumed. Squealing pigs hung suspended amongst the pelts, snouts smeared with yams. Perhaps, I thought, I should wait for another ship. My feet stuck to the deck planks.

A shout from topside: "Girls!"

The Bawd had reluctantly dispatched a canoe bearing her surviving quartet of slave women, who refused to go below. Blue beads, looking-glass mirrors, and the souvenir coins persuaded them to bestow their intimate favours, but only on deck, in plain sight.

The ship's orchestra assembled again, launching into a folk tune. Rested from their earlier performance on the occasion of the crossing of the bar, the musicians were pleased to learn they had been appreciated from atop the cape. They boasted an adolescent fiddler, talented but untrained, a slender lad named Filip with wild black hair and fire in his fingers. Another crewman played a batter'd accordion, another a triangular three-stringed lute they called a *balalaika*. Tambourines jangled.

The Cossacks leaped about, kicking & shouting. The Bawd's crew joined the dancing but found themselves hard-pressed to keep pace. The swivel-cannon blast'd salutes. The shores echo'd. Slobodchikov proposed a toast to the Tsar, causing argument. Fights broke out. A crew member was lost o'er the side, necessitating an emotional rescue and tearful reaffirmations of eternal brotherhood.

As twilight descended, the celebration caught its second wind, gaining renewed vigour. The village snuff'd its fires. Sunset bathed the river in a soft glow. The white volcano turned pink. Comcomly came out in his canoe and complained about the noise.

Slobodchikov apologized: "Sorry. We gather our courage for our voyage. Soon we go." A glance oceanward, a shudder. He clapped his hands and shouted: "All hands, up with the anchors. Soon the tides turn against us. We sail north, my brothers, for home."

The crew grumbled: "We have fallen in love with these kolosh girls. We must vote."

Slobodchikov didn't want a vote. Tugging his beard, he invited Comcomly to come aboard. He proposed a trade: "Your girls for our fur. A healthy girl is worth four sea otter pelts, I am told."

Comcomly, dubious: "Only slave girls we got. Bawd be angry."

Slobodchikov rubbed his palms and indicated the aft swivel-cannon: "How about the girls for our little cannon? Solid brass, like the plaque. Shoot three-pound cannonball. Big boom."

Comcomly scratch'd his scalp: "One girl, maybe. Bawd might trade that little one there for the cannon, couple powder kegs, dozen cannonballs. Take it or leave it."

The crew: "Take it."

The tender'd slave girl grovel'd at Comcomly's toes. A fate worse than death, she sobbed, begging her colleagues to intervene. The females advised Comcomly that the Russians should include some vodka in the bargain.

Comcomly narrow'd his good eye suspiciously: "Vodka?"

Slobodchikov offered a jug. Comcomly sniffed, wiped the jug's mouth on his furs, took a swig, made a face, stagger'd.

"Stars spin about in sky," Comcomly said. "Vodka bad medicine."

Slobodchikov nodded sadly: "Vodka is a thief. You let her in your mouth, she steals your brain."

With the anguish'd slave girl clutching his ankle, Comcomly ordered her sisters ashore, then directed his attendants in the off-loading of the cannon & munitions. Despite conditions aboard, I fancied I had a better chance of finding a friendly ship at Sitka.

Comcomly readily grant'd me my freedom. As he stepped over the side he nodded at my new shipmates and said: "Beware, John Williams. These men are *ho'kwat,* strange wanderers, lost spirits. They have no home. They drift on the wind. Men with no home go crazy."

# 3 | New Archangel

A CRY FROM THE MAINTOP: "I SEE THE FLAG."
The crew cheer'd as a southerly breeze pushed the *Tamana* into Sitka Sound, and the bay enfolded her happy prodigals in a green embrace, a welcome respite from the ocean's gray expanse. A sleeping volcano guard'd the sound's entrance and the sweet scent of spruce & cedar surrounded us. Smooth saltwater, rippled only by a whale's tail, reflected a backdrop of white mountain peaks, pristine teeth. An eagle's swoop, mirror'd.

Though we voyagers had enjoyed moderate weather for the past fortnight and a steady wind aft, we were nonetheless anxious for landfall and a respite from these close quarters. My shipmates had passed the time with vodka & wrestling. I had grown a splendid beard and master'd conversational Russian.

The musicians played a jig. My shipmates danced on the deck, their odyssey nearly ended.

Slobodchikov pointed toward the sound's inner shore: "Behold, Baranov's castle. *Novaya Archangelsk*, New Archangel, the Gibraltar of America."

Through my glass I could see a tiny log fort perch'd atop what the Russians called a *kekur*, a natural tower of rock sixty feet high. Stout timbers enclosed a two-story house with a steep roof. Smaller structures clustered below. The Tsar's flag, tho' worn & faded, provided a trace of colour.

Our ship had no flag. Slobodchikov said we'd approach cautiously, for Baranov fired cannon unpredictably. He gave me the helm and went forward to devote his attention to lurking rocks. Small islands sprouting tatter'd spruce observed our arrival. The crew shouted warnings to me from port & starboard. We furl'd our sails, drifting into the anchorage with just a jib up. The ribs of broken ships lay exposed on the rocky shore, a batter'd trade brig lay at anchor, and a rowboat came off to meet us. A boisterous crowd gathered at a cobblestone bay below the bastion.

Slobodchikov, relieved: "All is well. Our comrades welcome us. We must fire a salute with our small cannon."

The crew: "Where is our small cannon, Sysoi?"

"Also, Sysoi, where is the profit from our long voyage? Rotten fur and pineapples? What do we tell Baranov?"

Slobodchikov, muttering, fired a musket into the air. The mountains echoed. No response from the fort.

"Never do they see this ship," Slobodchikov told me. "Baranov reminds us to beware of our enemies who hate the peaceful men of Russia. He says every shadow hides a killer, every stranger is a spy." *Who did you steal that from?*

Slobodchikov pointed to the battlements, where we could see a bearded man in a black suit watching us through a telescope.

"That is Kuskov, not Baranov. Sometimes Baranov hides, to fool us. If so, you meet Kuskov the moment your feet touch Russian soil. Beware of Kuskov."

We dropped anchor and rowed ashore to a welcoming celebration. Slobodchikov's acquisition of the *Tamana* and successful return were toasted with guzzling from jugs. I jumped from the skiff and was greet'd by large & predatory mosquitoes, but my arrival went otherwise unnoticed amidst the revelry. The fort's denizens embraced their brethren with hugs & fervent cheek kisses. No women in sight. The men danced, wrestled, and shout'd. More musicians joined the *Tamana*'s. The dancers squatted on their haunches, arms folded across their chests, kicking & somersaulting.

A sturdy blond chap introduced himself and asked for my papers. "I am Timofei Osipovich Tarakanov, the elected *ataman* (leader, foreman) here" he said, offering a crumb of bread. "For you, bread with salt, a gesture of welcome, but not of trust. You are to be questioned by our temporary leader, Ivan Aleksandrovich Kuskov. Very temporary. Up there. Follow me."

Tarakanov squinted at my documents, then passed them to a black-haired ragamuffin, who sped off up the path and into the fort. We followed, entering a muddy interiour courtyard, where the two-story house dominated squat storehouses. An iron pot steamed amidst piles of clothes & blankets. The man with the telescope had vanish'd.

A large gray wolf ambled by, curled a lip at me and said, or seemed to say: "Fee, fi, fo, fum, I smell the blood of an Englishman."

What? More hallucinations? I did feel a bit dizzy. Doubtless the transition from the ship's fluid motion to solid ground had affected my ears. At any rate, my hearing had been doubtful since Trafalgar (*Stop right now and go find your hearing aid*), and I was increasingly uncertain of my mental bearings after my encounter with the whale, real or imagined.

I say: "Amazing, Mr. Tarakanov. You're a ventriloquist. The wolf, is he, ah, friendly?"

"No," Tarakanov said. "And he says he is a dog, named Kahmooks. A woman of the Malamute people, who live far to the north, she rescues him as an orphan wolf puppy. She takes him to her breast and with her milk she gives to him the words of people, so better he serves his masters. The Malamutes banish him, for mouthing off."

Kahmooks rolled soft brown eyes: "Ah, the memories. Awake before dawn tied to a stake under a blanket of new snow. Drag the sled across bleak wastelands. With luck, a frozen salmon to gnaw on. And the whips. How I loved the whips. They do not banish me, Timofei. I depart, without the long farewell."

Tarakanov shook his head: "Bad dogs and Englishmen." *No puns.*

The ground trembled. Approaching footsteps, something large. A furry goliath tower'd over me. Behind his bushy beard he was smiling.

Timofei: "John Williams, meet Kozma Ovchinnikov."

The day went dark as Mr. Ovchinnikov captured me inside a furry hug. His size & strength were astonishing, and he could have easily crush'd me. His smell was that of a wild animal, as tho' his fur grew from his own skin. I felt his huge heart thumping under the fur, and I imagined I was to be consumed again, as I'd been by the whale.

Tarakanov rescued me. "I take the Englishman to meet Kuskov," he said. "Remain here, so our brave leader is not frightened. Smoke the pipe beside the balagan."

Tarakanov indicated a small shed snuggled up to the castle. I could smell gunpowder inside. Bit moist, perhaps? I pointed to a sign posted on the door. I would never read Russian.

"'Dangers!,'" Kozma read, his immense finger tracing the words. "'Gunpowder! Not the fire to burn! Or else! By order of Baranov.' The greencoats, the navy officers, they tell Baranov that better the powder is stored in different places around the fort, for safety. Baranov says, 'Good idea. Every mutiny should have its own gunpowder supply.' The greencoats say, 'We will tell the Tsar. One bolt of lightning and his only fortress in America is explode.' Baranov says, "Tell the Tsar I fear the kolosh. Tell him I fear the fools and assassins he sends me. With the lightning I take my chances.'"

TARAKANOV & I ASCENDED TO A DARK, ROUGH-HEWN OFFICE scent'd by mildew. Kuskov, fat, bearded, bespectacled, sat at a wobbling desk wearing a threadbare undertaker's suit and a suspicious squint. He'd emptied my bag on his desk. He looked relieved when Timofei told him Kozma wouldn't be joining us.

"So," Kuskov said, "Slobodchikov brings us a spy."

I permitted myself a smirk as I survey'd my surroundings. Though it sat on solid stone, Baranov's castle, only a few years old, had already suffer'd subsidence: no true verticals or horizontals, no right angles. The office's floor, windows, doors all tilted slightly askew, nonetheless offering a panoramic view of both water and forest. A small library filled leaning bookshelves.

Kuskov, annoy'd at my disdain, slapped his desk. It collapsed with a crash, documents sliding to the plank floor. I feared for my compass & sextant, as well as my pipe & lamp. Kuskov leapt to his foot (a wooden peg-leg protruded from his left knee), braced himself with a cane and screamed for Yakov to come fix the desk. A native man rushed in and propped the desk back up on a stack of ledgers. My belongings appeared undamaged.

Kuskov sat again: "Confess you are a spy, or that moldy bread is your last bite."

I say: "Didn't expect the Russian Inquisition."

Kuskov jumped up again: "Nobody . . ." *Delete. Nobody gets your stupid jokes.*

Tarakanov indicated my portfolio: "Look at his journal, Kuskov. He draws a map. The mouth of the Columbia, with compass headings. He knows navigation."

Kuskov blink'd. "Oh? Maria, darling? Refreshments for our guest?"

Tarakanov & I took seats as a native maiden entered bearing a silver samovar, her long black hair tied back, her long black dress ruffled with Chinese silk. A Russian crucifix with three crossbars bounced on her bodice, a tiny rowboat tossed in tempestuous swells. She poured tea for us from the samovar and added a dollop of vodka, sending Tarakanov looks. Kuskov, watching with narrow'd eye, proposed a toast to the Tsar.

"Cheers," I replied. "And here's to New Archangel, his newest American colony. Me, I've had quite enough of America. Hoping for passage home, sooner the better, that's the ticket. How I miss dearest Elizabeth & the baby. Almost a year now since last I . . ."

"How sad," Kuskov said. "Some of us have not been home in, sniff, twenty years. Damn this wilderness. No civilized women. Joyously, we have our lovely Maria."

Maria passed by Timofei and touch'd his shoulder.

I changed the subject: "I'm told trading vessels call here. Marvelous stroke of luck, the *Tamana* coming to my rescue. I say, good show: first Russian ship to enter the Columbia. Feather in the Tsar's cap."

Kuskov coughed into his fist: "The Tsar prefers that Russian history is not written by escaped felons. Please provide the pathetic explanation for how we are finding you."

"Shipwreck'd at the mouth of the Columbia River. The *Emily*, Astor brig out of New York. Signed on as master at Mr. Astor's personal request. All hands lost but me. Taken in by the natives and soon restored to vigour, but still, there I was, maroon'd, on the other side of the world from England. Damn. Should've stayed home and heed'd my bride's tearful . . ."

"How sad. And your sword? You are the heroic naval officer?"

"Not likely. Drummed out of the navy. Not much for bloodshed & such, truth be told. Rather fond of the sword, though. Spiffy, what? Gad, what a fuss the wife made. Told her, 'Eleanor darling, when I'm home from the sea we'll . . .'"

"Wait. Eleanor? What happens to Elizabeth?"

"Eleanor Elizabeth."

"Liar. Spy."

When one's honour is question'd, one is required to rise and place a hand on one's sword. I did so. Kuskov sneer'd. I withdrew the blade an inch.

Tarakanov, a cautionary note: "Many desire to put the blade in Kuskov, Mr. Williams. We beg you to wait at the end of the line."

Maria offered the hors d'oeurves tray: "You would like to taste my sweetmeats?"

Kuskov snicker'd: "I assure you, Mr. Williams, no man tastes her sweetmeats. Our Maria is as pure as the snow on the mountaintop. From the priest at Kodiak, she learns religion. But, for too long, the sweetmeats roll about the platter, moist and tasty. Soon a husband must be found for our Maria, a gentleman with whom she will bear the little ones in the Tsar's honor. A mature, educated bridegroom, a good Russian with dignity and substance, not some mongrel rutting about in the yard below."

Tarakanov: "Treasure each breath, Ivan Aleksandrovich. Savor each heartbeat."

"I do, Timofei Osipovich. Especially when lovely Maria lingers obediently here at my side, lending beauty and grace to my dreary routine."

"Each touch, a missing finger."

Kuskov feign'd fright: "Threats of violence. See, Mr. Williams, how my nine remaining digits tremble? Timofei knows that his treacherous words and deeds are written in the Company records, for the benefit of those who can read."

"Burn your ledgers, Kuskov, while you have fingers to light the fire. Destroy the evidence. Enjoy the warmth. Soon your patron saint returns from Kodiak. Soon all your pain is gone."

Kuskov leer'd: "Pain? Maria soothes my . . ."

Timofei's hand was a blur. Kuskov scream'd. A hunting knife pinned his hand to the desk. His beady eyes bulged and his blood spurted, staining my portfolio. The knife vibrated with a low hum. Maria departed through velvet portières. Kuskov considered pulling the knife out. Timofei yank'd it free, wiped the blade on Kuskov's sleeve, turned to me and suggested a tour of New Archangel.

TIMOFEI GESTURED WESTWARD: "If there is not the cloud, we see Mother Russia."

We viewed the sound from the fort's seaward parapet. Clouds obscured the volcano's icy summit only twenty miles away, so he must have been joking about seeing their homeland. Bit far, wasn't it? Best not argue. I murmur'd amazement. The surrounding waters, the verdant islands and the backdrop of snowy peaks were a pleasing aspect at any rate.

A rising tide climbed the kekur's toes. Offshore the *Tamana* lay at anchor near the old brig *Kodiak*. Timofei said three Russian naval officers lived aboard, banish'd and confined to quarters by Baranov for refusing to obey orders. Timofei said they remained belowdecks unless the sun was out.

"The greencoats refuse to go on hunting voyages. They fear the kolosh. They write to St. Petersburg, saying that Baranov is mad, his methods unsound. Baranov intercepts the letter. He tells them, 'If you know I am crazy, that means you are sane. Therefore, you must cheerfully accept the hunting voyages I assign you.'"

A skin-covered rowboat he called a *baidara* labour'd back from the *Tamana*, offloading pigs & pineapples. A smaller, pointy-ended *baidarka* clad in sealskin ventured out for fishing, propelled with a double-bladed paddle by a native hunter in a cockpit sealed with drawstrings. Timofei said he had ventured out in a baidarka when the water was calm, but that the other Russians abstained, fearing the capsizings that trapped the paddler upside down underwater. The native paddlers, he said, capsized and right'd themselves just for fun.

We moved to the fort's landward side, overlooking the rude structures cluster'd below. Timofei pointed out the communal steam bath, a shed nestled amongst similar buildings, the largest a two-story barracks with sentries in top-floor kiosks, its stone foundation almost in the water. My erstwhile shipmates ran back & forth between these two structures, starkers.

No church. The only sign of religion so far was the Russian Orthodox crucifix on Maria's bosom, and if the Hereafter wasn't New Archangel's primary concern, the Here & Now certainly was. The fort devoutly guarded its earthly existence: sentries studiously scanned shadowy spruce, and a dozen small cannon were mounted in wheeled carriages, aimed at the forest a stone's throw distant. I inspected the flintlock firing-mechanisms. Obsolete, rusty, dubious reliability. *Clarify. You or the guns?*

At length, the welcome celebration ebb'd. As the music & shouting faded, we heard a blacksmith's hammer strike an iron forge. The breeze brought the aroma of fresh bread. Down at the cargo bay, Cossacks repaired a thick hemp ship's cable, splicing in what Tarakanov said were strips of cedar bark & spruce root. A few women ventured out of the buildings, black-haired, copper-skinned matrons shroud'd in multiple layers of linen skirts, aprons and scarves. They wield'd twig brooms and tended small gardens; Tarakanov pointed out a woman digging *sarana*, a Russian lily bulb he said was a delicacy. Others herded children & livestock on the bumpy slope behind the fort, amidst stumps & grave sites. A menagerie of pigs, goats and sheep grazed lush ferns, but kept their distance from the forest.

For good reason. Kahmooks sat staring at the trees, ears up, a low growl in his throat. At the forest's edge, a shadow moved.

I say: "Indians?"

Timofei shrugged: "Perhaps *leshiy*, the wild man. Big, hairy, shy, like Kozma. Kozma stays in the fort, leshiy stays in the forest."

Kozma: "Yes, Indians, kolosh. Always they watch. Always we must beware. If Baranov finds the sentry to be sleeping, he cuts off the eyelids. If the sentry sleeps, we die. Again."

I believed Kozma was referring to the massacre of 1802, of which I'd been informed by the *Tamana* crew. The Sitkas had attacked & burned the Russians' first fort a few miles north of here, slaughtering most of the occupants. Had Timofei & Kozma been there? If so, how had they survived? I resolved to learn more, albeit discreetly. If Kuskov was New Archangel's figurehead leader, these two Cossacks certainly ran the place, and I hoped to remain in their favour.

As we returned to the seaward parapets, I noted a small kiosk on the rocks below, perch'd above the churning tides.

"What's that?," I asked. "A guard post? A privy?"

"The Bird House, Baranov's steambath, the *banya* of the Little Bird Man. The kolosh seek to destroy it. They believe it holds Baranov's power. One day, from the trees, the kolosh shoot the small cannon, which they obtain from our friends the Bostons. The cannonball enters the window of Baranov's office. The desk loses the leg. Then, boom, another cannonball. It finds its mark, and hits upon the Bird House, but Baranov builds her strong. Joyously, her stout planks do not shatter. Sadly, not so good does she sit upon the rocks. The Bird House tips. Baranov screams."

"Egad. He was . . . ?"

"With a dozen hot stones. Thump, thump, thump. Splash."

"But he escaped, unhurt?"

"Often he is hurt. Always he survives, stronger than before, and more babies he makes with his Kodiak princess. Be warned, English spy, he is hard to kill. No, do not deny why you come. We know, someday, Baranov's assassin arrives. Perhaps already Baranov dies on Kodiak. If so, when we receive word, Kuskov feeds the ferns, and your errand is finish."

I say: "Good show. Just out of curiousity, who would your new leader be?"

Kozma thump'd his furry chest: "We are Cossacks, as free as the wind blowing across the steppes. Freely we vote for our leaders, our atamans. Every man chooses to vote for Timofei. Those who do not are spies and traitors, like you."

Timofei: "Who sends you, spy? Answer, without the joke."

I say: "Poppycock, old chap. Why would a spy come here? Why would anybody? I want to go home."

Kozma seized my wrist in his massive paw and bit down on my little finger. I shriek'd.

Timofei: "Kozma eats fingers, old chap. Bones and all. Ask Kuskov."

I say: "British agent. Ouch ouch ouch."

"What happens to the Astor ship?"

"Blew it up. Ten tons of gunpowder. All dead. No trace." *Delete mass murder. Is that true about the fingers?*

"You blow up your own ship? You blow opium smoke, British agent. They throw you overboard, yes? We suspect you plot with your rescuer Slobodchikov, who is not to be trusted. Nobody can we trust. Maybe you, if you stop lying to us."

"Come, we go talk to Mr. Lincoln, our Boston shipwright. Always he is angry. Maybe he likes you better than us."

BROKEN HULKS, THEIR BEST BONES SCAVENGED from their bowels, lay on the beach above the tide in attitudes of despair, never again to feel the rush of sea beneath their keels. Tho' it looked to be the aftermath of a violent storm, 'twas actually a little shipyard, the realm of a Mr. Lincoln, a grumpy expatriate American shipwright who, according to rumour, hid a cache of Baranov's silver 'neath the keel of his current project, the canvas-draped *Otkrytie*, which was encircled by steel-toothed bear traps.

Our approach was herald'd by shouting scamps & barking dogs, who took care to avoid the traps. The sound of tool on timber drifted from under wind-whipped canvas.

Timofei: "Perhaps today we are friends. Hello? Mr. Lincoln? Permission to come aboard?"

The sound of woodworking paused & resumed. We slipped between the embryonic ship's ribs, into a dark womb dense with sweat & sawdust. A bald colour'd man worked at the bow by lantern-light, shaping the knightheads with an adze. A furtive Cossack named Grudinin squatted amidships, hunch'd over a paint pot, mixing the oils of hemp seed & Sandwich Island coconuts.

I was introduced. The shipwright glanced over his shoulder but didn't pause from his labours.

Timofei: "Mr. Lincoln comes from Boston in search of fortune. Today he builds the beautiful *Otkrytie*. Three masts, 300 tons. The largest ship ever built in Russian America."

Grunt, puff, grunt, puff.

"Already Mr. Lincoln creates for us the brig *Sitka*, a symphony of seaworthiness, which sails from here last spring, perhaps reaching Okhotsk with a cargo of furs, God willing."

Grudinin, huddled amidst his pots, made the sign of the cross.

I addressed Lincoln's sweat-soak'd back: "Jolly good show, all things considered."

Timofei tried again: "Perhaps Mr. Lincoln shows to Mr. Williams his plans, the drawings? Perhaps Mr. Williams explains the modern ideas, from England?"

Veins popped on Lincoln's glistening skull. His jaw worked.

I ventured a polite suggestion: "Wide enough in the beam, Mr. Lincoln? Tad skinny for three masts, what? Big in the bottom, that's the ticket."

Lincoln, a groan.

Timofei: "We must find work for Mr. Williams."

Grudinin: "Put him on the crosscut saw. Maybe he grows some shoulders like a Cossack."

I say: "Manual labour? Rather envision'd myself in an advisory role."

Lincoln waved the adze at Timofei: "My contract says I get an assistant, but you send the imbecile Grudinin. You deliberately impede my progress. No more helpers. Be honest, Tarakanov. You don't want this ship, do you? If you wanted a ship, why would you send me Grudinin, who fails even at latrine duty? Why? So I won't finish. So Kuskov won't have to pay me. Look me in the eye. No longer can you deny it. Bloodthirsty savages, up there in the trees, licking their chops, wagering on who will add the African's noble head to his collection. But, still, as you see, despite everything, despite Grudinin, I progress. So now you drag in some washed-up Brit, and I should listen to him babble. 'A tad skinny'? She's a pig. What next, Tarakanov?"

Timofei woke me with news of the arrival of the trade ship *O'Cain*, a Yankee brig of 280 tons, stopping off on her way to the Canton fur bazaar, stuff'd with California sea otter pelts. She lay in the anchorage looking like a warship with her eighteen guns all rolled out, more than many frigates. The crew remained aboard, but the captain came ashore and offered a reward for information on the whereabouts of a young Englishman who, he alleged, had massacred a shipload of innocent Americans at the Columbia River last summer *(Delete)*, then departed aboard a Russian brig. Timofei told him they hadn't seen any Englishmen.

Clap this blackguard in irons, the captain said, hand him over and Mr. Astor will pay you a fortune in silver. Timofei said they'd keep an eye out. Fogged in by opium, I watched from the ramparts as the captain raised sail for China with a fortune in fur in his hold.

I sank deeper into the drug's depths, losing interest in food, drawing sustenance from stale bread & Chinese tea, visiting the steambath only when dragged there by Kozma. Baranov stock'd opium primarily as a medicinal painkiller, and the supply, tho' sporadic, was potent & plentiful, courtesy of the China trade. Vodka remained New Archangel's drug of choice, but I was not opium's only devotee.

Nonetheless, we all struggled to comply with Timofei's assignments for work & sentry duty. New Archangel teeter'd on the brink of starvation, and those who ate work'd. In the brief daylight some of the fort's denizens ventured out to fish and gather drift logs for firewood, but I remained fortbound, wrapped in my blankets, aware but blissfully serene. I was available if needed, and Timofei & Kozma often roust'd me for a chat, curious about the world outside. They readily admitted they planned escape from New Archangel, and that I played a role in that endeavour.

I remember little from this period, and my journal is not reliable. *No! Really?* One scribbled entry says a tipsy sentry fell from the palisade and broke his leg. Timofei & I restrained the bloke, we sedated him with a mixture of vodka & opium, and Kozma set his shatter'd bones. Date uncertain.

I undertook a study of the fog & tides, of the storm clouds that crowded in from the ocean, spilling their own oceans on us. Gusts pounded our shutters, churning the sound & forest. The islands & volcano hid in swirling mist. The world outside became three elements: the storm above, the water below, the forest surrounding. A wild triumvirate.

Timofei assigned me to nocturnal sentry duty, ordering me to report in coherent fashion. There was no arguing, and I found I liked the watchman's life. On stormy nights, Saint Elmo's fire danced on our bayonets, and if the dog couldn't sleep, he'd tell me amusing stories about our colleagues.

No storms tonight, and too cold for the dog, who'd abandon'd the frozen north in favour of New Archangel's wool blankets & wood-stoves. If the fleas & ticks farther south were tolerable, he said, he'd move to warmer climes when the chance arrived, which, he confided, might be soon. Kahmooks was a chronic & skill'd eavesdropper.

Freezing tonight. Clearing sky. Black clouds withdrew to the north as I reported for duty, revealing Big & Little Dippers. White peaks gleam'd in moonlight. Wolves lament'd from the forest, and the trees sighed, mourning their mates cut down and carried off by Cossacks, then stacked upon this rock like a funeral pyre. The *Kodiak* and *Tamana* slept in the anchorage, protected by vigilant deck watches with candle-lanterns. On previous nights, under the cover of fog, Sitka swimmers had attempted to cut their anchor cables.

Trouble often haunt'd a clear night as well, and a sniper's shot from the forest had disturb'd the garrison earlier. Timofei ordered the dog to sniff the breeze on the quarter-hour, for Kahmooks could scent & hear the shadowy Sitka sharpshooters as they crept about the forest's edge. The shooters knew it, and, like me, the dog had a price on his head. He moved about the fort carefully, never offering the Sitkas a target. He told Timofei he'd sniff hourly.

We sentries stood bundled, scarves tied under chins like grandmothers, our breath clouds mingling with wisps of sea fog. My fingers went numb but Kozma forbade us gloves; we might need to shoot in a hurry. My comrades huddled, blowing on their fingers. I kept moving, like Kahmooks. By the time the musket ball arrives, I told myself, I shall be elsewhere. I danced. Fiddler, fiddler, play us a jig, whirling dervish, blankets flying, sword swinging. My mukluks slapped on rough timbers. Bones gone numb. Senses a'tingle.

A flash of light flood'd the sky.

I was gobsmack'd. An explosion? Hallucinations? Should I sound the alarm? My mates were staring at the heavens too. Why were they silent? I could only gape as a thin ribbon of flashing green & red light snaked across the sky's black ice, shimmering, wavering as though buffeted by heavenly breezes. A spinning black hole, a whirling vortex, appeared within the waving ribbon. I stood stunned.

Would I be sucked up into the cold cosmos? Surely the end was near. Earth was to be destroyed by extraterrestrial forces. I could only stand, staring, awestruck. Would we burn to death, or freeze in the dark?

"Shut the mouth or the tongue freezes."

Kozma. He crept about with nary a sound, a 300-pound shadow. Woe to the sentry caught sleeping. He, Timofei and the Aleut called Yuri were out making rounds, checking on us.

Kozma gazed heavenward: "Some say the lights are the sun reflecting upon the northern ice, from where comes Kahmooks, which the Aleuts call Alaska. Right, Yuri?"

Yuri: "*Alakhskhak.*"

Kozma: "Bless you. But the kolosh here say the lights mean the Great Spirit is angry, that after the lights comes trouble. Other kolosh say the lights are ghosts of their ancestors. The priest on Kodiak, he says the light is made by God in Heaven, but Baranov says that Baranov is God, and he does not make night lights. So, who knows? Come, Yuri relieves you. Join us for tea."

KAHMOOKS, LOUNGING ON HIS FAVOURITE BLANKET: "Look what the cat drags in."

The dog loath'd Kuskov and could chase him from the office with a bared fang, so our temporary commander had barricaded himself in Baranov's tiny room in the attic, from whence he would not venture, not with both Kozma & Kahmooks present, and those two chose to stay close by the stove.

A goosebumpy breeze whisper'd through the Castle's dim interiour. The kekur had been a Sitka cemetery prior to Russian annexation, and the fort was said to be haunt'd by the ghosts of native chieftains. Maria tossed driftwood into the stove's roaring maw, then broke a chunk of brown Chinese tea from a brick. The samovar steam'd, as did the iron pot beside it, a gruel of fish & rice called kasha. No bread today, Maria said, not enough wood to fire the oven, tho' Kuskov's stove was never cold. And no venison: the hunters fear'd lurking Sitkas, but fish were plentiful. I licked my bowl. The stove spat sparks, lusting to consume the timbers that shelter'd it. I lifted my blanket and offered me bum to the iron sun, roasting one side, shivering on the other.

Timofei shuffled documents on Kuskov's desk and consult'd a curious calendar, a carved wooden disk covered with peg-holes, religious holidays marked by crosses. He & Kuskov had been arguing over an early spring hunting trip, one which included all the Aleut & Kodiak hunters, with Slobodchikov's Cossacks as supervisors. Two hundred baidarkas would be lashed to the decks of the *Kodiak* & *Tamana*, these vessels to be captain'd by Benzeman & Bulygin respectively.

Kuskov was desperate for fur, Timofei told me. When Baranov returned, he would demand results, and Kuskov feared the master's wrath, knowing Baranov might appoint Timofei to be his second-in-command, thereby reducing Kuskov to irrelevance. Kuskov begged Timofei to lead the hunt, doubting that Slobodchikov would push the hunters into dangerous inlets where the last sea otters had fled. Timofei declined, anticipating Baranov's imminent return, for which he hoped to be present. The hunt would threaten the fort's very existence by spreading its defenses too thin. Those who remained would do naught but sleep & stand guard, and would be hard-pressed to turn back a serious attack.

The Kodiak man nicknamed Five entered to report that the long-overdue firewood detail had returned safely, driftwood logs in tow. Five seemed always blissful, white-haired but ageless, his countenance carved from polished mahogany. I'd noticed the people from Kodiak looked like the Columbia River natives, while those from the Aleutian Islands, much closer to the Asian mainland, looked almost Chinese. Still, the Russians had been mingling for half a century, and their blood was evident in every copper-hued face.

When he was gone, I asked: "Why's he called Five?"

"Kodiak," Timofei said. "Long ago. Day after day, the wind blows. Waves like mountains. We cannot send out the baidarkas to hunt. Baranov reminds us, 'If the fur does not go back to Okhotsk, the Company does not send supplies.' Still the hunters refuse. On the beach, Baranov threatens with the whip, the cat-o'-nine-tails, but the hunters are angry. The Russians have taken their wives and daughters. They have nothing to lose but their vodka. They are ready to die.

"Baranov cracks the whip. The hunters spit. Never before do they defy Baranov. They see what happens to Cossacks who disobey, so this is serious. Baranov puts down the whip, picks up the big sea lion gun, a small cannon that shoots like a rifle. He tells the Cossacks to separate five leaders from the hunters, strip them, tie them together in a line, facing forward, chests to backs.

"Baranov says, 'Last chance. Do you still refuse?' He proposes a wager: 'If I shoot, how many hunters does the ball go through?' The Cossacks laugh and bet. Nobody believes he will shoot. Baranov loads a charge, tamps the ball down hard. The gun, she is bigger than Baranov. We cry out, '*Papochka*, little father, please, enough. We need our hunters.' Baranov hesitates. Kuskov snatches the gun from Baranov's hands. Before we can stop him, kahboom, four men fall. Five remains standing, tied to the four dead men in front of him."

Timofei fell silent. Kozma picked up the narrative. These two could converse between themselves without words, but when they talked, they told the same story.

"The mutiny is finish," Kozma said. "Baranov tells us, 'This is why Kuskov is my second-in-command. He knows about fear. I lose four good hunters, but I am willing to pay the price. This is your lesson, boys. Fear. When they show no fear, run for Russia.'"

Timofei said, "I told you, English assassin. Many desire to put the blade in Kuskov. Now you know why. He lives only because Baranov forbids his death."

"That night," Kozma said, "the sea rises. We swim inside our barabaras, our huts, thinking it must be a dream. In the morning, the sea ebbs away. The shore is washed clean. Only Five remains."

"Standing. Remains standing. Naked. The ball is lodged in his chest, under his skin, but no wound, no blood. He is slimy, fishy, stinky. He looks older, and his black hair is white."

"He says he is swallow by a whale."

"Look at him. Close the mouth, spy."

"He gulps like a whale. Now Five's guardian spirit is always with him. In times of danger, we touch the ball over Five's heart. Five protects us."

Nothing protects us. God hath forsaken us. Soon we die.

At dawn on a March morning the seascape filled with hundreds of canoes carrying a thousand singing warriors, all just out of cannon range. No doubt more gathered in the forest, but if so Kahmooks couldn't detect them.

A thousand, at least. They could take the fort. If they all came at once, we couldn't shoot them fast enough. We were seriously outnumbered; most of our men were off hunting in coastal waters to the north aboard *Tamana* & *Kodiak*, so we couldn't escape to the sea. The *Otkrytie* lay on the beach with half her hull planking on, her scheduled launch still months off.

Our breath-clouds mingled with the kekur's floating ghosts. We loaded three cannons on the seaward side, then stood in chilly silence, taking turns with the brass telescope.

Kozma, scanning our flock of little green islands: "They hide good."

The Aleuts named Vladimir & Petr had taken a baidarka out before first light to hunt seal, only to find themselves surrounded by this sudden surge of Sitkas. The Cossack fisherman Sobachnikov had narrowly escaped. He breathlessly reported that our lads & their boat lay concealed in dense shrubbery on a tiny island, waiting for a chance to hasten back inside New Archangel's cannon range.

Through the glass the Sitkas looked a fierce lot: sinister goatees & mustachios, nostrils pierced by bones. Long black hair, fur capes. They'd brought a variety of weapons, including a variety of muskets. Bows & arrows. Spears. They appeared to be dipping tree branches into the water. I asked when they'd attack.

Kozma reassured me: "Calm down, trembling puppy. See the white scum on the water? Herring eggs. In spring, when the tide is right, the herring makes eggs that taste like caviar. The whale, the seagull, they feast. No, the kolosh do not attack today. They come to harvest the eggs with the tree branch."

Timofei: "But they come in force. The kolosh remind us they can harvest us too, when they choose. They dangle us on their hook. Our fort is our prison. For the kolosh, time is nothing. The Russian arrives yesterday. Someday the shaman casts his medicine bones, and the bones will say the Russian must die."

I say: "Beware the tides of March." *No puns. Delete.*

The Aleut named Sergei had the telescope. He cursed & pointed.

Our hunters' baidarka burst from a brushy isle. A Sitka canoe had passed too near and spied them. Distant angry shouts reached our ears. We could only stare helplessly as our lads pumped their double-bladed paddles in staccato unison. They had a jump on the passing canoe. The Sitka paddlers paused in mid-stroke, surprised. Couldn't turn around in time. Other canoes gave chase. Vladimir & Petr duck'd Sitka arrows, spray flying from their paddles.

Still too far for the cannons. Would the pursuers dare to venture within our range? If so, we were ready. Timofei gripped the flintlock lanyard on the number-one gun. His fist was trembling. I aimed the gun, tapping the quoin wedge with a wooden mallet.

Only a lone black Sitka canoe now, slicing across at an angle to intercept the speeding baidarka. Eight vengeful paddlers, stroking hard, closing the gap.

I aimed twenty feet ahead of the Sitka's bow. Wait, wait. Still too far. Timofei looked at me, nodding frantically: fire, fire. No time to argue. Trajectory, wind speed. Target. Range.

I fired. A pause, and then a fountain spurted abaft the pursuing canoe. They were moving faster than I'd thought, and my shot prompt'd them to increase the intensity of their strokes.

Timofei stood shaking. Shoving him aside, I aimed & touched off the number-two gun. Another pretty fountain, just off the Sitkas' prow. Gave them a good soaking. Guns one & two reload. Sergei rammed the charges down hard.

The Sitka paddlers rushed their strokes, out of rhythm. That last shot scared them. Yelling over their shoulders at the coxswain in the stern. Turn back, cease pursuit. The whistle of flying lead hath chill'd their bones. Yea, fear me, Sitkas. Ask ye not my name. You know me. I am pale Death, come for thee.

I tapped the number-three gun to adjust elevation and sighted on the canoe's bow, leading it by a length. The Sitka at the bow had a musket at his shoulder, bracing the barrel on the prow, aiming.

I fired, but the cannon's flintlock shatter'd. Pieces of rusty iron flew.

From out on the water, the Sitka's musket boom'd. Vladimir dropped his paddle and slump'd. Petr had no chance. The Sitkas came up alongside, laughing. Petr raised his paddle. The morning sun glowed on the wet blade and on the sweeping arc of a whalebone club.

Aiming number-one cannon. Steady on. Fire.

A shower of splinters burst from the Sitka canoe. Direct hit on the wolf's-head prow, warriors in the water, canoe still afloat. The Sitkas retreated sans prow, waving two heads at us. A red slick spread around the empty baidarka.

WET & WEEPING GRAVEDIGGERS HUDDLED AROUND the barracks woodstove, passing a jug. Sealskins hung, dripping. Puddles on planks. I huddled shivering in my blanket. Vodka didn't quite dull the pain. I rather wanted opium.

Timofei & Kozma appeared before me, pale as ghosts. Timofei was still shaking.

"Good men buried with no heads," he said. "Satan comes. We must be gone from this place."

I say: "Balderdash. In what? You couldn't get out of here if you had to. Gone to where? Back to Kodiak?"

I had restrained myself from questions about my friends' plans. They treated inquiries with suspicion. Now I hoped I hadn't seemed too curious.

"No," Timofei said. "Not Kodiak. We remember Kodiak."

Kozma: "We come here from Kodiak fifteen years ago. *Bobri morski*, sea otter, everywhere. Big trees, good timber. The mountains protect from the wind. Baranov says, 'This will be our home.'"

"The kolosh fear Baranov. They see he is crazy. They believe his spirit is powerful. They let us build a little fort, six miles north of here. Their shaman says, 'The Russians wander far from their homeland. Soon they go away.'

"Baranov orders us, 'Bring me fur.' The kolosh say the sea otter belongs to them. When we hunt, kolosh, all around. We protect the hunters from the ship with the cannon. If the kolosh comes near, we sink his canoe. So, the kolosh scare off the sea otter. We must send our hunters into shallow water. The ship cannot follow. Our hunters become the hunted. The kolosh leave their heads, on poles, for us to see. Our hunters are caught between Baranov and the kolosh."

"We sail out in Baranov's little sloop. White flag. We wait. The kolosh come in canoes. They say, 'Still the Russian lingers. Our cousins laugh at us. We cannot be laughed at. Go now, or you die like your brothers at Yakutat.'"

"Yakutat is our first settlement on the mainland, three hundred miles to the north. The kolosh massacre two dozen Russians and Aleuts. Revenge, against us, because we take this kekur."

"Baranov screams at the kolosh, 'All this land belongs to Russia. You are subjects of the Tsar. You must submit.'"

"We decide we must talk to the kolosh on our own."

"Without Baranov."

"We are not telling you this."

"Baranov has spies amongst the kolosh, but we expose them, so we are not found out."

"We are not telling you this. Understand? Nod your head."

"Someday the kolosh come for us. We know this. But they know many of them will die. No more surprise attacks. They fear Baranov's powerful spirit. They believe if Baranov is here, the attack fails."

"So, we promise to them that Baranov will be absent. We promise, when the kolosh attack, the sentry sleeps. The kolosh promise that if Baranov is gone, they spare the two of us, the women, the children. They will trade us for guns to the Englishman, Captain Barber. He will return us to Kodiak."

"Ha. Look at him. The Englishman is horrified. He cannot believe it."

I say: "I didn't say anything."

"Yes, we betray our comrades. How can we do such a thing?"

"So the innocent can live. Because it is wrong for us to be here. Because why should we die for Baranov's mistake."

"The brave are in the grave. Sitka is a place of sadness. We want to leave."

"Alive."

"You think we are cowards? Tell us, how many die because of you?"

"He told you. He explodes the Astor ship." *Delete.*

"He explodes his shipmates. Kolosh women, says the Yankee captain. *Delete delete delete.* But somehow John Williams is still alive. Do the ghosts haunt you too? Why does Mr. Astor offer to pay us your weight in silver?"

"His weight? He is just bones wrapped in a dirty blanket. Don't worry, skinny Englishman, we protect you. Never do we betray our fearless navigator and cannon shooter."

"So, we say to Baranov that he should sail back to Kodiak in his little boat, make another baby. Baranov departs."

"The day comes. A holiday, saint somebody day. An extra cup of vodka for all. The sentries snooze in the sun. Barber's ship *Unicorn* lies at anchor down by the kolosh village. No breeze, flat water, no kolosh to be seen. We depart to hunt the seal. We tell Maria, when she hears trouble, gather the women and children in the storage cellar."

"We paddle out behind the island. We wait. We hear shooting, screaming. Smoke drifts on the water. When silence returns, so do we. Our fort is ashes. Our comrades lie dead on the beach. The simpleton Plotnikov, he laughs and waves the head of his father at the kolosh. The kolosh fear crazy people. If they cut off his head, the demons escape. Also, they spare eighteen women and two other men."

"They take us to their village. They dance, waving the heads of our comrades. We are tied up beneath the totem poles. They pass the women around, like slaves. Maria, we say she is Timofei's wife. They leave her alone. Aboard the *Unicorn*, the ransom begins, us for Barber's guns."

"But the kolosh discover that Barber's guns are not shooting. The angry tyee is on the ship, demanding that Barber takes back the broken guns. Barber seizes him, puts the rope around his neck, says he will hang him from the yardarm. The kolosh know Barber is crazy, and he has cannons, so they accept the bad guns."

"Barber returns us to Kodiak. Baranov pays him ten thousand rubles' worth of fur."

"The crazy men from Boston. Tell him."

"Before the attack, a Boston ship comes to trade. Four crewmen they throw over the side, escapees from a madhouse. The crazy men swim to shore, to our fort. One will work, so we keep him. The others, too crazy. Only Baranov can be crazy. He casts out the three who refuse to work. They become slaves of the kolosh."

"For the kolosh, they work."

"When the kolosh attack our fort, the crazy Boston men lead the charge. They see their comrade. They chase him down."

"Now the heads of our brothers call to us. Growling dogs drag white arms through the mud. The cow walks on her knees, spears in her side. On the beach, a pile of flesh and bone. Ravens fight, croaking, black wings flapping. Bloated gluttons, too full to fly."

"The Devil is real, John Williams, not a fairy tale. Some days he walks about under the sunshine."

"He has seen the Devil. The opium makes him forget."

"So, we return to Kodiak with Captain Barber. Baranov is happy. We, his protectors, return. Nobody asks questions. The fur dwindles, and never does the Company send supplies. Whispers of mutiny. We eavesdrop on the plottings. The smiling assassin approaches Baranov with the knife in the sleeve, but Kozma seizes him and breaks his bones. Baranov says, 'Drag him out on the rocks. Leave him for the crabs. He will sing to me while the tide rises.'"

"One day, a ship comes. No supplies, just a gold medal for Baranov and a letter from the Tsar. Baranov sobs with joy. We put him up on the table, we gather around. We sing to him that he is tall, noble, brave, and tall."

"The letter says a warship comes, the navy frigate *Neva*."

"Comes to Sitka, not Kodiak. Still the Tsar believes he owns Sitka."

I say: "Saw the *Neva* being built in the Thames shipyards. A beauty. Three hundred and fifty tons. Cruises at eleven knots."

Timofei nodded: "The beautiful *Neva* calls to Baranov from across the ocean, 'Meet me in Sitka.' The Tsar's medal whispers in his ear, 'We must have revenge on the kolosh. Assemble an army. When the kolosh sees you and the *Neva*, their red skins turn yellow.'"

"He says we will take everyone, all the hunters, all the Cossacks. Hundreds of men and guns, five little ships. We depart with a favorable wind. We attack kolosh villages along the way. First, we shoot the cannon. Ashore we go, yelling, shooting. We take furs. Food, we take what we want and throw the rest on the ground. We burn houses. Valgusov steals the mask of the Raven spirit."

"The kolosh fight back. A man stabs Shubin with a spear."

"Shubin cuts off his head."

"And keeps it. In a sack."

"We hasten on to Sitka. The *Neva* waits. Never do we see such a ship. Polished wood, polished cannons. The crew, clean uniforms. We go aboard. Baranov drinks with the captain, Lisianski, and dares him to shoot the cannon at the kolosh village, which was down there beside that little river. Houses, a wall of logs facing the water, children playing on the beach."

"Lisianski says he cannot turn his guns upon the innocent. Baranov and Lisianski argue. Baranov points, 'Look, a canoe with nine warriors. See the war paint? They taunt you.' Kahboom.

Lisianski's gunners sink the canoe. Baranov bets Lisianski a ruble he cannot hit the biggest longhouse. Kahboom. The cannonball hits the house, goes through the roof, kills the children. Little bodies carried out, laid upon the ground. Lisianski sees through the telescope. He weeps."

"Baranov says, 'Bah. The greencoat has not the stomach for this. Come, boys, to the boats. We attack while the kolosh mourn.'"

"Baranov leads a charge against the village. The kolosh hide behind the log wall. When we get close, they shoot a Boston cannon loaded with scrap iron. We are wounded. With haste we return to the *Neva*."

"Baranov has a rusty nail in his shoulder. He runs about the deck, waving his sword. He orders Lisianski to fire on the village. Many times the cannons shoot. They destroy the kolosh houses. The tyees paddle out with a white flag. Baranov shouts, 'See, kolosh? Baranov returns. Go away from this place, abandon your village.'"

"Next day, all is quiet, no kolosh to be seen. Baranov says, 'Ha. They sneak away in the night. Now I build my fort atop their sacred rock.'"

"The *Neva* departs for the Sandwich Islands, where the women are without clothing. We stay. We build Baranov's fort. Half stand guard, half work. Cold, hunger, exhaustion. The weak, the sick, they perish. The forest gives us a thousand trees, but still, it hides the kolosh. We shoot at shadows. We run low on gunpowder. Again, we must speak to the kolosh."

"In secret."

"You understand 'secret', Englishman?"

"We tell them we will leave Sitka, but they must give back our fur which they capture at the massacre. At our new home on Kauai, we will have fish, fruits, a garden, pigs, goats. But other necessities, such as gunpowder, and . . ."

I say: "Opium."

". . . and medicine, these things we must trade for, when the ships come. But if we have no fur, we have nothing to trade. The kolosh must give us a parting gift. They agree, but they say, 'Also, we are sad if Little Bird Man flies away forever.'"

I say: "Why do they call him that?"

"Never mind. So, if we give them Baranov, they give us back our fur."

"Which we take from their waters."

"Then the Russian goes away forever."

Timofei spat on the stove's black belly. The spit sizzled.

"Now you know, English spy. Yes, we conspire with the enemy. But the enemy is also the subject of the Tsar, like us. But they resist against the Tsar's rule, so . . ."

"So, tell us, what should we do? Before, Little Bird Man tells us. He says fly, we grow wings. But now his mind is fly away."

"Baranov abandons us. Why is he not here? He knows the kolosh fear him. Why does he leave us, helpless, in our lofty nest, waiting for the kolosh to snatch us up?"

"Baranov no longer loves us. If he dies, he gives us new life. We fly away."

"And the curious English spy asks, 'Fly to where?' No, not Kodiak. And not Russia. In Russia we are nobody. The Tsar would take our fur."

"We fly to Kauai."

I say: "Good show."

"Yes. For a long time, we wait. Someday, the Tsar man comes. He will say we are going to California, or to the Columbia River. He will find us ready. Bravely we embark, as our Tsar commands, but we encounter storms, or headwinds, or Spanish frigates. We cannot reach our destination. Do we limp back to Archangel? No, never does the Cossack surrender. We are beyond the point of no return. We press on, heroically, to Kauai."

I say: "You're aware that King Kamehameha has a small army."

"With the king we are friends. Years ago, New Archangel is starving. The kolosh will not let us hunt or fish. Baranov writes a letter to Kamehameha, sends it with a Boston ship. Months pass. We eat our boots. Then, behold, the ship returns, full of pigs, sweet potatoes, sugar cane, cabbages, goats, chickens . . ."

"And a beautiful long cloak of tiny feathers, and a helmet shaped like the head of a bird. And a letter. Kamehameha writes to Baranov, in English, with the help of an English shipbuilder. Lincoln, our Boston shipbuilder, translates. Kamehameha writes that the bird costume gives power to he who wears it. He says he smiles down upon his little Russian brother. They say Kamehameha is bigger than Kozma."

"So, Slobodchikov and his crew, before they rescue you, they sail to Oahu from California with the help of a Boston sailor. They ask if Russians can live there. The king says, 'Not on Oahu. Too much the cavorting. Perhaps Kauai. Bring me fur. We will see.'"

"The king will trade our fur to the Bostons, so what is left for us?"

"We get a Russian outpost, the only foreign flag in the Sandwich Islands, in the center of the Pacific."

I say: "Just out of curiousity, what's the Tsar's punishment for mutiny?"

"If his flag flies over Kauai, maybe not so bad."

"So how do we sail to Kauai? Small island, big ocean. Maybe we fall from the edge of the world. Therefore, our trustworthy navigator must join the mutiny."

I say: "In for a penny, in for a pound." *Cliché delete.*


I AWOKE HUNGRY AND VENTURED OUT wrapped in my blanket, hoping to find a biscuit in the bakery, where I was startled by a strange little old man mumbling & scuttling about behind the oven, an elderly leprechaun with a frightful wig. Was this wizen'd elf a remnant of my druggy dreams?

I hasten'd off in search of my mates, finding them in the cargo bay. Through bleary eyes I noticed a stubby little sloop I'd never seen before, bobbing at anchor amidst the *Kodiak, Tamana,* and the floating-but-still-mastless *Otkrytie.* A skilled sailor could leave New Archangel in that wee boat, single-handed.

Yes? And go where?

Had the mysterious elf arrived in that boat?

Timofei & Kozma fell silent when they saw me coming.

Kozma: "Go to the steam bath. Come back when you are clean."

I say: "Who's that in the bakery? Wee chap, bad wig."

Timofei shush'd me, glancing about: "It is a kolosh scalp, and he is not here unless he chooses to be. For us to speak of this burdens the men with confusion."

"What's confusing?," I asked. "He's here, but he isn't. Is that his boat?"

"Baranov is like the father returning home from a long journey. First, he fondly peeks in the window at his family gathered by the hearth. He observes the many mistakes we make in his absence, and he eavesdrops on our whisperings. Then, at the proper moment, he bursts through the door, to save us."

"From?"

"Us."

"He's barking mad," I said. "He's hiding behind the oven, beady little eyes darting about. Shouldn't someone . . .?"

Timofei shook his head: "When the time comes, he is revealing. Then we are surprised that he slips in amongst ourselves, the sheep in the wolfskin, disguising himself as a wandering fool. Ha! We are the fools. This is how he teaches us."

"But . . ."

A wild scream ripped the air.

Above us, on the parapets, a burst of colour flash'd against a somber sky. A tiny figure scampered madly about the battlements, leaping, squawking wildfowl noises, trailing a cape of luminous scarlet & gold.

Baranov (for this was surely he) stared reproachfully down at us through the fierce aquiline eyes of an exotic ceremonial mask, a primitive representation of a parrot's head, a crude bird-of-paradise with hook'd beak & tuft'd crown.

A shout arose from his followers: "Behold. He returns."

With flamboyant plumage rippling, this *rara avis* shriek'd & spread his stubby wings, leaping up on a cannon as tho' preparing to take wing, to swoop above the fort's company, to enlighten us with his grace & beauty. The crowd urged him on, but at the last moment he was restrained by an alert sentry. With another shrill cry he scampered off, regalia sweeping.

His audience, enraptured: "Baranov is among us."

On the parapet, their diminutive leader spread his wings, proclaiming his splendour to the forest.

Timofei elbow'd me: "See? Baranov taunts the kolosh. To them, he is the devil. They can only hide in the shadow, trembling."

From the trees, a puff of gunsmoke. A musket ball zipped.

A loud whack. Tropical plumage fluttered. The regal headgear had been grazed, knocking Baranov on his tailfeathers, but the shot had ricochet'd, failing to penetrate the mask's crown, formerly the shell of a sea turtle. Baranov sat stunned.

Pandemonium. Women screamed, snatching up children. We ran up to the Castle, just in time to see a Cossack tripping over a pig and falling into the laundry pot fire, spilling the steaming iron kettle, scattering glowing embers. All hands seized up muskets, pistols, shot pouches & powder horns, as well as a variety of swords, daggers & cutlasses, and hauled this weaponry to the ramparts facing the forest. A crew loaded three guns with scrap iron and, without waiting for Timofei's order, fired off a thund'rous volley.

I failed to cover my ears in time. The blast jolted my bones. I choked on thick billowing smoke. I yawned & swallowed, stabilizing the air pressure. My ears popped. *Find your hearing aid. Where did you have it last?*

Only two guns had fired. The middle gun sat silent. Damp powder. The crew tried again to fire it, without success. They looked at Timofei, who looked at me.

"Let her sit," I said. "She might still be burning. You've no target, and she might go off while you're unloading."

Timofei shouted to hold fire. Gunsmoke mingled with fog. The mountains echoed. Spruce, shredded.

Baranov regained his feet and, with a cry of vengeance, shook a stubby, iridescent wing at the silent forest.

A sentry cried out, pointing at the foggy sound: "Three masts. Russian flag."

Excitement again swept New Archangel. We ascended to the parapet just as a pretty frigate burst from the fog a league out and begin a slow jibe into the anchorage, Russian flag rippling.

The fort's denizens remembered her. A cry went up: "The *Neva* returns."

A cannon boom'd from the frigate, a cautious salute. She must have heard our guns and was puzzled about our situation. Signal pennants ran up & down her mizzen.

Kuskov, from the window: "Well? Do we return their salute? No, better we ignore them. Perhaps they go away."

Timofei ordered us to load the three seaward cannons with salute charges. Kozma rallied a gun crew. I focused my telescope on the *Neva* as she sounded for an anchorage she fancied. The trill of a boatswain's pipe drifted to us.

The excitement restored Baranov's manic vigour. He dashed across the courtyard squawking, flapping his little wings. His costume, flowing majestically, swept over the embers of the laundry pot fire. Wisps of smoke waft'd. Cossacks pursued, slapping at the smoke with blankets, but flames reached Baranov's flesh, and his avian cries became human. The Cossacks lifted their smouldering leader aloft and ran out the gate, headed for the water, leaving tropical feather smoke in their wake.

The *Kodiak* lay at anchor with no movement on deck. She had hosted a raising-of-the-mast party the previous evening, and Bulygin had been tied to the new main mast, where he remained slumped unconscious in his bonds. He'd previously beaten his head on the deck in a fit of wretch'd melancholy and had been restrained by his concerned colleagues, the lieutenants Vasilii Petrov & Khristofor Benzeman, who had not yet appeared on deck, tho' the sun was o'er the yardarm, or would have been, if not for the fog.

As we watched from the parapet, Timofei confided that Baranov and the *Neva* had departed Kodiak together, with Baranov's little sloop arriving first. He took my 'scope and peered at the frigate. He caught his breath. He'd seen something.

I snatched my glass back. The *Neva's* deck was a nautical beehive. Sailors in striped shirts swarm'd, furling sail, hoisting a longboat to the gunwale. Eight oarsmen snapped to attention. Officers in green dress coats. Two older men in dark suits. In their midst, a blonde queen bee in a long blue dress with gloves & matching bonnet.

*Mommy!*

The *Neva* swung on her anchor in the currents like a kite on a string, showing us her pretty stern, drifting closer to the *Kodiak*. Those on the *Neva's* deck saw a naked man tied to the *Kodiak's* mast. His face was bloody, and above him hung a human head.

The *Neva* people heard shouts from the fort. Cossacks burst forth, rushed down to the cargo bay, and cast a small costumed figure into the water. It was kicking & screaming.

On the *Kodiak*, the truss'd-up Bulygin awoke to the sound of cannon, and through bleary eyes saw smoke rising from the fort. He winced at the pain pulsing in his forehead. Struggling in his bonds, shivering in the morning chill, he blinked at what he supposed to be a ghost ship, an apparition of a splendid Russian frigate. It couldn't be real, could it? Had his prayers been answered? Had the frigate fired upon the fort, or vice versa? He saw what appeared to be a Russian flag flying from the mizzen, and comrades in green uniform coats on the quarterdeck. He nearly fainted with joy. He noticed he was naked save for remnants of his bloody shirt, but his appearance didn't concern him. His colleagues on the frigate would surely understand. He tried to call out for rescue, but could only croak, his throat dry from lack of vodka. Where were Petrov and Benzeman, his steadfast brothers-in-arms? Why was he tied to the mast?

Bulygin blinked again. He saw a tall officer on the frigate who resembled that German ass Leonty Hagemeister, whom Bulygin suspected was complicit in his precipitous departure from St. Petersburg seven years ago, and, clinging to the officer's arm, none other than the attractive and talented Anna Petrovna, his beloved long-lost bride. Again, he lost consciousness.

The *Neva* ran more signal pennants up & down. No response from the fort. The ship's company mustered at battle stations. Their boat hung suspended above the water on its davits.

Up in the Castle, Kuskov consulted a manual on naval signals. The fort's company abandoned their defensive positions and gathered at the cargo bay, buzzing with restless anticipation: New Archangel's first white woman had arrived.

On the *Kodiak*, the officers Petrov and Benzeman, awakened like Bulygin by the guns, rushed topside in their underwear to free their comrade from his bonds. Bulygin staggered to the rail. He called to the people on the *Neva*, who chose not to respond.

The *Kodiak* officers conferred, agreeing that they should report to the *Neva* as soon as they could make themselves presentable. They noticed their boat was beached in the cargo bay. How could they retrieve it? Was that Baranov's little sloop? Petrov waved and shouted at the *Neva*, to no avail. Benzeman began searching for his uniform. Bulygin fell to the deck, sobbing.

Two of our men ventured out to the *Neva* in a baidarka and upon their return reported, "They ask where is Baranov."

Baranov was in the Castle being treated for burns and a possible concussion, and, after sedation, found himself unable to greet our visitors. Baranov was frequently injured, Timofei said, and like me took opium to numb his various pains. Kuskov feared the Cossacks would steal his peg-leg if he ventured out of the Castle, so Timofei would greet a shore party from the *Neva*, should one be forthcoming.

Kuskov, unable to discern a response to the *Neva's* signals, ordered the gun crew to fire a belated salute from the seaward wall, one which erroneously included a rusty ten-pound ball, which splash'd harmlessly out beyond the ships. The jolt of the blast awaken'd the misfiring cannon facing the forest, which also boom'd, belatedly, just as I'd predicted, giving us all a fright and showering the trees with more scrap metal.

The *Neva*, still uncertain as to the fort's disposition, fearing she'd sailed into an ambush and realizing she was a sitting duck under the fort's guns, considered raising anchor. She brought in her boat and remained at battle stations.

Sitka canoes gathered like vultures out beyond cannon range.

The *Kodiak's* officers discussed whether the fort had fired at them, or the *Neva*. Was this another insult from Baranov, another provocation? They voted unanimously that if put to the test their loyalties would lie with the Tsar's navy, not Baranov. They realized they should remove Shubin's head from the rigging where the partiers had hung it (the head, an expression of outrage frozen on its countenance, allegedly offered prescient warnings when given a sip of vodka), but they were afraid to touch it. They remembered their dress uniforms might be ashore, perhaps in the laundry pot. They considered swimming to shore, but were troubled & confused by the Cossacks' baptism of the costumed Baranov and were uncertain as to the fort's disposition. What was going on up there? Another mutiny? They called & waved to the *Neva*, again without response. They voted unanimously to fire at the Castle as a means of demonstrating their loyalty to the Tsar, thus hopefully winning the *Neva's* approval, and went below to find their gunpowder.

Through my glass I watched an animated multilateral discussion on the *Neva* involving the woman, the two suits, and the tall officer. The woman appeared to prevail. *Well duh.* She stepped into the longboat, lifting her skirts above the ankle, revealing stylish hunting boots. The officer assisted, then joined her. Sailors elbow'd for a view. The suits followed the woman into the boat.

At the fort, Kozma shook a fist at the sentries, who returned their eyes to the forest. The gun crew discussed the loading of salute charges, as to whether or not they should include an actual cannonball. Maria brought a silver platter with a mildew'd slice of salted bread on it and we joined the others at the cargo bay.

Eight oars flashing, the *Neva's* longboat approach'd, negotiating the nearshore currents, oarsmen pulling smartly on the coxswain's count. Two officers sat on the aft thwart. The tall one stood behind the woman, a gloved hand on her shoulder and a brocaded tricorner under his elbow. He blocked the coxswain's view.

Alas, a boulder loiter'd in the boat's path, just breaking the surface. A Cossack shouted & pointed, too late. The longboat lurch'd. The standing officer pitch'd with a cry of dismay over the port gunwale and into the water, a glossy boot caught under a thwart. Aghast at his predicament, the oarsmen lunged to his assistance, and the sudden redistribution of weight caused the boat to heel sharply, shipping water. Arms windmilling, sailors dutifully followed the officer over the side. The boat swamp'd. Sailors &

passengers shouted & splashed. Another cannon salute boomed from the Castle, punctuating the aquatic drama.

No sign of the woman. Wait, there: a glimpse of blue silk. She'd climbed on a sailor's back and gripped his hair, to the lad's distress. Timofei tore off his shirt, waded into the maelstrom, grasped the woman to his chest, carried her to shore and set her down before us. Rivulets of seawater trickled from her bonnet, which lay askew, tipped saucily over one eye in the manner of a Parisian courtesan. Water also dripped from her dress, which molded itself to its occupant's torso.

We stood in silent awe. The woman spat curses in French, ripped off the bonnet, hurled it to the stones, stomped on it. Timofei stared at her, trying out different syllables, hoping to form words. She allowed herself a discreet glance at Timofei's baggy but clinging trousers, which were tuck'd into his boots, which squirt'd water. Both breathed heavily from their exertions, his muscled chest rising & falling in rhythm with her swelling bodice.

Neither noted the approach of Hagemeister, who spat German curses and limped on a wrench'd knee.

"You, Cossack," he shouted at Timofei. "Take us to Baranov."

Timofei couldn't take his eyes from the woman. He nodded vaguely toward the Castle. Offended by Timofei's impudence, the angry officer put his hand on his sword, causing Kozma to step forward, causing the officer to step back behind the woman. Kozma explained to her that Baranov wasn't feeling well, and introduced Timofei, our designated spokesman, who remained speechless.

"Where," she asked, "is Mr. Kuskov?"

"He is afraid to come out," Kozma said.

The woman considered this for a moment, then asked: "The man tied to the mast on that ship? With blood on his face?"

"Bulygin," Kozma said. "A naval officer. He harms himself. He despairs. His friends restrain him. Seven years ago, on his wedding night, he is transferred from the navy to here. Since then, not one letter. He desires to return home to his beautiful bride."

The woman & the officer had a quiet word. Kahmooks, eavesdropping, said the officer was advising a retreat to the ship.

Sailors & Cossacks struggled with the *Neva's* boat, endeavouring to get it bailed & beached. The two suits sat coughing, recovering from their ordeal. Hagemeister shiver'd in his wet uniform. The woman's teeth chatter'd. The wet blue dress continued to cling. Her audience observed.

She gathered up her dripping skirts and bolted for the Castle. The limping lieutenant pursued, his hand still on his sword as though he feared we might snap at his haunches. Grunting sailors fell in behind, hauling a teak sea trunk trimmed in brass. The junior officers assisted the older of the two suits, who had lost his eyeglasses. The other had lost his wind, but when air returned he too trudged off up the path. Gallons of water went with them, and a small creek formed in their wake, washing over the forlorn blue bonnet. Our Tim snatch'd it up and waved it at the woman, making odd vocalizations.

Kozma shook his head. "She befuddles him. He cannot speak. A bad omen."

Most prescient, Kozma. But, just before she disappeared into the Castle, the woman did pause on the pathway to adjust her squishy boot, and Timofei might have received just a fraction of a backward glance. Perhaps not. If so, she might have noticed that he clutched her bonnet to his pounding heart.

Timofei: "She smiles at me?"

I say: "A grimace, I think, poor thing. She's endured a rude welcome."

A wet but jovial sailor approached, his eye on our jug: "So, comrades, is America as bad as they say?"

"All you have heard is true, comrade. Our vodka eats your insides, the kolosh eat your outsides."

The sailor elbow'd Kozma, a dangerous gambit: "Vodka first then. Pass the jug, big boy."

Kozma put an arm around the sailor's neck, seized his nose, and poured into his mouth. The sailor's struggles were futile.

Timofei: "Who are they? Why are they here?"

The swabby gagged & choked: "I swear, we know nothing. The old man is Zacharov, a commissar of something. The other is Dr.

Mordgorst, a complete mystery. The woman is Madame Bulygin, a cultural attaché from the Tsar's court. Watch out for her. She is trouble. That is terrible vodka."

Timofei: "We know. 'Bulygin'?"

"You've heard of her."

"No. Yes. Why do they come here?"

"Top secret. Not a word to the crew. Let go of me, you . . ."

"Drink. Do not be rude."

"Please. I know nothing. We have a priest on board. He says the Church tells the Tsar that his American subjects are born out of holy wedlock, so they are not true Russians. Madame Bulygin orders him to go ashore, splice the lines, give all your children the good Russian name, but he sees you through the telescope and secludes himself below. If he obeys, you become husbands, and the Christian names of your red babies are written in the church book."

Timofei: "No priests. Baranov's orders. Does she sleep with your captain?"

"Ha. She occupies the captain's cabin, and the captain waits in line to see her. The young sailor prances in with downy cheeks and crawls out with a beard. The rest of us, we just sail the ship."

The Cossacks piped up: "She is bored with the sailor boys, Timofei. Perhaps she is free this evening."

"Not free. Beware, Timofei, you pay a price."

"But why is she here? Never before does a white woman come to New Archangel."

Timofei: "What is in your hold?"

"The Tsar's cargo. Guarded. Separate from the ship's stores. All we know is the ship rides heavy in the waves. Perhaps the Tsar sends you a load of rocks. Please let me go."

Timofei thanked him: "Keep the jug. Our lovely hostess Olga waits to greet you in the goat shed."

The swabby staggered off, his spine realign'd. The Cossacks debated.

"Heavy cargo? Have they sent us cannons?"

"Does this Hagemeister come to replace Baranov? He told us, when he dies, the Company sends a naval officer to be our leader."

"Yes, but a Russian, not another useless German."
"They will tell Kuskov their secrets. Kuskov will tell us."

KUSKOV LAY TETHER'D FACE-DOWN AT AN AWKWARD ANGLE across his collapsed desk like a walrus carcass about to be render'd. His clothing had been ripped away and his bottom reared its mottled flesh. An ink bottle, spill'd. Ledgers & letters, scatter'd. Kozma unstrapped Kuskov's wooden leg. Kuskov struggled & protested to no avail.

I perused the bookshelves. Timofei said the Tsar had sent New Archangel a thousand books, but literacy was not a priority here, some books had not survived the firewood shortages, and only half were in Russian, with the rest a potpourri of French, German, Latin, Swedish, Dutch, Spanish and Italian. Thirty-five were in English, including a worn copy of *Gulliver's Travels*, which featured a Lilliputian battlefield on its interiour pages: a green mold resisted the advance of a black scum.

I pretended to read, sipping my tea in a wobbly chair beside the woodstove. Though disinterested in the vulgar proceedings playing out before me, I was nonetheless curious about what Kuskov might confide about our visitors, hopefully before Kozma reinstalled his prosthetic in an inappropriate mannour.

The delegation from St. Petersburg had caused us great anxiety. After a tour of the fort and consultations with Kuskov (Baranov remained incoherent), Madame Bulygin announced that Maria was to be her personal assistant and that they and the party's menfolk would return to the *Neva*, which then repositioned herself beyond the fort's cannon range but closer to the Sitka canoes, which retreat'd to safer waters.

Kozma brandish'd Kuskov's leg at the bookshelves: "The Tsar's friend Rezanov teaches Timofei to read the book."

My ears perk'd up whenever they mentioned Nicholai Petrovich Rezanov, who was known to be an influential agent of the Tsar. Upon arriving in New Archangel two years ago, Rezanov had purchased a visiting American brig with just his signature, which was considered as good as the Tsar's gold, and sailed south to claim sites for colonies. Coincidentally, and unbeknownst to Rezanov, the Lewis & Clark expedition was fortified just a few miles inland from the river's mouth, preparing to return home overland, at the same moment that Rezanov was endeavouring unsuccessfully to enter the Columbia River. Lewis & Clark had given up on the ship Astor had sent for them, which, like the *Emily*, had vanished en route.

Russians & Americans never met. Rezanov, frustrated, gave up on trying to enter the river's mouth and sailed on south to San Francisco, where he visited the Spanish mission, got himself engaged to a fifteen-year-old girl, and immediately cast off on the return voyage to St. Petersburg without her. Timofei & Kozma expected his imminent return.

Kuskov writh'd in his bonds: "Fools. Timofei can't read, Rezanov never returns, and if you hurt me I will tell the Tsar's woman. Untie me. Please."

Kozma slid a thumb along the shaft of Kuskov's appendage. Tooth marks, possibly left by a large dog.

"Ouch," he said. "Splinters. Where is the bear grease?"

Kuskov moan'd: "They tell me nothing. She can read a ledger. Many questions she asks."

"She?"

"Mostly she. Zakharov, Mordgorst, not so much. Baranov just babbles. She asks about fur, ships, men. I say, 'Yes, Madame, the men are a disgrace. Mother Russia wants profits, but never does she send us good men or enough supplies. If not for the Boston traders we would starve. How can we build new forts?' I plead, I beg, but she ignores me. She expects to find the men of New Archangel ready and eager for a hazardous voyage, and she will select the best from amongst them. If they are not ready, a tribunal will find me, your beloved brother-in-arms, guilty of mismanagement of Company assets. Also, of treason against our beloved Tsar. Baranov will serve as the government's chief witness before he returns home to a well-deserved retirement.

"Zakharov is old and ill," Kuskov continued, sobbing. "Dr. Mordgorst trembles at the howling of the wind. They tell her the

American colonies are hopeless. Soon the sea otter is gone. The two men return to the *Neva*, but she sits here with my books, like a schoolmistress. She says, 'Your ledgers are fairy tales, Kuskov. Show me the storehouses.' We go, we look. 'These are good pelts,' she says. 'Why have these not been sent back to Okhotsk?' What am I supposed to tell her? 'Oh, Madame, we must save the good fur for the Bostons, who will get rich trading it in Canton, so they will bring us sugar so we can distill vodka so the men won't mutiny'?

"And what is Maria telling her? Maria hates me. She will say the books are my responsibility. She will say Baranov pleads with St. Petersburg to bring him home, that his old eyes can no longer see the little numbers, that he must rely on me. All is lost. My career is in tatters. Never will I see my home in Vologda again. I will be executed. No, I will shoot myself. No, I can't, I'm afraid."

"Tell us more."

Kuskov sobbed: "She reads the fort's roster. She asks who is reliable. Her husband, can he function? The Tsar desires that Bulygin returns home a hero. Who knows why? She asks about you, Timofei. And Petrov, and Benzeman. And you, Englishman. She is curious about you." *She could tell you were bogus, dude.*

I say: "You informed her it isn't mutual."

"Of course. I tell her, 'Williams, a spy? Ha. He only consumes our meager opium supply. She looks at your papers. Closely. Many questions she asks. She knows how to get answers."

"So does Kozma," Timofei said.

Kuskov whimper'd. "She tells me I must prepare for a long and difficult mission. Impossible, I say. She pulls from her sleeve the small pistol. She cocks the hammer. She says, 'We do not disappoint the Tsar, Kuskov. If you cannot fulfill your duties, you are not useful.'"

"Mission?"

"Top secret. Not of interest to the promyshlenniki."

Kozma, gently: "Open wide."

"California. They want a fort at Bodega Bay. And the Columbia River. She asks me, 'When is the *Otkrytie* ready for sea? How long does the *Kodiak* careen on the beach? The *Tamana*, how much cargo can she carry?' I say, 'How do I know? I am just the bookkeeper.

Ask Lincoln, the Boston shipbuilder.' I tell her Lincoln demands payment in Spanish silver, no more rubles printed on sealskin, but even if I had silver I cannot pay him, or off he goes on the next Boston ship, and no more sturdy vessels does he build. She says, 'Lincoln's contract is written in Russian, so it says what I say it says.' She has a letter from the Tsar to the mandarins of Canton, asking that Russian ships be allowed to trade there, as the vessels of other nations do. She says the Tsar is willingly to pay for this privilege, in silver. She says, 'Bring to me the angry shipwright. I soothe the dark moods.' So, Lincoln meets with her privately, at which time they sign the new contract, in which Lincoln promises that soon the ships are seaworthy. She pays him, in silver."

MADAME BULYGIN, WEARING A SHRUNKEN BLUE DRESS, presided from behind Kuskov's wobbly desk. Her fair hair was an intricate construction of prim braids & errant locks. A disobedient curl fell over her brow as she read leatherbound *Rossiĭskaya-Amerikanskaya Kompaniya* (Russian-American Company) ledgers. She brushed it back. It stayed. *Do I look like her? Be honest.*

Maria, clad in gray woolens, sat in gray light beside the north window, watching gray water. The seated officers squirm'd in faded green uniforms trimmed in tarnish'd brass, with Petrov & Benzeman bracing a glassy-eyed Bulygin like book-ends. Kuskov hover'd at Madame Bulygin's shoulder, perspiring despite the chill. Hagemeister stood, fidgeting. Baranov, still costumed but somewhat the worse for wear, perched atop the bookcase armoire, preening. His charred plumage drooped to the floor, where a disciple crouched, one Afanasii Valgusov, a wiry Cossack who called himself "The Raven." Valgusov had foresworn clothing, instead attaching his namesake's feathers to his flesh in a manner we hoped not to learn. His wild black beard protruded from beneath a black bird mask of native design. He hopped & croak'd.

Timofei & I arrived late. Kuskov saw us and bent to whisper in Madame's ear. Her blue eyes continued to move up & down the pages, but at length she stood, adjusted cuffs of Belgian lace, and swept us with a stern gaze.

"All present? *Très bien.* You know who I am. An imperial envoy on an important mission. Therefore, I am the virtual embodiment of our beloved Tsar."

The officers, in unison: "Long live the Tsar."

The Raven croak'd: "Long live Baranov, the Tsar of America."

Madame Bulygin ignored him: "As you know, two of the Tsar's emissaries, Commissar Zakharov and Dr. Mordgorst, accompany me on this mission, but now prefer to remain aboard the *Neva.* They intend to return to St. Petersburg, where they will report to the Tsar that our situation in America is hopeless. They may be right.

"But they will also report that I, Madame Anna Petrovna Bulygin, remain. Why do I exchange the comforts of St. Petersburg for these forlorn premises? Why do I linger here, when others retreat in despair? Why does Madame Bulygin risk her impressive diplomatic career on this, this 'republic of drunkards', as comrade Rezanov so charitably described it?"

Quoth the Raven: "Alas, poor Rezanov, we knew him well."

She raised a scroll'd document like Joan of Arc's crucifix: "I remain in New Archangel because of this letter. It is signed by the Tsar's own hand. If you read it, you would share my determination, but the letter is secret. Besides myself, only Mr. Baranov reads it, and he is sworn to . . ."

Baranov squawk'd from aloft the armoire: "It says, 'By this order, I, Tsar Alexander the First, do hereby commission an armed expedition of colonization, to be conducted under the guise of . . .'"

Madame Bulygin glared at him: "Silence. We reveal our orders only to those who are necessary. I can tell you that this letter bestows upon us the most noble quest the Tsar can offer his minions, that of expansion of his dominion to new regions. For two centuries, since the reign of Peter the Great, we march east across the wastelands of Siberia, to the Pacific, to Kodiak Island, and now to New Archangel, where we gather our forces for the extension of Tsar Alexander's beneficent rule to the mainland of North America. You all remember Mr. Rezanov, how he dreamed of a Russian America. Sadly, he has perished in service to the Tsar, but his dream, our dream, lives on. We, the servants of the Tsar, prepare to make that dream manifest. Today, New Archangel's best men and women will volunteer to build two new forts on the fertile land to the south."

She smiled: "Two forts? How can this be? You can barely defend this little pile of logs. Gentlemen, let me confide that in addition to food, clothing and tools, the *Neva's* cargo includes sixteen cannons, a dozen crates of infantry muskets, and more ammunition than the Tsar thought prudent to part with. He desires that his new forts be well-defended from our many enemies. Tomorrow, at first light, you will supervise the transfer of this cargo, from . . . "

Petrov, a question: "Madame? Our contract with Baranov says the officers can be, ahem, elsewhere when the Cossacks handle gunpowder?"

"Contract? *Qu'est-ce que c'est?* Gentlemen, the Tsar's orders are the *raison d' être* of your insignificant and temporary existence. Prior agreements no longer exist. All cargo handlers remain sober. No *faux pas, s'il vous plait.* Not once does the gunpowder explode. Any further questions?"

Petrov: "The Cossacks will not load gunpowder without a cup of vodka first. Too hard on their nerves."

Madame Bulygin: "Hmmm. Vodka and gunpowder. A hazardous mixture, it would seem. But perhaps better than the alternative. Very well then. But no horseplay, and no smoking. Sorry. Careful smoking only. Now, assignments. After much consideration, I decide Mr. Kuskov is to be the deputy commander of the mission. He will sail aboard the *Kodiak*, with Mr. Petrov serving as ship's captain."

Petrov slapped his forehead and moaned: "Why not Benzeman? He . . ."

Benzeman groveled: "Madame, I beg you, I must return on the *Neva*. Not another winter in this madhouse. Please."

Madame Bulygin: "Courage, Mr. Benzeman. I too yearn for civilization, but the Tsar has other plans for us. Due to the colonial nature of this mission, he directs that only true Russians may embark upon it. Also, the Tsar's faithful Aleut and Kodiak subjects. Our Mr. Benzeman is, yes, a loyal servant of the Tsar, but he is also a citizen of Germany and a former officer in that country's navy, so he will remain on duty here.

"The crew of the *Kodiak*, I have decided, will be made up primarily of Mr. Slobodchikov's men, the first Russians to enter the Columbia River. On the second ship, the *St. Nicholas*, Mr. Bulygin is to be master of the vessel, and . . ."

A murmur. Smirks. Bulygin glowered at the floor, appearing not to have heard his name mentioned. Benzeman sobbed quietly.

". . . and the trustworthy employee Timofei Tarakanov will serve as both quartermaster and second-in-command, as a reward for steadfast service to the Company. And other duties. To be specified. Later."

Eyebrows, snickers.

"A reminder, men. Your Tsar assumes that his orders are obeyed without question, with enthusiasm. Any disrespect to an envoy would be an insult to the Tsar, to be reported as such. Nothing interferes with the tasks the Tsar's envoy assigns you. No longer will your men vote on whether to obey orders. Understood?

"Now then. I need twenty good men for each ship. Can you meet my requirements, Mr. Tarakanov?"

Her husband staggered to his feet: "What? You need Tarakanov to find men for you?" His mates pulled him back to his chair.

Petrov: "What about the *Neva*? We will need protection from the Spanish frigates."

Madame Bulygin: "The *Neva* has other orders. This is a sensitive mission. We do not seek attention, so we will not sail in company with a warship. We are ambiguous. We are peaceful visitors. We are civilians, not military. The structures we build will be fortified, but we will call them trading posts. We conduct the Tsar's business under arms, but not in uniform. Do we represent the Tsar's navy, or his fur company? Are they different? Remember, in St. Petersburg, London, Paris, Madrid, nobody cares about a spat between fur hunters, but a bloody uniform can prompt precipitous realignment of important alliances, and, thus, needless . . ."

Petrov had another question: "Ah, Madame? When you say 'we', surely you do not mean that you yourself plan to accompany us? Rigors of the voyage?"

"'Accompany'? I command, Mr. Petrov. I cannot in good conscience allow you to go blundering off by yourselves. The larger vessel, the *Kodiak*, will carry most of our cargo. I will, ahem, command, from the swifter *St. Nicholas*."

"Blunder off to where, might we be so bold as to inquire?"

Baranov flapped his stubby wings: "Fool. Where else? The letter says, 'a sturdy fort north of San Francisco, limiting Spain's future northward expansion, and another at the mouth of the Columbia River, a major portal to the interior of . . .'"

A petite bang. In the blink of an eye, a slender French pistol had slipped out of Madame Bulygin's sleeve and fired, nicking the armoire just below Baranov's bare toes. The shot's report echoed from the log walls. A petite puff of smoke floated angelically. We sat speechless. Bulygin toppled over backwards in his chair. Round-eyed Aleuts peered in through the heavy velvet portieres.

Baranov, defiant: ". . . through which hundreds of hardy Russian settlers shall soon . . ."

Madame Bulygin handed the smoking pistol to Maria: "*Vite. L'autre.*" Maria passed her a matching weapon.

Hagemeister, a hasty intervention: "Madame, this is the stuff of common scuttlebutt. As I warn you, there are no secrets in zis place."

Madame Bulygin held her fire: "A leak, *peut-être*? A breach in our security, Mr. Kuskov?"

Kuskov accused Timofei: "He makes me talk. He and that monster Ovchinnikov, they . . ."

"Mr. Tarakanov?"

Timofei explained: "We must tell the men where they go. The book cannot be missing the page."

Madame Bulygin smiled faintly: "How sad. I imagined Cossacks would embrace my adventuresome perspective. Where is our *joie de vivre*, our cheery spirit of adventure? Why, a journey with a mysterious destination is an opportunity for spiritual growth, a dancing lesson from God. As Voltaire would say, our voyage may not be predictable, but it will be interesting. Please tell the men of my distress upon hearing that they hesitate to embark with me this month, on . . ."

Gasps: "When?"

"*Mais certainment*. September the 28th, 1808, to be precise. Why? Previous engagement?"

"We are doomed. The storms."

Madame: "We must depart soon. We have been awaiting the arrival of another ship, one bringing more people and more supplies, but we . . ."

"'People'? You mean . . .?"

"A dozen robust women of childbearing age. We . . ."

A cheer from the courtyard below. She didn't notice and continued: "We pray that they reach Sitka by now, but . . ." A pause, a wistful glance out across the sound, as though a sail might appear. "So, when they arrive, they will follow in our wake. Already we tarry too long. I study the Company's meteorological records, gentlemen, and I discover that a brief autumn respite in the weather may allow us to slip down the coast before the winter gales are upon us, perhaps with a north wind to push us along. If not, if the storms catch us on the open sea, why, we will simply 'lay to', as the sailors say. We will put our bow into the weather, batten our hatches, and ride the tempest out. Already I experience the storm at sea, as the lieutenant remembers."

Hagemeister sighed fondly: "*Liebchen*, ven you vitness the *sturm und drang* of the sea's fury, you tremble, and cling to me."

"I cling to my flask of cognac, lieutenant. I retired to my cabin, to bask in my crew's attentive pampering, while you remained on deck for the duration of the storm. Yes, I am ready for adverse conditions, and I expect the same of . . ."

Benzeman: "Madame? Speaking of adverse conditions, if you take forty men from New Archangel, you leave the fort in great danger. Even now . . ."

"Perhaps I do not make myself clear. We devote everything to this mission. The Aleutians, Kodiak, Yakutat, New Archangel, these are but stepping-stones. Your affection for this miserable pile of logs touches me deeply, but we have no room in our hold for sentiment. New Archangel is simply a forlorn monument to the squandering of the fur trade. The sea otter vanishes from here to

Cook's Inlet. You allow foreign ships to sail without permission in the Tsar's territorial waters, where they trade guns to the Tsar's native subjects for the Tsar's sea otter pelts, guns these natives then shoot at the Tsar's fur hunters. After half a century of Russian rule, we Russians have no safe haven. Even our Aleut and Kodiak hunters would turn on us, had they the strength. According to Mr. Kuskov's records, over 700 of them perish in the last ten years, most of them lost far out at sea in their little boats, where they go to seek the last remaining sea otter. Two hundred souls in one storm, and not a Russian ship in sight. And, since you confiscate their women, they find themselves hard-pressed to replace themselves at the rate you kill them off.

"No, we depart with no regrets. We could be, should be, in California by now, farming fields, tending flocks, sending Russian pioneers ever deeper into the interior. Instead, we cower atop this pile of rocks. Only the natives' superstitious fear of Mr. Baranov separates us from disaster."

Valgusov flapped his wings: "Caw! Behold the great Aleksandr Baranov, an eagle among sparrows. King of Kodiak, conqueror of the kekur, sultan of Sitka."

Outside, a faint cheer drifted up: "Long live Baranov, Tsar of America."

Baranov preen'd.

Hagemeister, a thoughtless gaffe: "Heh heh. Ven Madame vurst meets Baranov, she vispers to me, 'He is not much bigger than your . . .' Oops."

Hand on sword, a sputtering Bulygin rose to confront Hagemeister.

Madame Bulygin waved him back to his chair: "Yes, New Archangel may fall in our absence. If so, so be it. This fort is but a pawn, one the Tsar is prepared to sacrifice. We pray that Mr. Baranov can hold New Archangel together, but already I hear rumors of mutiny plots in the barracks, of . . ."

Baranov flapped angrily: "Treachery. Who dares conspire against me? Drag the rats from their holes. Lash them to the whipping post. Fetch my cat-o'-nine-tails."

Valgusov: "The men remain loyal, little father. The traitor is Kuskov. He . . ."

Kuskov, flush'd.

"To the contrary," Madame Bulygin said, "I have confidence in Mr. Kuskov. He patiently takes time to explain to me the inventory of the storehouses, that I might become more knowledgeable of our assets. Previous cursory inspections have raised more questions than they answered, and Mr. Kuskov has reason to believe that, without my support, he fares poorly in a Company audit. Therefore, at my request, he devotes himself to scrutiny of his accounts. When the record books are reconciling with the inventory, Mr. Kuskov assumes his new duties. As he has reason to fear bodily harm, as does the supervisor Sysoi Slobodchikov, the Tsar therefore assigns them new quarters aboard the *Kodiak*, under the protection of armed and trustworthy . . .'"

Valgusov screech'd: "Slobodchikov? Why, that . . ."

Hagemeister: "Ha. Ven Madame questions Slobodchikov about the Sandwich Islands, and where is the profit from his long voyage, the good soldier Slobodchikov sings like the little birdie. Tveet tveet tveet."

Little Bird Man, puzzled: "Tveet?"

Kuskov, perspiring: "Madame? Why do we discuss Company business in the presence of the foreigner?"

I say: "Me? Or the Germans?"

Madame Bulygin: "Ah, yes. Mr. Williams, our friend from England with the dirty blanket and the rusty sword and the *aire de mystère*. Is this, how do you say, the British cloak and dagger? Mr. Kuskov believes you are a spy, a secret agent of some sort, bent on some nefarious mission. Mr. Tarakanov allows you bask in our hospitality but remain otherwise indolent, whining for passage home, even as your unpaid bills overflow the Company's ledgers, now totaling . . ."

Kuskov handed her a ledger: "Not including his opium consumption."

Baranov, from on high: "Pass the pipe, comrades."

Madame Bulygin sighed: "*Quel dommage.* You have l'attachement, Mr. Williams, *le penchant*?"

I say: "Rubbish. If Mr. Kuskov could produce a credible account of my expenses, my employers would happily reimburse as soon as I'm returned home. Sadly, however, his past attempts at such an invoice have been, like his tabulations of the inventory, fraught with error."

Kuskov whined: "Lies, Madame. This, this provocateur, he seeks to sow the seeds of doubt and mistrust. Do not be misled by his glib tongue, I implore you." *Good advice.*

"Mr. Williams does not fool us," Madame Bulygin said. "I order him to attend this meeting to remind him of his debts and to inform him of his new duties. No longer does he languish while honest Russians toil to make him comfortable. He sails with us, and he will work. Pending resolution of his debt to the Tsar, he serves as the ordinary seaman."

Kuskov: "But you just said only Russians are to go?"

I say: "Egad, Madame. A British citizen, forced to serve aboard a foreign vessel? Whitehall shall have questions for the Russian ambassador. Deplorable."

"Calm yourself, sir. Just as we provide you with a ration of opium, so also do we ration your freedom. Too much of either brings trouble. Together, disaster. We fear that if you return to England, you will tell false stories about us. It is my duty to protect the Tsar's friendship with King George, and also to collect the many rubles you owe to The Russian-American Company. Therefore, please do not attempt to depart from us before you have paid your debt, in which case . . ."

Hagemeister pointed at me, wiggling his thumb: "She shoots you vis the teensy Vrench pistol."

Madame Bulygin: "I'm sure it won't come to that. I now control the medicinal stores, so Mr. Williams will behave himself. We welcome you to our little crew, sir. The Tsar appreciates your enthusiastic assistance, and he regrets, for perhaps obvious reasons, that you will not be listed in the Company records.

"Understood? Questions? Good. Our course is clear. All hands on deck. The Tsar assigns us a staggering task. The weak may perish along the way, but Russia must strengthen her fragile grip upon this continent. We venture south, toward new horizons, into wild lands, to a risky destiny. Valuable fruits lie within our reach, ripe for plucking. While England fights France and Spain, while the United States quarrel amongst themselves, Russia will act. We will plant our flag in American soil, and soon heroic Russian peasants will spread bountiful pastures across the Tsar's new wilderness. It is our moment. America awaits us.

# 4 | The Voyage of the *St. Nicholas*

OUR SHIPS AWAIT'D US IN THE ANCHORAGE, ready to depart, but the cargo bay still teem'd with reluctant seafarers and distraught well-wishers. The sleek little schooner *Tamana*, newly rechristened the *Sv. Nikolai* (*St. Nicholas*), pulled at her tether, impatiently awaiting her crew, which was to include me. After a year & a month here, I would leave on the same ship I sailed in on.

Her fat sister *Kodiak* would depart first. Baggy-panted Cossacks hung from the yards, shaking out her canvas. On the quarterdeck, her captain, Petrov, and Kuskov, deputy mission commander, observed the shoreside bon voyage party with disdain. Boats scurried to & fro. Anchors prepared to be hoisted.

The *St. Nicholas'* crew linger'd ashore. Passing of jugs, tearful embraces. The ship's orchestra lightened the mood with a farewell jig. Comrades linked arms, stumbling in the cobblestones. Madame Bulygin wore a gray wool ensemble that blended with the sky & water. Timofei stood at her side, inhaling her atmosphere.

I had not yet had opportunity to discuss our impending voyage with Timofei & Kozma. It appeared they were abandoning New Archangel to the mercy of the Sitka and thereby risk the loss of the fortune in fur they'd need to establish themselves on Kauai, assuming they returned from this voyage. What of Madame Bulygin's rumour'd treasure chest, the value of its contents still unknown?

She kicked a cobblestone impatiently: "The inspirational message, please, then the reading of the ship's roster."

Timofei addressed us, reading from a prepared statement: "Hear me, brothers. A parting word from our beloved Tsar. Ahem: 'Heroes! You who have been chosen for the glorious crew of the insert name of ship, step forward!'"

A voice from the crowd: "Yes, hurry off to your doom."

Madame Bulygin glanced at the ebbing tide.

Timofei: "Are the Aleut and Kodiak crew members present? Five? Yakov? Sergei? Yuri? Pavel? Olga? All here? Good. Kahmooks, ship's dog? Speak, boy."

Kahmooks: "Bow. Wow."

Madame Bulygin: "Skip the animals, Noah. Call the Cossacks."

Timofei flipped a page: "Ivan Bolotov."

Bolotov, a queasy tone: "Not me. I cannot go to sea. I fwo up."

Timofei: "Get in the boat, Ivan. Is the apprentice Filip Kotelnikov with us?"

Filip's mother, a sob: "He is only thirteen. Please do not take away my innocent . . ."

Little Filip groaned, palm to forehead, then tucked his fiddle under his arm, kissed his mother's teary cheek, and hastened for the waiting boat.

Timofei: "Good lad. Ivan Kurmachev."

Kurmachev called out from the back: "Kurmachev could not be here."

Timofei: "Get in the boat. Where are the evil twins?"

Abram Petukhov regarded his twin brother Iakov with disgust: "He is the evil one. He should not be on the same ship as young Filip. Remember what . . ."

Timofei: "Dimitri Shubin."

Shubin, disconsolate: "I told you. I go nowhere until I get it back."

Madame Bulygin: "Sick, loathsome . . ."

Shubin threw his fists into the air, revealing sweat-soaked armpits: "Mark my words, brothers. You are cursed. My head warned us, you all heard. Misery befalls us, especially those of you who have taken part in, or have knowledge of, the disappearance of my head. Beware the Tsar's whore. Heed her not. Those red lips are the mouth of hell."

Timofei: "Khariton Sobachnikov."

Despite a shadowy past, the portly, red-faced Sobachnikov was New Archangel's best fisherman and an accomplished accordionist as well. He bade farewell to his weeping wives, who thrust babes at him. Children clung to their skirts.

The women wailed: "We need him here, to provide for us. Again, we are with child."

Timofei, a nod at the boat: "You need rest, comrade Sobachnikov. A peaceful sea voyage. Bring your accordion. Next, Afanasii (The Raven) Valgusov."

A forlorn cry from the battlements. We turned to observe a sorrowful Baranov flapping his wings on the parapets above. From within his gaudy mask, a plaintive plea: "Have pity, Madame. You take Timofei and Kozma, my protection. Must you abduct my loyal Raven, too?"

Madame Bulygin called back: "Birds of a feather should flock together, Mr. Baranov. Time for Mr. Valgusov to leave the nest, to try his wings against a different breeze. Do you agree, Raven? Do you join our voyage freely?"

Valgusov turned, displaying blown-away tail feathers: "The Raven is endangered. The hunters, too much they drink."

Timofei: "We have a safe place for you aloft, Afanasii, a perch they call the crow's nest. Next: John Williams, ordinary seaman."

Madame Bulygin: "Debtor. Malingerer. Addict."

I say: "Present, but under strenuous protest."

Madame Bulygin: "Noted, *avec amusement*. Next?"

Timofei: "Savva Zuev, and his melodious balalaika."

Zuev: "Present, but under protest, like him. How can they force us to go on a dangerous voyage? Why do we allow the Company to oppress us? I refuse."

Kozma was moving silently toward Zuev.

Timofei called out, "Kasian Zypianov."

Zuev kept shouting: "Brothers, sisters, hear me. We are not slaves. We can be free. Rise up, throw off your chains of servitude.

Why have you been shackled to debt since the day you arrived? What have they done with the pelts we fought and died for? Why must we plead like beggars for our vodka? If you call yourself men, you must demand your share of the profits. We have won this rock with our blood, our sweat, our tears. We bury our comrades up there amongst those stumps. Listen to me! If we rise up, together, as one, now, then we can live here, in America, to work, to have families, to be free, forever. If we defy these slave-drivers, if we refuse to be dragged aboard these ships like bleating sheep, if we remain here, in this fort we have built, with our loved ones, we can! Resist! If we unite, if we stand bravely as one, they cannot oppress us. What do you say? As for me, I will have freedom, or death. Who will join me?"

A frenzied Baranov hopped about the palisade, demanding Zuev be arrest'd. Zuev noted Kozma's approach and hasten'd for the boat.

Timofei repeated: "Kasian Zypianov."

Zypianov arrived late with his bear in tow: "Here. Also my old lady wants to come."

Madame Bulygin smiled: "I'm sorry, Mr. Zypianov. No more womenfolk. How sweet: a tame bear, and so affectionate. You have raised it from an orphan cub?"

Timofei: "Better is not to talk of this."

Madame Bulygin: "*Au contraire*. I am curious. Folksy anecdotes provide me with valuable cultural perspective. Please enlighten me."

Kozma spoke up: "When comrade Zypianov arrives in New Archangel, he seeks to join the Brotherhood of Yermak, the followers of the great Cossack leader. But, to become a Brother, one must prove himself by completing The Triple Troika, a demanding test of strength and endurance. First, he drinks three cups of vodka. Second, he wrestles the angry bear, winning two falls out of three. Finally, what is left of him makes romance with Olga, the large Kodiak girl. Again, best two out of three, according to the judges' ruling. So, Zypianov, he gets the vodka down, but then, alas, he becomes confused."

His friends recalled the incident clearly: "Actually, Zyp is lucky to be alive, not to mention . . . dare we say it . . . loved?"

The bear embraced Zypianov's leg.

Kozma: "But they live privately, behind the carpentry shop. She sleeps all winter. They are fond of each other, as you can . . ."

Madame Bulygin quivered with indignation: "Depravity. The Church shall hear of this. Poor innocent creature. No more animal husbandry. Return her, it, to the wild, immediately."

Hagemeister giggled: "Zis place is vild, jah?"

Zypianov: "She is bored by the wild, and I fear to leave her behind in New Archangel. She cannot resist the spruce beer. She will fall into disrepute the moment I am gone."

Kahmooks: "If she goes, I stay here."

Madame Bulygin: "She is not going. *Sacre bleu*."

I told Zypianov: "Beastly luck, old chap. You'll just have to bear up somehow."

He sobbed & hugged his furry mate. Tearful hugs all around. The last of us pushed off. The Tsar's flag waved. Below it on the ramparts sat a forlorn pile of feathers.

Madame Bulygin stepped daintily into the last boat. "*Au revoir,* Mr. Baranov," she called. "*Bon chance.* May the fort be with you." *Delete lame pun. Bear anecdote in poor taste. Delete.*

At dawn on October the 10th, Cape Flattery rose from the sea, its green summit cresting a thousand feet above the waves. I knew where we were.

Our voyage had been tedious: we'd struggled against a relentless southwest wind, tacking far out to sea, then running back in, to the continent, glimpsing snowy mountains. This morning I had scent'd forest on the breeze.

Our fishermen hauled halibut lines through clouds of red krill. Olga banged iron pots below. Whales follow'd in our wake.

Yesterday, at noon, with the cape unseen, I shot the sun as best I could, a white orb behind the gray. Forty-eight or 49 degrees north. At midnight, in utter blackness, I woke the deck watch and we came about on a beam reach due east, bounding landward through leaden swells. Our slim English lass loved to run with the wind on her beam. At dawn the sea's colour changed, became violet, then rose. The sky cleared, and through bleary eyes I saw the cape, our landmark. I felt I'd been drawn to it just as I'd been to the Columbia River.

The wind came west, moving north, blowing us south on a calmer sea through flocks of auklets. On the coast, signs of habitation: plumes of wood smoke blend'd with foggy forest. Mountains, above the clouds.

Filip played whale songs. Long notes, off-key, held 'til the strings could not sustain. The whales danced frantically around us on wing'd tails.

Treacherous waters, these, uncharted. Sea otter lounged in kelp beds, regarding us with dog-eyes. Kahmooks regarded them with disgust. The Aleuts wanted to put the boat in the water, to hunt. Timofei ordered us to press onward.

Kozma scanned the seascape: "No sails to be seen. The *Kodiak* returns to New Archangel."

Bulygin slumped mumbling against the rail, nightmares raging unabated, his coat pulled over his head.

Kozma: "Why does Bulygin not yet fall overboard?"

Madame Bulygin & Maria appeared at the companionway behind Kozma. He didn't see them. Timofei performed warning signals using only his eyes.

Kozma, oblivious: "Well? What? Does our plan change?"

Madame Bulygin peer'd landward: "Good morning, employees. All is well? Have we raised the cape?"

Kozma jumped. At the sound of his wife's voice, Bulygin's salt-crust'd eyes cracked open. Blinking, he struggled to his knees.

My report: "Cape Flattery indeed, as my countryman Captain Cook dubbed it thirty years ago. He said the cape flatter'd him with hopes of finding safe harbour nearby."

She smirk'd: "*C'est vrai, monsieur?* Cook finds the cape, but misses the strait? *Regardez, s'il vous plait*: the mouth of a strait leading into the depths of the continent, fourteen miles wide, possibly the entrance to the fabled Northwest Passage, yet somehow Cook fails to notice it. He was here, was he not?"

I say: "Vagarious fogbanks, no doubt. Rocks. Closer now than we really should be."

"Cook also fails to find the Columbia River, as I recall. No, better we refer to this inspiring promontory as the Cape of Juan de Fuca, after the mariner who explores these straits for Spain in 1592, long before . . ."

I say: "Long after England's Sir Francis Drake visited in 1579, according to . . ."

Valgusov, from the main-top: "Kolosh! To arms!"

OUR EYES FOLLOWED THE RAVEN'S OUTTHRUST WINGTIP. Timofei scanned the waves with the telescope. Madame Bulygin snatch'd the glass from him. With my own 'scope I saw canoes a mile to landward, bounding through the swells. Yellow paddles flash'd in rhythm. Already we could hear them singing.

Madame Bulygin: "Our first encounter with the natives of the region. Captain, let us furl our sails and come up into the wind. Mr. Tarakanov, tell the men to behave peacefully."

The captain did as ordered. Timofei shouted, "Battle stations. Bolotov, to the maintop with Afanasii, two muskets each. Five, Zypianov, quick, up to the fore-top. Swivel crews, man your guns. A double load of shot. Set your fuses. Olga, light the slow-match."

Madame Bulygin glared. The singing armada stayed well off, casting eagle feathers and red mineral dust upon the sea. The canoes, like those at the Columbia River, were reminiscent of Venice's gondolas: a high prow topped with a wolf's head, broad of beam, a raised stern where the steersman stood. The paddlers' faces were painted red & black, with bones through their noses. Some wore sea otter robes, one sported a Yankee sailor's jacket, and most wore conical hats, bulb-topped and wide-brimmed, woven with images of whales & faces. All were heavily armed with English flintlocks and the American .58-caliber trade musket, as well as whalebone clubs, steel hatchets, bows & iron-tipped arrows, spears & double-pointed pitchforks. They circled, singing, at a distance, balancing on the waves like ducks, their paddles scarcely touching the sea.

THE *ST. NICHOLAS* BRISTLED WITH MUSKETRY, porcupinish. Timofei shouted a greeting: "*Klahowya, sikhs.*" Hello, friends.

No response. More singing.

Timofei: "After the singing, I offer another greeting."

Madame Bulygin: "They seem nervous. I suggest we refrain from pointing the guns. How beautiful they are, in their primal state, so innocent. *La bete sauvage.* Such strong chests and shoulders. Are they singing to welcome us? Should we respond?"

Timofei shrugged: "They summon their guardian spirits, for protection. They discuss us, decide what to do. We are a strange ship, and we come after the trading season."

Madame Bulygin: "Perhaps a small coin will get their attention."

The crew: "Coin?"

Madame Bulygin: "Yes, I shall now confide that the Tsar has entrusted us with a chest full of fine Spanish silver, which we . . ." *Delete.*

Timofei: "The chest with the imperial seal? In the cabin, behind the loose plank in the bulkhead? Not silver. Pewter tax tokens." *Delete everything about silver.*

Madame Bulygin blinked, turned on her heel, disappear'd down the companionway. Maria, Timofei and curious onlookers followed, finding Madame Bulygin in the cabin kneeling before a padlock'd chest, discovering that a skilled hand had surreptitiously picked the lock, sliced the crimson wax seal joining lid to box, exchanged the contents for pewter trade tokens, and then concealed the cut.

Timofei: "Kuskov opens the chest before we leave New Archangel. On your orders, he said."

Tokens clatter'd through her pale fingers. She rushed from the cabin up to the deck, seeking air at the rail, where she held fast to the rat-lines, staring expressionless past the circling canoes to the snowy mountains beyond.

We rocked in the swells. The schooner's bones creaked. Cold sea sloshed against our hull.

A small canoe bearing two boys and a large glistening halibut bobbed in our lee. The smaller boy had scars that bespoke violence, one on his nose from a knife and another on his thigh, from a bullet. He also had some white blood in his veins; the coastal natives displayed a variety of skin colours, but this lad was several shades lighter than average. He & his mate gazed up at Madame Bulygin as she gripped the lines.

The singing ceased. A canoe bearing eight men drew near, its occupants addressing us in the jargon: "*Tsolo? Tseepe ooahut?*" Are you lost?

They repeated that word Comcomly used: "*Ho'kwat?*"

I translated: "They ask if we're homeless wanderers."

Madame Bulygin, a defiant tear in her eye: "Tell them that we have a purpose, a destination. Tell them that this is the Tsar's ship *St. Nicholas*, and that . . ."

The crew: "*Tamana*. Bad luck to rename a ship."

". . . and that we come on a mission of peace and friendship. Inform them that their Tsar extends to them his love and protection, and that we, in his name, accept their humble gratitude."

Timofei pointed north: "Sitka."

The natives backed their canoes off, tapping their temples, making bird-noises: "*Tenas kalakala*." Little bird.

Then: "*Kah mika klatawa?*" Where are you going?

Timofei pointed south: "*Hyas chuck*." The big river.

"*Kahta?*" Why?

With proud gestures, Timofei described a structure of extensive width and height: "*Mamook hyas illahee, kopa mahkook nawamooks*." We will make a large house for trading sea otter.

The natives bounced their pluck'd eyebrows at each other. A tyee inquired about our trade goods.

Timofei: "Bring up a barrel of blue beads. Also, some pearls. Drop the cargo net over the side." He held up three fingers, motioning to the natives: "*Klone klatawa chako, klone klatawa keekwullie*." Three men come up, three go down.

The natives declined. Dozens of canoes, perhaps a hundred, had come out laden with furs, women paddling with the men. None were eager to come aboard. A man stood in his canoe, displaying a five-foot-long sea otter pelt that shimmer'd lustrously in anaemic sunlight. Timofei ceremoniously withdrew a length of blue beads from the barrel. Suppressed snickers from the canoes. Undaunted,

Timofei proudly held up an iron wood-chopping chisel, only slightly rusted. Canoes turned shoreward.

Madame Bulygin: "The chisels are good enough for Russians, no? How rude."

Timofei displayed a bolt of Nanking cotton, only slightly mildew'd. The remaining natives coughed behind their paddles, remembering pressing engagements. One, lingering, pointed at Kurmachev's bulky wool greatcoat: "*Kloshe capo.*" Good coat. Kurmachev clutch'd his garment protectively.

Madame Bulygin: "He has a canoe full of fur, and he wants a coat? We will not trade coats. We barely have enough as it is. Better the natives wear their traditional costumes."

Timofei shook his head. The native pointed at Shubin's gun: "*Sukwalwal.*" Shubin clutch'd his weapon protectively.

Madame Bulygin: "No guns. Our orders forbid us to trade firearms. Express to them my disappointment, that they will not exchange their musty old pelts for our fashionable trade goods. I myself might wear these beads. What is wrong with these people?"

THE REMAINING CANOES DEPARTED, PADDLERS SINGING. We bobbed alone on the ocean with the canoe bearing the two boys & the halibut.

Timofei smiled & pointed: "*Hyas pows.*" Big fish.

The fair-skinned lad proudly showed us his hook, a smooth, curved splinter of polished hardwood on a fine line of kelp fiber, his bait a tiny wriggling octopus. He indicated the fish, rubbing his tummy. Did we fancy a trade? Timofei nodded, measuring off nine feet of blue beads. The boy shook his head and gestured for more. Timofei added a foot-long string of glass pearls and the deal was consummated. We hauled the fish aboard. The boys scrambled up the cargo net behind it.

Madame Bulygin, annoyed: "Timofei? All those beads? Why did you do that?"

The crew: "Just for the halibut." *Delete dumb puns. Not funny.*

Madame Bulygin: "The crew can fish, and the beads must last us for as long as possible now. I defer to your judgment in these matters, Timofei, but . . ."

The fair-skinned youth stepped forward with outstretch'd hand and spoke in English: "Better to trade a little something when strangers meet," he said. "Bad luck if nothing passes between the hands. I am Yutramaki of the *Qwidicca-atx* (he pronounced it kwee-ditch-chuh-aht), the People of the Cape."

So this would be the tyee Comcomly mentioned? Yutramaki had five wives, think he said. This might be a son, then?

Madame Bulygin eyed the naked lad with interest: "I am Madame Anna Petrovna Bulygin, and I represent Tsar Alexander of Russia, who conveys, through me, his warmest . . ."

Yutramaki: "But who wears pants? Who is tyee of ship?"

The crew: "Good question."

Madame Bulygin: "You may address yourself to me, Mr. Yutramaki. Tell me, the color of your skin, your features. How is it that you, ah . . . ?"

Yutramaki pointed at our maintop: "How is it that the raven has black feathers?"

The crew murmur'd: "He speaks in riddles."

Valgusov called down: "Again, good question. Why does not The Raven have pretty feathers like Little Bird Man? Hey?"

Yutramaki's chum piped up: "Little Bird Man big Roosky tyee."

Madame Bulygin, a patient smile: "Our beloved Tsar is the big Russian tyee. The Tsar rules over all of us, including Mr. Baranov, but the Tsar lives far away, on the other side of the world, in a lovely city we call St. Petersburg, which has beautiful, warm buildings, and bright lights, and music and dancing and delicious food and French wine, and hot soapy water, and charming, witty, clean people in nice, clean clothes, and clean, warm beds, and . . . And so, the Tsar asks us to come here, to build a fort, as Mr. Tarakanov said, and to live amongst you, at the Columbia River, as your protectors and benefactors. But . . ."

Yutramaki: "But why? You have no home?"

Bolotov: "I vote we go to California. I am cold."

Madame Bulygin: "Because we bring civilization with us. Wonderful things, such as guns, which will rid these lands of wild animals, and bring civilization to your people."

Yutramaki, hand covering eyes: "Wait, wait . . ."

The chum: "Yutramaki see vision."

Yutramaki held his head as though it pained him: "Why? Why does Tsar banish Madame?"

The captain gasp'd.

Madame Bulygin teased him: "Mischievous rascal. You would have us believe you are clairvoyant. A fortune-teller, a seer, preying on gullible seafarers such as our unsuspecting captain. Now, no more hocus-pocus, young man, or . . ."

Yutramaki indicated our commander: "He is captain?"

Bulygin huff'd: "Yes, I am Captain Bulygin, and . . ."

"Same name as boss lady?"

Madame Bulygin: "It is complicated. I bring a letter of introduction with the Tsar's signature, Mr. Yutramaki. His name, written by him, on paper, in ink, and in a moment, we go below, to my cabin, for cognac and a friendly visit, but first I return to my question. Now, all of us are as God chooses to make us. You can see that our crew is a harmonious blend of white men and persons similar to yourself. So, my question, again, is . . ."

The chum: "Fishbelly in the firewood, many moons ago." *Delete.*

Madame Bulygin: "I see. I would not pry, but the Tsar is tantalized by persistent rumors that sixteen Russian sailors lost sixty-seven years ago from the Chirikov expedition might have mingled with resident populations, meaning that you, young Mr. Yutramaki, might already be a de facto subject of His Imperial Majesty. Therefore, captain, you will remain on the quarterdeck as we hold our present position relative to the cape, pausing in our voyage to press our inquiries into the fate of Chirikov's gallant castaways. Maria and I will query the boy further, in my cabin."

She led her youthful guest below. Maria followed. Captain Bulygin watched, distraught. The chum draped blue beads around his neck and preen'd. Our halibut glisten'd, sliding about the deck listlessly with the roll of the swells. Kahmooks sniffed it and gnaw'd off a chunk. The crew loiter'd at the aft rail, eavesdropping on the cabin below.

"It's so quiet down there. Too quiet."

"Just like the weather. Beware, brothers. I feel a storm coming."

"Bite your tongue. A storm is the last thing we need."

AT DAWN WE BEAT TO WINDWARD before a violent southwest gale, pitching, rolling, struggling to maintain our equilibrium. Hobgoblin howls haunt'd the masts, storm clouds skimmed the sea, white beards sprouted from black waves. Maria, venturing to the bowsprits, pluck'd wisps of eagle feathers from her medicine bag, offering these tufts to the storm spirits. Alas, they ignored her. The storm strengthen'd.

Where are we, I wonder'd. How far from shore? Hadn't the foggiest. But we could sense the continent's mass to the east, just as the compass sensed the north. We looked toward land first when we came on deck, not out to sea. We wanted the earth beneath our feet again, but we feared it too. We had to maintain leeway, a sufficient distance, a margin for error.

That said, we hoped for different landfalls: Madame Bulygin desired California but would settle for the Columbia River. Timofei dreamed of Kauai. I'd settle for Kauai, but if that was not to be then I'd rather bring us up on a soft beach with friendly natives. I should put a pistol to my head before I sink at sea again.

Kozma rallied a grumbling deck watch and we came about close-hauled on the port tack, beating back out into deep water. I wished I had fat *Emily* from Boston beneath me again. This slim lass came up into the wind nicely, but she was too light in the bottom for heavy weather, even with the cannons & cannonballs packed tight below.

A rogue gust knocked us over on our starboard rail. Water gurgled in the scuppers. Loud curses from the hold. I decided we would shorten sail when Bulygin relieved me. The storm-demons screamed louder in the rigging, their spine-tingling cries rising from a moan to a shriek, pitched an octave higher every hour.

A ghost appeared in the gloom, a shimmering spectral spirit. I exclaimed, startled. The ghost became Kozma, blowing on two cups of steaming tea.

He laughed: "More ghosts, poppyhead? Please, no more screaming. You make me to burn myself. Only the frightened weakling smokes the opium. The brave drink vodka. Also, tea. Tea and vodka."

I say: "Better go tell Timofei that the weather's coming up faster than we expected. Hope Bulygin's sober enough to take the helm."

Kozma grumbled: "Bulygin steers better drunk. No, you go. You tell Timofei. Before, Timofei and me, we sleep back to back, one eye open. When the knife comes in the night, one of us awakens. Now my back is cold. So be it."

"Take the helm then."

"He betrays me. He carries her blue bonnet under his shirt, a bandage on his broken heart. She makes him crazy."

He had a tear in his eye as he took the tiller. Back in a jiffy, I told him. He wasn't a skilled helmsmen, so I wouldn't linger below. I scrambled down the companionway and, leaning on the bulkhead to stay upright, knocked discreetly on the cabin door. Yesterday, Yutramaki the Younger spent hours in conference with Madame Bulygin (*I was conceived on the ship? With everybody like right there? She just met him. He was what? 15?*), sometimes but not always with Maria present, and he & his chum departed the ship before we resumed our voyage south. Now Timofei took Yutramaki's place, sheepish in a nankeen-cotton dressing gown. Feminine scents wafted from the cabin's dark sanctum. A bleary Timofei absorbed my weather report in silence.

I returned topside. Kozma was struggling with the helm. The morning watch was struggling to the deck, regarding the weather with dismay. The forces of light struggled with the dark.

Bulygin lunged about, coat-tails flapping, his officer's tricorner lashed on with a handkerchief knotted under his chin. I suggested we get some sail down while we had both watches on deck. He scoff'd, spat, wiped his beard with his sleeve.

He sneer'd: "A storm? How frightening. No, all sail stays up. We must hasten on to our secret destination." He searched his pockets. "Where is my tobacco? Curse these thieves. They rob their captain while he sleeps. In my dreams I feel them poking, probing . . . Williams, come back."

I hasten'd to my hammock. My shipmates stumbled about the hold, arguing, shoving, edgy. The storm's approach brought trepidation. Unease hung heavy in the air. I thought I'd nod off straightaway, but sleep was a stranger. Even opium failed to calm my nerves.

Voices. Madame Bulygin visited the crew's quarters unannounced: "*Mon dieu*, the smell. Is that the captain's tobacco? Well, give it back to him. How does he fare? Did you feed him?"

"He keeps both hands on the helm. I throw fish stew at his mouth."

She said something I couldn't hear and departed, leaving her French perfume to linger in our fetid atmosphere. The ship climbed, plunged, rolled. I noticed water glistening on the windward bulkhead, which seemed to bulge inward. We came about unannounced on a new tack, raising havoc with our centre of gravity. Unsecured bottles and barrels assaulted the unwary. I gripped my hammock's hems.

Feverish. Blanket soaked with sweat. Couldn't sleep. A soft lullaby kiss from my Lady sent me floating on gentle waves through her misty kingdom, and a soft fog soothed my fevered brain, flooding my soul with warm languor.

SOMEBODY SHOOK ME AWAKE: "COME TAKE THE HELM. Soon she shoots her husband."

I peek'd out of my hammock. The ship was heeled well over to starboard, fighting for balance. The pitch was worse: deep into the troughs, high against the crests. Breaking waves pounded the deck above as I lurch'd aft along the bulkhead to the ladder and cracked open the companionway hatch. The storm roared. Instantly I was soaked by cold spindrift. Blinking, I peer'd about the dark deck. The angle was sickening. Shiver me timbers: ghosts gathered amidships around the longboat, muttering.

Was this to be the end? The storm stomped upon the sea with smoking feet, annoyed by the day's last light. She meant to bury us, and she wanted no witnesses.

I crawled with rubbery legs to the mainmast, which I embraced, sealskins flapping. Bulygin stood at the helm, face splatter'd with stew, steering with one hand, waving his sword in wicked arcs with the other. Timofei, Kozma & Madame Bulygin leaned back against the rail, watching the sword.

Madame Bulygin sought to distract her husband, but he wasn't fooled. Timofei & Kozma waited for a chance to lunge, but Bulygin knew how to handle his blade. Timofei & Kozma kept their distance. Madame Bulygin kept her pistol dry under her cape.

The captain cried out a warning: "Monsters, I tell you, drool dripping from their fangs. They infest these waters. Am I the only one who sees them?"

Alas, no, I do too. As my countryman Samuel Taylor Coleridge noted, "Slimy Things did crawl with legs upon the slimy sea."

Bulygin wouldn't leave the helm: "I am not going below. Fingers, in my mouth."

Madame Bulygin pleaded with him: "You are exhausted, Nikolai. Rest in the cabin. We will lock the door."

"In the captain's cabin? With you? You treacherous, back-stabbing . . . Stay back. Do not touch me."

"Mr. Williams," Madame Bulygin called. "Could you . . .?"

Could I what? Couldn't hear over the wind. The deck pitched frightfully. Good lord, the sea: acres of ocean rose, topped with white gardens of froth. We should have been running away under bare poles, but Bulygin had us headed into the teeth of the gale, as close to the wind as he could get. The tattered main sail whipped, unreefed. A gust ripped the foresail and sent it flapping, held only by frayed lines. Lightning crackled betwixt the masts. A continuous green flood washed the deck, too much for the scuppers to drain. The ghosts loiter'd by the boat, lifting their faint feet above the flood, biting wispy nails.

I returned to my hammock for a quick puff. I hoped I'd be left alone, but footsteps approached.

Kozma reached in, seized my ear: "Show to me the happy face. I worry about you. Loosen the grip on the hammock."

"Go away, there's a good chap."

"Bulygin will sink us. Put away the pipe. Show us what to do."

"Can't be heel'd over like this. Deck watch has to shorten sail."

"They vote not to go aloft."

A gust slammed the ship. Kozma slipped, fell, cursed.

"Put her stern to," I said. "Get the wind on the aft port quarter. That might push us away from the eye of the storm. The sails will blow away, but we've a spare mainsail."

"The wave, she is big. What do we do when the sea breaks over the stern?"

I shrugged, curled up, drifted off. Fog set in. Time dissolved. Despite the storm's shrieks, despite the ship's pitching & rolling, I floated, suspended, aware only of an ethereal whale song, of a leviathan lullaby reverberating through the hull. Only this eerie music pervaded my sanctuary.

Voices woke me in my warm womb. The hold & its contents adopted strange angles in relation to my hammock. I could hear the fore & aft bilge-pump crews working their levers. I shivered, feverish, body stiff, mouth wretch'd. I drifted between sleep & consciousness. Bumps & curses.

Voices: "Here, Dmitrii, a cup of tea. How goes it topside?"

"Still our brave captain remains at the helm. She tells him if he gets us through the storm, he sleeps with her in the cabin."

"Damn. Then how do I pull his tooth out?"

"Ha. A tooth of gold, from the jawbone of an ass."

"The gold tooth is not for you. Kozma says I am to yank it out when the mutiny begins. Sobachnikov gets the coat, Kurmachev gets the shiny boots, and . . ."

"You lie. Kozma!"

"Shhh. He sleeps."

I couldn't sleep. I counted the glistening drops of water popping through the bulkhead in the lantern's dim glow. No such thing as a watertight ship, I told myself. In a storm the hull bends under the ocean's pressure, cracks widen between planks, caulking falls away. Pensive, the sea rolled our delicate egg in the palm of her hand, deciding whether to break us or save us for another day.

Steady on. Fear not. Englishman built this ship. Britannia rules the waves.

Drip.

If a God exists, 'tis not a wise God. Whoever made this planet erred grievously, for the brine covering most of Earth is naught but wasted space. What purpose hath the sea? Earth should've been created as just that: sweet soil refresh'd by rain. Let the oceans be reduced to babbling brooks & languid lakes, and all else be solid ground. Let the storm subside. Lay me down beside still waters, to sleep, to dream.

THIS IS MY DREAM (MEMORY?) ABOUT A STORM: Night falls over our sinking man o' war. The storm strengthens. The pump crews lose their battle with the leaks. Our ship's belly floods, and I feel her shudder of surrender vibrate the deck underfoot. Men swim in the sea, clinging to broken spars. I find a seat in the last boat as my shipmates battle with knives, cargo hooks, belaying pins. Oars thrashing, overloaded, we fight each other and the swirling vortex, the ship's awful gravity. Water rises around our ankles. The man beside me clutches his chest and slumps on his oar. We push him over the gunwale. Others fight to take his place. Pull, pull again. We keep pulling until we capsize in thund'rous surf.

Between the waves, a distant light, a candle, a window, a stone hut. A girl with long black hair, framed, her warm palms press'd to cold glass.

Riptides sweep us back to sea. Faint calls, lanterns bobbing. Barefoot angels in nightclothes rush out into the night.

'Tis all for naught, I feared. So near, so far. So cold.

I sink into the sea and am reborn, my dead head resting in the lap of the black-haired girl. She weeps, and each teardrop becomes a tiny sea where the shimmering ghost of her lost bridegroom swims. Vanish'd in a storm, he did, left a wee one wailing in the crib, left his bride watching from the window. Here, a blanket, young sir, a cup of tea, dry clothes. His clothes. He's not been gone long, still washes up in her dreams, and she wakes with wet spots left by a clammy phantom. Sleep, sir, she tells me. Sink into slumber like a ship into the sea. Press thy cold, fearful soul against my burning breasts. Sleep, dream.

When you wake, the sea will have cleaned out her closets, leaving lifeless shipmates on the shore. Sand crabs will scuttle, clutching stolen bites of sailor flesh, purloin'd loins. The black-haired girl will turn away, threadbare shawl pulled tight across slender shoulders. The wail of fisherwives drifts on bleak strands.

Did that happen? To me? Is it a memory? A sailor's story? Just rubbish, an opium-inspired dream? A vision of heaven & hell?

Heavenly harmonies drifted through my blankets. Angelic choirs? No. Ship's orchestra. We rolled over a swell. Gravity shifted from port to starboard. Leaping Cossacks and unsecured cargo slid, coming to rest against bulkheads. The wave surmount'd, a brief moment of equilibrium. The dancers regained their balance. Filip, black hair in his eyes, elbow flying, fiddle bow burning a blur on smoking strings. Brow furrow'd, Zuev hunker'd over his balalaika. Sobachnikov's squeezebox wheezed. Dancers squatted & kicked, arms folded on their chest.

We slid into a deep trough. The dancers pitched forward. We stayed down too long, but our bow finally climbed the next wave. I gripped my hammock. The dancers slid past, shouting, clapping, banging tambourines. I was rudely bumped. Madame Bulygin's bathtub slid by with Sobachnikov and his accordion inside.

"Come, Williams. Cavort with us."

No, thanks. Dreadfully sorry. Not feeling well.

Music, darkness, dreams. Adrift. Time stood still. No present, no past.

Nothingness. Then light. Air.

Fresh breeze. Open hatches. No more music, and the sound of the wind had gone, but the swells still felt big as they rolled under us. I dared not peek from my cocoon. Voices from above, on deck. Someone approaching.

Timofei's voice: "How is he?"

"He fears the storm. He weeps."

Timofei poked me: "Good morning. No more storm."

Kozma was behind him: "No more fear. Life is good again. Come up and point the device at the sun. Bulygin has not the focus in the eyes. We see mountains, but where are we? Move, or Yuri soaks you with the piss bucket."

Pretty day, clear & cold. The sun, so long restrained, illuminated snow-covered mountain peaks backdropped by the dark storm that had passed o'er us and left us reeling in her wake. Forests swept down steep slopes from lofty snowfields.

Where were we?

Big swells, but dead air, not a whisper. The tattered mainsail flutter'd. Bulygin gripped the helm, glassy-eyed, muttering angrily. All hands on deck, as though gathered for an announcement.

Madame Bulygin clapped briskly: "Crew, we are eager to express admiration and gratitude to our brave captain, who remains resolutely in command these past three days, disregarding his own comfort. A heroic feat, noted in the log. So, a cheer, please?"

"Huzzah."

Bulygin waved his pipe at us: "Thieves. You would steal my gold tooth, were I not so alert."

Madame Bulygin said, "Ah, a visitor. Mr. Williams favors us with a personal appearance. Are you feeling shipshape, sir? Prepared for a demanding navigational assignment?"

I ignored her and stood resolutely at the rail with my sextant, labouring to reach agreement between sun & horizon. Forty-nine degrees, thereabouts. Timofei & I studied the chart, tracing the continent's edge as artfully illustrated by Vancouver's cartographer, determining that this mountainous coastline might be Vancouver's Island. If so, the storm had blown us a hundred miles back north.

Surf boom'd. We eyed the shrinking interval between our vessel and the rocks against which the swells crash'd, noticing that these nearshore waves & currents were no longer pushing us north, but now moved us landward.

"Dmitrii, how deep?"

Amidships, Kurmachev cast the sounding line: "Ten . . . make that nine fathoms."

"Again we are in trouble."

"When were we not in trouble?"

Madame Bulygin: "This is all we can do? Simply drift ever closer to the rocks? Why do we not pull the ship back out to sea with the boat?"

Timofei shook his head: "Too big is the wave. If we drop the anchor, and it catches, the cable breaks. Better we put the guns and food in the boat and swim it to shore. With luck . . ."

Madame Bulygin, aghast: "What? We survive that dreadful storm and then abandon our ship in calm weather?"

Kurmachev sound'd the sea floor: "Seven fathoms, six . . ."

Kozma shook my shoulder. Had I missed something?

Madame Bulygin: "Mr. Williams? Nodding off? I ask if the Vancouver Island natives are friendly."

I say: "If that's where we are. They torched an American brig five years ago. Trade dispute. Behead'd all but two of the crew."

The crew scratch'd their heads thoughtfully.

Timofei turned to Maria: "You must call the spirits of the wind."

Madame Bulygin sniff'd: "Young ladies who expect to marry into polite St. Petersburg society do not engage in hocus pocus."

Timofei gaped at Maria.

Kozma, helpfully: "Maria makes the wind to come. Her *babushka*, her grandmother on Kodiak, she talks to the spirits, to the gods of wind and rain. Maria learns from her. On Sitka Sound, when we sail our little boat, Maria touches the feather to herself and throws it into the air, and then always the wind is behind us, anywhere we want to go."

Kurmachev: "Five fathoms . . ."

Madame Bulygin relented: "Very well. Call the wind, Maria."

The crew broke into song: "Way out here, they got a name for the wind and rain and . . ." *Delete. That song wasn't until 1951. This is an example of why people don't take you seriously.*

"Be serious," Maria said. "The spirits must believe we are sincere."

"We could sacrifice a virgin."

"Not little Filip. Who else can make the fiddle sing? How do we live without music?"

"Besides, Olga fiddles with Filip. No more the virgin."

Maria: "The wind spirit demands the feather of a wild bird. All my eagle feathers I give to the storm."

Rather a lot of birds in sight, and close at hand. Thousands of gulls & terns preen'd on the nearby surf-pounded rocks, so close we could see their feathers.

"The seabirds fly ashore, seeking shelter from the storm. We shoot them."

"We throw rocks. No tern shall go unstoned." *Delete.*

"Thousands of birds, millions of feathers, just out of reach. Perhaps Afanasii will contribute."

We appealed to our feather'd comrade in the crow's nest: "Raven, we are in peril. Save your shipmates."

Valgusov, partially hidden behind the drooping sails, declined in a wounded tone: "Stay down there or I shoot."

Timofei: "One feather, Afanasii. Soon."

Valgusov: "What are you sleeping on, Timofei? Rip open one of her pillows."

Maria: "I need the feather of a wild bird."

Madame Bulygin: "Mr. Valgusov, my bedding contains down plucked from the Tsar's finest domestic geese. *Comprende*? You will be compensated for your loss."

Bulygin blinked at Timofei: "Sleeping?"

Valgusov, intrigued: "Compensated? How?"

Timofei: "Afanasii, Kozma is coming up to teach you how to fly."

Valgusov: "No. Ouch. Here, take the damn thing."

Maria: "Filip, hasten up and fetch Afanasii's feather. The rest of you, be quiet. John, from which direction should the wind come?"

I pointed nor'west. Maria ripped open her bodice and chanted a primal hymn in the Kodiak tongue, her untamed countenance raised heavenward in supplication. Filip, arriving with a long black feather, gaped, tripped, sprawled.

Valgusov screamed: "Clumsy kid. You almost lost my feather."

"It is a sacrifice, Afanasii. We are supposed to lose it."

Eyes shut tight, Maria shook her lustrous tresses, sang beseechingly, kissed the feather, pressed it to her naked breast and cast it to the winds. The feather flutter'd off with Valgusov's anguish'd sobs in pursuit.

I held up a moisten'd finger: "Hark, a breeze."

First a puff from the northwest, then a sudden gust balloon'd our slack sails, pushing the ship over on a slight heel. Bulygin windmill'd his arms, lost his balance, disappeared with a forlorn cry down the companionway. I alertly rushed to the helm and threw the rudder hard over, putting this fresh air on our starboard beam. Timofei & Kozma rallied the crew. The men hauled mightily on the sheets, and our sail trim began to improve. Another gust. Our torn canvas strain'd against its tethers, but we made leeway in a seawardly direction. My mouth was dry, else I could've spit on the nearest rock.

DESTRUCTION ISLAND. FLAT, ROCKY, A LEAGUE OFF THE COAST, barren but for tatter'd shrubs. Ragged reefs broke the waves on the seaward edge. Seabirds swirl'd like flies over a messy table.

Weather: cold, cloudy, intermittent precipitation. Wind from the south: five, ten knots. The sun, cold & dead. I shot it: 47° 33' north latitude.

We cruised landward. Clouds rose o'er lofty inland glaciers, Olympus coat'd in cream. Between mountains & sea, a deep blanket of evergreen forest colour'd in hues ranging from dark olive to soft jade. What secrets lurk'd within this wilderness? Was it too alien for man, too extreme? Comcomly had told me the coastal natives dread'd the forest, fearing carnivores & demons, and ventured therein only grudgingly, and not without beseeching their guardian-spirits to hover at their shoulders.

Sobachnikov's melancholy accordion tunes haunt'd the deck. Madame Bulygin hugged her shoulders, inhaled sea breeze, studied her chart. Bulygin, beard trimmed, gaze resolute, squared his shoulders and authoritatively ordered course corrections to the trainee helmsmen, Zypianov & Sergei.

Madame Bulygin bid me a cheery good-morning: "So, Mr. Williams, on deck before noon. Most impressive. When the cobwebs clear, you will note that our captain has brought us to Destruction Island, a landmark situated just a hundred miles north of the Columbia River, as the crow flies."

From aloft, a squawk of protest.

She waved her scroll'd chart at me: "Tell me, why do the English call this Destruction Island? My map says the Spanish named it Isla de Delores, the Island of Sorrows, in 1775. I prefer that *nom de géographique*: so haunting, so bleak, so Russian. Perhaps we go ashore, bury a plaque, stake a claim."

I say: "Bone dry, and the anchorage is unshelter'd."

Madame Bulygin pushed back wind-blown hair: "Again Mr. Williams enlightens us with his *anecdotiques trivial*. He is our constant source of edification, and we do miss him when he flees our dull company and withdraws into his cocoon. Now hear this, crew: we must find a river soon. Our firewood is nearly gone and our water falls low in the barrels. Consequently, I am reduced to tepid sponge-baths, and I would enjoy a good hot soak in my tub, now that the seas are calmer."

My note of caution: "Bit dodgy hereabouts. 'Tis said the natives slaughter shore parties, some Spanish in 1775, thus the Island of Sorrows, and a British boat crew back in 1787. Their captain named it Destruction Island in their memory. Rather doubt anyone's gone ashore since."

Madame Bulygin: "Nevertheless."

Quoth the Raven, aloft: "Nevermore."

Kurmachev whined: "We must follow our plan. Find water and set sail for Kauai."

Madame Bulygin blinked: "Excuse me? To where?"

"Oops."

"Not yet does Timofei tell her the plan, fool."

Madame Bulygin: "A plan? About Kauai?"

"Never mind. Kurmachev babbles."

Kurmachev spat on the deck: "Weaklings. I will tell her. We decide for ourselves now, your ladyship. No longer do we go to the Columbia River. We go to Kauai. First we toss your husband in the ocean. Am I right, Timofei?"

Madame Bulygin, baffled: "Husband? Ocean? Mr. Tarakanov?"

Timofei, speechless. Kozma the shaggy lion prepared to pounce on Kurmachev, the trembling gazelle.

Kurmachev: "Brothers, all in favor of telling her now, say . . ."

The crew intervened: "Spare poor Ivan. Timofei, tell her our plan. We are beyond the point of no return."

Madame Bulygin coughed discreetly and pointed a pistol at Kozma's head. He blinked, froze in his tracks, his huge, outstretched hands only inches from Kurmachev's scrawny neck.

Madame Bulygin held her aim: "I bore easily, Timofei. As you know."

Timofei's eyes flew from the sea, to the deck, to the sky, to Kozma: "We . . ."

Kozma: "We change course."

Timofei: "Please, do not shoot Kozma, or the Brothers must throw you to the oceans. Please."

Madame Bulygin: "I see. Employee Kurmachev, come, stand behind me. Employee Ovchinnikov, kindly step back a few paces, and please do not regard me with such an angry expression. Now what is this nonsense about Kauai?"

Timofei: "The Tsar's fort. We agree to build it, but at a better location. As you know, already comrade Slobodchikov secures King Kamehameha's permission to . . ."

Madame Bulygin sputtered: "'We'? Enough of this foolishness. The Tsar studies the choices carefully, and he chooses the Columbia River. Yes, the Sandwich Islands do figure in his long-range plans, but any departure from his timetable could cause irreparable damage. Such foolishness. If we can conclude this discussion now, the ship's log will report only that you were misled by fanciful tales of balmy tropical beaches and slant-eyed sirens. In that regard, I remind you that comrade Olga stands ready to subdue your lusty appetites, assuming she finishes her cooking chores. We will not besmirch future accounts of our heroic expedition with any hint of shipboard grumbling, and certainly not with the m-word. Perish the thought. The Tsar deserves your . . ."

A question, in the back: "'M-word?'"

*Please don't start.*

"She means you, moron."

"No. Madame means the *mal de mer.*"

"Madness. She refers to her husband, the maniac of the merchant marine. She wants no more malicious mumbling about his mental maladies, his missing marbles, his macabre monsters in the murk."

"You are much mistaken. Remember comrade Zuev's mawkish message a month ago, when we depart New Archangel? Almost poor Savva becomes a martyr."

Zuev, ruefully: "Almost Baranov and his whip makes me into mincemeat. Where are my comrades when I need them?"

"Ha. My motto is, mustn't stick your miserable neck out."

"She means we are a motley, malcontent mob of mangy misbegotten mongrels."

The malamute murmur'd a menace: "Speak for yourself, mutt."

"M is for Madame's marriage. We are not to mention her merry *ménage*."

"Maternity. She becomes the mother."

"Maybe, but who is the man? Muster the multitudes of suspects." *Who yo daddy?*

"The gunner's mate? Mikhail, her muddled muscle muffin from Minsk?"

Madame Bulygin, mortified: "*Merde*."

"She means our meals, our malignant malnutrition. Our menu is but meagerly-measured morsels, and we have maggots in our mush. Soon the morbid scurvy runs amuck."

"Maximum? For the level of punishment our magnificent monarch would impose upon us, if, God forbid, we should foolishly dare to, to . . ."

"Mouth off? Mock her? Malinger? Mope? Mutter?"

"Mother of mercy. Not us. We meekly mind our manners."

"Maybe the m-word is for what Kozma will soon do to poor Ivan. Maim? Mutilate? Mangle? Maul?"

Kurmachev, from behind Madame Bulygin: "Kozma, have mercy."

Madame Bulygin: "You already said 'mercy.' Please conclude this nonsense."

*Yes. Please.*

"We give up. The m-word mystifies us."

Madame Bulygin sighed: "For a moment, I feared my menial minion Mr. Kurmachev would be dismembered. *Et maintenant,* may we resume our mission, maintaining our momentous maritime march to the Columbia? *Merci, monsieurs.*"

"You must tell us the m-word."

*Murder, by John Williams.*

Madame Bulygin: "Employee Tarakanov, please have Williams mind the helm. The captain and I must go below. Set a course south, for the Columbia River. The wind vanishes, mysteriously, but perhaps it materializes again momentarily. And keep an eye out for fresh water. You know that if I do not have my bath, my mood becomes morose."

Timofei: "Kauai."

Madame Bulygin: "I must say, Timofei, this conversation lends disturbing weight to a rumor just brought to my ears, that our captain's wardrobe has been assigned to the crew."

Bulygin hastened to assure her: "Everything I have is yours, my love."

Madame Bulygin: "Mumbo-jumbo, I assume. Surely you would mop up any such mendacity as soon as you learn of it. I do not mince words, Timofei. I . . ."

"Wait," Zuev said. "I had 'mincemeat,' a metaphor for what happens to my back if that malevolent midget martinet had managed to . . ."

Madame Bulygin: "You have your mandate, Mr. Tarakanov, the Tsar's maxim: his mighty fort must be made manifest at the Columbia River, if you do not mind. Meanwhile . . ." She took the captain by the elbow. "Come along, my musky marauder."

The Bulygins departed the deck. I took the helm.

*M-words is really stupid. Delete.*

The crew turned to Timofei: "Well?"

Timofei, through gritted teeth: "Our plan still holds. The Brotherhood of Yermak hereby takes command of the *St. Nicholas.* I, Timofei Osipovich Tarakanov, your ataman, shall assume the blame for all our wrongdoings. Any man who has cold feet, he should say so now, so that . . ."

"Me. I need boots."

"A vote, Timofei? Perhaps we are still unsure?"

Timofei: ". . . so that, like brother Ivan, he can meet now with brother Kozma, to discuss the risks of uncertain loyalty."

"Now we are sure."

Timofei pointed sou'west: "Then we set sail for Kauai, to a new life, as masters of our own ship, our own destiny. Today, for the first time in our lives, we are free men."

Olga & Maria: "Ahem?"

Timofei: "Free people."

Kahmooks & The Raven: "Ahem?"

Timofei: "All of us, free as the wind."

Doldrums. The sails flopped. We languish'd in low swells a league off the island.

"When Maria brings the wind, we sail to Kauai."

Maria declined. "Only do I bring the wind if we go to the Columbia River."

The crew pleaded: "Kauai, Maria. The Raven will sacrifice another tailfeather."

From aloft: "Not a chance. Kauai has not the ravens, but at the Columbia I am amongst my own."

"Also they have slave girls at the Columbia. Or did. Right, Williams?"

I say: "Four. Three. Slobodchikov bought one."

Discussion ensued. The Columbia River lost favour as a destination.

"I say we go to Kauai. Yes, the ocean is big, and the winter storm is upon us, but our ship, she is sturdy, and her crew, she is brave."

"Also, after Bulygin falls overboard, we have comrade John Williams to navigate."

The crew shuffled its boots.

I say: "Gad. Have a little faith, boys. Been to Kauai before, you know." *Really? When?*

"So you say."

"Better we go first to the Columbia River, just for the winter. We build a shelter. We rest. In spring, we sail for Kauai."

"It is almost November. The river will eat us alive. We must go south to nice calm Bodega Bay. Later, if anybody asks, we say we try to enter the Columbia, but the wave is too big."

"Slobodchikov and his crew did it, and in this ship, too."

"In summer. Barely."

"California. Sunshine. Señoritas."

"Spanish frigates."

"This is hopeless. We should go home."

"Where is home? Like the kolosh said, we are aimless drifters. I am too sad to continue."

"I am bored. When begins the adventure?" *He's got a point. Pep it up, geezer.*

A SCREECH FROM THE MAINTOP: "ROCKS! STARBOARD bow!"

Bulygin lunged about, raving. All except the women were on deck.

"Rocks," the captain cried. "No wind. The waves, the currents, they push us ever closer to this harsh, forbidding coast. I am uncertain how to proceed. I will seek advice from the crew."

The crew: "Jump overboard. Leave your coat and boots. And tooth."

An offshore cluster of black rocks loomed, the wind had vanish'd, and the current swept us north to our apparent doom.

Bulygin waved his hands: "I know. I will eyeball a course through these rocks like they are not even there. Old navigator's trick I am just remembering."

The crew was glum: "We are done for. Soon we are wrecked on the beach, simply some savage's salvage."

Bulygin peer'd over the side and saw submerged rocks: "Drop the stern anchors. Stand by to drop the bow anchors."

"We could tie the captain to an anchor."

"Wait. Fetch me the pliers. Please to open the mouth, captain. Williams, take the helm."

While the crew chased the captain, I steered amongst what Vancouver had called "many detach'd rocks, of various Romantic forms." Some barely broke the water, little frothy-mouthed mastiffs waiting to bite a hole in the seat of our pants, but some loom'd higher than our masthead. Some were rounded, some were sharp obelisks. Rocks guarded little beaches backdropped by evergreen forest, others stood offshore, shredding the sea. They could've sunk us in a second, but they were indifferent to our passage, caring not whether we wreck'd on them or missed by an inch.

The rocks might be the death of us, but they reek'd of life. As we approached, we could see greenery blooming in every niche, topped by scrawny, tortured bonsai spruce with exposed roots clenched like claws, their branches twist'd by storms. Orange & purple starfish clung to Easter Island stone-faces, to boulders bearded by barnacles. Eagles atop rocky spires, white-hooded gargoyles, spread fathom-wide wings and screech'd at the sight of the Raven in his perch.

A bump, a lurch. Dead in the water. A smooth rounded rock. We'd been dragging all four anchors, and two caught, briefly, but then their cables broke. Turmoil, shouting, running about. We couldn't bump up against even a smooth rock for long.

Timofei shouted orders. With nothing to do at the helm, I wandered about watching the others. The captain followed me, clutching his jaw, tugging at my sleeve, begging for opium. Apparently, I possess'd the ship's entire supply. Candle-lanterns swayed, flickering, casting shadows. The crew skidded the boat across the deck to the port rail and dropped it over the rail. Kozma lifted me by my belt and tossed me into the boat. I found an oar and slid the pin into a forward lock. The seats around me filled. Kozma came last, dropping his bulk on a sagging beam-thwart, seizing an oar in each hand. Swells splashed nearby rocks, cold spray on my face.

Timofei called down: "Good. Tie it off."

We knotted a thick line to the boat's stern-post and began to pull the ship's bow around. We hauled mightily. The tow-line stretched, dripping.

Kozma: "Pull. Pull or swim."

We pulled, but something bump'd against the boat. We heeled and began to capsize. Sea rushed in. A dark mass rose alongside.

Pungent spray pervaded the atmosphere. A huge eye peered down. At me.

After that I remember nothing until Timofei was slapping my face. I lay on deck, naked & wet.

Timofei: "Open the eyes. Say my name."

Whale poop in the windpipe: "Gurgle. Spitooey."

My mates rejoiced: "A miracle. We thought you were dead. The whale, she turns the boat over and you disappear but, praise the saints, you return, alive."

"An omen. What does it mean?"

"Stinky, all over him. The slimy limey. He looks older."

"Quiet. He tries to say something."

I cough'd. I was anxious to tell them. "Listen, the whales, they . . ."

"Rest easy, brother. No more fears."

I was off for another swim. "It's, it's . . . Come, we can all go."

"Grab him. He has gone mad." *Got that right.*

"You grab him. Why does he want to jump back in?"

Kozma ordered my mates to wash me down, and I was drench'd with buckets of icy sea water. Whale poop permeated my every orifice. I trembled, glowing rapturously.

A SHOUT OF ALARM, FROM AFT. The port stern anchor cable, worn from rubbing on the rocks, had parted.

The crew pleaded with Maria: "Only one anchor remains. You must bring back the winds."

Maria: "Only if loyalty is sworn by all. No more talk of mutiny."

"We agree. Onward, to the Columbia."

The Bulygins appeared on deck: "Madame, Captain, your devoted crew pledges undying allegiance."

Madame Bulygin: "There was doubt?"

From aloft, sounds of a struggle. Another feather, obtain'd. Maria repeated her earlier performance and was rewarded with a vigourous southwest wind. The ship lunged forward, snapping the cable of our last anchor.

The crew wasn't concerned: "Who cares about the anchors?

The wind returns. We are saved. Praise the saints. Set the sails. Williams, set a course for Kauai."

"Wait. Maria causes the wind to come from the wrong direction."

Maria: "You said southwest. Make up your mind."

"We have to sail southwest. We can't sail straight into the wind. The wind must come that direction. Or maybe ... ."

"Once more Maria must call the wind."

Valgusov, a muffled sob: "He comes up here again, I shoot him. I swear it. No more talk of brotherhood. The Raven's dignity has been violated. No more feathers."

Dawn broke, shapes took form. We drifted on northbound currents, thumping, bumping like a drunk in a graveyard, dancing with rough headstones. An unseen reef ran its tongue along our keel.

"Our captain says the direction of the wind does not matter. We simply look at where we want to go, and make a wish, and if we truly believe, with all our hearts, then somehow . . ."

"Moor the musky marauder to the mast. The captain must go down with the ship."

"First we swing him back and forth across the deck."

"What fun. Come, we catch the captain."

A report from above: "Rocks. Big rocks."

Stone spires as tall as churches, an eerie giants' graveyard. Crest'd tides rushed between these brutal obelisks, and we wandered through this Stonehenge with a vapourous zephyr fondling our sails.

Bulygin's pursuers paused to peer at the passing pinnacles, allowing the captain a chance to return to the helm, where he frantically aimed the ship at an opening in the rocks. We rolled on a surging wave, the masts leaned too far over, and the foretop yardarm struck an overhanging ledge. The next wave thrust us between the rocks on a northbound course.

The pump crew reported from below on the integrity of our hull: "She bends, but not yet does she break."

The crew again captured Bulygin: "For the moment, we have escaped the rocks. Yank the captain's boots off. Williams, take the helm."

Our situation deteriorated. The captain, relieved of his duties, clothes & boots, was inverted, gurgling, with a line knotted around his bare ankles. A scuffle broke out over who should get his boots. Kozma ruled that Kurmachev had prior claim.

Shubin dissented: "Already Kurmachev has boots. I have nothing but these stupid walrus-hide *torbasy*."

"Your shoes are *bakhily*, peasant's boots."

"What? You call me a peasant? See this knife, swine? I am Cossack. I . . ."

"Mukluks," Kahmooks said. "The tops should be caribou hide, for warmth. Sealskin on the bottom. Waterproof."

"Quiet. The proud Cossack does not take advice from dogs."

"Not about boots, anyway."

"I vote we share Bulygin's boots equally. We all risk our lives. We work, we play, as brothers. Why should . . .?"

Olga: "Ahem?"

". . . Why should some get more than others? Because they are greedy?"

"I wish we had a way to distribute things fairly, from those who have, to those in need, to share the things we . . ."

"Fine. Here, he gets this boot, you get that boot. Share and share alike. Satisfied?"

"There. The rope is tied securely around our captain's ankles."

"Hoist him up. Good. Now, we grab hold, and we pull him alll the way over to . . ."

"Wait. Look, the rope is caught on that long wooden thing, the yardarm. The spar will break."

"Rest easy, brother. The yardarm is strong. Now, we . . ."

"Almost it breaks when it strikes against the big rock."

"Too much you worry. Here, take hold of Bulygin's arm. We pull him all the way over to this side of the ship, and then we . . ."

The captain was launch'd from the port rail; his sweeping path across the deck described a clock's pendulum. He snatched at the deck, then at the starboard rail, then at the darkness into which he disappeared.

"Get ready. More push this time."

A wide-eyed Bulygin returned from the gloom, a pale spectre gliding back across the deck with a scream caught in his throat.

"Catch him. Now, all together, heave."

The captain again departed from view, his terrified cry piercing the night. At the apex of his swing, the foreyard, a vital spar necessary to our escape from these close quarters, crack'd & shatter'd, with the outer portion disappearing into the void, taking block, tackle and Bulygin with it.

The wind came back west, blowing us toward the dark coast. The foreyard was shatter'd beyond repair, and we had no spare spars. Without the foresail, we couldn't tack against the westerlies and move away from shore, which was beginning to loom in a threatening mannour. *Try "manner." Better yet, delete everything after "loom."*

We readied the boat at first light. Vodka, food, gunpowder, bags of shot. We looked to our guns, wrapping them in sea lion skins. Those who weren't assigned to the boat would tow it ashore, swimming in frigid seas. If I volunteer'd, I'd rejoin the whales.

A thin dawn appeared behind the continent, lighting the rocks around us. A steeple of stone stood apart, sculpt'd smooth & sharp, a sheer black fang rising a hundred feet above the sea. We slipped between tall tombstones on a tenuous beam reach, begging the westerly breeze for leeway, aided only slightly by the northbound near-shore current behind us.

"Look. Feathers."

A trio of fat brown pelicans flapped sedately past, low over the water, a stone's throw off to port, northbound. They were taken under fire. A cloud of gunsmoke hung o'er the deck.

"Well, anyway, we scare them pretty good."

Timofei, Madame Bulygin and Maria rushed to the deck, concern'd. Madame Bulygin, wearing layers of coats & blankets, scream'd when she saw the captain, still wet and lash'd to the mainmast like Odysseus. He struggled against his bonds, blood drooling from a swollen mouth.

Madame, aghast: "Free him. This instant. Cut him loose."

The crew declined: "The Brotherhood of Yermak now commands this vessel and votes to restrain the captain, due to our lack of confidence in . . ."

"Treason," Madame said. "Last night you proclaimed your devotion to our beloved Tsar. Has the Brotherhood thought carefully about the crimes it commits? About punishment? Medical research involving removal and inspection of still-functioning organs? Do not imagine yourselves to be mere minnows, so meaningless that you might slip through the Tsar's nets. Remember, I record the names of your kinfolk and villages of birth in my most-recent report, which returns, as we speak, to St. Petersburg, with the *Neva*."

The crew shuffled. A mutter: "With the Tsar's silver." *Delete.*

Madame Bulygin: "I promise you, those responsible for the disappearance of imperial funds have but a grim future. That crime is serious. In contrast, I consider this morning's horseplay to be but an awkward attempt to relieve the anxiety of our current predicament. I cannot, in fairness, expect you to display the same nerve I do. However, should you persist in these antics, your names will be added to the Tsar's enemies list, which is, yes, a lengthy document, but one that is, nonetheless, revised, regularly. A question, in the back?"

"Was that true about the organs?"

Madame Bulygin: "If the Tsar's interviewers determine that your heart is pure, you may keep it. Traitors, however, should fear the Tsar's scalpel."

Zuev: "The Tsar fears Napoleon. The Tsar fears *liberté, égalité, fraternité*."

Madame Bulygin: "No political discussions. No talk of fear. Russians fear nothing, not even these monstrous rocks, for we . . ."


"BIG ROCK," VALGUSOV SHOUTED FROM THE MAIN-TOP.

A high island appeared off the starboard bow close to shore. Sheer cliffs vault'd two hundred feet to a forest summit from whence smoke drifted. Villagers gathered atop the precipices. A sand spit joined the island to a beach covered with canoes and people. Houses in the forest. No good anchorage visible.

Not the place to run aground. We would not be welcome. With luck, if the scant breeze held, I could reach us out around the island.

Maria stood with us at the rail. She said this miniature Gibraltar looked like a Kodiak refuge called Sitkalidak.

"In times of danger," she said, "we flee to the top, and we throw stones upon our enemies. Before Baranov, before Timofei and Kozma, the Russians force our men to be their hunters. Wives, girls, they become the property of the Russians. We run away, retreat up to the top of Sitkalidak, but a traitor tells the Russians about the secret cove where boats can land at low tide. They come, they shoot at us with cannons, then they try to capture us. Mothers jump from the cliff into the sea, with their children in their arms. My mother jumps, but leaves me behind."

She held her crucifix, her eyes fastened on the rock: "After that, never again does the Kodiak fight the Russian. The priest tells us to wear the cross, like this, to protect. One night I carry the slop bucket to the pigs, and the bad Cossack, he laughs at the cross. He pushes it into my mouth. He says, 'Here, little Maria. Chew on Jesus while I make you into a woman.' I spit it out. Timofei, Kozma, they hear me scream. They nail the hands of the bad Cossack to the pig shed, like Jesus on the cross."

Madame Bulygin didn't comment, instead focusing her glass on the village's inhabitants.

"Much the same as young Mr. Yutramaki's people," she said. "I adore those pointy hats. *Tres asiatique, n'cest ce pas?* Is there a suitable anchorage, Mr. Williams? Perhaps we could go ashore to cut a new yardarm. What do we know about these people?"

"The rock is a landmark," I said, "but the natives are mentioned unfavourably. Dangerous, ill-humour'd. No one's ever gone ashore, but 'tis said they'll come out with good pelts to trade."

Hundreds of souls now lined the lofty island's seaward cliffs. Timofei raised a hand in greeting. No response.

To the north, smaller rocks & islands. A river rushed from the forest, and seabirds circled the mouth's churning stew. We sailed at the edge of the sea, almost in the surf. The weight of my thumb on the wheel might be enough to send us landward, were I so inclined.

Madame Bulygin studied the Vancouver chart: "Hmmm. An island, close to shore, halfway between Cape Flattery and Destruction Island. If this is that island, we know where we are. So let us sail on to the cape under that assumption, searching for safe anchorage. In the meantime, a log entry. I shall need a reading, Mr. Williams? When you're rested?"

I say: "Almighty Saviour, we are but forlorn & helpless orphans, cast adrift upon Thine angry . . ."

"Mr. Williams, take your little sextant thing in hand and tell us where we are. You are a hazard to civilized navigation." *Which is why you don't go out in the boat.*

I say: "Dreadfully sorry. Let's see. Make it 47° 56' North."

"So noted, for my entry of November the 1st, 1808, with the addendum that this reading is provided us by a foreigner under the influence of opium."

A vote of confidence from Bolotov: "Quit picking on Williams. What do you think your husband takes for his toothache?"

Bulygin sniffled: "You gathe me an abtheth. It hurth."

A second from Zypianov: "I say we blame the captain for our predicament. Not only does he almost sink us during the big storm, but also he steers too close to the rocky shore, knowing that the wind might fade at any moment and we would be cast up on the rocks."

Shubin pointed an accusatory finger at Madame Bulygin: "Yes, but who tells him to venture in so near? And why? To look for a river. Because she thinks she is a French lady who bathes in a tub. If she is truly a Russian woman, she takes a steam bath with the men. Brothers, in New Archangel, my head forewarned us about her. Why do you not take heed?"

"He's right. Also, where is our wind, Maria?"

Maria: "You want wind? Climb up, bring me a feather."

"You go. He will shoot us."

Aloft, the defiant Raven brandish'd his brass blunderbuss, a

Belgian fowling-piece with cornucopia muzzle: "Double load of birdshot," he croak'd.

But then he gasp'd and pointed down, silently thrusting a wing-tip at the water.

What now? We ventured to the port rail and peer'd o'er the side.

# 5 | Shipwreck'd

FOUR FROLICSOME HUMPBACKS SHOVED US SHOREWARD, push-ing our little brig from the open sea into breaking surf. They splash'd as they bump'd their enormous black snouts against the hull, bending the planks inward. Soon we were caught broadside in the breakers. The whales would soon run us aground, but where?

The fog thinned, revealing a soft welcoming beach stretching two miles from the river mouth north to a rocky headland. A stone spire the size & shape of a cathedral rose from the shoreline. Rocks large & small graced our approach.

We would arrive, fortunately, at high tide. We could see the surf running up to the forest's gnarl'd toes. Storms had hurled drift logs back against an evergreen wall.

The whales' bumping ceased. A loud crunch shook the ship; a rock had pierced our hull. Our transition from water to land would not be smooth. We struggled in a frothy purgatory, between liq-uid & solid, not floating, not quite aground. We could hear our hull rupturing, the sea rushing in. *Wait. The whales caused the shipwreck? I thought you wrecked the ship by steering into the surf. Which is it? Get your story straight.*

Timofei & I wrestled the tiller. The pumpers abandon'd their posts, the Raven his perch aloft. Pandemonium on deck.

A roaring green surf, streaks of creamy froth across its face, hit us on the port beam, tipped us on edge, hurl'd us shoreward.

Rocks, all around. We struggled to bring the ship stern-to, lest we roll. Kozma spat over the rail into the next wave's maw.

Another crunch. The helm went limp in our hands; the rudder was gone. The next wave cupped us in her palm and flung us into the shallows, where we shudder'd to a soft stop, tilted over on our starboard beam.

A wave roared past streaming strands of kelp in its wake. As it reached shallow water it paused as though noticing that we were no longer in its clutches, then returned seaward with full force.

The brig groan'd but didn't budge. Stuck tight, hard aground. The firmament held us, recognized us, claimed us as her own.

The deck was too steep to stand on. We slid to the starboard rail, clawing at the deck for purchase. Surf pound'd the hull and flowed over the rail, flooding us. The ship shudder'd. Her joints, twist'd, scream'd in pain. She was tearing apart. We struggled in a mess of fallen sails, sheets and hemp lines. Moans & curses. Bulygin fought his bonds, kicking at the air.

Madame Bulygin clutched the rail: "Timofei, prepare the men to continue our mission ashore."

Timofei yelled orders: "Coats and blankets. Cooking pots. Sails. But first, guns, powder, shot."

He led the first party over the rail: the Aleuts, plus Bolotov, Shubin and Zuev, guns strapped to their shoulders, a watertight powder keg under each elbow. Immediately they sank to their necks. Zuev, floundering. Sergei released a powder keg, jerked Zuev back to the surface, shouted in his face. They recovered their burdens and moved landward, breaking into a trot when they reached the shallows. The next wave could only lick at their upturned heels.

The second group loaded the boat, fighting the ebb & flow, clutching the boat's gunwales. Their plan was to push it ashore. Kahmooks, not much of a swimmer, jumped into the boat, balancing anxiously atop shifting powder kegs. Zypianov was swept under the hull and disappeared with a forlorn cry but was collar'd & retrieved, spitting, choking.

I lay on the deck watching cargo erupt from the hatches. Maria & Olga appeared carrying iron kettles, black hair matted to their faces. Olga, surprisingly agile for her size, leaped over the rail in a lull between waves and disappeared with kettles in each hand. Maria hesitated, waiting for Madame Bulygin, who apparently remained below. Kozma ordered the third group ashore with the furl'd mainsail & foresails.

What was keeping Madame Bulygin? I crawl'd below. Cold sea flooded the hold. Dark moving shapes. Kegs & crates bobbed & bumped. A wave shook the ship, rushed through the cabin, tore the door off its hinges, knocked me awash. Madame Bulygin was in the cabin alone, wrestling with her sea trunk, wearing several layers of clothing. She called over her shoulder for help. The Petukhov brothers struggled past, pushing powder kegs, but didn't stop.

Madame Bulygin was pointing her pistol at me.

She was shivering, couldn't keep a level aim: "My trunk, Mr. Williams. Now. Abram, Iakov, help him get my trunk on deck, then carry it to dry land. Guard it with your lives."

Our vessel shriek'd, her spine twist'd. Another chill rush of sea. I'd gone numb.

Madame Bulygin held the pistol above the water: "I am authorized to perform an emergency execution, *sans* hearing or trial, as necessary to imperial business. Who refuses to help save the Tsar's sea chest?"

We heaved the chest up through the hatch, heard it slide off across the slope of the deck. The Petukhovs & Madame Bulygin followed. I hung back, grappling with powder kegs. When next I looked, Madame was at the rail and the Petukhovs were swimming with the sea trunk. A wave engulf'd them. The twins surfaced, sputtering. No sign of the trunk.

Madame Bulygin climbed to the rail and jumped without a backward glance. Timofei, on the beach, saw & rushed out to her. She surfaced, gasping, but was weigh'd down by her water-soaked clothing, couldn't get her footing and was swept under. Timofei, running, plunged, stroked hard, reached her just as a wave hit them. They disappeared, reappeared, were swept into shallow water locked in desperate embrace.

The Petukhovs recovered Madame Bulygin's trunk. Timofei stood in rushing tide with Madame limp in his arms. Green breakers spread cold white sheets across a soggy mattress. The ship groan'd in agony. Bulygin & I held fast to her mainmast.

WE TOOK REFUGE IN AN ELEPHANT'S BONEYARD of driftwood logs stacked high on the beach by storm surf, their vertical siblings a green wall behind us. We scavenged dry branches, Olga's tinderbox birth'd a spark, and we drew near, teeth chattering, offering our dripping coats and goosebumpy skin to the reluctant fire.

No sign of the natives, but we feared attack was nonetheless imminent. We bolster'd our defenses by propping up the two swivels on the logs and stuffing them with pebbles. Timofei set us to drying, cleaning, priming and loading two muskets each.

From the forest, birdsong. Kahmooks sniff'd, ears twitching. Just birds, he said. We spread the mainsail & a foresail, rigging these canvases aloft with ropes & poles in the manner of the bedouin tribes. We stumbled about, our wet clothes sucking away at our bodies' last remaining heat. We would have to get dry soon or die. Madame Bulygin claimed the jib and duck'd inside to change. Maria dragged the sea trunk in behind her. Olga's samovar steamed on a small fire inside the tent. The crew passed a jug, toasting our survival of our arrival.

Kozma muster'd us, counted heads: "All here? Good. Kahmooks, ears on the trees. Afanasii, back him up with your bird gun. Keep a fuse burning. The rest of us will save what we can of the cargo while the tide goes out. Kahmooks, if you hear something, if the twig snaps, tell Afanasii and he touches off the swivels."

He formed us into a ragged line, wind-chilled derelicts stumbling back & forth between camp & ship. After an hour we'd secured the muskets, most of the shot & gunpowder, the last half-dozen jugs of vodka. Much remained aboard. We'd saved two axes, but the other tools were still in the hold. The musical instruments had survived.

The tide withdrew beyond the rock garden. The wind subsided. To the south, the rocky islands loom'd under a low sky. Kiss of drizzle.

Our poor ship careen'd like a broken toy. She lay on rocky muck surrounded by tidepools, damaged beyond repair, masts groaning under the weight of her rigging. She was a little mare with a broken leg, terrified by her pain, yet dreading the cock of the pistol.

Again & again, we returned to her, climbing the pitch'd deck, venturing down into a dark pool of floating cargo. We fashion'd slings from sails & spars. Bulygin, rescued from his bonds, stood beside the ship demanding the topmasts be lowered. His speech was slurred, due to his swollen jaw, but with gestures he indicated that the next high tide would rock the hull, causing the heavy spars to snap. He ordered us to lower the masts and remove the cargo, then haul the hull up on shore for repairs with the aid of an elaborate block & tackle arrangement he would devise from the ship's rigging. The crew pelted him with mud. Timofei, indicating gaping holes in the hull and the missing rudder, insisted that the ship was lost, that the cargo necessary to our survival must be high & dry as soon as possible.

Timofei & Kozma climbed inside the hull and tossed barrels of grain & goat cheese out at us. Bulygin stomp'd back to camp, vowing to return with a vote of confidence from Madame Bulygin. We shoulder'd our burdens. I hoist'd a cask of *iukola*, dried fish, and arrived in camp just as Madame Bulygin was ordering Five, Pavel, Yuri and Sergei to assist the captain. These four returned to the ship, seeking Timofei's confirmation. Bulygin gleefully followed, waving a cannon fuse.

IN RETROSPECT WE WOULD WISH THAT WE HAD QUESTIONED Bulygin's possession of the fuse, but at that instant the eagle-eyed Raven noticed several hundred visitors approaching on the beach to the south. They were singing.

All hands scrambled to defend our barricades. Timofei hurried back to camp, hoping to learn why Madame Bulygin had sent four good shots away at such a critical juncture. En route he passed Bulygin & his crew, who continued toward the ship.

Our warbling welcomers approached leisurely, still distant. They sounded like a flock of tropical birds, but their gestures indicated their song was more discussion than music. I imagined them saying, "Look at the ho'kwat hiding in the logs. Look at that ship. What do you suppose they have brought us?" Men in sea otter robes up front sport'd elaborate mustachios & chinwhiskers and carried whalebone clubs & spears. Conical hats woven from cedar bark, high cheekbones painted red & black. All barefoot, wearing a variety of furs, blankets, and the ubiquitous cedar-fiber tunic. Shorter in stature than we, but, like the Sitka natives, bigger through their torsos, a physical feature attained from shoveling large quantities of sea water. The men were crowd'd from behind by at least as many women, elderly and children. Ragged slaves brought up the rear.

Timofei, squinting through the glass, counted under his breath: "A hundred men, no guns, but all with weapons. Even the male slaves have spears. But if they come to fight, why do they bring the women, the children?"

Kurmachev, patting the swivel, suggested a preemptive warning shot. Timofei said no. I agreed. If they meant to rush us, our swivels might take down a dozen, including women & children. Each of us might drop a warrior, maybe two, with our muskets. Then they'd have us. Shouldn't want to be captured alive after that. If there's to be a fight, let them start it. Brace of pistols in my belt. I jiggled my sword in her scabbard. Tiny grains of sand scraped against smooth steel.

The delegation ceased its singing, coming to rest a hundred feet off, indecisive, arguing. Where first? The ship or the camp? Three tyees in elegant sea otter capes departed from the crowd and approached our position. One packed a whalebone club, the others carried long copper-pointed spears. They stopped on the far side of the creek, singing like birds. Timofei, Kozma and I walked out to meet them, smiling, holding our muskets across our chests.

Timofei greeted the tyees in Chinook: "*Kloshe tumtum mika chako.*"

Timofei had just welcomed the tyees to their own beach. Behind us, Madame Bulygin stepped up on a log, with the breeze ruffling her skirts around her ankles.

"Timofei, she said, "inform them they are invited for tea."

She demonstrated a china cup & saucer. Maria held the samovar. Our hosts splash'd across the creek. One snatch'd up the crockery, examining it with interest.

His mates examined Madame Bulygin & Maria. A tyee fondled Maria's breast, causing her to pour boiling water on his hand. He cursed. Cup & saucer flew. Madame Bulygin took the shrieking tyee by the elbow and led him into the jib-tent. The other two followed, then Maria, then Timofei. I brought up the rear, invited along as translator, and we all squeezed in for a go at afternoon tea. Madame Bulygin kneel'd in *pique-niqueuse* fashion, cup & saucer held daintily in her lap, pinkie extended. Maria hover'd behind her, chin on Madame Bulygin's shoulder. Our guests squatted on their haunches, sniffing chunks of salty bread only slighted mildew'd. Timofei & I sat on our rumps, knees drawn up to our chins. We noticed a favourable omen: the tyees had smear'd their hair with bear grease & duck's down, meaning they came in peace. The burned tyee dabbed his burn with grease from his feathered coiffure. One of the tyees and I were actually seated somewhat outside the tent, a position which permitted us a view of events transpiring both inside & out.

ACROSS THE CREEK, THE NATIVE DELEGATION SPLIT: one group ambled off toward the hulk of the *St. Nicholas*, into which Bulygin and the four Aleuts had vanished, the other to our camp, where they began to examine our possessions.

Inside the tent, a tyee sniffed his tea skeptically and asked: "*Kah mika illahee?*" What is your country?

Timofei: "Russia? Baranov?"

The tyees winked, nudged, tapped their temples: "Tweet tweet."

A tyee indicated the ship: "*Mamook kloshe?*" Can you fix it?

Timofei shook his head: "*Kokshut.*" Broken.

The tyee put it nicely: "*Hyas kokshut.*" Very broken.

Timofei: "*Klonas nowitka.*" Probably so.

Madame Bulygin: "Mr. Williams? Do you agree? The captain insists that the ship is salvageable."

I say: "Don't know how we'd make a new rudder, let alone repair the hull. Can't work on it out there, and we'd need a hundred men to haul her up on the beach, comes to that. Doubt the natives would help us. Either they'll strip her to the bone, or we'll lose her at the next high tide."

Madame Bulygin: "Then why is the captain so convinced?"

Timofei: "The ship is his reason to be."

A tyee sipped from his teacup, grimaced, spit, dumped the tea, scratched at the cup's delicate floral design with his thumbnail. Madame Bulygin protested. Timofei took a deep swallow from the vodka jug and in comradely fashion offered it to a tyee, who felt obligated to follow Timofei's example. Liquid flame sear'd his throat. He decided to make a speech, but found his tongue had gone numb. While he made odd noises & faces, his colleagues explained that we were at loggerheads with the mighty Quileute for running our ship aground on their beach without permission, and they demanded that Timofei accompany them back to the village for unspecified punishment. Our men, eavesdropping outside the tent, vehemently rejected the Quileutes' suggestion.

Timofei attempted to soothe them: "Better I should go, brothers. It is my duty as ataman."

Kozma: "We vote that you stay here."

Madame Bulygin had a suggestion: "Send Mr. Williams. Tell them this is his fault."

I refrained from translating. Timofei held up a tea cup and instructed me to explain that we came bearing gifts. "Also, tell them we leave much behind when we go. Warn them, better is not to quarrel with the Brotherhood of Yermak."

The tyees weren't impressed. They said we must surrender all but the clothes we wore, including & especially our guns, and depart. They weren't picky about where. They believed we were possessed by *mesachie tumtum*, demons, evil spirits.

Timofei handed the tyee a pewter token: "A gift, from the Tsar."

The tyee carefully placed the token on the sand beside his cup & saucer.

Madame Bulygin, an addendum: "His Tsar, his personal sovereign ruler, who extends his merciful protection even unto those aboriginal peoples who do not fully appreciate the many benefits accruing to heathen savages who find themselves so fortunate as to be . . ."

A tyee began to wail a plaintive dirge, which went on & on.

Maria presented the samovar, attempting again to pour. The tyees recoiled in fear. We fell silent, pondering the impasse. The tides ceased ebbing and began their return, promising to reach high water by mid-afternoon. The group out on the beach continued their slow pilgrimage in the direction of the ship.

Madame Bulygin was impatient: "This will never do. We must be firm with these people. Thank them and dismiss them. Such impudence."

The tyees scowl'd behind their face-paint.

I say: "Madame, they add that you, Maria and Olga will remain, as their servants. They say they will, ahem, *mamook tenas moosum*, 'make the little sleep' with you, even though they already have wives. The rest of us are to be gone forthwith."

Madame Bulygin: "No, we stay together. Also, we keep our guns. A gift, yes. An ax, a cooking pot, but no guns. Tell him we would appreciate it very much if they would make a few of those large canoes available to us. And a guide, and . . ."

I asked politely, "*Moosum yukwa tenas laly*?" May we sleep here a short time?

I was informed that we'd sleep elsewhere. Confrontation loom'd.

Kozma growl'd to Timofei: "I say we seize these tyees as hostages until their people find us a ship."

The tyees sensed opposition to their plan. To lighten the mood, one ceremoniously withdrew a polished stone smoking-pipe from within his garments and lit it with a twig from our little fire, inhaling and exhaling with gusto, his nostrils emitting dense plumes of smoke. The tent's atmosphere thickened. Gagging, Madame Bulygin sought fresh air from under the edge of the sail, thrusting her bottom up in a manner that was probably not meant to be provocative, but was nonetheless so interpreted by the tyees, who sighed and fondled themselves appreciatively. Timofei distract'd them by resuming negotiations.

A brouhaha began outside, hand to hand combat. A stone thump'd Kozma's skull.

Our hosts, believing they held salvage rights to our cargo, had begun an informal inventory, which led to argument, both amongst themselves and with us, which led to snatching and counter-snatching, which led to hitting, pushing and stone-throwing. The Quileutes proved expert at the latter.

Timofei excused himself, departing the tent to check on Kozma and to restore calm. He returned and spoke sternly to the tyee with dramatic gestures. To ease tensions, we puffed on the tyee's pipe and drank from the jug. Timofei & I cough'd. The tyees choked on the vodka.

Madame Bulygin cursed: the native women were looting her sea trunk. We had removed it from the tent to make room for the tea party, thereby giving the natives the erroneous impression that Madame Bulygin no longer claimed possession of its contents. She had appointed Filip & Yakov to guard the trunk, but they soon abandon'd their post for a bit of rough & tumble with members of the host delegation. The blue silk dress, the one she wore for her arrival at New Archangel, disappeared into the crowd, as did the brown English tweed. Dressing gown. Silk lingerie, Paris tags. Infant's dress. Tiny pair of shoes. *WTF?*

These items, like our cargo, soon attained widespread distribution. *Wait. She had a baby before me?* Madame Bulygin observed the lace collar of her French paisley settle on the naked shoulders of a giggling maiden. *Why am I just finding out she had a baby before me? Why doesn't anybody ever tell me anything?* She seized up a tyee's club, and, with the weapon held aloft, hasten'd off in pursuit. The club's owner, distracted by the jug, was alert'd by his colleagues.

Outside, Sobachnikov, tussling with a native man over possession of a musket, smote his adversary on his painted nose, but in so doing relinquish'd control of the gun, the hammer of which was prone to self-release without warning.

A shot. A hush fell.

No cries, no screams. Flesh had not been disturbed.

Kozma, recovering from the thrown stone, evened the score, seizing Sobachnikov by the collar, thumping him a stout blow on the noggin. Sobachnikov slumped. Kozma dropped him and spread his hands in supplication.

Timofei and the tyees emerged from the tent to join us, with our leader pleading for restraint: "*Wake mamook kahdena.*" Please, no fighting.

The tyees chose to view Kozma's punishment of Sobachnikov as a meritorious display of voluntary sacrificial retribution. Sobachnikov's adversary wobbled to his feet, dazed, still clutching the smoking gun, but a tyee clubbed him senseless in imitation of Kozma's gesture. Timofei and the tyees returned to the jib-tent for further negotiations, our hosts to their plunder, the crew to their futile defensive efforts.

OUT ON THE TIDEFLATS, THE QUILEUTES APPROACHED the wreck with expressions of awe etch'd upon their weatherbeaten faces, as though our ship was from another planet. They didn't rush, but paused to laugh at chortling urchins splashing in a tidepool.

A cannon fired.

An unseen hand swept the beach, just as the chessboard is cleared by the embittered loser, the pieces tossed & scattered. The boom echoed from the forest's soft ramparts.

A gentle breeze. Rumble of distant tides.

On the beach, limp bodies lay strewn. A low moan rose, cries of shock & pain. People struggled to stand, wobbly, as though awakening. A woman hid her face in bloody hands. A sullen cloud of gunsmoke slunk off down the beach.

Believing himself under attack, Bulygin had ordered the four Aleuts to fire a ten-pounder loaded with small stones & scrap metal from a hole in the starboard bow. A dozen Quileutes lay motionless, but some were at least moving, some now staggering to their feet. The native women in our camp dropped their newfound acquisitions and rushed out to aid the fallen. Madame Bulygin chased down the occupant of the paisley dress and wrestled the garment away.

We fellows stood staring, first at the defrocked lass, then at each other. For a brief moment we teetered on the brink of an epiphany, a shared realization that we might yet escape our bestial nature, that now, mutually appall'd, we might reach out across this chasm that yawn'd between us. Had Bulygin's atrocity satisfied our lust for further bloodshed? Could we now confront our differences peacefully, as men of goodwill? Surely, they could see we were as shock'd as they.

But, nay, the orgy of blood & bruises resumed, and we were again beset by multiple adversaries. Our guns had fired warning shots and then been dropped, reducing the combatants to fists, driftwood, knives, spears, clubs, and the buzzing stones.

Timofei emerged again from the tent intending to rally us, but a flying spear tore open his shirt, gashing his chest. He duck'd back into the tent to get his musket, only to bump heads with a departing tyee who'd had a taste of vodka. Though the tyee was needed outside, though his council might have soothed the turmoil, he instead seized his head with both hands and sat down again.

Timofei, with blood in his eye and on his torn shirt as well, snatched up his gun and returned to the fray, spitting curses. He noticed with relief that a bellowing Kozma was still on his feet, flinging screaming foes down upon rocks & logs. Timofei spied the blackguard who had wounded him lurking behind the mainsail tent, with now yet another spear and an apple-sized stone, which he hurl'd at Timofei, who at that moment fired his musket. The ball & the stone passed in flight. Each found its mark. The assailant's chest sprayed a pink mist. Timofei cried out, clutching his brow.

I crouch'd behind a log with Kahmooks, who likewise viewed this brouhaha with profound disdain; we believed ourselves best advised to take shelter whilst the storm spent itself. Yet, though senseless danger prevailed, when we saw Timofei fall I ran to help him, finding him moaning & unfocused. Another passing stone whisper'd in my ear. Madame Bulygin & Maria rushed to help me, seizing Timofei up under his arms. I took his feet and we hauled him behind the sea trunk, to which the women had restored some of Madame Bulygin's plunder'd wardrobe. Documents with crimson seals flutter'd in the breeze, weight'd by stones.

THE TYEES CONFERRED AND ADVANCED, WEAPONS IN HAND. We begged them to desist, to no avail. One tyee swung his club in a murderous arc, the other rushed at me with a spear. I drew my sword but tripped, lost my balance and fell on me arse. *Your default position.*

Frantically I kicked at my assailants' legs just as he thrust his spear down at me. Its iron point sought to bury itself in my chest but only sliced me and ripped my coat. The tyee tripped over my boots, fell forward, and, with a cry of dismay, impaled himself on my upturned sword.

The tyee behind him had a whalebone club, a white blur ripping at the air. I tried to flee, pushing my gurgling assailant off me. My sword went with him. My boots churn'd pebbles. I turned, pulled the pistol from my belt, cock'd the hammer, raised it to . . .

The tyee flung the club underhand with a flick of his wrist. My vision went black and my pistol discharged. I fell again, experiencing pain remarkable in its intensity. My darkened vision filled with brilliant flashes of light, and I was reminded of the nocturnal heavens over New Archangel.

Maria scream'd. My vision cleared. The tyee had seized up his club and, with vengeance burning in his eyes, lofted it o'er his head. The cudgel loomed, vivid with detailed carvings of animal faces. Tiny dark lines veined the club's blunt leading edge, old black blood forced into tiny fissures under great pressure.

Blood? Good heavens. I was about to be killed. Might display a bit of dignity. I rose to my knees so as to provide a better target. The camp tilted, spun. As I watch'd, the tyee's left eye retreated into his painted face like a child's ball sucked down a gutter. He paused, mid-stroke.

Madame Bulygin's arm lay braced across the sea trunk, her spent pistol languishing in her delicate fingers, smoking insouciantly. First, she threatens to kill me, I thought, and now she saves my life. The tyee extruded gray brains on his furry shoulder. He dropped his club and carefully placed a hand over each of his new apertures.

The donnybrook continued, with the Brotherhood receiving the short end. Timofei continued to be unconscious, hors de combat behind the sea trunk, reclining in heroic repose like Nelson on the deck of the Victory. The third tyee, the only survivor of the original trio, fled homeward, bare legs churning beneath his furs, with Kahmooks in dogged pursuit.

Reinforcements arrived from the ship in the form of the gun crew, which had deserted Bulygin. The captain appeared at the stern, followed by an angry mob of Quileutes. Cornered, his back against the shatter'd hull, he waved his sword. The Quileutes gave the blade ample space, but threw stones, with effect. Blood squirted from the captain's ear. He made a desperate break for the camp, but a stout matron flung a barb'd fishing spear into his departing backside. Impaled, Bulygin shriek'd, summon'd renewed vigour to his step, and continued, the spear stuck securely.

The ship exploded. The boom nearly ruptured my ears. *Go. Find. Hearing aid.* The masts vaulted skyward like heaven-bound crucifixes. Deck planks flew. The fleeing Bulygin & his pursuers were knocked flat. Multiple secondary explosions, the last of the powder kegs. Fires smoulder'd within the sodden wreckage, which was reduced to ribs, bowsprits and lower hull. A cloud of smoke rose.

Our adversaries in camp recovered their senses first. With anguished shouts they hoisted up the tyee with the vanish'd eye, causing more brains to slurp out the back of his shatter'd skull, and they rushed off, leaving us with the bloke Timofei shot, who was still sucking air through the hole in his chest, and my tyee, whom I was loathe to part with, 'ere (?) I retrieved my sword, which seemed to be stuck tight between his ribs. I braced both feet against his chest and pulled with all my might until he gurgled & relax'd. The blade slid from the wound with a gentle sucking sound. Jack the ripper, *c'est moi. Delete. Anachronism.*

The dead & wound'd, mostly women & children, still lay on the beach. We dropped to the sand, exhausted. Our camp was scatter'd

& spatter'd with blood. All of us, even Madame Bulygin & Maria, had suffered at least bumps & bruises. Kozma got Timofei sorted, then assessed the damage. We'd lost cargo, but somehow retained most of our guns & ammunition.

A bloody sun set behind a cloudy horizon, and a shadowy sea swept her shroud over the remains of our shatter'd ship. The natives retreated carrying their casualties, shouting promises of revenge.

TIMOFEI SHOOK ME FROM MY SLUMBERS. Dawn glow'd pale behind the forest. The dark sea rumbled. Our camp slept, snores mingling with moans.

Our leader had a nasty lump on his forehead and a finger on his lips: "Wake up. Join Zypianov on the north side. Kozma and I go up the beach to the archway, to see if we can get through. If we are captured, they might offer to trade us for guns. If so, demand to see us, then shoot us. Do not trade guns."

Kozma thumped his furry chest: "Shoot me here. And do not miss, poppy-puffer."

I say: "Wait. Coming with you."

Kozma's heavy hand restrained me: "We return, but maybe in a hurry. Stay awake."

They disappeared into the drift logs, each carrying a musket, another slung across their backs, a pistol stuck in their sashes. Kozma carried a heavy bag over his shoulder.

What was in the bag? The Tsar's silver? *Delete*. Had they stolen it? Did they plan to bury it?

I scanned my surroundings. We'd been granted a reprieve from the sea's deep dungeons, only to be cast up on this sandy purgatory. Sunrise lit a seascape of remorseless grandeur: gray sky & sea, black rocks & forest. Flash of white breakers, a swooping gull. On the southern horizon, the Quileutes' huge rock and an umbilical sand spite merged. Distant dogs danced.

Offshore from our camp large rocks rose from the sea, one with a sharp point, another looked like a flat cap with a button on top. To the north, the spired cathedral and a headland bored through with a natural arch wide enough for two carriages to pass abreast.

No sign of Timofei & Kozma.

The dead white roots of my log grasp'd at the moist breeze. The ship's exposed ribs likewise curled in black rigour mortis. I gripped my teacup's dying warmth.

Everything hurt. Sympathy would not have been wasted on me, might I have evoked such in some tender heart. Many of my mates were worse off than I, but my nose felt broken, and the crudely-stitched spear gash on my shoulder throbbed. Pain, proof of life. I hurt, therefore I am. I should like a smoke.

Those feeling no pain included the two slain tyees laid to rest under a pile of cobblestones. Madame Bulygin & Maria slumber'd under the foresail with Yakov & Filip curled at their feet like faithful hounds. From the mainsail tent a symphony of suffering, a crescendo of groans & snores. Captain Bulygin, bandaged buttocks bared, was banish'd from the tent.

Zypianov, nearby, stirred behind his log. We sentries were shrouded mummies, muskets clutch'd to our chests.

The evanescent seascape swirl'd, sought shape. On the beach a heron posed on one leg, a feather'd ballerina admiring her mirror'd reflection.

Three shots.

The heron took flight. We kicked away our blankets, yanked our guns from their protective skins, looked to our firing-pans, peeped over the logs, thumb'd back our hammers.

I remembered my instructions: "Hold fire," I shouted to my mates, "Timofei & Kozma are out there."

Scarcely had these words left my tongue when these two burst into view, hurdling logs. Kozma was minus a musket. Sand spurted from their heels as they plunged headlong into our midst. No sign of pursuers, nor of the bag Kozma had carried. *They buried it. We found it. Thank you Jesus.*

Olga wiped a nasty slash on Kozma's leg with vodka, our all-purpose disinfectant, and thread'd a sewing needle with fishing line, just as she'd done for the gash on my chest.

Kozma gritted his teeth: "Damn the kolosh. They get one of my guns, but we kill two of them."

Timofei nodded sadly: "Our debt grows."

Madame Bulygin & Maria, bleary-eyed, joined us, blankets draped over their coats, native hats tied under their chins with bright blue ribbons.

Madame Bulygin confronted Timofei: "Why do you provoke the natives? Did I give permission for this *sortie d' reconnaissance*?"

Timofei: "We seek to go north. We can, at low tide, through the archway. But beyond, big rocks, cliffs."

Kozma: "We plan to return to New Archangel. On foot. We do not ask permission. Maria comes with us."

Madame Bulygin, concerned: "Mutiny, desertion, kidnapping. What next? No one desires rescue more than I, but we must not waste what we have won. We survive our first challenges on these shores. We rebuff our tormentors, we prevail against the elements. The storm, the shipwreck, yesterday's battle, all these dangers we surmount together. Adversity unites us. We are a tight-knit and disciplined corps d' conquest. In our solidarity lies our strength. One for all, all for one. In contrast, see how the savages leave their fallen behind? We leave no one behind."

The crew begged to differ: "We vote that the captain stays with the ship."

Madame Bulygin ignored this, flourishing a scrolled chart: "I now reveal our plans, which are secret. Russia's many enemies would pay dearly to hear that our orders, from the Tsar, are that we will rendezvous with the *Kodiak* at Gray's Harbor, then sail with them to California, where we will build a fort at Bodega Bay, claiming the surrounding territory for Russia. Then we sail back north to the Columbia River, where we construct yet another redoubt. The Tsar desires that his flag should fly over both California and the Columbia River, and he orders Mr. Kuskov to meet us at Gray's Harbor. Also, the Tsar desires that Captain Bulygin continue in his role as our captain, and not be left behind."

She unrolled the chart, spread it on the pebbles, placed stones on its corners, poked it with a stick: "Here we are. Approximately. Here is Gray's Harbor, our destination. In between, a pleasant stroll on the seashore."

The crew was skeptical: "Where on your map is this river we see to the south? Or the river north of Destruction Island?"

Madame: "Rivers can be crossed. We cannot walk back to New Archangel, and we can't stay here. If we take our muskets and gunpowder, they will fear us. If we give them the ship and this great pile of loot, they will not pursue us."

Kozma: "Me and Timofei they pursue. Almost they catch us."

Zuev picked a mournful melody: "Not me. Soon I am playing balalaika for the grateful dead." *Anachronism.*

Despondent, we contemplated suicide, but voted to finish the vodka first. All quiet in the forest.

We peered into the trees: "They hide. They fear us."

Bulygin stabbed the southern horizon with his sword, declaring he would lead us to Gray's Harbour and a rendezvous with Kuskov.

The crew: "Lead on, captain. We are behind you all the way."

Timofei: "We go north, back to New Archangel. Any man who wishes to do otherwise, the Brotherhood releases him without punishment."

Madame Bulygin stood firm: "Gray's Harbor, Timofei. The Tsar's orders. I am sure the *Kodiak* sailed past us in the night and rests at anchor in Gray's Harbor at this very moment, waiting for us. If Mr. Kuskov fails to reach our rendezvous, or if he departs it without us, he must answer probing questions."

The Brotherhood rubbed its collective tummy, mulling its options: "If the *Kodiak* comes to Gray's Harbor, we sail her to Kauai. If not, still there is a chance of rescue by another ship."

"North. The cape. Sooner or later, a ship comes to the cape, and the cape is closer."

"Closer, but big rocks. Cliffs. Easier going to the south."

"The kolosh will have a path around the big rocks. Look at the map. The distance to the cape is half of what it is to Gray's Harbor. We cannot go south. Never do the kolosh let us pass their village. Not now."

"We sneak around behind the village. The kolosh fears the forest."

"I fear the forest. The bear, the wolf, they eat us alive. Tell us what you think, Timofei."

Timofei shook his head. "How do we cross this river? Swift current. Many trips our little boat must make, over and back. When we are divided, the kolosh attacks. But, to the north, no big rivers between here and the cape."

Debate ensued: "No rivers that we know of. If we go south, each man carrying two guns, they must let us pass. Coats, blankets, a week's food, these we carry in sails slung on poles. Everything else, we leave. Cannons, cannonballs . . ."

"And gunpowder. With a slow fuse burning. Kahboom goes the kolosh."

"No. If again we kill them, never do they let us escape. But if they see we leave treasures behind, maybe they fall to fighting amongst . . ."

Kahmooks, from his sentry post: "Ahem? Bark bark?"

We hastened to our ramparts, peering into the forest. A leaf flutter'd, even though the breeze had died.

Timofei: "How many?"

Kahmooks, ears up: "Everybody and his cousin."

Short fuses lay curled on the cannons, awaiting the slow-match's sizzling kiss. Silence, just the whisper of the surf. We crouch'd behind our logs, clutched our guns, licked dry lips, and listened to our hearts thumping under our coats.

Maria stood up and faced the forest, apparently unafraid of flying arrows. "Hear me, Quileutes," she called. "Leave us in peace. We will walk away from this place."

No response from the forest. Mumbling in the ranks.

Madame Bulygin stood beside Maria: "We prepare for departure, Mr. Tarakanov. South, to Grays Harbor. I will dash off a log entry before we go, noting our desperate circumstances. Mr. Williams hopes my pen does not linger on yesterday's episode."

I say: "But you'll mention the captain's heroic role?"

"You are so tragique as you kneel in the sand, gallantly awaiting your execution, accepting your fate. A poignant scene, reminiscent of Cook's demise at the hands of the cannibals. I hesitated to intervene. My finger, poised upon the trigger, a poetic *intervalle*, a pause to savor the subtle facets of the violent scene playing out before me. Then, luckily for you, I choose to alter your executioner's viewpoint, with my little French paintbrush."

I say: "Nick in the bloke's arm might have sufficed, what?"

"Your gratitude overwhelms me. Why do you impale that man through his chest? Why not a gentlemanly nick in the arm?"

Maria's dark eyes flashing, intervened: "Write in the book that the cannon shoots the women and children."

Silence. Maria had never before taken issue with her benefactress, at least not in our presence.

Madame Bulygin smiled: "The log shall note that by firing the cannon, our brave captain and his men turned the tide of battle in our …"

"Write in the book that the captain kills," Maria said. "Write down the dead babies."

WE SLEPT, SHELTER'D BY SCENT'D CEDARS. Awakening, we sniff'd the sweet stink of tidepools.

Timofei & Kozma prodded us with gun-butts. We stirred, moaning, remembering the battle. Shipwreck & cargo, distant memories, three miles behind us.

When we departed the ship we spiked the cannon, pounding iron nails into the touch-holes, and we loaded food, vodka, coats, blankets, cartridge-boxes and three kegs of musket powder into sailcloth slings. The tools we left beside the cannon, the surplus powder we scattered on the sand, and we set off southbound at water's edge, pulling the boat through the tidewash, each man packing a pair of muskets. When we looked back, the camp teem'd with plundering Quileutes, their shouts buried in the surf's roar.

At the river's mouth we turned inland, with Quileute men & women silently watching us from the opposite bank. We ventured a half-mile upstream, reached a defensible crossing, and ferried ourselves back & forth. No sign of the natives. When we were safe on the far bank, we gave our little boat to the current, and as it swept past the village naked boys swam to catch her. Little Filip watched them, mixed emotions playing on his tender features. If we were captured, he'd be their slave.

The wilderness looked impenetrable. Huge trees, thick undergrowth. I took a compass bearing. Giving the village a wide berth, we plunged into a green cathedral, a quiet abbey of hemlocks, immense cedars, firs, spruces. A soft glow filter'd down from the canopy a hundred feet above, where choirs of birds herald'd our passing. No Quileutes visible, but we felt watched. Squirrels cursed us. Shapes in the shadows, faeries in the ferns. A wail echoed, chilling us. A wolf? Leshiy, the wild man?

The Cossacks crossed themselves.

Wet to the skin, we waded in soggy vegetation, on a dewy sponge of moss & leaves spread over the soft bones of the forest's fallen ancestors. We made slow progress, detouring around great reefs of fallen trees, through clearings their descents had created. Infant seedlings sprout'd from the logs, miniatures of their parents. Colonies of lichens & toadstools burgeon'd. The fallen trees left splinter'd stumps rising thirty feet above the forest floor, their hollow wombs large enough to accommodate us all.

We stumbled on, fearful not only of ambush, but also the damp cold that sucked the life from our flesh. Must keep moving, we told each other, keep bearing back toward the coast. We marched 'til nightfall, then slept exhaust'd in a pile.

At dawn, without tea or breakfast, we stumbled on, emerging hours later from the forest atop a headland with an expansive view. Gray sea swept out to an obscure horizon. Empty cobblestoned beaches.

Descending to the shore, we built a fire in the lee of a stone spire. Above us, a thin white waterfall dropped a hundred feet, its wee creek running with what looked like tea. Brownish, but good water. Olga fired up the samovar and made some real tea. We steamed our wet woolens on sticks while breakfasting on sea-soaked sausage. As we ate, we regarded the massive headland blocking our way south. Scouts returned from the surf-washed rocks at its base, shaking their heads: no passage at water's edge, even at low tide.

So, we climbed the headland, ascending steep slopes of thick brush, hauling ourselves and our cargo up on ropes belay'd on trees. Scrambling down the opposite slope, we reached another rocky beach with another pretty creek, banks strewn with driftwood. Our travel had been more vertical than horizontal. Scratch'd, bleeding, we paused to regroup.

Kahmooks, an ear, cock'd: "Footsteps."

We seized up our guns just as two native men emerged from the forest. One we recognized, a tyee from the fight at the camp. He and his companion wore protective elk-hide and the red & black face-paint. Both carried bows & arrows, spears & knives, whalebone clubs. They approached with smiles & greetings. I translated.

The tyee: "Why walk on the beach in the wind and rain? Dry path up in the forest. Come, we show you the way."

The crew responded rudely.

The tyee: "You cannot escape. Surrender. Return with us to our village. Why make misery last longer?"

The crew: "We are Russian. We like misery."

The tyee pointed south: "You come to the right place. Next river belongs to Hoh people. Crossing is *mesachie mitlite*, very dangerous. Can't do it on your own. Better give up now."

Madame Bulygin: "Ask him to send word to our friend Mr. Yutramaki."

The tyee: "This is Quileute territory. Yutramaki stays away. Give us the four who kill our people. The captain, his wife, the Englishman, and that man." He pointed at Timofei.

Shubin stroked his scraggly beard: "How about just the captain?"

The tyee, an accusatory finger: "Nobody kills a Quileute and walks away."

Madame Bulygin had an idea: "Timofei, impress the tyee with your marksmanship. Filip, see that piece of driftwood lying on that rock? Run down, draw a circle around the knot with this pencil."

Filip did so. Timofei aimed his musket & fired. The driftwood jumped into the air. The tyee and his companion solemnly marched down the beach, picked up the target, and poked Timofei's bullet hole, which was off the knot by only inches. The tyee replaced the driftwood on the rock and returned. We hadn't noticed he'd strung an arrow in a short bow under his furs, and with barely a glance he whirled and let fly. The arrow was a blur as it knock'd out the knothole, passing through cleanly.

They bade us farewell: "Storm comes. Big cave up ahead you can sleep in. Watch out for bears."

Black clouds approached from seaward, rumbling with atmospheric menace.

The tyee: "Reminds me. How much you want for that talking wolf?"

Kahmooks, a fang, reveal'd: "How much you want for that fat butt, chief?"

The natives departed in haste. Storm clouds boom'd, breakers crash'd, cedars bent in the moist breeze. We covered our guns, even though we should thus be slow to respond to ambush, and set off again, soon arriving at a cave in the face of a rocky cliff, its mouth open to the sea. Moss & miniature ferns grew from fissures in smooth stone. Fat raindrops splatter'd. Kozma tossed pebbles into the cave's dark recesses.

He shoved Zypianov in first: "Crawl back and look for bears. If you fall in love, keep it quiet."

THUNDER TREMBLED OUR TOMB. ROCKS, PERHAPS loosened by the deluge, perhaps by human hands, tumbled down past the mouth, and we limited our departures to the necessities, conducting our business with a wary eye on the precipice above. Around us the ancient forest wept, its moaning limbs burdened by the monsoon.

In the afternoon, three naked Quileute men ran past southbound on the pathway, no doubt carrying news of us to the Hohs. Madame Bulygin, finding the cave's interiour air objectionable, sat near the mouth wrapped in her blankets, watching the runners with interest. Gusts hurl'd waves of rain against the cliff, and the storm's violence left her wide-eyed, awestruck.

Morning dawn'd with a clear sky. We summit'd the next headland, then traversed a rushing creek below a pretty waterfall. The next stream, pouring through a narrow, alder-lined ravine, was too swift to wade. A well-trod path led inland along the bank. We could see fish in the water, and supposed that people might live upstream. If so, they might have a log that bridged the torrent.

The sun sank into dark clouds. The unseen sea was a quiet roar.

Timofei: "Either we follow the path, or we camp here."

We debated. Kahmooks noted a faint whiff of smoked fish, evidence of upstream habitation. Our tummies groaned audibly, but we knew the natives might be lying in wait for us. We couldn't go back the way we'd come. Somewhere upstream, a crossing must await us.

Timofei: "Afanasii, scout ahead."

Valgusov advanced, his beady gaze probing the foliage from within his ebony mask, the muzzle of his fowling-piece protruding from his plumage. We followed, hammers cock'd under our gun covers, deafen'd by the stream's roar.

Eventually the path opened into a pretty clearing complete with rustic cottage, fragrant smoke issuing from a hole in the roof. A log spanned the stream above a fish trap made of lash'd branches.

We were watched by unseen eyes. We halloo'd. Silence. The roar of the water drown'd our words. Timofei approached the house, poked the mat covering the door, peeked in.

"*Kizutch*," he said. Silver salmon.

Dark inside. Desultory alderwood fires smoulder'd in pits. Fishing gear draped the walls. The ceiling was hung with bundles of fish, each containing twenty-five suspended salmon, beheaded, cleaned, gutted, smoked dry. Timofei cut a bundle down.

Kozma was worried: "Fires, but no people. Kahmooks?"

The malamute sniffed: "They just left. Four or five people. Give me a fish."

"Speak, boy. Say please."

Kahmooks: "Just the boy in the bushes, other side of the stream. Now give me a fish or I will eat your leg, please."

We turned as one to scan the opposite bank. A wide-eyed boy jumped out of a fern and dash'd up a path into the forest.

"Ha. Run away, little boy. We are the big scary Cossacks."

"See? The kolosh fear us. Tonight, we feast on their food. We sleep in their house, safe and dry."

Timofei: "We sleep in the clearing, and no more fish do we take. As payment, I leave three fathoms of blue beads. Also, a handful of glass pearls. In the morning, we cross the log. Not to wear out the welcome."

AT DAWN, OUR GUARDS RETREATED HASTILY TO CAMP, pointing at painted faces in the trees. Quileutes, all about us. Singing birds swoop'd through slanting beams of fine light.

Timofei fired a shot into the treetops. The birds fell silent. The Quileutes faded into the forest, laughing. They'd tested our defenses, toying with us, and found that when the dog slept they could approach within bow-and-arrow range.

We calmed ourselves. Olga prepared tea. Timofei reloaded. Madame Bulygin sat on her trunk, sleepy-eyed, swath'd in blankets, pistol at the ready.

She fixed Kahmooks with a withering glare: "Our faithful guardian."

Kahmooks yawn'd: "Not my watch."

She survey'd the bushes, announcing she would like to relieve herself.

Kahmooks sniffed the air: "They're still close. Lift your leg on a fern."

Madame Bulygin opened the ship's log: "Perhaps our countrymen will understand the challenges we face when they read the piteous lament that I compose for my forthcoming book, which reads as follows: 'My God! Who will believe that there might exist on the face of the earth such a cruel, barbaric people . . . They plundered and burned the ship and, still not satisfied, chased us down to take our lives. To them we were neither a threat nor a danger. But it seems they begrudged our very existence.'" *Owens and Donnelly. Cite source.*

The crew: "But why? Perhaps because your husband kills their women and children? Write the truth, Madame. It is not the kolosh who destroy our ship."

"She cannot. She is forced to fabricate fictitious fibs, flagrant falsehoods, and feeble fables. *F words! I love F words!* Violence can only be concealed by a lie, and lies can only be maintained by violence." *Anachronism, uncited quote from Solzhenitsyn. Fix or delete.*

"Truth," Madame Bulygin said, "is a relative commodity, like beauty. Truth changes from moment to moment. It is fleeting, depending upon the eye of the beholder. As the French writer Sébastien-Roch Nicolas de Chamfort remarked, 'Man may aspire to virtue, but he cannot reasonably aspire to truth.' *See how she credits the people she quotes?* No, the only truth that need concern you is God, your Tsar, and Mother Russia."

"God is just opium for the peasants." *Anachronism, stolen quote.*

"Vodka is the opium of the peasants."

"Vodka is the truth. All else is lies."

"The truth is lies soaked in vodka."

"Other way around, idiot. A lie is the truth soaked in vodka."

"But then," I asked, "does Lord Byron's point'd query fall far from the mark? Could a lie, he asks us, be but the truth in masquerade? *See? That wasn't so hard, was it?* What, forsooth, is a lie?"

"What is a forsooth?"

Madame Bulygin closed the logbook: "No more discussion. My version stands as written. The natives were belligerent in their demands, and their assault on our camp is not forgiven. If they suffer losses, they have only themselves to blame. Our captain's sterling record remains without tarnish."

Bulygin sneered: "An daff da troof. Ow." He finger'd the gap where his missing tooth had been.

Madame Bulygin stood, smoothing her soiled skirts: "The truth is that we are tired, hungry and wet. Now that we know we can cross this stream, we will rest under the sails today, resuming our journey at first light. Agreed, Mr. Tarakanov? Good. Mr. Williams, kindly provide our captain with medicine for his pain, *s'il vous plait*. Maria, cover me, would you please, while I tippy-toe off to the ferns."

WE STUMBLED THROUGH WET FERNS, CHILLED TO THE BONE. We'd left food behind at the shipwreck so we could carry more guns &

powder, and now our rations dwindled and the powder was damp, as were our clothes & blankets. We marched on, fearing to pause for rest. If we sat down, we would fall asleep, our bodies would lose what remained of their warmth, and we would not awaken.

We descended from steep headlands, drawing closer to the boom of unseen surf below. A startled deer leaped from the bushes. Timofei, in the lead, had his gun up first. His flint spark'd, but his powder only sputter'd. The deer vanish'd. Timofei cursed under his breath, yank'd his powder horn and shot bag from under his great-coat, grumbling. We rested as he reloaded, sagging on our muskets, sweating under soggy sealskins, scanning the surrounding sylvan scene. *S words! I love S words!* Green-gray daylight filtered through the high evergreen ceiling. Birds & breezes.

We assumed they watched us. What were they waiting for? Why didn't they attack? They knew now our powder was damp. Did it amuse them to watch us stumble about?

We reached a lofty promontory with a view of the ocean. A forested headland jutted from the coast a league to the south. Vancouver's chart recorded a similar feature, but in our view this coast was just one wretch'd headland after another. On the beach a pair of gargoyle eagles perched atop a stone tower, ignoring our approach. The sea's horizon was broken only by a sheer-sided loaf of stone a mile offshore, seabirds swirling above its summit. Madame Bulygin named it Alexander Island in honour of the Tsar.

We rested at a clear stream where it rushed from the forest. Sea lions clustered on offshore rocks. Sea otter frolick'd in kelp beds. The Aleuts wanted to shoot them from the rocks, then wait for the surf to wash fresh meat ashore. Timofei shook his head: no poach-ing. Shouldn't want to cause offense.

We crossed the stream and continued in a ragged column, limp-ing & cursing. Yuri & I shared a pole from which four kegs of gun-powder hung in a sail-cloth sling. A knot on the pole gouged deeper into my shoulder with every step. Madame Bulygin, wrapped in her long black cape, complained of blisters but kept pace with the aid of the shaft of a Quileute fishing spear. The captain brought up the rear, mumbling threats at scuttling crustaceans.

Another stream rush'd from the forest across the cobblestones. This one was bigger, faster, deeper, maybe chest high. We sat on driftwood tree trunks, watching the torrent, gathering courage. Timofei appointed me to cross first. I waded, poking the rocky bed with my toes, pair of muskets held high. Kozma belay'd the rope tied around my chest. The cold drained all sensation from my nether regions. I stumbled but found footing and emerged on the far bank, numb & dripping. I tied the line fast to a log. Timofei & Kozma crossed, then the others.

A shout. Little Filip, swept away into the surf. He vanished, buried in the breakers, weighed down by his coat. Dumbstruck, we stood gaping with our boots buried in the sand.

Kozma recovered first. Bellowing, he dived into the waves and flounder'd about like an enraged sea monster until he found Filip and hauled him ashore. The boy coughed and gulped for air. His muskets were lost, but his fiddle case was still clutch'd tight. Kozma stripped the shivering boy of his wet clothes, wrapped him in a blanket and poured vodka down his tender throat, then hugged him to his chest until the boy stopped shaking.

Out beyond the surf, a dark shape breach'd, blowing a foul stink into the onshore breeze.

A distraught howl from behind us: the malamute didn't swim well. I waded back to fetch our furry hundred-pounder, carrying him draped over my shoulders. When we reached safety he froze, ears up, fur bristling, staring at the trees, a low growl in his throat.

Four natives blended into the shadowy cedars: three men with spears stood behind a woman in a long fur cape, her black hair streaked with silver. She approached, offering us a basket of berries.

Timofei raised an open palm: "Klahowya."

The woman's forehead had been flattened, bespeaking membership in a family of noble status, and her bearing was authoritative. She introduced herself as Yutramaki's sister and told us in a combination of Chinook & English that her brother could not personally attend but had sent her in his stead. She explained that though she was of the Cape People, one of her husbands lived at the Hoh village and thus she & her entourage traveled safely on these shores, as the Hoh were related to (though not necessarily friendly with) the larger Quileute clans, whose territory we had just traversed. She said they had paddled down to the Hoh village from the cape, and, after negotiations regarding us, had been dropped off here at the creek. Though they found us amusing, they refrained from ridicule. They would not trifle with an armed raven or a talking dog.

The woman was curious about our womenfolk. Madame Bulygin, changing clothes behind the sea trunk, invited her to sit for tea. The samovar steamed over Olga's little fire. We men built our own merry little blaze, endeavouring to dry our clothes & blankets while we sat smoking, passing a jug. The spear carriers stood apart, observing us with reservation. The women nibbled berries and spoke in low tones.

Kahmooks eavesdropped & translated: "The sister woman says we just crossed into Hoh territory. Her brother wants us to surrender to the Hohs. Watch out for the Quileutes. They are very angry. The Hohs and the Cape People want to split us up between the villages. Madame and Maria will go to the cape."

The crew grumbled. Timofei shush'd us.

The dog, ears twitching: "Yutramaki wants Madame Bulygin, but so do the Quileutes, because she shot their tyee. It will cost Yutramaki much whale oil to buy her. Mumble mumble. Back and forth. Madame says the captain and Maria must return to Russia with her. Madame asks, 'Are there no ships on the coast?' The sister woman says no ships."

The crew moaned. Yutramaki's sister glanced at us and said something. Madame Bulygin laughed.

Kahmooks: "Madame says, '*Les miserables*? Never mind them. They lament their many wounds.' The sister says, 'Wounds? The Quileutes have dead *tillicums*, family. They are a violent people.'"

Long silence. The captain squatted in the stream, pants around his ankles, his festering spear-wound exposed. Olga poured from the steaming samovar. Yutramaki's sister reached out and put her hand on Madame Bulygin's belly.

Kahmooks: "The sister says, 'Ha. Thought so. Now you must think about your baby.'"

*And here she is, the star of our show . . .*

Maria shriek'd. Madame Bulygin sat dumbfound'd.

Kahmooks: "The sister says she's a midwife. 'I feel your daughter,' she says. 'She is strong. She comes late in summer. The medicine man in Russia says that never again does your belly hold a baby, and many men plant their seed, but only my brother's grows. Now your blood is joined with ours. Soon snow falls, early in the new moon. You need food and a warm house. When I tell the Quileutes that you carry Yutramaki's baby, no one will argue. He will buy you, and also Maria. Olga too. A captive woman from a high-up family needs female slaves.'"

Winds sigh'd, waves crash'd, gulls screech'd.

Our captain lost his balance and splash'd in the creek. We failed to assist him. Madame Bulygin, hands on abdomen, looked pensive.

Kahmooks: "The sister says the Hohs will demand we give them guns to take us across the river. Maria says, 'The men believe that if they give up their guns, they will be captured and tortured. They will fight to the death.' Madame says, mumble mumble, a bargain, an understanding. The sister says that the men who did not kill a Quileute, those who kiss the feet of the tyees, maybe they will not be tortured but will serve as slaves until a ship comes with ransom. Madame asks, what will happen to the captain? The sister says, if the Quileutes get him he will swallow small stones, like those which kill the people on the beach, until his belly is full.'"

Bulygin, breathing heavily, dragged himself out of the creek, clutching cobblestones. His wife glanced over her shoulder at him with an odd look in her eyes.

Kahmooks: "Madame says, 'I cannot go back to Russia without Captain Bulygin.'"

*Why not? If they wanted him back, why did they exile him in the 1st place? Why did she even marry him? Also, we need to have a serious talk about her first baby. You & daddy are withholding info and I do not appreciate it.*

WE WAITED, PUFFING OUR PIPES. The women chose their words. The stream gurgled. Captain Bulygin cast stones at unseen tormentors. The women spoke, too softly now for the malamute's ears, eventually agreeing on something. Madame Bulygin, nibbling berries from the basket, summon'd Timofei, who had been staring at the ocean. Kozma nudged him and told us we'd all attend this meeting. As we approached, Maria pointed me out to Yutramaki's sister.

Why me?

Madame Bulygin seemed pleased: "Excellent news, men. We arrive at the Hoh village by nightfall, and they will take us safely across the river. This good woman expresses sympathy for our mistreatment at the hands of the Quileutes, and she says neither the Hohs nor the Cape People were involved. She brings us these delicious berries to ward off scurvy. *Mahsie*, many thanks, Sister."

Yutramaki's sister spat in the sand: "Quileutes *mesachie tillicum*." Bad people.

Madame Bulygin: "But, she says, the Hohs await our arrival with open arms. Tonight, as a reward for your steadfast loyalty, a hot meal, a dry bed. Yes, I see your haggard faces fill with joy. A respite from our journey, a gracious stay with new friends, a kindness we shall reward with gifts. A few of the extra muskets will suffice. And then . . ."

Timofei: "No guns. As you say, the Tsar forbids."

"Gifts, Timofei. Appreciation for services provided to the Tsar's emissaries. Necessary services."

The sister: "Each Russian who crosses river, one gun that shoots. Don't like it, build a boat."

Madame Bulygin beamed with confidence: "So we are assured of a river crossing. Soon we rendezvous with the *Kodiak* at Gray's Harbor, and we focus our resources on the Columbia, not on . . ."

Timofei: "If we find the *Kodiak*, we go to Kauai. And we keep our guns."

". . . not on an island out in the ocean or some obscure bay in Spanish California. The Columbia, men, one of America's great rivers. *C'est magnifique*. And to achieve our goal, we lighten our burden, divesting ourselves of superfluous items from the vast array of armaments we lug about. Our Tsar understands that sometimes his rules must be bent, that his ambassadors must adapt to local circumstances."

She pointed down the beach: "And then, having done so, the goodwill we create here will flow before us like a welcoming carpet. Someday, historians will rank the heroic crew of the *St. Nicholas* with Russia's great explorers. Our saga will be engraved on monuments of bronze and marble, and your names will tumble from the tongues of schoolchildren. Courage, men. Immortality still lies within our grasp. Our fort on the Columbia is so close we can almost touch its sturdy ramparts. We are nearly there."

Timofei: "Kauai."

"The Columbia, by order of the Tsar."

Breakers boomed. A hungry eagle screamed. Sea winds sighed in cedars. Timofei stared at his boots.

Madame Bulygin: "*Tres bien.* Lead on, Sister."

Again, a whale surfaced out beyond the surf, its blow blooming. I sniff'd cetacean stink.

Yutramaki's sister touched my arm: "The whale, she tastes the boy. Almost she gets him, but the big man finds him first. Now Filip's smell is in the ocean, his song is in the sea. Now the whale dreams about the sweet boy who makes the music."

THIS IS THE DREAM ABOUT THE RIVER.

I lie down in darkness on smooth rocks beside a rumbling river, but at dawn a warm & gentle tide rises, carrying me off in a driftwood cradle, and though I'm swept away, I don't cry or thrash about, for the dawn's light warms my trembling flesh, pain & fear ebb away, and I swim through placid currents, through wreckage & body parts, through bloody splinters of pure white oak, the pieces of my cross. My hand was burned, disfigured. Now, before my very eyes, 'tis heal'd, made whole.

I'm almost to the sea. The whales await me, singing.

I woke in a black hole roaring with nearby surf. We were still on the north side of the river, which had risen with the tide. Perhaps we would cross this morning in the Hohs' canoes.

We had arrived at riverside in darkness and were informed that the currents were too hazardous for an immediate crossing. The Cossacks refused to cross in the dark at any rate, fearing the ghosts of the drown'd floating on the surface at nightfall. Timofei & Madame Bulygin argued again over whether we should trade guns to the Hohs in exchange for transport across the river. She ordered him to do so. Timofei refused. Impasse.

We bivouack'd on open beach just inside the mouth, equidistant from sea, forest & river. Kahmooks & I volunteer'd for first watch and hunker'd down behind a log upriver from the camp, one of four outlying sentry posts. Kozma & Five stationed themselves above us at the tree-line, Timofei was at water's edge. Zuev faced the ocean. We weren't covert: our pipes & whistled signals advertised our locations, and I started a small fire with my tinderbox. We feared the natives might creep close in the dark to probe our defenses, supposing us too tired to stay awake, but Kahmooks could discern nothing afoot with two feet.

I'd freeze before I was slaughter'd. A wet breeze blew from seaward, and the dog & I had nothing but a scrap of sailcloth to shed the persistent dampness. Kahmooks also shed persistently, enough to make a blanket. I had two loaded muskets wrapped in skins, a pistol, my sword, my lamp & pipe, and a small brown chunk of opium.

No, mustn't smoke. Stay alert. Cossacks on nocturnal guard duty placed a knife's point just under an eye, with the handle braced against a log. If they nodded off, they'd awake half-blind. If Kozma caught them snoozing, their fate might be worse.

Wolves chorus'd from the forest. Kahmooks listened. Across the river at the Hohs' village, a worried dog woof'd. Glacier water wash'd the rocks. The night had nary a glimmer, save the glow of our campfire floating in cold space. If intruders approach'd while Kahmooks slept, I hoped they'd kick a cobblestone loose, for I shouldn't see them until they were upon us.

In camp, Olga nursed her own infant blaze. A window opened in the clouds. Bright stars (Leo, Auriga, Gemini, the two Dippers) twinkled. Moonbeams draped a sleeping sea in silver sheets, and the ocean's round breast swelled. A fishy stink merged with the fragrance of rotting rainforest. Down by the river, a feminine silhouette rose from Timofei's post and tiptoed through moonshadows, returning to the big tent. *Do not imply this might have been my mother. She was pregnant. With me. Not showing, but still. Delete.*

The wolves sang "Ah-rooo."

Just off the river's mouth, a whale answered: "Skreeek."

Kahmooks thrust his cold nose at the moon: "Ah-rooo."

I say: "Call of the wild?" *Anachronism, reference.*

"Never do they smell white men. They have a fresh elk. There's some left."

"Weary of our company? Fine. Run off. See if we care."

"Come with me. They want to have you for dinner."

"The British don't consort with wildlife."

"Do again the sound of whales, please."

"Ahem. Skreeek."

The offshore whale heard me & replied: "Skreeek?"

The wolves called to the whales: "Ah-rooo."

From the distant village: "Woof."

The Raven, abed: "Quiet, damn it."

Kahmooks: "Good night, John boy." *Reference.*

Dawn revealed an ancient wilderness that had given birth to a young river, still restless in her snug bodice. She hadn't had time to grow wide yet, but she could evidently rise high, for her upper bank was bulwark'd with uprooted logs. Her currents twisted like jungle vines, rippling sinews intertwining, bursting into white blossoms on sinister sandbars, finally rushing out to hurl themselves into a reckless embrace with the pounding surf.

Destruction Island took form again on the southwestern seascape, flat & bleak. Close by, foggy ghosts roamed the beach and woodsmoke mingled with mist, daylight with drizzle. A reef of forest shield'd the village from the onshore flow: a half-dozen longhouses emerged from their family trees. Canoes made of logs crept up the bank, seeking refuge from the river. Overnight, the native fleet had increased by a dozen canoes, including a pair of fifty-foot ocean-cruisers, eight feet wide at the beam. Had they passed our camp in the night, undetected?

The fog thinned. Two hundred men. No women or children. Nose bones, faces painted red & black, sea otter robes over elk-hide body armour. Spears, bows, clubs. An array of muskets, including several antique Spanish blunderbusses. They stood silent, watching us.

Timofei watched them through Bulygin's telescope, fur cap down over his ears. I abandon'd my post and joined him behind his log. I refrained from asking how the newly-arrived canoes could have slipped past him.

Our camp stirred. Bulygin lament'd his wounds. The Aleuts huddled over a bowl of fish mush, dipping their fingers.

Madame Bulygin emerged from the sail-tent with Maria in her wake. If their relationship had suffer'd a strain after their debate over the log entry, it wasn't apparent now. The women knotted their scarves under their chins and set their Quileute whaling hats at jaunty angles.

I crouch'd beside Timofei, hiding from the breeze: "Rough lot."

He grunted without taking his eye from the glass: "Four different villages. See how each group stands apart from the others? But still, they join together to capture us. Are we worth so much?"

Madame Bulygin & Maria approached with the captain & crew in tow. Madame Bulygin asked Timofei for a report.

Timofei: "We are in trouble."

"Yutramaki's sister says we alarm the Hohs," Madame Bulygin said. "Doubtless their neighbors have come to ensure we behave ourselves."

Shubin, offended: "What do they take us for? Pitiful poltroons, plundering the pantries of peasants?" *P-words! I love p-words!*

Madame Bulygin, amused: "Are we perturbed, Mr. Shubin? Do we not have a peaceful slumber?"

The crew guffaw'd: "So much the tromping about last night. Somebody cannot find their assigned berth. Do you sleep soundly, captain?"

Bulygin, nursing his jaw, scowled, suspicious: "Wike a wog, fanks."

Madame Bulygin regarded the village with narrowed gaze. She asked Timofei if he could see Yutramaki's sister.

Timofei: "All men. War party."

Madame Bulygin: "Sister must be inside, parleying. We will show them we are ready to cross."

We assembled our gear at riverside. Timofei shouted across: "*Inati chuck?*" Over the river?

The natives stood like carved totems.

Kozma: "I have the bad feelings."

Timofei agreed: "Shoulder your burdens, brothers. We march upriver, to a safer crossing."

Madame Bulygin stretched a smile across her teeth: "Timofei, I . . ."

Timofei ignored her. Kozma took the lead.

No sooner was our little caravan underway than two of the wooden statues sprang to life, launching a long canoe. They sliced across the current and in a moment were at our bank. The stern paddler held his boat in place with a pointed yellow paddle. The man in the bow smiled reassuringly and held up nine fingers: "*Kwaist tillikum.*" Nine people.

Timofei stared at the two Hohs, attempting to discern their intentions. They nodded & beamed benignly. The stern paddler pointed at Timofei's gun: "*Sukwalwal?*" Timofei shook his head, offering instead a pewter token. A murmur from across the river, audible above the river's rumbling.

Madame Bulygin hissed: "One gun, Timofei."

The crew dissented: "Give them your little French paint brushes."

"Give them your husband."

Madame Bulygin: "They do not want my pistols. They want your clunky old army muskets, of which we have enough to equip a small army. Give them a gun, Timofei. Just so it shoots."

"Who do you think it shoots at?"

"She's right. Unless we give them guns, how do we cross the river?"

"What if they attack while we are on the river? How do we shoot and paddle at the same time? How can those on the riverbank cover those who are on the water?"

"A trap, brothers. They seek to divide us. We must send scouts upriver to find a safe crossing."

"What can dead scouts tell us? If we go, we must all go together."

"A raft. We go upriver, find a safe crossing, build a raft, get across. Then, like before, we travel through the forest to reach the coast."

"The river is too swift for a raft. We have no paddles, no oars. We are swept away, drowned, captured."

"We camp here in the logs for a few days. We need rest. The fish is in the river, the fat deer comes down to the creek. Soon the kolosh lets us go."

"Hostages. When the sister comes over to talk, we grab her. If she has a knife at her throat, perhaps her people help us."

"A raft. Remember, at New Archangel, when we build the sturdy raft, for hauling the cargo to and from the ship? With a raft, we are the masters of our own destiny. No need to bargain with the treacherous."

"Lincoln builds the sturdy raft, remember? We have one ax, we leave the nails on the ship, and we bring only one rope, so how do we fasten the logs? And we need a big raft, if all are to cross at once. To build such a raft would take two, three days. Soon we run out of food. And then what? What about the next river?"

"We go upriver, deeper into the forest. Soon the river becomes narrow. We chop the tree down so it falls across."

"Bah. The kolosh get there first. They shoot arrows as we cross on the log."

"We can't stay here. Too exposed to the weather and the kolosh. The Quileutes will not let us go back the way we came. Better for us if we had remained with the ship. We would have food, cannons . . ."

"Patience, brothers. We cause the kolosh to be absent from his lodges. The squaw at home, she worries. Winter comes. Soon they decide to be done with us."

"One way or the other."

"If they attack, more die. The squaw, she weeps. Better they let us go."

"Never do they let us go. We are a fortune on foot. Many guns. Three women. If they let us go, we fall into the hands of their enemies."

"Fifty Quileute men over there, all the dead people's male relatives. Not so soon do they go home."

"Timofei, maybe we should trade a few guns, like she says. What can be the harm?"

"Tell us what you think, Timofei."

Timofei was thinking. Madame Bulygin waited.

Kozma had a plan: "I take the best shots over first. We dig in behind that big log. Then the rest cross. If the kolosh attacks, we shoot, then jump in the river with our guns, swim away. That way, they lose some men and they do not get you, the captain, or the women."

Timofei didn't like it: "Swim? When do you learn to swim? Too swift is the river to swim. And maybe the kolosh does not attack. Maybe he walks up to you like back at the shipwreck, with the smiling face. What do you do? Shoot him? Push comes to shove, he has you and half the guns. Over here, we are eight men, three women, and Bulygin. And perhaps more Quileutes lurk in the forest behind us. What do we do if they attack while you are over there?"

Madame Bulygin sensed uncertainty: "Men, the Hohs do us a good deed, at Sister's behest, at the risk of offending the Quileutes. The Hohs have but a dozen old guns amongst them, and, according to Sister, very little fresh gunpowder. It is spears and arrows against modern infantry muskets, and we still have two guns per man. I assure you, the Hohs are but peaceful fisherfolk, and they are impressed with our abundant weaponry. We may find their good will useful in the future, so let us be on our way to Gray's Harbor. Timofei, offer them your gun, then tell them we require another big canoe."

Timofei kept his gun. Madame Bulygin fumed. No response from the other side.

BUT THEN THE CROWD PARTED. The sister stepped forward, and, despite the chill, doff'd her furs, revealing a short smock, a risky choice for active boating. She appeared to be younger than she'd been at our previous meeting, and her dress revealed that her arms & legs were covered with downy feathers.

Her entourage portaged a slim canoe down to the riverbank, its polished gunwales encrust'd with gleaming white seashells, and she embarked alone, paddling from the stern, crossing as easily as the two Hohs did. Upon her arrival she spoke to them in their own tongue as they hauled her craft ashore.

The crew was uneasy: "Bah. Just a little canoe. Only four at a time. They scheme to separate us so we will be easier to capture. See how the sister conspires with these two kolosh? We should take her hostage until we are safe."

Madame Bulygin, frustrated with us: "This is embarrassing. Give them a gun."

Timofei shook his head: "If we give them one gun, they demand more. Soon they have more guns than we do."

Madame: "What else would they want? Give them the gun with the faulty flintlock. Do not tell them that it does not always shoot."

"Ha. Give them the faulty captain. They know he shoots."

Madame Bulygin's green eyes brimmed with angry tears: "Why must you be so stubborn? Remember what comrade Zuev told you on the day we sailed from New Archangel? You are not dumb animals."

Zuev scoff'd: "Yes, you are. If you listen to me, we are still safe in our snug little fort."

Kurmachev: "Listen to you? It was I who foresaw that the Tsar's whore would betray us."

Madame Bulygin: "Fools. Timofei Osipovich Tarakanov betrays you. Why does he cling so desperately to all these guns, when only a few will buy us safe passage? Think for yourselves, men. Our only hope is to lighten our load, to leave the natives a payment for their losses. Instead, your ataman, who demands your undying loyalty, not a single gun can he part with. And does he lead the first group across the river? No. He remains here, with the women. Bulygin should lead the first group across."

"We need not ridicule our captain," Madame Bulygin said. "He suffers the loss of his vessel, and he deserves our sympathy, not the taunts you inflict upon him. Listen to me. Let me tell the sister that we will surrender a few guns as gifts of friendship. What do you say?"

Silence. She stomp'd her boot: "Are you sheep? Do you follow Timofei blindly, without question, to the slaughter?"

Shubin: "Be calm, Madame. Think of the little one."

The captain had distanced himself from our deliberations, hurling pebbles at predatory ducks. Timofei exchanged stares with Madame Bulygin, with much going unsaid. We waited. The river thrust an emerald sword into the sea's gray belly.

MADAME BULYGIN SLIPPED A BIT ON THE STONES, then squared her shoulders: "I see. My private life, the stuff of scuttlebutt. This is your appreciation for the delicate negotiations I conduct on your behalf. You will be interested to know that, because of the relationships I establish, the Cape People now offer the Quileutes a large quantity of trade goods in exchange for us, and the Quileutes may accept, despite their anger. So, therefore, our plans change. No longer is our destination Gray's Harbor. Instead, most of us will spend the winter with the Cape People, where we will await rescue by a trading vessel in the spring. Yes, I know, Timofei tells you that the natives, the kolosh as you call them, are cruel and treacherous, but I believe the Cape People are a better class of people and can be trusted. If you follow Timofei, you will die. I will get us rescued."

Timofei: "Say what you said last night. You bargained with them. You agreed that those who shoot the cannon become captives of the Quileutes. Except Bulygin."

Madame Bulygin set her chin: "Unfortunately, at this point in the negotiations, the Quileutes are not willing to forgive our Aleut comrades who fired the cannon. Yes, they also want Captain Bulygin, but he is an officer of the Tsar and is indispensable to our mission. Our brave and loyal Aleut employees, however, may be asked to remain behind, that the rest of us might . . ."

Timofei: "We stay together."

"The Tsar's armies willingly charge against Napoleon's cannons, joyous that they have been chosen to sacrifice their lives. Therefore, those of us who become captives of the Quileute will offer themselves as martyrs to a cause far greater than they can imagine. Immortality awaits them. Their story will be carried home by those of us who must grimly press on."

Silence. Green glacier water snaked, writhing, hissing. Maria pulled Madame Bulygin away by the elbow. Yutramaki's sister joined them in quiet but vigourous discussion.

Kahmooks cock'd an ear: "The sister says the tyees argue over who gets which captive. They all want The Raven. He is magic."

Valgusov, black feathers all a'flutter, ran to river's edge and, waving his wings, hailed the village.

Kahmooks: "Madame says, 'Aha. So Valgusov is their eavesdropper. We will have to quiet our voices.' The sister says, 'Yesterday those no-good Quinaults from down south show up. Troublemakers. They want a share. We told them, keep clam, be patient, but they . . . No, clam, like oysters. A joke.' She says her in-laws have treachery in their brains."

Kahmooks: "Madame says, 'At least they have brains. Let us be done with this.'"

She called for Yakov & Filip to haul the sea trunk down to the sister's canoe, wherein it was secured amidships. Madame Bulygin & Maria reef'd up their skirts, found seats in the canoe and prepared for the crossing. Girl chums, off for a row on the pond. The sister, in the stern with her paddle, beckoned, pointing. More room here. Madame Bulygin called to Filip & Yakov, who were knee deep in the river. They looked back at Timofei.

"Wait," Timofei shouted. "Do not cross until the men do."

The river rumbled, too loud to hear. Madame Bulygin ignored him as if she hadn't heard. Timofei yelled at Filip & Yakov. They nodded, wary, slung their muskets over their shoulders, waded out to pull the canoe closer to the bank. Yutramaki's sister gestured impatiently: hurry up, climb in. Yakov & Filip considered wading back to shore. Yakov slipped, almost swept away, almost lost his gun. Timofei, shaking his head, preparing to wade out and drag them back. Madame Bulygin ordered Yakov & Filip into the canoe. They hauled themselves over the ornate gunwales, but saw Timofei coming and had second thoughts.

Filip called to us: "My fiddle. Bring my . . ."

Timofei: "Get out of the canoe. Come back. Wait until . . ."

Madame Bulygin spoke to Maria, who took up a paddle and helped the sister turn the bow into the current. Yakov & Filip looked confused & forlorn.

Timofei grabbed Kozma: "Quick. Take eight others, two guns each. Catch up to the women. Stay with them, no matter what. We cover you from here. If the kolosh attack, it will be when the second group is on the river. Hold fast until we join you. If you must, fire a warning shot. Make them keep their distance."

The sister's canoe, overloaded, made headway at midstream. Kozma assigned me to the first canoe. Clutching our guns, we rubbed the hard lump on Five's chest and boarded. The Hoh paddlers sat fore & aft. Timofei urged them to hasten. They responded with trustworthy smiles of warmth & friendship.

"Savva, a tune for the crossing, for good luck."

Zuev, in the bow, launched his balalaika into a melancholy lament. The river was a thick milky jade, viscous & vicious. Swirling white eddies churn'd, breaking on obscured logs & shifting sandbars. The paddlers made but slow progress.

A cold green tongue slipped over the gunwales, licking our legs.

Kozma told us to keep the guns dry. I seized a bailer, a scoop carved from cedar, and put some water back into the river. The two hundred men at the village remained motionless. The sister's canoe reached the far shore just as our canoe reached midstream. The Hoh paddler behind me shouted to his chum in the bow. They yank'd plugs from drain-holes in the bilge and plunged overboard, paddles in hand.

WATER ROSE AROUND OUR ANKLES. WE stuffed fur caps into the bubbling drains and stomp'd on them with guns held high. The currents caught our bow, sent us spinning. We tipped. The river poured in.

The warriors at the village threw off their furs, brandish'd their weaponry, and, with a dreadful shout, rushed to the riverbank. Arrows & spears arc'd across gray sky.

Kozma, an arrow in his arm, shouted: "Shoot, then paddle with the guns."

Iakov jerked & gurgled. A spear's shaft protruded from his chest.

We got off a ragged volley. I fired at a man with a bow. He yelp'd and grabbed his thigh. I seized my warm gun-barrel, dug the stock into the river. No effect. We continued spinning & sinking, some of us still in the canoe, some clutching the gunwales. The archers on the opposite bank again whirled into my field of view, their short bows horizontal, bent back. They let fly.

Sharp pain in my back. Little black fishing arrow. Couldn't quite reach it.

More shooting. Our lads on the north bank, trying to help us. From the Hoh side, a slender spear swam through the air, a straight snake, and it buried itself in Sobachnikov's belly. He cried out and clutched the shaft, toppled backward into the rushing torrents with the spear point protruding from his lower back. His blood was a scarlet ribbon lacing green currents. Flailing, he seized my outstretch'd musket.

Spinning, sideways, stern down. Archers & spear-throwers, leaps & bounds over logs & rocks. Our comrades behind us, firing, reloading. The canoe lurch'd, throwing the Raven from the prow into the river. Sobachnikov, screaming in pain, climbed my musket, hand over hand, seized my leg, pulled me in with him. The river closed over my head and the chill water suck'd the warmth from my flesh. A peaceful stillness prevailed amidst the rushing currents, a deep & eerie quiet under the roar.

Then, faintly: whale songs. I'd nearly reached the sea.

My feet found a muddy sandbar near the north bank. Sobachnikov still clung to me, moaning. The current pulled me seaward. Only the canoe's stern remained visible. I crawled up out of the muck, clutching sword & gun, dragging Sobachnikov, who left a bloody trail on the stones. The arrowhead in my back poked a nerve. Angry black snakes zipped past, hissing. My comrades stumbled about, confused. Sobachnikov gurgled, eyes rolled back. Iakov lay nearby spitting blood, a broken spear shaft lodged in his chest.

We reassembled in logs on the high bank. Wet guns, powder horns, shot bags, all scattered across blood-spattered stones. Timofei yanked the protruding arrow from Kozma's arm. Some of Kozma came with it.

Timofei spat on the wound, then knelt & shouted into Sobachnikov's blank face: "Are you still with us, brother? Can you hear me?"

Sobachnikov gurgled pink foam. "Blood fills my chest. I cannot breathe," he moan'd. "Shoot me."

"Soon he dies. Is Iakov alive?"

Iakov gasped: "The pain. Shoot me first."

"Sorry, Iakov. We must save our dry powder for the kolosh."

"Damn the kolosh. Look, they cross the river."

Kozma: "Those with dry powder, share. Olga, a fire, quick. We must dry the powder."

I walked in circles, looking for a place to faint. Kozma put his hand against my back and yank'd the arrow out just as Timofei had done for him. He showed me a barbed arrowhead with soft pink tissue snagged on it. A kaleidoscope of river, forest and ocean spun around me, then darkness, then daylight again. Must rest a bit. I told myself I should assist with the defensive efforts, but I could only lie face down in the stones.

The scene across the river came into focus. Madame Bulygin & Maria were halfway up the bank to the village, pausing to watch the show. The natives left them unmolest'd, but Filip & Yakov were hauled off kicking, their guns brandish'd by new owners.

Raising my head, I saw Bulygin standing on a log, waving his sword, oblivious. Timofei rallied a firing line behind a log. Olga, mothering a pile of twigs, created a little puff of smoke. My mates & I began crawling toward it. Kozma set some of us to frying moist powder on tin plates. Others fired across the river at the advancing enemy, with limit'd effect.

I took a personal inventory. I was shaking uncontrollably and should want dry clothes if I was to live much longer. My wound required attention, but I'd decided that besides these annoying arrows, my next most urgent problem would be a charging warrior with a spear or a club. Didn't feel much like standing up, so my sword would be of little use. I wanted a dry gun but couldn't find one. Wished they'd leave us alone for a bit, let us get squared away.

Timofei grabbed my sore arm, pulled me to my knees, thrust me into his firing line behind the log, shoved a musket under my nose. Couldn't seem to grip it.

Timofei told us: "When they get in range, pick out a tyee, shoot him in the leg. Then two of his friends must carry him home. We must push them back to the other side."

The natives advanced cautiously into our firing range, brandishing their weapons, making a dreadful racket, getting their courage up. Some were still crossing the river, others remained on the opposite bank. A musketeer dropped to one knee, aimed, fired. I ducked. Shubin shriek'd as pieces of his hand went flying. Five braced his gun on the log, aimed down the beach, fired. A native jerked backwards and fell, leg kicking, blood spurting from his chest. His mates halted & stared down at him; battle cries caught in their throats.

"Good shot, Five. That should stop them."

"Oops. Here they come again."

Our adversaries advanced. One appeared to be related to our friend Yutramaki. Middle-aged uncle, perhaps. Same face, same colour. Nothing on but a loincloth & whaling hat. No weapons. Same scars on his nose & thigh.

Yakov saw him too: "A shaman. Big medicine, to go into battle with no weapon. If we make that one bleed, maybe they go away."

"Who has a dry gun? John?"

Though still a good distance off, the unarmed tyee stared right at me, smiling, a challenge. Blighter stopped to give me a better target. Bit cheeky, must say. A little respect for English marksmanship, if you please. I aimed for his head, squeezed the trigger. His hat flipped off, pin-wheeling down the beach. He didn't flinch, but again the natives halted their advance. Some still huddled around the man Five had shot. Argument ensued. One launched an arrow at us. Angry shouts.

Three warriors broke from the huddle and charged; spears held aloft. Their mates called to the trio, begging them to reconsider. Two paused, realizing the futility of their act, but the third charged harder. Tears smeared his face paint.

Kozma cranked his hammer back, squinted.

Timofei: "His leg. Make them carry him home."

Kozma, aiming: "He wants to die."

He fired. The crying man's legs went wobbly. He flung his spear, clutched his chest and crumpled. His two reluctant chums rushed out to drag him back, and others, chanting, carried wounded comrades to the canoes. Some stayed, arguing for another assault.

MORE ARROWS FROM THE FAR SHORE. Musket balls whack'd our logs and spray'd sand in our eyes. Bulygin stood on his log and waved his sword at our tormentors.

Just upriver from our position lay a thicket of ferns, berry-bushes and skinny alders. Beyond that, behemoth cedars, the forest primeval. Timofei ordered us to run for the trees. Bulygin ordered us to stand & fight. We departed with as much dignity as we could muster, abandoning precious goods so we could carry Iakov & Sobachnikov.

A faint path appeared before us, narrow but well-trod. We ran for a few minutes, gasping & staggering, then paused to catch our breath at a pretty creek burbling under ferns. Bulygin caught up, mumbling, stumbling, glassy-eyed. Sobachnikov & Iakov lay moaning on their litters, clutching their wounds. Our hearts pounded as we struggled to breathe the moist atmosphere.

Sobachnikov: "The agony. Shoot me."

Iakov: "Shoot me first. My soul hesitates to depart my flesh, unsure of its destination. I linger too long in this sinful world."

Kozma: "We must slide the spear all the way through his chest, pull it out the back. Abram, push on the shaft. I will pull. Ready? One, two . . ."

Iakov, a bloodcurdling scream: "Leave it, please. My lung, she comes out with it."

Sobachnikov whimper'd. Sergei dripped water on his lips. It was a slender, barbed seal spear, like Iakov's, lodged deep.

"We have to cut into him. We need bandages."

"No time. We cannot leave him here alive. Should we shoot him?"

Sobachnikov: "Yes. Bless you."

Iakov: "No. Shoot me first."

"But who pulls the trigger? Not me."

"The ataman must do the deed. Here, Timofei, my pistol."

Timofei took the gun, kneeled, kissed Sobachnikov softly on his cheek. Trembling, he cock'd the hammer.

Shouts from the trail behind, louder. Warriors visible across the river.

"Time for us to go, Timofei."

Sobachnikov, mumbling: "Yes, hurry. Shoot me. I cannot remember my prayers. Say goodbye to my wives and numerous little ones, whose names escape me. Timofei, please, must I help you? Here, give me the pistol."

"No, brother, to kill yourself is a sin. Timofei must do it for you."

Timofei's hands shook.

Sobachnikov clutched the pistol. "Williams pulls me from the river. He should shoot me. Better is not a Russian."

A shot from down the path. A ball whistled over our heads, burying itself in the tree against which Sobachnikov reclined, showering us in fragrant flakes of cedar bark. Kozma cursed, returned fire, ducked. An arrow struck beside the bullet hole, its shaft vibrating. Pavel snatched it out and snapped the shaft.

Sobachnikov, impatient to depart: "Timofei? A gentle nudge into the next world? Too much to ask?"

Timofei's tears dripped on the pistol. His hands shook.

Kozma: "Gather around, brothers. All must put their hands on the pistol."

We huddled about. Sobachnikov gurgled happily, grasped the pistol's muzzle and drew it to his mouth. Bloody drool flow'd down the barrel and into the flintlock.

Sobachnikov: "Anytime you are . . . slurp . . . ready."

A fizz, a smoky poof. A black-faced Sobachnikov stared at us dumbfound'd, his beard smouldering. Blood squirted from his lip. He spat first a tooth and then a pistol ball into his hand. He staggered to his feet and with a disgusted glance at us stumbled off back down the trail toward our pursuers, soon disappearing from view. Smoke linger'd. Timofei sat staring at the pistol lying in the mud before him.

Kozma was the first to find his voice: "If anybody asks, Sobachnikov begs us to leave him behind, so the rest of us can escape. Agreed? So be it. Now we run."

Despite our burdens we turned up our heels, running like pickpockets through a marketplace, one eye on the faint path ahead, the other cast back over our shoulders. We leaped tree trunks, sank into stinking oily mud.

A clearing. Daylight linger'd. Then dark forest again, air thick with rotting vegetation. We remained in lowlands, not gaining altitude. The river twisted & turned, smooth, swift. No waterfalls yet. Half the crew up ahead of me. Kahmooks led, sniffing. Iakov sobbing, bounced on his litter. We were all wounded, our path of broken branches splattered with crimson dewdrops. Run, stumble, fall, get up, run.

Natives ran single file like a wolf pack on the opposite bank.

Again, the forest opened, again the rumbling river met us. We regrouped on a tiny beach of smooth stones. We knelt, seeking the river's sustenance, and it snatch'd at our tin cups. Timofei & Kozma counted heads. Bleeding wounds demanded attention. Bulygin brought up the rear, stumbling, mumbling. The far bank was a green wall. The last daylight linger'd.

"Arrow!" A humming shaft flew, seeking the stumbling captain, who fortuitously chose that moment to trip & fall. The arrow passed over him and continued on in search of new prey, finding Iakov on his litter, lodging in his knee. Iakov shriek'd.

We responded with a desultory volley. No targets. Our powder-smoke merged with fog. The echo of our fusillade faded into the river's roar.

Iakov writhed, clutching his knee: "I beg you, brothers, shoot me. My sins, they pass before my eyes. If you truly love me, you will end this torture. Please put my soul to rest."

"Careful. Maybe we shoot your tooth."

"Be patient, Iakov. God wants you to suffer for a little while longer."

Iakov moaned. Darkness descend'd. We pawed our belongings.

"Where is the food? What have we lost? What do we have?"

"We have Filip's fiddle, Zuev's balalaika, and Sobachnikov's squeezebox. The dead can dance. Also, we have forty guns, four barrels of powder, the shot bags, glass beads, pewter tokens, the ax, two sails, and a bag of clothes. Timofei, look, your dressing gown."

We mourn'd our lost comrades: "Poor little Filip. And Yakov, always cheerful and dependable. Sobachnikov, so strong, so steadfast."

"And our faithful Maria, who would never betray us."

Kozma's blade glinted in the last light: "If you speak ill of Maria, stick out your tongue."

"She forsakes us, Kozma. She sleeps with the Tsar's whore. Am I wrong, Timofei?"

Timofei sat silent, face between his knees. The river tossed & turned in her bed. We huddled by her side.

Iakov gurgled: "Brothers, I beg you."

Kozma nudged Timofei: "Camp here?"

Timofei shook his head. No rest for the wicked. *Cliché*.

# 6 | The Winter Palace

WICKED WOODS, THESE. WITCHES' THICKETS. Black branches festoon'd with fungi fingers investigated our coats as we pressed upriver. Curious ferns touch'd our cheeks. Silent streams slither'd. Moss moved.

The sky's tides ebb'd & flow'd. Black clouds rushed inland, southwest to northeast. The forest floor, spongy, suck'd at our feet. Huge cedars dug their roots into this fickle morass, lamenting the scattered bones of their siblings, victims of the river's rampage.

Thunder rumbled. Lightning. The Raven abandon'd his sentry perch and joined us beneath a benevolent cedar, where we huddled under the main sail. We could not glimpse our tree's foggy summit, and its circumference was like a rough wall. Yesterday (the day before?) we circled the tree, pressed our faces into its bark, and tried to join hands. Couldn't reach.

A food-gathering detachment returned. Foragers found fungi. "Taste these mushrooms," they said. "Up from the elk poop they grow." *Nothing about mushrooms please.*

We roasted mushrooms on Olga's smouldering fire, and when I closed my eyes, it became a roaring hearth. Memories rose unbidden. I sniff'd aromas of a feast. Visions of sugarplums, pudding bowls, a steaming goose. Tarts on platters, too close to the edge of the table, guarded by apple-cheeked aunts in aprons. Chubby children: cousins? Siblings? A pile of scarves, caps, coats. A cold night, stars a'twinkle. A snowball starred a cellar door. Sleighbells, hoof-stomping, wet snorts. Horse lips snuffled a slice of apple.

A voice, from above. Snowflakes settled on a beaverskin tophat, melted into a furry beard.

The beard said: "Tomorrow you're off to your new home, lad. A ship. You're to be cabin boy."

Ever since my home has been a ship. I am ho'kwat.

But are these real memories? Or daydreams, fantasies? Another man's reminiscences, overheard, read, borrowed? Had I gone mad? My passage through time seemed to leave no trace, no wake. Was John Williams my real name? If the past is a parent, was I an orphan, cast adrift, unable to distinguish between my lies and my dreams and what might have once been true?

Olga's smoky little fire became a burning warship, and I remembered war, of trading broadsides with enemy frigates, first a Spaniard, then a Frenchman. Our guns were too hot to touch. I looked out a gun port into the barrel of a French cannon just as it fired. I threw my hand up before my eyes.

A blast, then darkness, then lying on the gun deck, breath knock'd out of me, smoke & flames all around. A gaping black hole where the cannon had been. My crew, just bloody bits. I couldn't hear. *Where did you leave your hearing aid?* My coat was black & smoking. Flames danced on my hand, the hand that had saved my face.

Grenades flew through the black hole, bouncing, exploding around me. Frenchmen tried to climb through the hole.

My hand couldn't grip my sword. I stumbled topside, seeking water to stop the burning, finding Frenchmen on the rail wielding boarding sabers. Our bowsprit was ensnarled with theirs, trapping us in a deadly embrace. Explosions from below, amongst the guns & powder. The bulkheads heaved; nails pulled from beams. Surely, we would sink. The cold ocean will soothe my hand, I thought.

Signal pennants flutter'd from Nelson's flagship Victory, half a league distant. A boatswain's cry: we're winning, lads. Three cheers. Stand up & fight. Officers required to stand. Sharpshooters in the Frenchman's crosstrees, aiming for the officers. Musket balls zipped through the smoke, drawing blood, slick & slippery. Our tars tossed buckets of sand across the deck for traction. My fellow officers stood in the blood, dodging shots, shouting orders & encouragement. A musket ball tugged at my coat sleeve. I fell to the deck again, embracing the sand and the bloody boards. My mates thought me dead. I did not argue.

Nelson's dead, the signals said. Our captain perish'd too, and a dying sun sank into a dark & sharky sea. Light breeze, big swells, storm coming in from the ocean. Men in the water all around us, ours & theirs, crying out. Couldn't hear them.

I made myself useful. I stumbled through smoke with a roster in my good hand, tripping on bloody pig-tailed boys in blue jackets. I added up the butcher's bill: twenty-seven dead, 123 wounded. The papers slipped from my grip and fell to the deck, soaking up blood. Blood dripped from the bulkheads & overhead. Crimson waistcoats, bloody. Straw sailor hats floated in blood. Bloody hands reached for my ankles. All hands accounted for, but we were missing legs, and a tar without a face wouldn't stop screaming. Couldn't hear him. Another, neatly cut in two at the waist by spinning chain-shot, top half dead but his striped trousers twitching as tho' he were dancing a jig, still alive.

A gunner passed me: "Thought you was dead, Mr. Williams."

No, not dead, not quite alive. Damaged, the surgeon said later, not fit for duty. He gave me opium for my pain. My pain liked opium. I gave my pain what it wanted. Pain, proof of life.

The forest was alive. Raindrops, tiny spheres of water & light, tumbled merrily, sporting bulbous bellies, pulsating with anticipation in their rush to the river. The raindrops sang to us. Zuev reported raindrops dancing on his fingers. He fanned his grimy hands back & forth before his eyes, amazed.

Unexplained phenomena. Something was amiss, incoherent, askew. Our bodies were weak & wounded, but our minds were oddly tilt'd. We couldn't sleep nor quite awaken. Newton be damn'd, gravity did not rule in this kingdom; perforce, a raindrop would fall or remain suspended, or even return to its original position, singing all the while. Whales swam above us in moist atmosphere.

Delusions, we told ourselves. Symptoms of fatigue, loss of blood, stress of battle. Starvation was a monster in our bellies. We stripped crumbling bark from rotten stumps, then gobbled plump beetles as they fled, screaming tiny beetle shrieks. Did they think us monsters, vengeful gods? We chew'd our sealskin boots, kamleias and the gun covers made from sea lion skins. We scavenged afield for mushrooms, especially the juicy morsels that bloomed from elk droppings, but otherwise remained stormbound, prisoners of both the deluge and this odd mood into which we had descended, our souls but tenuously joined to our bodies.

We huddled under our tree. Bulygin stood in the clearing before us, trying to rally us, waving his sword, plotting revenge against unseen tormentors, wet forelocks obscuring his unfocused gaze. He outlined his strategy in detail, his performance unaffected by lack of attentive audience, but he was menaced by knife-wielding Cossacks and fled off to my right, disappearing from view, reappearing hours later on my left, a smaller version of himself, a mud-caked leprechaun, clothes in disarray. His words were visible, floating in air, but delayed, out of sequence. He approached, breathing hard, gradually returning to normal size, but taking ever so long to arrive. I could only stare in astonishment. His blood-stained eyeballs bulged. Worms writh'd in his beard.

A call from the bushes: "Captain, please, a pound of flesh. *Cite reference, Shakespeare.* You have plenty."

Bulygin shudder'd, crawled in under the sail, fell asleep. Hours passed, a day, two days. The forest throbbed with bright & muted greens, sport'd a hundred, nay, a thousand viridescent hues. I examined tiny leaves, watched liquids surging through tiny veins. Zuev got some of the others interested in watching raindrops. Reports of inner contentment, tranquility, an enhanced sense of well-being. Mild euphoria.

A chorus of raindrops lined the sail's hem, singing our requiem. We were dying.


THE RAVEN SQUAWK'D AN ALARM. THE FLYING whales had vanish'd, but now an eagle as big as a ship swoop'd low above us, a terrifying raptor with wings the size of mainsails. Thunder boom'd from its wings and lightning crackled from its mighty talons. The air lay on us cold, wet, heavy. The fearsome fowl hover'd, peering down at us with reptilian eyes, then disappeared into the murk.

We huddled, trembling, unprepared to discuss this monster.

A hallucination, like a ghost ship in fog? Was the giant bird a chimaera, mutually imagined, like the flying whales? A phantasm, produced inside our muddled minds by fear, hunger, pain?

Our attention was diverted by a pathetic scuffle: Bulygin, attempting to relieve himself in the bushes, had been captured and was being prepared for slaughter.

Kozma raised a hand, forestalling the butchers: "Wait. Still Bulygin can walk. He is a moveable feast (*Bible*?), the meat that marches. *M-words! Let's play m-words again! I love m-words!* Better we save him for later. Iakov dies within the hour."

Iakov, a pitiful rattling in his throat: "Give or take."

We had stopped his external bleeding, but he continued to deteriorate within, begging to be delivered from his earthly travails. Weapons were placed beyond his feeble reach.

Abram Petukhov, knife upraised over the captain's pale, twitching thigh: "Yes, go ahead, sink your teeth into my dear dying brother. But what about me? Someday, if God is willing, I return home to my poor mother, who awaits her twin boys who have gone to America to make their fortune, and she will greet me, saying, 'My dim eyes can see my honest and trustworthy son Abram, but where is chubby little Iakov, the naughty one?' And I will reply, 'Iakov? Hmmm. I forget, mama. Perhaps, my comrades and I, when we were shipwrecked and starving, maybe we ate Iakov?'"

The crew wept, remorseful.

Abram: "No. I cannot. A man is not to eat his own family. Not in any country or religion. Am I right, Williams?"

I say: "Quite so. Gastronomic incest."

Abram: "Besides, Iakov's flesh has the taint of sin. I shall eat Bulygin."

Bulygin struggled in Abram's grip, sobbing.

Iakov, faintly: "Abram, tell our dear mother that my death was truly that of a martyr, that in my final moments I thought only of my brothers."

Olga licked her lips: "Ahem."

"Ahem yourself, fat girl. You could miss a meal."

Iakov: "No, a full share for Olga, who has always been generous with her own ample body. Following her inspiring example, I share myself with all but the captain."

Kozma reassured Iakov: "Your gesture is recognized, brother, but our ataman decides who eats who when he returns, perhaps with the fat deer."

"A long time he is gone. Why does he go alone? The kolosh will get him."

"Kahmooks smells no kolosh for days now. Maybe they forget we are here."

Iakov coughed up blood: "A farewell to my pain, that is all I ask. That, and to decide who is to get what."

Shubin waved his wounded hand: "I must receive a whole arm. With my remaining good hand I help to carry you from the mouth of the river to here. If not for me, the kolosh are chewing on you. Instead, you spend your last moments in the arms of your comrades. So, therefore, an arm is all I ask."

"We all help carry him, Dimitrii. An equal share for each. Also, Kahmooks."

Iakov: "Now I am dog food?"

Kozma, a ruling: "If anybody eats Iakov, all must. As Abram reminds us, when we go home, we all tell the same tale, and stories about Russians eating Russians do not go down so good. No more the discussion."

Iakov: "Agreed, but I too must partake of the feast. Even before the last breath escapes my lips, my brothers will fall upon my flesh like wolves on a bleating sheep, and my blood will drip from their beards. Does not the host sit down at his own table? (*Bible again*) Am I not to share in the repast?"

"You are delirious, Iakov. Imagine the pain."

"I have pain. Williams, light up your little lamp. A puff or two from your pipe, and a tight tourniquet. Yuri, put an edge on your knife. Olga, stir the coals. Prepare to cook meat, brothers. Cut me a big slice of calf on a stick. I want only to die with a full tummy, my loving comrades by my side."

Kahmooks threw a paw over his eyes and whined.

I consoled him: "'Tis a dog-eat-dog world, Fang. You're . . ."

The dog: "So to speak."

". . . You're either the eater, or the eatee. We might have lunch, or be it. Today the customer, tomorrow the merchandise. But now Iakov says you can take it with you, that you can have your cake and . . ."

*Delete everything about eating people. Trust me on this.*


A GUNSHOT ECHO'D FROM THE FOREST. CLOSE? DISTANT?

The crew speculated: "Perhaps Timofei shoots a fat bear for our dinner."

"Perhaps the bear gets dinner."

We waited, anxious. Despite constant rain, our green glade glow'd. Beyond, dark forest. Days or minutes passed. Hard to tell.

After ever so long, a halloo from the trees. Timofei, bedraggled, returned, proudly displaying the moldering carcass of a small furry animal.

Kahmooks wrinkled his wet nose: "We don't need no stinking badger." *Delete.*

Timofei collapsed on the moss: "A badger, maybe, or a river otter. Yes, we need it. This is strange country, brothers. I got lost out there. I eat the mushroom from the elk poop. The bird-monster flies over me, with lightning shooting from the claws. From the wings, thunder booms. The bird-monster dives down to snatch me up. I shoot. The bird-monster is not harmed, but turns into a little mama owl. I say, 'I am sorry I shoot you. I am afraid. We are cold, starving. The people here deny us their fish.' She seizes my collar in her beak and picks me up. We fly through the trees. She puts me down beside the river. I peek through the ferns. I see two houses. I smell the smoking of the salmon."

The crew drool'd.

"The owl says the river overflows with abundance," Timofei said. "She says we are not to harm the creatures of the forest, but only to find animals like this one and make masks from their pelts. Then, when we wear our fur caps, we will appear unto the kolosh as leshiy, whom they call sasquatch. The kolosh will run away in fear, leaving the salmons to appease us."

The crew cheer'd. Bulygin, frantic, elbow'd Timofei aside, renewing his argument for a strategic rescue-by-force of our captives, but to no avail. The crew ridiculed him. He began to sob. Timofei embraced him in comradely fashion.

"I have almost lost my mind," Bulygin wailed. "No longer do I have the strength to lead you. Tarakanov will command you, and I will also obey him myself. If he is not to your liking, then choose another leader from among your comrades." *Another paraphrase from Owens/Donnelly. Cite reference.*

Bolotov nominated Kahmooks. The dog declined.

Kahmooks: "How about Olga? The Brotherhood's first female ataman."

The crew: "See, captain? We cannot accept your resignation. We insist you remain our commander-in-chief."

Bulygin, chin quivering, blinked back a tear: "Men, it is with deep gratitude that I . . ."

"I move we eat the captain."

Timofei said no: "Patience, brothers. Soon we eat like real people."


THE EARTH TREMBLED. A great tromping in the shrubbery. Were the natives attacking? We seized up our guns.

Elk. They stampeded through our camp on their way to the river, great wild-eyed honking elephants, antlers wide as yardarms. They proved benign, gentle, vegetarian, but awkward creatures nonetheless, unaware of their size & strength.

We hasten'd out of their way, calling to them as they passed, "Elks, where is the poop?"

The lumbering beasts paid us no heed. We returned to a late brunch of watercress & lichens, but as soon as we had settled down another rumbling shook our camp. Not elk.

Thunder. A flash of lightning. Close by. Our beards curl'd. We blink'd, astonish'd.

No monster eagle this time. 'Twas a small brown owl with big round eyes, perch'd above us on a limb, hooting.

We gathered about. Timofei donned the furry mask he'd made from his rotting pelt and slipped into a trance, only to awaken moments later with what he said was an announcement from the owl: the people in the houses were ready to give us some fish.

Jubilant, we stowed our gear under the sails, slung our muskets over our shoulders, and ventured off into the forest. Kozma led, hacking at the foliage with the ax. The owl hopped from branch to branch above us, leading us upriver, eventually bringing us within hailing distance of two riverside dwellings from whence a smoky aroma waft'd, the scent of salmon curing over coals. We experienced gastric rumblings.

Nobody in sight. The owl disappeared. We crouch'd in the ferns discussing strategy. A youth emerged from a house and waved at our hiding place. We ended our surveillance and approached, albeit with caution, in as much as both longhouses were expanding & contracting as though they were breathing. Turned out the boy spoke the Chinook jargon, but his words flew about his head like sparrows and it was difficult to understand what he was saying. Pantomiming, he indicated that his people had heard of a marauding band of sasquatch in the vicinity and had hastily departed, but that he, being extremely courageous, had remained behind to assist us with our food shortage, assuming we were willing to trade guns for salmon. We gripped our guns and crowded into the smoke-house, emerging from the dim interiour with bundles of fragrant fish dripping with fat.

We scanned the forest as we devour'd our booty. The trees moved, changing colours. We eyed our surroundings warily.

"This is strange. Kahmooks? Smell anything?"

The malamute was wolfing down a salmon and couldn't be bothered. The boy dashed about, catching our errant fish bones on a cedar tray. All bones must be returned to the river, he explained, else the salmon might not return.

Timofei was anxious too: "Hurry, brothers. Something is not right. The forest has eyes that tickle the back of my neck."

"That's your mask."

We prepared to depart. Each of us shoulder'd a bundle of fish. The boy offered to trade a fish bundle for a gun, straight across. Timofei counter-offered: one pewter token per bundle. The boy snort'd scornfully.

The crew was hurt: "The rude boy declines Timofei's sincere offer of compensation. Just for that, we take the fish and we leave nothing."

"Beware, kid. We are Cossacks. We eat little boys."

"Ha. We only eat each other."

"He looks like a brave lad. Maybe he wants to join us. Tell him that we are the Brotherhood of Yermak, and we come to America in search of adventure. Soon we sail away to a tropical island."

"Yes, right after we find our way back to camp."

Timofei chose a trail leading off into the forest and we departed, gobbling on the run, soon reaching a resting spot beside a babbling brook in a ravine. No sooner had we dropped our burdens and seated ourselves on soggy moss than we were hailed by a native man waving a salmon skeleton.

We were baffled: "What does he say? His words float about in the air."

"We should shoot him."

"Perhaps he tells us we take the wrong path. Are we lost?"

The man with the salmon skeleton hasten'd off back the way he'd come.

"Never is the Cossack lost. Always our ataman knows our exact position. Right, Timofei?"

Timofei, mouthful of salmon: "Gulp. I will climb to the top of this ridge and look around."

Kozma scrutinized the vegetation, which continued to change both colour & shape: "I have the bad feelings. Yuri, come. We go first, make sure it is safe."

These three, each carrying two muskets, crossed the creek and ascend'd the steep slope opposite us, huffing & puffing, with Kozma in the lead.

A shout. A flash in the air. Arrows, from the slope behind us. Many arrows. War party. Kozma & Yuri had arrows protruding from their backsides.

Timofei shout'd to us, pointing up the slope. A dozen shouting natives charged down at our mates, intending to cut them off from us. Where had they come from? How had they gathered so fast, so quietly? We observed, concerned, knowing we should snatch up our guns, but we were astound'd, and our hands & mouths were full of salmon.

Timofei fired at the attackers, hitting one in the thigh, and the bloke fell writhing in the ferns. Kozma & Yuri likewise agonized as they tried to yank barb'd fishing arrows from their bottoms. More arrows flew across the ravine. Timofei snatch'd up his comrades' guns and threaten'd to fire again at the charging assailants, who wisely opted to pick up their wounded mate and withdraw, whooping & singing.

Our lads tumbled down the hillside, tearing out brush as they slid; we cheer'd their safe return. The native warriors withdrew from view, but continued to sing. Clouds obscured the sun and the deluge returned. Cedars overhung the stream. We removed arrows from Kozma & Yuri, finding that neither wound appeared critical, then posted guards and resumed our feast.

WE DISCUSSED OUR SITUATION: "I vote we go back to the houses. Perhaps they let us stay for the winter."

"Fool. They just attack us, remember?"

"Yes, because we steal their salmon, fool. Perhaps if we ask their forgiveness . . ."

Timofei: "No. We must take responsibility for ourselves. The owl says we are to go up the river until we come to a beautiful lake with rainbows and leaping fishes. There we will build a sturdy little *dacha*, snug and warm. Wild berries will become wine. We will trap, hunt, fish. The kolosh will see that we are peaceful. Life will be good again."

"'Again'? When was . . .?"

"Never mind. We agree, Timofei."

Timofei: "In spring, we vote. Do we stay in our warm, safe house beside our bountiful lake, or do we risk death in a doomed attempt to escape? We make that decision then. Today, we need food for our journey to the lake. We return to the houses by the river."

We reached the river again and hail'd two women in a small canoe. They had a basket of fish. Timofei bargain'd, hoping to establish a food source, but they wouldn't come near the bank or tell us where they lived. Finally, Timofei persuaded them to trade a small salmon for three fathoms of glass beads. As we prepared to resume our journey, Kahmooks sniff'd the breeze from upriver and informed us that the houses were close by.

Timofei ordered us to approach in a neighbourly manner. A dozen natives emerged, regarding us impassively.

Timofei addressed an elderly party: "Greetings, old man. The owl said you . . ."

The elder shouted: "*Klatawa.* Go away. You shot one of our men. No more fish for Rooskies. We don't care what the *waugh-waugh* (owl) says. We had a bad fishing season. River rises up over our fish traps. Salmon swim past, all the way to the mountains."

"But we . . ."

"No. Drop your guns and become captives, or go away. You look like sasquatch. Smelt you coming yesterday."

Shubin brandish'd his musket: "Give us more fish, kolosh, or we shoot you."

Timofei: "Quiet. Remember, we are Cossacks. Proud, dignified. Listen, kolosh. We are hungry, and we have guns. We did not ask to be here, so give us some fish, or we shoot you."

That did the trick. The natives brought forth bundles of fish, and we each seized one up. Timofei dragoon'd two native men to carry sealskin bags of salmon eggs, which tasted like caviar, and we retreated into the forest under a barrage of intense criticism. Fearing we might be followed, we guarded our rear and trudged a mile upriver before pausing to release our bearers. In parting, Timofei gave each man a used handkerchief as a gesture of our appreciation. We'd been using them as bandages.

"All the way from China," Timofei assured them. "The blood-stains are symbols of our brotherhood."

"Ask them how far to the lake."

"Bah. They seek to deceive us. They say there is no lake, that the river rushes down without sleeping from high in the mountains, where the snows of winter lie deep even in summer. They say Timofei's owl lies to us, and we should beware of the mushrooms."

"What? Do they think we are fools?"

WE WERE FOOL'D BY SOUNDS. The visuals astound'd us, but the sounds left us dumbstruck too. The river seemed to roar into one ear, then out the other. The cedars and rain sang in harmony. When we spoke, our voices seemed near, then far away.

A strange voice invaded my slumber. I peeked bleary-eyed from under my wet blanket. Avast, what's this? Visitors?

Two elderly native men sat beside our fizzling fire, both cloak'd in fur. How had they slipped past our guards? One was the elder we'd encountered at the smokehouse. His companion was a dead ringer for Yutramaki, only this version was a hunched grandfather with wispy white chinwhiskers and twinkling eyes buried in walrus wrinkles. Same skin colour as Yutramaki. Same scars. Three generations of look-alike Yutramakis.

Olga, wrapped in a blanket, offered them tea. Old Smokehouse declined, but Yutramaki the Elder accepted, holding the cup with his little finger stuck out like a bowsprit.

Our camp stirred. We glared accusingly at the slumbering watchdog. No movement in the forest.

Yutramaki the Elder offered Timofei a small sealskin bladder of whale oil. A favourable portent, this, a traditional opening-gesture for auspicious trading sessions.

The old man croak'd: "Keeps the scurvy away. Goes good with salmon eggs."

Kozma: "Tell us, tyee, our people who were captured . . .?"

"Filip and Yakov got traded to the Chinooks. Could be anywhere by now. Maria is with the Quileutes. Madame Bulygin is living in my house up at the cape."

He shook his fingertips: "Woman's a handful. Want her back? She's waiting, other side of the river. Four guns and she's yours again."

Hearing this, a chortling Bulygin scamper'd about camp in his long-johns trying to gather guns, but these were kept from his frantic grasp. The crew taunt'd him. Desperate, he hurled his soggy green officer's coat down on the soggy green moss at the tyee's feet, then snatch'd up clothes drying on bushes, including Timofei's dressing-gown, and threw these down upon the coat. The crew found itself caught up in the spirit of the occasion and likewise offered their own attire, even dumping the reeking laundry bag out before a baffled Yutramaki.

The tyee found the pile appalling: "Heap big stinkum."

Bulygin, offended, fists on hips: "Thath a Wuthan offitherth dweth coat."

Yutramaki, weary sigh: "Three guns."

Timofei: "No guns."

Bulygin, sobbing: "Gib deb da gubs. Thath an ordo. Leb me thee her."

Yutramaki & his chum walked down to the river and signal'd to the far bank. Men in canoes appear'd, as did Madame Bulygin, wrapped in blankets, hair tied back beneath her whaling-hat. She embark'd in a canoe with a pair of paddlers who brought her to midstream, where they held fast to a snag. Bulygin tearfully waded out with arms outstretched and was washed in the water's flow. We had all acquired a coating of mud & leaves.

Madame Bulygin, downwind, caught our aroma and sniffed, dabbing her nose with a silk handkerchief. The captain supposed her to be weeping and likewise wailed pitifully as the water rushed about him.

Madame Bulygin called: "Do not worry so, Nikolai. The Cape People attend to my needs. *Mon dieu*, you look awful. Surely you do not intend to stay in the woods all winter."

Timofei shouted back: "We journey upriver to build our fort at Rainbow Lake. We invite you to come along."

Madame Bulygin: "Would someone assist the captain, before he is swept away? I assure you, our good friend Yutramaki will provide for your comfort. We come here hoping you will listen to reason."

Timofei: "Your good friend Yutramaki just offered to trade you for three guns."

Madame Bulygin: "He jests with you, Timofei. He will protect me. I carry his child."

Bulygin emitted a sorrowful cry, lost his balance, went under, and was nearly swept away.

Timofei called to him: "Come back to shore, Nikolai Isaakovich. We cannot bargain with the kolosh in good faith. The old man toys with us. His words fly about in the air. How can we be sure he is truthful?"

Timofei turned to us. "Hear me, brothers. No more guns can fall into the hands of the kolosh. When we left the ship, each man had two muskets. Now, only one. The other guns are lost, broken. If we trade guns to the kolosh, they will shoot us, and somebody cannot shoot back. Perhaps I should surrender, live amongst them as a slave. If they torture me, if I die in agony, it will be penance for our sins."

Madame Bulygin: "You could be warm, sleeping under a roof, eating good food, performing simple tasks."

Shubin: "What do you perform?"

Madame Bulygin performed a double eye-roll: "It is too cold to argue. When you reconsider, send word to the village."

"When you reconsider, come visit our dacha by the lake."

Madame Bulygin beckon'd to her paddlers. "We are sorry to hear that Iakov died. He would still be alive if you had treated our hosts as friends, not enemies. They are our only chance to escape this place. Please do not shoot at them again. Agreed? Very well. I hope to see you all in the spring, if not before. Soon Mr. Baranov will send a vessel to rescue us, or a friendly vessel will arrive. We must be ready to go when a ship appears."

An eagle sat on a snag screaming at Pavel & Sergei as they spear-fished in chilly torrents, wielding alder branches tipped with arrowheads. The raptor swoop'd and returned to its perch with a twisting salmon in its talons.

Guard duty. We sentries commanded a view of the surrounding terrain through gun ports in our redoubt's corners. The landscape throbbed & undulated in sensuous waves & shimmers. Shapes & colours, transform'd. The river rose & fell in its banks, flooding to our very doorstep, then narrowing to a distant trickle. Our perception of distance was alter'd, making spearfishing difficult. When we walked, ghostly images of ourselves drift'd in our wake.

Our nearest neighbours lived an uncertain distance downstream in the two longhouses we'd visited earlier, but we believed another smaller settlement lay upriver, perhaps at scenic-but-unseen Rainbow Lake. Kahmooks scent'd salmon smoke on the downriver breeze. Canoes had passed our fort moving in both directions, despite our vigilant blockade.

Through my gun port I observed a tangled, overgrown morass: rough-barked evergreens draped in moss, frost'd by the thin blanket of wet snow which had stopped our upriver pilgrimage in its tracks and prompt'd frantic construction of the Winter Palace, with we builders paying tribute to the architectural spirit of the *barabara*, the Aleutian family dwelling. We covered an excavated pit with a driftwood dome caulk'd with moss clumps, but eschew'd the Aleuts' traditional circular design, finding ourselves strongly influenced instead by the Russian preference for a rectangular dwelling. Ours turned out to be a compromise, joined at odd angles due to hasty construction, impair'd depth perception, and the mismatch'd logs & branches we gathered from the riverbank. The river was cold & dangerous, but her fish & driftwood proved to be our salvation.

Speaking of which: Timofei called a meeting. The owl had asked him to pass along her thoughts regarding our deliverance from these desperate circumstances. We gathered inside our new dwelling. Snowflakes fluttered through the smoke hole, fizzing in the fire. Melting snow dripped.

A thump, a curse. Kozma rubbed his shaggy noggin: "Ouch. More downwards into the earth you must dig. Still I bump my head."

"You dig. Our heads do not bump."

"Dig, or they do."

Outside, a distant "Mooo."

"Elk?"

"Zypianov. He sees the lady elk rubbing her bottom against the mossy tree to attract the male. He gets an idea: maybe if he smears himself with the smelly moss, soon the foolish bull elk comes running. Then, Zyp makes the moo sound, wiggles the patootski, and hot-foots it on all fours past our palace, where our alert sentries await, guns at the ready. Kahboom. Red meat for dinner."

A faint cry from the woods: "Help!"

"So, we ask, 'But, Zyp, when we get home, what do you tell your old lady? When she gets jealous, she can be a real bear.'"

"Better we get the elk before the elk gets Zyp."

Bellows, snorts, pounding hooves in the snow. A terrified scream.

"Did you hear something?"

"The wind sings in the cedars."

"Williams, wake up. Anybody out there?"

My report: "Zypianov, struggling home through the snow. Big elk on his back."

My mates rejoiced: "Zyp returns with fresh meat. Our hunger is solved."

I say: "And there's a canoe coming down around the bend, with three men in it."

A great hub-bub: "To arms. Defend the river. Where is my gun?"

We rushed forth, ready to turn back any trespasser who travelled our tributary without tribute *(T-words!)*, but slipped in the slush.

Our visitors, unarmed, nudged their canoe into the riverbank. Two were strangers, probably slaves, judging from their demeanour & attire, but the boy in the stern looked familiar.

"That boy, Timofei, he is the little smarty-pants from when we raid the smokehouse. I bet his father is a tyee."

With narrow'd eye, Timofei cock'd his hammer: "You know the fee, boy. One salmon for each person who passes. Also, you must partake of the mushroom and accept the teachings of the owl."

From out back, sounds of a struggle.

The boy nodded upriver: "Father says owl sends foolish Rooskies on wild goose chase."

Bolotov threatened to smite him: "We told you, we are the chosen."

Kurmachev defended the boy: "Have pity, brothers. Behold his befuddled face. Timofei, let me talk sense to them. No longer can they turn away from us in our hour of need. They must understand that there is a purpose to their miserable lives."

"Yes. To provide us with fish."

Zypianov, unseen, cried out: "Beast! Go away!"

The crew mull'd Ivan's proposal: "Maybe Ivan is right, Timofei. Maybe he can discover more about Rainbow Lake and return with fish for his hungry comrades. What could go wrong?"

Timofei, suspicious: "Only if this big kolosh remains here as our hostage."

The boy: "My father's best slave?"

Timofei: "We promise not to eat him. Now take Ivan home with you. Tell your father that we need more fish."

The slave wailed piteously. The boy & his remaining companion assured him and shoved off upriver with an unarmed Ivan seated amidships, his thin bespectacled face aglow.

A victorious bugling echoed, the triumphant mating call of the bull elk. We heard Zypianov's plaintive wail: "Brothers? Do you abandon me?"

Timofei turned to us: "Somebody must put the elk out of his misery. Volunteers?"

Timofei paced the riverside in the rain, brooding, hands clasp'd behind his back. His bloodstain'd dressing gown flapped in the wind.

A worried Kozma confided in us: "The owl is angry about the slaying of the elk. We were wrong to kill him. The big fellow just has the lonesomes. Rutting season comes and goes, but not yet does he meet the lady elk."

"Woe is us. Look, two canoes coming down the river. The boy, two more kolosh, and Ivan. It is as we fear. Ivan returns, but with the long face and no fish."

Kurmachev disembark'd looking sorrowful: "Nine men, three women, one longhouse. I try to reason with them, but they scorn me. They mock the glass beads. Also, no lake. Nothing but river."

"And still the kolosh insist that we are the fools, not them. Timofei, are you sure that what the owl says comes straight from the horse's mouth?"

Timofei, affronted: "Does your faith waver, in the hour when I most depend upon you?"

Our faith was indeed wavering, but our hostage, having tasted the Fruit of Truth, was babbling ecstatically about the owl, pointing at the treetops. His mates ridiculed him, so Timofei ordered us to take them hostage as well, then left for another visit to the owl, absences which were becoming increasingly frequent. He returned at eventide, his brow furrow'd with foreboding. We gathered about.

He outlined our situation: "The owl cannot forgive the kolosh. Also, she is angry with us, for the killing of the elk. She chooses six of you to paddle upriver. You will punish the kolosh for their indifference. Kozma will take Bolotov, Abram, Valgusov, Five, and Sergei. Those chosen for this mission must not fail, as brother Ivan did, as did those who slayed the gentle beast of the forest, who came to us with only love in his heart. The owl fears that maybe I, her disciple, do not convey the message. Perhaps the time comes for me to throw myself upon the mercy of the kolosh, and seek redemption in suffering."

Kozma: "Not yet, brother. You are still our leader. Your work is here with us. Remain near the camp. No more wandering barefoot in the snow. Rest. Meditate. Soon we return."

Timofei placed a reassuring hand on Kozma's brow: "Fear not, for even though we anger her, the owl protects us, and guides you upriver. When the sun rises behind the mountains, take the two canoes. Do what you must. Soon our blue beads turn into fishes."

He smiled upon us. "Not by accident do we wash up on these shores, brothers. We come here for a reason. I think we are . . . invited."

The chosen six prepared to push off upriver at daybreak. The rest of us readied our muskets and assumed defensive positions. As we parted, I urged Kozma to take care.

He growl'd through his beard: "Tell Timofei to take care. He thinks we are invited?"

An hour passed. Or a day. Hard to tell. Maybe two days. Kozma's crew returned safely, each man carrying a salmon-bundle. We gathered on the riverbank to welcome them.

Kozma reported: "The kolosh cry out in anger when they see that the hostages do not return, but it is as Ivan said: they have hearts of stone. They run into the forest and will not listen. We call to them, 'Give us fish as the owl told you, or we burn the house.' But they are silent, stubborn, not accepting of this abundant love we offer. Also, the logs of the house are too wet to burn."

Timofei sighed: "Send the boy home with his slaves. Maybe he can explain."

The native males departed, soon returning with a party led by the boy's father. The tyee had a hundred dried salmon in his canoe.

The old man jabbed a spear at Bulygin: "Brass buttons. Yank them off."

The captain meekly did as ordered.

The elder: "Give them here. Now make this fish last until a ship comes, understand? And don't shoot the elk, and don't shoot at us. *Kumtux*? Understand? I know you didn't hit nobody. You hit somebody, you find out about it."

He prepared to shove off upstream: "No lake up there. Owl lies to you. Nothing but river."

Nonetheless, several days hence, the tyee's son, defying his father, returned, drawn by an unquench'd thirst for enlightenment. He left his slave in the canoe and strode confidently into the Winter Palace, finding us housebound, despondent, morose, weigh'd down with unspoken anxiety. Timofei was out looking for the owl.

We responded to his concern: "What troubles us? We worry about Timofei, young friend. We ask to ourself, is Rainbow Lake really up there?"

The boy shook his head: "No. No lake. But the owl speaks to Yutramaki of the Cape People, in his dream. Owl tells him, when ho'kwat come, we must feed them."

A halloo from the woods. Timofei returned with a message: the owl wanted us take the tyee's son hostage again until his family brought us four hundred fish & ten bags of salmon eggs. The boy agreed to be captured and bade his slave depart with word of Timofei's demands.

Days passed. The boy's companions visited, conferred with the tyee's son in whispers. More days passed. The companions returned, informing us that canoes would be coming downriver.

We were unprepared for the armada that descend'd upon us. Thirteen watercraft sped past on the current, the faces of the occupants (some seventy unarmed men & women) set in stone. The next day, four canoes struggled back up against the currents, laden with salmon & sealskin bladders filled with roe, which the natives dumped on our riverbank.

We gathered to inspect this cornucopia. Timofei gruffly commandeer'd a canoe at gunpoint, ousting its occupants. Muttering, the native contingent departed, but not before the tyee regained custody of his wayward son, now clad in authentic Cossack garb and sporting a broken gun. The elder stripped his son naked, seized him by the ear and cast him into the river. The youth swam hard to regain the bank.

The tyee turned to us: "No more fish. When that's gone, you are too. And remember where you got that canoe."

TIMOFEI GATHERED US FOR AN ANNOUNCEMENT: "Brothers, I smell springtime on the breeze. Soon our pilgrimage to Rainbow Lake continues. If the kolosh can paddle upriver against the current, we can too. Our new canoe holds only four of us, so we will make two more canoes by chopping and burning out these logs, as the kolosh do. Also, again all our food is gone, so we will send the good canoe out upon the river, that the fishes may leap into it."

"Timofei? The kolosh swear this Rainbow Lake does not exist. Maybe we should, ahem, vote?"

"Voting just makes us argue. Timofei trusts the owl. I trust Timofei."

Yuri spoke up: "Timofei? Sergei and I volunteer to scout upriver, to discover how far is Rainbow Lake."

Timofei turned away: "I cannot hear of this. If I knew of such a plan, I would have to tell the owl, and she would worry that we do not trust her. We must believe the lake awaits us. When we go up the river, we all go."

"Yuri and Sergei could leave after you go to see the owl. She does not have to know."

"Timofei? If the owl is so wise, why does she depend on you to tell her what we are doing? And why are you the only one she talks to?"

Timofei snapped: "You ask me? Ask her. Yes, go now, into the dark forest. Look up into the trees. Wait. Maybe she shows herself. Maybe not. If she appears, lavish praise on her. Thank her for the salmon she bestows upon her hungry children. Remind her that the kolosh lurks, waiting to pounce upon us. Tell her that, yes, we understand, if not for her, we would no longer survive, that our hearts overflow with gratitude, but now, all of a sudden, we who have been saved are not sure we can, ahem, trust our beloved guide and guardian. We do not know from where comes our next food, and we would be happy if the kolosh bring us more, so that we do not have to find food for ourselves, but if she should inquire in the roundabout way if her children still love their . . ."

"Timofei, please, I . . ."

"Go, tell her. I stay here by the fire. Tell her we love her until we get hungry. Tell her the Brotherhood is loyal to whoever feeds us. Come back, tell me what she says."

Kozma comfort'd Timofei: "Go in peace. Seek patience to lead the fearful. When you return, share with us the wisdoms."

Timofei spat on our earthen floor: "Hear me. He who does not trust the owl, abandon this house that she provides us."

He departed in a huff. Kozma conferred with Yuri & Sergei, and these two wrapped a salmon in salal leaves and their guns in seal-skin, were hugged & kissed by all, and departed upriver on foot. Timofei eventually returned. Yuri & Sergei did not.

The daylight began to last a little longer. Snow crept back into shadows.

On a windy day, a gust toppled an old cedar. The soggy earth shook.

"That was close. Hmmm. I wonder . . ."

"What?"

"If we had not heard the tree fall with our own ears, would it . . .?"

"No. You need three things: one something to make the sound on another something, and, also, the ear, to hear. First, the ax chops the log. Then the sound comes to the ear. If you have the ear and the log, but no ax, or if the tree falls to the ground, but the ear is elsewhere, then, poof, nothing. Right, Timofei?"

Timofei: "The owl would say that the sound happens, even if our ears do not hear it. We are cursed by our lack of awareness, but the owl hears our hearts beating as we sleep, for the tree in which she perches has its roots in the same mud in which we slumber."

A canoe appeared on the river bearing the tyee's son, who jumped ashore with advice for the captain regarding his dental distress: "Lick butt of yellow-belly slug."

Bulygin blink'd & sputter'd, offend'd. The boy pointed at a four-inch mollusk lurking under a fern.

"See trail of slime? Suck slug's butt or lick up slime as he crawls. Pain go away pronto. If slug is sluggish, annoy with stick." *Delete everything about slugs.*

OUR FOOD WAS NEARLY GONE. We couldn't catch a fish to save our lives.

The crew grumbled. "I am so hungry I could eat an elk."

"Not to shoot the elk."

"We could shoot the dee-o-gee. By mistake. While clumsily cleaning our weapons."

"But then who would guard us? The kolosh would capture us in our sleep."

"Ha. Remember when the two old kolosh walk past him and sit down at the fire? Also, he catches the rodent and refuses to share."

Kahmooks: "Help. Man bites dog. By the way, somebody just stepped on a branch out there."

Kozma duck'd: "Get down. Eyes on the trees."

"Not this again. Every time we threaten to eat the dog, he says, 'Wait. Listen. What was that?' Me, I hear nothing."

The birds had ceased their chatter. We looked to our firearms and peered into the forest, which throbbed & undulated. We had long believed ourselves to be watched, but we couldn't allow the natives to approach too near, lest we be picked off by arrows. A defensive volley, perhaps, an overwhelming display of firepower if our powder was not moist. Zuev, on sentry duty, had a dry gun at the ready.

Kozma: "Savva, a warning shot."

Zuev unwrapped his musket from its partially-chew'd walrus skin cover. He cock'd his hammer, aimed.

Kahmooks, ears twitching: "Left. Left. Back a tick. There."

Zuev fired into the forest. A distant yelp, a curse. Silence.

"Hmmm. Better we let sleeping dogs lie." *Cliché. Delete.*

Kahmooks wagged his fluffy tail: "What great friends."

"Only the joke we make, Kahmooks. Never would we eat you."

"Let's eat Bulygin."

Bulygin, morose & silent for weeks, shriek'd, waving a salal leaf laced with slug slime: "You have all gone mad, but I, your captain, am still strong, in body and mind. And look, thee? Even by abtheth hath healed. I, your captain, can see where Tarakanov steers you wrong, and I know how to get us back on course. Yes, surprise, you think your captain is not listening. You talk as if he is not here. But, as you can see, once again he strides proudly across the quarterdeck, strong, confident, more alert than ever before. Employee Tarakanov, I hereby inform you that I resume my rightful place at the helm."

Timofei, standing in the river with his dressing-gown hitch'd up: "At last. My burden is lifted."

Bulygin giggled: "See how Tarakanov casts his duties aside at the first opportunity, devoting himself instead to his religious studies? Command is not so easy in times of crisis. But, luckily for you, I am a professional. Thanks to the slug slime, I recover from the horrors which strain my sanity to the breaking point. I suffer torments no man should face, yet I endure."

A cheer: "Hooway. Ow bwave weedo."

Bulygin: "Thank you, men. Now, here is the plan. Thinking back, we can all agree that everything was fine until our beloved Madame Bulygin and the others were forced to leave our party down at the village. Therefore . . ."

Shubin: "Everything was fine until the Tsar's whore (*delete*) arrived in New Archangel. Remember, brothers? As you may recall, my head foretold that . . ."

"Wait. Bulygin has a point. Perhaps we reach Gray's Harbor by now if we give the kolosh a few guns to take us across the river."

Bulygin: "Yes. And whose idea was it, to refuse? Who talks to the birdie in the tree? Who tells you a fish story about Rainbow Lake? Not I."

"Blasphemy. Punish him, Timofei."

Timofei stared into the river rushing past his knees.

"Timofei? Do you doubt?"

Timofei gazed upstream: "Still I believe in Rainbow Lake. I know, the kolosh deny that it exists, but . . ."

"But what if we cannot find the lake? What if the river forks, and we take the wrong branch? What if the owl chooses not to reveal the lake to us? What then? At least if we go down the river, we know what awaits."

"Yes, death or slavery. Better we head for Rainbow Lake, with our hearts singing a song of hope. If we do not find the lake, we walk south to the Columbia River, where perhaps the kolosh is friendly."

"Of course. A walk in the woods. A hundred miles of mountains in winter. Fool. We get lost when we poop in the bushes."

"And what would we eat? How do we keep the guns dry? How do we keep us dry? How do we walk? Nothing to put on the feet but these moccasins that Olga makes from the skin of the lonesome elk."

"Bah. We are Cossack. We roam wild and free, living off the land, masters of our own destiny. Like the wolf, we eat through our feet."

"We should push the canoes up the river as far as we can. If we do not find the lake, we come back down. If we get past the village and out to the ocean, we head south, perhaps meeting a ship. If we don't, no matter. Luck was not with us."

"Luck? Our guns are our luck. Forget about the lake. We should paddle stealthily down the river under the cover of nightfall. We sneak up on the village. Kahmooks asks the barking dogs to please be quiet. We steal a cargo canoe, big enough for all. Then . . ."

"Sneak up? Steal? Bah. We are the Brotherhood. We take what we want. We attack with the sun at our backs, guns blazing, screaming our fearsome . . ."

"Sun?"

Bulygin, ecstatic: "Yes. Yes. Frontal daylight amphibious assault. Exactly what I . . ."

"We steal the big canoe before the kolosh awakens. We paddle south to the Columbia. Soon a ship rescues us."

"And, while we wait, we build a fort. We claim the river for our beloved Tsar."

"Think, idiot. Maybe does the kolosh suspect we might try to steal their canoe? Always they watch us. You think not? Where are Yuri and Sergei? When do they return?"

We gazed upriver at the spot where our Aleut comrades had last waved farewell before disappearing into the forest.

"We were crazy to let them go."

Bulygin frantically licked his leaf: "See? You admit you have gone mad, so my strategic cunning will be of the utmost . . ."

"We are afraid to attack the village, Bulygin, and your wife is not there anyway. She is shacked up in Yutramaki's wigwam."

Bulygin sniffled. One minute he was happy & excited, the next, depress'd, suicidal.

"So?," he cried, "You do not understand her like I do. Despite everything, I still love her. Have you seen any slugs?"

"Me, I love the owl, but when the going gets tough, she abandons us. Why does she test our faith, Timofei?"

Timofei sighed: "Owl doubts that we are strong enough for the journey to Rainbow Lake. She feeds our bodies with kolosh fish, but I must feed your souls with her words, and she says I have not yet prepared you for the dangers which lie in wait. When I walk in the forest, I see demons in the shadows with sharp teeth and claws, slinking through the bushes without even does the leaf move. My spine tingles. Only our faith in the owl keeps these creatures at bay. If we falter, our blood will soak the ferns long before we see Rainbow Lake. But, if I fail as your ataman, when the time comes, if you choose, you may surrender with me, and accept whatever fate that . . ."

"'Whatever fate'? We are dead or slaves the minute we drop our guns. Tell him, Kozma."

Kozma stared at his boots. Night & rain descended. Melting snow dripped. Out in the woods, beyond the palace walls, the wolves gathered to sing.

Kahmooks, wet nose in upright position, eyes closed, deep breath, tenor voce: "Ah-rooo."

From the darkness, the wolves answered him with a chorus of anguish'd moans. We huddled around our smoky fire, eyeballs rolling like gaming-dice, tugging our thin damp blankets tight about our ears.

I told the dog: "You scare me when you howl like that."

"Feels good. You try."

"The British don't howl."

"Werewolves of London. Ah-rooo." *Reference.*

"If they do, they bloody well don't enjoy it. Ah-roo."

"You'd howl if I bit your bloody butt. Ah-rooo. Deep throat. Ah-rooo. Feel it? The singer becomes the song. Try again. Let the message and messenger merge, blending as one. Become the howl."

I WADED THE RIVER'S MURKY SHALLOWS, stabbing at fishes with my sword, the image of a pagan hunter-gatherer reflect'd, beard'd & barbaric. Have we met, sir? Am I you? Is he me? Are we all together? Goo goo g' joob.

We slept in the river's embrace. Rivers hold memories, memory lives in dreams, and I dreamed the river rose in its banks, carrying me down to the sea, to a tidepool, a tiny ocean where I floated, serene, ecstatic. Above me, feath'ry wings flutter'd: the owl poop'd on my upturn'd brow, and each white splatter became a page, its words all true & beautiful. Let loose your hold upon this earth, the owl said. Swim away. All rivers flow to the sea. The ocean is all oceans, all life is one.

I sobbed with joy. My teardrops flood'd the tidepool.

A snoozing sentry awaken'd: "The river rises!" I was lying in cold water.

Groggy, we scrambled to secure our watercraft. All about us the river rumbled & churned with uprooted trees and bobbing boughs. The distant alpine snowfields we'd sighted from offshore had melted, sending an ocean of slush sliding down the river, stranding our house on an island of diminishing dimensions. The dripping trees, once a short stroll away, now seemed distant. Bowing in the rain, they lamenting their swept-away siblings sailing seaward.

An uprooted cedar the size of a ship bore down on our humble home. The Winter Palace was about to fall. Our dwelling groan'd & trembled beneath us, lamenting its demise. Structural failure was imminent. Cold torrents flooded in.

Kozma: "Prepare the canoes. Get some clothes on Timofei."

Timofei called to the trees: "Why do you not warn me of this flood? Is it time for me to go?"

Our purloin'd canoe, the good one, bobbed obediently on its tether, but the two we'd made rolled awkwardly. We threw in our possessions and just as our house collapsed, I jumped into the good canoe. Kozma pushed Timofei in behind me, Kahmooks followed. Five had the stern paddle, then Shubin, Abram, Olga. Overloaded, we flounder'd but remained buoyant. We roped the canoes together and cast off, propelled downstream by a vigorous current.

Soon we sped past the smokehouse & its attendant dwelling, noting both were situated well above the flood, with the inhabitants emerging to observe us from beneath the hoods of their fiber woven capes. We swept around bends, soon approaching the rocky beach where we last spoke with Madame Bulygin and Yutramaki. Timofei motioned to haul the canoes up on cobblestones. A quick inventory: we still possessed guns, powder, shot, and a sailcloth bag of mixed clothes & food.

Kozma told Timofei we needed a sheltered resting spot: "Too much wind and rain here. How can Olga get a fire going?"

Timofei spread his hands to the weeping heavens: "Brothers, the owl reminds us that our thin flesh contains a warm ocean within. Most of the Earth is water, just like our bodies. We are as one with the rain. The owl says that soon a guide approaches, with refreshments."

We searched for dry driftwood. We'd lost our ax, so with numb & bleeding fingers we ripped splinters from the innards of a broken log. Olga's flint sparked. Timofei paced at water's edge, dressing-gown plaster'd to his chest. We pulled the last few scraps of sail over our heads and huddled.

"Kozma, you must accept command. Break it to him gently."

Kozma shook his head, stared down at little rivers trickling 'twixt cobblestones.

"Who tells him, if not you?"

"If Timofei surrenders," Kozma said, "so do I."

"And us?"

"He is your ataman. You have sworn a blood oath. Like me, you will follow Timofei."

Timofei called to us, pointing upriver: "Our guide appears."

A WIZEN'D GNOME APPROACHED IN A SLENDER CANOE. He beach'd his craft, hopped ashore, took a swig from a fiber woven jug and offered us a drink. The crew accepted.

"Tastes like *kvas (Russian fermented drink)*. How does a kolosh have Rooski brewski? It must be poison."

"The old man drinks it. Me, I can drink anything. Glug, glug. Yum. Not bad. Like spruce beer, only without the woody bouquet."

The gnome introduced himself: "Name is Liuliuliuk. Where you going?"

"Down the river."

"Really. And then?"

Boot-shuffling, beard-tugging.

Liuliuliuk, helpfully: "*Delate siah*? A long distance?"

"Kauai, maybe."

"I see. Word to the wise?"

"You mean us?"

"Never mind. How come the fat girl is trying to start a fire out here in the rain?"

"Our leader says we are as one with the water."

"You boys sit tight. I'll go see what I can find."

Liuliuliuk left us on foot, soon returning with two cracked house-planks with which we sheltered our beleaguer'd fire. In gratitude Timofei offered him a blood-stained handkerchief.

Liuliuliuk declined. "Better follow me down to the village," he said. "Dangerous today."

We agreed to disembark with Liuliuliuk leading the way. Sullen torrents churn'd, flinging broken logs against our pitiful craft. We fought to remain afloat & upright. Liuliuliuk, observing our struggles, waved us to a resting place on the north bank. Just below us a forest'd island divided the river; the wider branch rumbled off to the south. The narrow north channel was studded with broken snags, some floating, some rakishly protruding from the bottom at odd angles. Liuliuliuk paddled off alone to scout the larger stream, slipping effortlessly through the angry currents.

We waited in defensive positions, albeit with damp powder. I scanned the island with my glass, soon spying a warrior with a bow ducking behind a tree. I alert'd my mates, but we could discern no further movement.

Liuliuliuk returned against the flood, tuck'd in close to the riverbank: "They're laying for you along the big channel. We better go down the narrow passage."

The crew objected: "You lead us away from a kolosh ambush? We are not as dumb as we look, old man."

"Yes, we are. Dumb pigs, fat for the slaughter. Sly old Liuliuliuk warms our bones with kolosh kvas while his friends sharpen their knives. Those kolosh hiding on the island are decoys, brothers. Not by mistake do they show themselves. The main force awaits us on the narrow passage."

"We are fools. Why do we not suspect Liuliuliuk before? Let's beat him up."

Timofei intervened: "Harm him not, for the owl sends him to us. We shall follow Liuliuliuk without question, even if the route he advises seems more hazardous."

"Ahem? Perhaps, Timofei, a vote?"

Kozma: "I vote we follow Liuliuliuk down the narrow passage. Who insults my honor by rudely voting against me?"

That settled, we embarked again, tuck'd in close behind Liuliuliuk's canoe. The narrow waterway's brushy banks had been ravaged by the flooding, and we were buffet'd by rampaging logs, spun by violent currents, whipped by overhanging alder branches. We saw nary a native and soon regained the river's swift mainstream. Rounding a bend, we ceased paddling and fell silent.

The ocean opened before us. On the north bank, our old campground, vacant. On the south, the village and its canoe fleet, pulled up high & dry. A silent crowd observed our arrival.

Liuliuliuk beached directly across from the longhouses. Timofei motioned for us to do likewise, and we gathered to bid our guide farewell. He demanded a gun in payment.

"No gun. We will give you a pewter token. It's engraved. It's . . ."

Liuliuliuk: "It's *cultus*, worthless. Give me a gun."

"No, see? Timofei has scratched the date on it with his knife-point, and an eagle, the symbol of the Tsar. If white men ask about us, you show it to them. They will give you a gun."

Liuliuliuk: "An eagle? A little bird with big round eyes? Ain't nobody coming to look for you. Where would you be, wasn't for me?"

"No guns for kolosh. Hey, look, a canoe is coming. The sister crosses the river with two companions."

"And the whole village is coming with her."

DOZENS OF VILLAGERS LAUNCHED CANOES and traversed the river. They were unarmed, but we nonetheless retreat'd to the drift logs, dragging our canoes behind us, and prepared to defend those rude ramparts.

Yutramaki's sister, accompanied by a woman & a young man, advanced bearing food baskets. The sister greet'd us. She'd matured.

Her hair was all silver now, and downy feathers peek'd from under her deerskin dress.

"Seize her," Timofei said. "Tie them up. Make her eat a mushroom. Then she will see the owl. If her people object, we shoot."

"Only a few mushy mushrooms remain, Timofei. Better not to waste them."

"Also, nobody do we shoot, Timofei. Still our powder is wet."

Timofei: "Pretend your powder is dry. If you believe, maybe they believe."

Ergo, after a brief-but-furious struggle, Yutramaki's sister and her two companions lay bound hand & foot. The villagers grumbled. We brandish'd our guns. They refrain'd from attack.

Timofei: "Hold the knife to the sister's throat."

He turned to address the villagers. "Kolosh, hear me: these people are our *elitees* (captives). Now return Filip and Yakov to us, or else."

The crowd parted and a worried tyee approached, introducing himself as the sister's husband: "Within four days, all your people return to you. Also, two ships are in the strait. Soon you sail for home. Let our people go."

The crew guffaw'd: "His tongue drips with treachery. He seeks to buy time."

The sister called reassuringly to the villagers and they reluctantly retreated across the river. We settled into the logs to await developments, feeling a bit more confident now that our hand held a queen. Our captives sat with their backs against a log, muttering.

The villagers brought fish & berries. The floods abated. A week passed uneventfully, with no unusual activity in the village, until one morning fifty men, some familiar, some strangers, emerged from a longhouse and marched down to water's edge at the narrows. Madame Bulygin, bundled in coat, scarf and whaling hat, walked with a still-elderly Yutramaki, who wore what appeared to be an English gentleman's suit, one made for a larger man, with matching top hat.

The flood was spent, the river now only a stone's throw across. Conversation would require no more than a raised voice.

Timofei prepared to converse with them: "Kozma, John, come with me. Cover us, brothers, and keep an eye on Bulygin. No more the outbursting."

We approach'd the narrows with guns at the ready.

Madame Bulygin called out to us over the river's roar: "Timofei? Can you hear me? It is important that we untie Yutramaki's sister immediately. That was not a good idea."

Timofei pointed at Yutramaki: "Who hides inside the suit?"

The tyee tipped the brim of his hat: "Tag says Savile Row. Spiffy, what?"

Madame Bulygin: "Well?"

Timofei: "Not yet can the sister leave us. Still she says the owl leads us astray. Also, we have no more mushrooms from the elk poop. Nowhere can we find them." *Delete everything about mushrooms.*

Yutramaki: "Forget the mushrooms. Can't be gobbling them down like you been. Now turn my sister loose and we'll get you back on a ship."

Kozma shook his head: "Our captain orders us to hold your treacherous sister until you return his devoted wife to his loving and protective arms."

I say: "From whence she was so rudely wrest'd."

Madame Bulygin rejected that proposal. "I will remain with the Cape People, thank you. You should join me, men. Mr. Yutramaki is an upright *(Did she really say that?)* and virtuous man. I'm told two ships are in the strait. Soon we depart."

Kozma: "Take pity on your unhappy spouse. See how he despairs. Come over and say something nice to him."

Madame Bulygin wiggled sensuously: "Ooo. And get tied up? Threatened with a knife?"

DEADLOCK'D, WE RETURNED TO THE LOGS. Kozma broke the news: "We are not out of the woods. Madame Bulygin says nothing good happens until we let the sister and her companions go, and give up ourselves. Then we go to the Cape. Our sins are forgiven."

Timofei: "But how do we know we can believe them? You see

how their words fly from their mouths and flit about like sparrows. Again, they say that two ships sail the strait, and if we surrender, soon we return to New Archangel. Also, Madame says she is happy living with Yutramaki, that he is virtuous and upright."

Bulygin shook a fist at his distant wife: "Upwight? You ho. God dab id, gib be dad gub."

The captain, frenzied, grabbed a gun and started towards the riverbank with the intention of shooting his wife, but then stopped short, weeping, shoulders shaking.

Timofei embraced the captain: "Peace be with you, Nikolai Isaakovich. Let it pass. What does she give to you but the breakings of the heart?"

Bulygin blinked teary eyes: "Sheeb good id bed."

Kozma extracted the gun from the captain's grip: "So we hear. Now listen, everybody. We three will go back down to the river. We will tell them we must discuss some more. Cover us. Do not shoot unless they do."

We returned to the river. Madame Bulygin tapped her boot on a stone: "This is embarrassing. You men look awful. The captain is covered with mud."

I say: "The mud has sedimental value. *Delete*. He is romantic, as you know."

Yutramaki: "He keeps pointing that gun, somebody will put an arrow in him."

"His wife drives him mad," Timofei said. "He threatens to shoot her."

"I do not fear death," Madame Bulygin said. "It is better for me to die than to wander about with you in the forest, where we might fall into the hands of cruel and barbarous people. I am living with kind and humane people. Tell my husband that I scorn his threats. *Owens/Donnelly. Paraphrase and/or cite reference*. Now set these people free so we can go to the cape. Consider how your appearance reflects on me."

Kozma: "Behold Timofei Tarakanov, the messy messiah. Tyee, listen, we will trade your sister for that big canoe over there. We give it back when we are done with it."

Yutramaki nodded: "Anything else? Salmon for dinner? Steam bath? Couple days head start?"

We trudged back up to our camp. When Timofei passed along Madame Bulygin's comments, her husband faint'd and fell to the stones, but then regained consciousness and lay weeping.

Timofei: "Well, brothers, now we must decide. Never do they let us cross the river unless we trade guns. Even if we escape to the ocean, our canoes will sink in the surf. If we march north, the Quileutes will capture us. If we go back up the river, we can carry with us only a few days' food. Here, as long as we have Yutramaki's sister, they will feed us, but they are angry, and the longer we wait . . ."

The sister cursed, struggling with her bonds.

"Timofei, we should try for Destruction Island. The tyee's son said nobody lives there, and it has pools of rain water, crabs, bird eggs. We could make a signal fire from driftwood and watch for ships."

"You babble, brother. From here to the island is four miles of ocean. Only by the grace of God do we get down the river."

Timofei had an announcement: "The owl says I must surrender. Yes, I know, maybe they torture and kill me, maybe I will be a slave. I must atone for our sins. As for you, my followers, I will ask them to free you without harm."

Bulygin, swollen-cheeked, sliced the air with his sword: "Bah. We cwoff the wivo add daybweak. A weckless waid, a defpwit gambo, a wisky supwise stwike. A bwaze of gwo-wee."

"Easy for you to say."

"Here, captain, lick the slug slime. Nobody can understand you."

Timofei continued: "Therefore, dearest brothers, I bid you farewell, knowing that soon . . ."

"Kozma, tell him he is crazy."

Kozma shook his head: "I surrender with Timofei."

Five & Pavel: "Us also. We follow Timofei."

Bulygin licked a leaf: "Slurp. Count me in. Yum. This is good stuff. Before, I was crazy with jealousy, but now I agree that to attack the village is suicidal. Obviously, further resistance is pointless, so I surrender too, hoping for the best. Certainly, the Quileutes forget about that silly cannon incident by now. Bygones be bygones, right? Yes, my Anna Petrovna is one clever girl, and if she says we should surrender, then who am I to . . ."

Kozma: "Anybody else? John?"

I nodded oceanward: "Rather prefer Kauai."

The crew murmur'd.

"Me, I paddle for the Columbia in the good canoe. Who joins me?"

"Look at those breakers. You will drown."

"Better than whatever awaits us over there."

"Look, the old man."


WITH COAT SLEEVES SWALLOWING HIS PADDLE-HANDLE, Yutramaki power'd his canoe across the currents, then beached & approached with rolled-up pants cuffs flapping about his gnarly toes. He tipped the beaver-hat again, shook hands with Timofei, had a quiet word.

Then he turned to me: "Them two ships in the strait? One's British, the *Otter*. Other one is the *Hamilton*, out of Boston. They ain't on speaking terms, but they both been asking the Nootkas and the Clayoquots about you. Appears the Chinooks told them about an Englishman name of John Williams who got off an Astor ship right before it goes boom. The captain of the *Hamilton* says Astor wants this Williams dead or alive, and the British say King George wants to give him a night hood. Is that for sleeping?"

"Different chap," I said. "Common name. A ship exploded, you say? Dreadfully sorry, old boy, haven't a clue."

Yutramaki smiled: "The Americans said you was a liar and a scoundrel. And a murderer. The captain of the British ship is offering a dozen army muskets to he who brings you in, and the Yankees on the *Hamilton* will double that. When Madame Bulygin hears that, she swears in French and she says, 'All along I suspect Williams is a British agent. Why do I not shoot him when I have the chance? He sabotages Astor and now he runs the Tsar's enterprise aground. But wait,' she says. 'Perhaps Williams can extricate us from our predicament. Yutramaki, tell the Americans they can have Williams if they return us to New Archangel, but he must not reach the English ship.' Her very words. However, way I see it is, yes, you might be a fork-tongued backstabber like they say, but you might also be the messenger the owl's been waiting for, ever since the last ice age."

Timofei: "The owl comes to my dream, not John's. She . . ."

Yutramaki: "Owl's old, Tim. Confused."

Timofei's broad shoulders slumped. The moment of truth arrived, sudden, quiet. Without another word Timofei handed me his musket, knife, shot bag & powder horn, then stood staring upriver as though awaiting instructions. Kozma, Five and Pavel likewise divested themselves of their weaponry. Yutramaki cut the strips of sealskin that bound our hostages, who rubbed raw wrists & ankles. Timofei stepped up on a log to address us, his beard & dressing-gown flowing in the sea breeze, his background the Pacific panorama.

He spread his palms. A psalm: "Go forth upon the waters, brothers. Spread the story of the wonders we behold. Tell the world that Rainbow Lake is up there, awaiting better men than we. No tears, brothers. My heart is not heavy. I go to a better place, with only my most faithful followers by my side. Just when all seems lost, the owl will appear to those who truly believe in her."

Kozma hugged & kissed us all farewell, his words catching in his throat like leaves caught on stones in a flowing stream: "Somebody must go back, tell them . . ."

Yutramaki waved his hands in our faces: "Last chance. Do what I say, everybody goes home."

"Home? Where is . . ."

"Listen," Yutramaki said. "You are not paddling out of here. Look at them waves. What's the matter with you? Figure it out while you're still alive."

Timofei: "Soon we are more than alive. A wonderful world awaits, just beyond this cruel existence. The eyes in our heads may never see Rainbow Lake, but our spirits shall dwell on its bountiful shores forever."

Yutramaki, exasperated: "Ain't no lake up there. Owl said that just to get you through the winter. Quit eating them mushrooms, things clear up pronto. You want to live through this, do what I tell you."

His plea fell on deaf ears. Timofei, Kozma, Five and Pavel departed with Yutramaki. Once across the river, the natives clustered around their captives and marched them off to the village, but did not bind them, and we discern'd no roughness. Timofei walked with his eyes on the forest. Kozma turned, gave us a sad wave. Madame Bulygin, Maria and Yutramaki brought up the rear. At least half of the native warriors remained at the narrows, two dozen or so, waiting to see what we'd do.

We hunker'd down to discuss the same topic. Eight men, Olga, the Raven, and the dog.

Zypianov dabbed at tears: "I am the eldest, so I will be acting ataman, if there is no objection. I will paddle the bad canoe. Olga, good canoe. Abram, you can still paddle, you will be with me. Savva, good canoe. Afanasii . . ."

The Raven: "I will stay here, holding out for the previous offer. So far, they keep their word."

"Ha. What happens when they find out Raven Warrior is a crazy Cossack in a crow costume?" *C words? Let's do M words again.*

Zypianov shook my shoulder: "Coming with us? Yes? Then you are in the bad canoe."

I rubbed the malamute's soft ears: "Doggy go swimmies?"

Kahmooks, chin on paws, brown eyes upturn'd: "Surrender. I'll put in a good word for you."

Whales were out beyond the breakers, black on gray. Dizzy, light-headed, giddy with a fearful joy, I unbuckled my sword and asked the malamute to give it to Yutramaki. He took the scabbard in his teeth.

A strange silence fell over us. We could hear no roar of surf, no rumble from the river, no wind, only a whale's distant song. We hauled two canoes down to the river as though we were in a dream. The canoes seemed weightless, but we moved slowly, entranced by the moment's tiny details. A gull, aloft. The clouds parted. The people across the river glow'd in pale light. Our own faces, luminous.

Five bared his chest. One by one we touched the lump, the old musket ball under his skin. We embraced tearfully and pushed off, paddling with our guns tied to our backs. In my canoe, Zypianov was in the bow, Abram mid-thwarts, me aft. My paddle was a delicate feather in my hands. The water was vaporous, offering no resistance to our strokes. We paddled out of the narrows into the first big breakers.

The good canoe led. We would hide in her lee as long as we could. A breaking wave rose above her port beam, and her prow bit defiantly at the sea's green paw. Then her paddlers were in the water, splashing, choking, their canoe bottom up. Somehow, we stayed upright. They swam to us, grasping at our gunwales.

The next wave capsized us too. We flounder'd, grabbing at each other. For a brief moment we clung together, a little island of warm flesh bobbing in a cold ocean, but the next breaker buried us all, and the songs of whales filled the sea.

# 7 | Village of the Whales

I FLOATED IN A SOUP OF PROTEAN PROTEINS, tiny creatures neither fish nor fowl. Around me sheer pinnacles vault'd skyward through mist. Quicksilver lightning crack'd a thund'rous sky.

Slave girls swam to my rescue, black tresses swirling, finding me snarl'd in kelp. They pulled me to the banks of a stream, but a horrible beast emerged from swirling smoke, baring its teeth. Was I to be sacrificed to this creature? Would these fangs tear me limb from limb? I was too exhausted to resist.

I lay naked in a dark chamber with whale poop in my mouth. Was this the monster's lair? Below me was a fiber mat, then smooth ground. A muttering girl scrubbed my flesh with spruce needles, angry that she'd been assigned this foul job.

On the walls, furs & fishing gear. In the corners, sleeping platforms. Bundles of dried salmon & bulging whale-oil bladders dangled from a plank roof, its beams supported by cedar posts thick as a mainmast, all carved with beastly faces. Foodstuffs in wooden bowls & bentwood boxes. Curious children scamper'd in gray light. A fire crackled, smoke drifting up through a hole in the ceiling. The menacing monster became a wall carving, its ferocious face moving in the fire's flickering shadows.

A fur-clad Yutramaki squatted beside the girl, grooming himself with a whalebone comb. The scar on his thigh remained, but his appearance (dramatically punctuated by an ornamental nose bone) was now youthful. Could this be the lad we'd first met?

He poked me with a stick of kindling: "Welcome back. You aged up. Me, I'm getting younger again. Be sixteen by summertime. Five wives keep young brave busy. Woo woo."

I say: "Patooey. Whey ebb I?"

"Gets in your mouth, don't it? Your whereabouts is Neah, the village of my ancestors. We have five villages on the cape, and most of your people are close by. Every high-up tyee has at least one of you. Cost us a fortune in whale oil, buying you from the Quileutes and Hohs, and then the two ships that were looking for you gave up and sailed away. Now we are stuck with you."

He said the Quileutes had traded The Raven to the Chinooks at the Columbia, along with Yakov and little Filip. "But they still have Maria, trading her around. Timofei belongs to me, same as you. He's out wandering in the woods, and your dog is sleeping over there in the corner. Kozma belongs to a tyee named Tatoosh. The Bulygins were both here for a while, but the captain is crazy, as you may know, and Madame Bulygin don't get along with my wives, and I feared for the baby *(Thank you daddy)*. Then me and Tatoosh, the one that has Kozma, we *mamook hiyu wawa*, had a big argument. Tatoosh Island out there is named after his family, so he thinks he's highest-up, even when I'm older than him, meaning he gets first pick of any captives, which, he says, includes both Bulygins. So now the captain is weaving baskets at Tatoosh's, Madame Bulygin is living with my sister, couple houses thataway, big as a house with my daughter, and I got five wives giving me the evil eye. What a mess. Oops."

The house shook. We looked up. A huge eye peered down at us through the smoke-hole.

"That's the old gal that brought you back. Everybody else washed up safe on shore. She's worried about you. Smile or she knocks the house down."

A joyous warmth flood'd my veins, stronger than opium. I smiled through the gunk coating my face.

"Whale poop smoothes the passage when you come back," Yutramaki said. "The other side is real close out here, which is how we get whales swimming through the village. However, this side don't match up with the other side time-wise, so when humans pass between, their age changes. Or not, in your case. The other animals have been around longer than us so they can pass back and forth on their own, but humans must be carried over by the whales, and they're picky about who they take and who they bring back. Coming back can be rough, as you know. Not everybody makes it. More poop you got on you the better. The owl thought my father was her chosen one, but he drowned coming back, so you are not going anywhere 'til she makes up her mind. Problem is, upkeep on you is *hyas mahkook*, expensive, and the legend says we only need the owl's messenger."

"Legend?"

"Owl Man Meets Lovely Maiden," Yutramaki said. "Girl goes berry-picking in the forest, and she sees an owl perched up in a tree. Turns out this dumpy little bird is a spirit who can change into a handsome brave right before her very eyes, so lo and behold, pretty soon she has a baby, a little girl covered with soft downy owl feathers. Her people believe the young mother is crazy, so they turn their backs on her and banish her from the village, but they keep the baby girl because they see she is a powerful spirit. She turns out to be my mother, but we say she's my sister because sometimes I'm older than her.

"Anyway. The baby's mother has nowhere to go, so she returns to the forest and gets back together with Owl Man, who's been very lonely. He welcomes her with open wings and changes her into an owl-person like him so she can live in his tree with him, but he sees that she misses her people and he's afraid that she will leave him, so he casts a spell on her so she can't change back to human. She says, 'Very well, I will stay, but only if I can turn into a big scary Thunderbird whenever I want.'

"He agrees, and she likes being a Thunderbird, but she is still sad because she misses her baby and being a human, so she changes back to a mama owl and goes and sits on her family's house. She cries out, 'Whooo? Who forsakes me? Let those who are blameless cast me out.'

"But her people are arguing and nobody pays attention. Every family thinks it's better than the others, all the tyees act like big shots, every potlatch is bigger than the one before. The tyees kill their slaves just to show off, like, 'Look, I have so many slaves that I can kill a few for fun and not even miss them.' The people have fat bellies, and they gamble on *lahal*, the bone-game, and with beaver-tooth dice.

"So the young mama owl is sad. She foresees hard times are coming, so she tries to warn her people. She finds she can perch on their houses at night and talk to them in their dreams and offer them wisdom, so they name her Owl-Who-Knows-All. But they still don't do what she says, and they run and hide when she turns into a Thunderbird, even when she drops a big fat whale on their beach, so she decides to find somebody else to speak her message for her. She cries out, 'Whooo? Who will help me? I must look beyond you, my people, for you are stupid and greedy. I will wait until some *klahowyum* (wretched) *babalid* (Qwidicca-atx language, meaning similar to ho'kwat) pass by who are desperate for salvation, and the whales will push their canoe ashore so I can choose my messenger from amongst them.'"

Yutramaki imitated a high-pitched feminine harangue: "'Yes, I must look elsewhere for my messenger, someone who will believe in me as you have not, maybe a tall bearded blond guy in a flowing white robe, someone who will learn my words of hope and courage and then speak them to you so you can understand, and my message of courage will carry you through the coming troubles. My messenger's tongue will be a river that joins the villages, and his words will be like canoes crossing seas of deep sorrow.'"

Yutramaki let this sink in, then resumed.

"So, something bad is coming, but maybe one of you ho'kwat is a shaman, an oracle who will guide us through the hard times. The legend says the whales will push the messenger's canoe ashore at the Hoh's river, where the owl lives, but the whales got their rivers confused, which is how you ended up with the Quileutes. The legend says the rival families will bury the hatchet and send forth their strongest warriors to capture the messenger, but he fights his way up the river into the owl's sacred forest, where he eats the fruit and wanders around all winter, receiving wisdom. In spring, he appears upon the river on a great flood, riding in a canoe, and he speaks to us. Timofei says he's our man, and he might be right, but Owl-Who-Knows-All remains silent. So, think hard. Did she give you any prophecies you can recall?"

"Yes. Morning of the flood. Vivid dream. She poop'd on my head. Please, tyee, feeling a bit wobbly. Walk me down to the beach, would you? There's a good chap."

"Call me Yutramaki. Tyees have different names. Young names, old names, summer names, winter names. And nobody but another slave can touch you. You're unclean."

Another poke from the stick: "Hey, cheer up. You been saved. Don't happen to just everybody. If owls or whales poop on you, that means they like you. So, let's keep the old gal happy. If you break a rule, she gets mad, she tells the whales to splash their tails and make big waves that wash away the village and we have to start all over. Rule is, 'No whoopee during whaling season.'"

"You hunt the whale?" *Oh, jeez. Here we go. Ahab of the North.*

He took a long harpoon down from the wall, a *dupuyak* he called it, an eighteen-foot-long shaft of yew, the length of a small canoe. He showed me the polish'd spearpoint: sharp mussel shells with barbs of elkhorn.

Yutramaki stroked this fearsome tool lovingly: "My family been whaling since The First Light. Every tyee has his own crew, all taught from boyhood. We prepare for the hunt by swimming at night in the streams and the ocean. Makes our minds and bodies strong. The night before the hunt, the crew sleeps together, and we share a dream in which our whale appears."

His hand swept oceanward: "Before dawn we paddle out over the horizon and sing our whale prayers. The whale we dreamed about looks us over and usually finds us unworthy, but sometimes lets us approach. The *hoachinicaha*, the harpooner, a tyee like me, we all have this scar on our noses, he stands in the bow like this. When the moment appears, when everything falls into place like it was in the dream, he beseeches his guardian spirit for strength, he throws the dupuyak and sticks the whale behind the fluke. She blows, poof, and the crew backs the canoe off so she don't swamp them with her tail. The hoachinicaha crouches down under a bear-skin to show her he's sorry, but the whale don't care. Usually, she dives with the harpoon stuck in her, and the point breaks away from the shaft at this joint here, and it has this rope attached, with these sealskin floats, which she drags along behind. If the harpoon hits her heart, pretty soon she slows down. Finish her off with spears, stick a plug in her blowhole, dive in, sew her mouth shut so she don't fill up with water and head for home, dragging her along behind. Haul her up on the beach at high tide, divide the meat and blubber up amongst family and friends. Boil the blubber, scoop the oil off the top with clamshells. All there is to it."

The tyee said each whaler usually brings home three whales in a season, unless the whales are angry, in which case the hunters seek their prey's forgiveness by performing mystical rites involving the resurrection of deceased former whalers by their old chums, who carry the mummified cadavers down to the beach and prop them up on logs so the whales can swim by and see them again.

I say: "By Jove. Necromancy."

"Least we don't eat people. We use almost the whole whale. Mostly we're after the oil, which is what's in them big bladders."

He indicated the bulging sealskin bags hanging from the rafters. A whale yielded about three tons of various grades of oil, which the natives used for a variety of purposes, including fish sauce, lamp oil and face paints. Most of the oil remained in the village; the rest was traded up & down the coast.

Whaling season was soon to begin, Yutramaki said, and the crews would relocate from the sheltered winter villages to their remote summer outposts, which offered faster access to the open ocean. Yutramaki & other tyees launch'd their hunts from stations out on the cape, others from tiny, barren Tatoosh's Island off the cape's tip.

"You and Timofei are coming, but we leave the wives behind. Whalers need solitude. No whoopee. When whalers go out on the ocean, their wives stay in bed and lie real still, and they don't eat. If a whaler's wife has a bite to eat, her old man brings home a skinny whale. If she gets out of bed, the whales might keep her husband."

Ergo, on a splendid spring morning we removed thick planks from one end of the winter house, stacked these weighty timbers crosswise on the beam thwarts of two parallel canoes, and departed, our craft resembling Polynesian catamarans. When we were offshore but still within the bay, I turned to view the village. Tiers of longhouses terraced from the beach, a two-mile-long crescent. Several thousand souls found shelter in its curve. Behind, dense evergreen forest. Distant glaciers.

Our convoy encountered a bit of chop as we entered the strait and turned oceanward, but we soon reached a pretty site clinging to the cape's steep & forest'd northern slope. White creeks splashed into the strait. Evergreens backdropped a forlorn cluster of bare house frames.

Yutramaki directed the unloading of the planks and their attachment to his house's posts & beams, first the roof boards, then the overlapping siding, all secured with twisted cedar-bark withes. Our abode was soon transferred, and at eventide the whaling crew bathed in the ocean before curling up on the earthen floor in a spartan ball. Timofei & I and a support staff of over a dozen sank into slumber around them.

AWAKEN'D IN DARKNESS, I WAS TOLD TO FETCH the harpoon from the wall. I stagger'd outside with thirty pounds of lethal menace clutch'd to my chest.

A cold dawn lit the foggy strait and the sleek black forty-foot whaling canoe. The white seashells decorating the gunwales gleam'd. Yutramaki's crew huddled to pray & sing beneath wind-whipped torches, then stowed their gear in assigned niches. Inflated sealskin floats marked with the tyee's personal logo nestled between the paddlers. Other floats, soaked overnight in the creek to increase their air-tight buoyancy, were stored deflated. Watertight bentwood boxes held tackle, food, drinking water. Killing-lances were lashed down forward with the harpoon, its deadly point safely sheath'd.

The paddlers sang as they launched, taking ordained positions, three to a side, one in the stern with the long steering paddle. Yutramaki stood at the wolf's-head bow; the wolf spirit would guide them to the whales. A slave launched a small canoe and hastened back to Neah with orders for the whalers' wives to commence their obligatory fasting & passivity, and the hunters embark'd upon a rolling sea, chopping a white wake through granite rollers, soon disappearing into drifting fog. Their ghostly chant linger'd on the shore.

My fellow slaves drifted back to the house. I fell asleep standing up, my feet washed in ripples. Time stood still, the world seemed oddly tilt'd, and the songs of whales seemed to rise through my body from the water.

The whaling canoe emerged from the mist, returning with an immense black bump in tow.

My mates rejoiced. The hunters' prayers had been answered. The people might now be nourished. I had come to know the whales as vessels that took me to another world, beings that transcended the corporeal. Had this great dead thing ever held a human?

We launched canoes and followed the hunters into the bay. A celebration commenced on shore, with thousands of villagers chanting a welcome. High tide lifted the whale up on the beach, revealing all fifty feet of it. Thirty tons, I guessed. A flipper a dozen feet long, more a wing than a fin, pointed skyward like a sail. Barnacles encrusted the behemoth's flanks, even the grooved pleats on its throat. The first whale of the season demanded a sacrifice, and Yutramaki calmly killed a native slave with a swift blow of his club, then ordered us to lay this unfortunate thrall to rest beneath the whale's blank gaze. The sacrificial death prompt'd jubilation. *Delete slave-killing please.*

The slaughter of the whale commenced, with we slaves pitching in enthusiastically. Yutramaki, exchanging his club for a sword, carved away strips of blubber six inches thick, assigning choice slabs first to crew members, then his family, then specific villagers. He directed the poking of holes in the whale's back, wherein we poured cold sea water, lest the meat spoil in the heat of its insulating blubber. Wives stood at a distance, advising. We slaves waded in red tides, laden with slabs of pink blubber as big as ourselves. Staggering, we hauled the meat to steaming cooking pots and buried the offal for the swarming sand crabs.

At day's end we'd reduced the whale to its bones. Shrieking gulls swirl'd & swoop'd as a blinding sunset bled across the sea's smooth horizon. Exhausted, caked with gore, we waded out to the shallows for a cleansing rinse, black silhouettes against a fiery sea.

I found myself splashing beside the four Japanese slaves, and we conversed in the Chinook jargon. Years ago, their erstwhile cargo boat had been dismasted by a sudden typhoon and swept from their homeland's coastal waters; the woebegone sailors caught fish and captured rain in a sail whilst strong currents whisk'd them across the Pacific, fetching them up here at the cape a fortnight later. Their boat became firewood.

They weren't the first Asians to be stranded here, and the village had acquired a collection of Asian relics, which included Yutramaki's whale-butchering sword. The Japanese confided that it had been previously owned by a passenger of theirs, a *samurai*, a professional soldier who had departed the vessel in mid-Pacific under circumstances which would remain unclear. The Japanese resided in Baadah, the bayside community just to the east of Neah, all owned by the same tyee. They spent their days scouring the tidal rock gardens for octopi; occasionally, to their anguish, they would find Japanese bamboo in the detritus, and they would sit & stare, morose, westward. Alas, they were hopelessly maroon'd, naught but common sailors lacking ransom value, and at any rate their homeland's ports remained forbidden to occidental traders.

Like me, they'd forgotten how long they'd been here. The seamless gray days played tricks with my sense of time, and the whales bewildered me with their changes in my age. I slipped about within my lifetime like a bar of soap on a wet deck, and my days became a book of disarranged chapters.

Yutramaki's age likewise varied, as did Sister Mother's, but the villagers appeared not to notice. Were they polite, discreet? Had they become accustomed to this phenomena?

THEY NOTICED THE QUILEUTE CANOE.

A breathless runner descended from the cape's summit with a lookout's report: a Quileute canoe with four paddlers was rounding Tatoosh's Island, entering the strait.

The village, abuzz: a brazen daylight slave-raid? Suicidal. Did the Quileutes intend to visit the Clallams, their cousins, on the strait to the east? Should they be slaughter'd, or allowed to pass in peace?

The visitors entered the bay but did not beach, instead waited bobbing in the surf, just offshore, singing. A young tyee we had encounter'd at the shipwreck stood in the canoe and serenaded us, bellowing out his fervent desire to wed the niece of Sister Mother. This lusty suitor wailed his plaintive entreaties, sonorously petitioning the girl's father, who stood silent on the beach. The Quileute sang to us that he had acquired ownership of our Maria but wanted to trade her, and these serendipitous circumstances encouraged him to press his suit anew: he offered Maria as a bridegroom's present to his prospective father-in-law.

The village found itself divided. Some, remembering unsettled scores, gestured rudely at the waiting Quileutes. Others saw potential profit in the lower'd trade barriers & reduced hostilities that the proposed marriage might promote. When next a trade ship appeared, Maria was sure to bring her owner a generous ransom. A delegation of free-trade tyees counsel'd the girl's father to consider the young tyee's proposal, and at length the visitors were granted permission to beach their canoe and enter the prospective bride's home, where they sat down by the fire to a hearty stew of boiled salmon heads.

The host greeted his guests: "Gets nippy out there, don't it? Here, this will warm you up."

In an extravagant welcoming display, he poured a bladder of whale oil on the fire and the blaze roared, lighting totemic carvings. The Quileutes, not being noted whalers, valued oil dearly and were suitably impressed by this profligate gesture, so awed, in fact, that they forgot to keep an eye on their canoe, negligence which allowed mischievous youths sufficient time to bury the watercraft bow-down in the beach, its stern suspended at a rakish angle.

The daughter, a slender lass of haughty demeanour, also responded unfavourably. Upon being informed of the young tyee's proposal she inserted a dainty finger into her throat and performed odd gagging vocalizations, retreating forthwith to distant berrybushes from whence she would not be summoned, not reappearing until the Quileute delegation had disinterred its canoe and departed under a scornful rain of hoots, catcalls, and small stones.

SMOOTH STONES LED US DOWN TO THE OCEAN. At night Yutramaki & I swam in the creek, and it carried us seaward in darkness, fresh water turning to brine. Sometimes we encountered Sister Mother, her moist feathers ablaze with St. Elmo's fire. Rapturous, she disappeared into the black roar of the nocturnal sea. When she returned, she was older, or younger, depending.

I remained old, an ancient pilgrim seeking sanctity, my brittle bones burning with a fire that threatened to consume my very being. As we swam my master & I raised our trembling hands to the heavens, steamy spectres rising from our tingling skin. We gulped water and like the whales we blew hard against the night, joining water to air. He prayed as he swam to the sea, murmuring, crying, singing. I drifted silently, rapturous like Sister Mother, but with an inner fire.

My age drifted but the whales preferred me old, and they were happier if I remained close to water, refraining from venturing inland. They keep me young. They like the way the water tastes when I'm having my period. I paddled in tidepools. I was a member of anemone, a sibling to starfish. I had planktonic relationships. I heard the fishes when they cried. *Cite reference.* I frequented sea caves lined with petroglyph faces carved in sheer stone, and weedy wave-washed wocks where whales wubbed *(stop it)* barnacles from their noses. I loiter'd in slimy, moonlit rock gardens, shouting & weeping. I was bloodied by salty stigmata.

The whales healed my wounds. I bask'd, submerged, suspended between stone & ocean, waiting, body burning. The planet spun in the heavens, the moon pulled, the tides flowed, and again the whales came for me.

O! The joy! *Reference.*

A RUMOUR: A SHIP HAD BEEN SIGHTED.

Where? On what course? What flag? Nobody knew. The rumour was an orphan.

Yutramaki nonetheless posted eagle-eyed sentinels on lofty spars atop the cape, left them suspended four hundred feet above sea level from dawn to dark, peering into the onshore flow of moist marine air. If weather permitted, they could see south to the Columbia River, north along the outer coast of Vancouver's Island, and far out to sea, but alas, the atmosphere was as dense as the ocean. No sight of sail.

Still, we told ourselves, we hadn't long to wait, neither for our ransom & rescue nor the return of Maria from the Quileutes (negotiations proceeded favourably, we learn'd), nor the birth of Madame Bulygin's daughter (Sister Mother, the midwife, guaranteed a healthy girl). *Oui. C'est moi.*

A custody battle loomed. A teenaged Yutramaki explained his point of view.

"My daughter stays here. If her mother wants to leave, she better deliver before her ship comes in."

Suffice to note that Madame Bulygin felt otherwise, and the principals weren't speaking. Sister Mother acted as liaison. The suspense was palpable. What if a ship arrived, say, today? Yutramaki's five wives waved knives at Madame Bulygin, voicing threats; she turned up her delicate nose *(Daddy says I have her nose)* in defiant response. She moved ponderously and tired easily as she strolled the seashore, scanning the strait, belly swaying. She was joined on these walks by Sister Mother and the girl desired in matrimony by the young Quileute tyee. They took target practice on floating logs with the French pistols, scattering flocks of terrified gulls.

Fatigued by these exertions, Madame Bulygin retired to her platform-bed in Sister Mother's longhouse, where she swaddled herself in furs & woolens and passed her time tidying up the ship's log, writing with the quill of an eagle's feather by the light of a stone whale-oil lamp. These revisions consumed the log's dwindling blank pages, and our precious ink supply *(klale chuck kopa mamook tzum*, black water to make marks) fell low in the bottle. Charcoal thinned with whale oil proved a messy substitute.

She occasionally shared her writing with us, often finding us down at the beach, taking respite from our chores behind a canoe, sharing a pipeful of dried *kinnikinnik*, a noxious local herb, listening to Zuev plink out plaintive tunes on his warped but still melodious balalaika. Yutramaki urged us to gather every day, for Timofei seemed calmer when his mates were near.

Kozma joined us too, physically. Our hulking comrade had transcended earthly cares and become mute, a bearded buddha in rags, his gaze fixed on a distant horizon. He'd been task'd *(Not a verb)* by his owner Tatoosh with hacking a canoe out of an immense cedar, but apparently hadn't displayed the expected enthusiasm, and had been beaten, with clubs. He cared not. Like all of us, he'd become gaunt and his knees & knuckles were raw, but his countenance remained serene, blissful, radiant.

Madame Bulygin, blanket-clad, rosy-cheeked, seated herself on our sheltering canoe. She rubbed elk marrow on her lips to heal chapping, positioned her belly and opened the logbook. Like us, she was barefoot.

Like Kozma, she seemed happy: "I have a title, men. *Shipwrecked On Savage Shores: A Russian Noblewoman's Adventures in America*, by Madame Anna Petrovna Bulygin. Imagine: storms at sea, the loss of the *St. Nicholas*, desperate battles, captured by naked Indians . . . *Quelle aventure, n'est ce pas?* Why, I shall tour, and speak."

Kahmooks: "Arf."

Madame Bulygin: "Thank you. Now, new business. While you toil at menial tasks, I negotiate for the return of Maria from the Quileutes, a delicate matter which brings my considerable diplomatic skills into play, as I describe in my forthcoming book. Sister has been of great assistance, and her Hoh in-laws act as go-betweens. Soon, I believe, our efforts bear fruit."

Timofei offered a ripe mushroom: "Behold the fruit."

Madame Bulygin: "Timofei, what would you say to an outing? Whose turn is it to take him? Feeling spry, Mr. Williams? Timofei, would you like to go duck-hunting tomorrow morning? Sister has secured permission for you to hunt up the river from the Waatch village, if you point your gun away from the houses. *Comprende?* Crack of dawn, Mr. Williams? Questions, anyone? Very well. We adjourn. Back to work."

The crew shuffled off. The malamute languish'd, belly up. I tickled his tummy.

I say: "Up for an outing, Rover? O, how I long for the sweet baying of hound in field. Tally ho, what? You could use some exercise."

Kahmooks snort'd: "Tim shootum duck, Tim fetchum. If you think I'm . . . Wait."

The dog cock'd an ear, listening. The crew had moved away, but Madame Bulygin had pulled Timofei aside for a quiet word. She held his hand and whisper'd.

Kahmooks eavesdropped: "She says, 'Timofei, listen. Tomorrow morning, if fortune is with us, we get Maria back. We send word to the Quileute tyee that we will trade Sister's niece for Maria. We meet him on the beach at dawn, on the other side of the cape. This is secret, Timofei. Say nothing to anyone. I cannot walk that far in my condition, but Sister says the sea will be calm, so we women will paddle around the cape in her canoe. Meanwhile, you and Williams will get up early, walk over, and be ready to help. We assume there will be trouble. Stay out of sight until we need you. Sister's niece won't go with the Quileutes willingly, so it will be we women and you and Williams against the four of them. Sister and I will have my two pistols. After we shoot, we will not have time to reload, so you and Williams must each bring a musket. What? I know he is old, Timofei, but he's the only one who can go without arousing suspicion. If anyone finds out, Maria may be lost forever. Can Williams shoot, do you think? Very well then. Hide at the rocky point at dawn. If the Quileutes see you, they will smell something fishy, so . . .'"

Madame Bulygin's whisper was too low for the dog to hear, but he was concerned, and he agreed to tag along.

TIMOFEI WOKE ME IN CHILLY DARKNESS. We'd borrowed Yutramaki's Yankee muskets, two good .58-caliber flintlocks, brass plates engraved with dragons & such, walnut stocks. We slung powder horns & shot bags over our shoulders and departed the sleeping village, Timofei clad in wolfskins, me in my blanket, sword lashed securely to me hip.

Once on the trail Kahmooks took the point, his elegant, plumed tail waving. He sniffed dewy bushes & dripping ferns, thoughtfully lifting a leg when he encountered a compelling scent. Timofei urged him on, impatient. Me & my creaky bones brought up the rear. Bird choirs herald'd our passing, and after two miles the trail opened to a cloudy oceanscape lit by the ascending sun behind us. Brackish bogs lined a narrow, mile-long tidal estuary, marshlands teeming with fish & fowl. Women in canoes patrolled with nets. All but the bravest paddled off as we approached, returning downriver to the village of Waatch at the estuary's mouth, where a dozen longhouses lined the cape's southern slope.

Flocks of fat ducks, *haht-haht*, paddled quacking in the rushes, but Timofei ignored them as a matron poling a flat-bottom canoe ferried us across the placid waterway. Timofei fidget'd in the bow. Once we reached shore he began to jog toward the sea, telling us over his shoulder what we already knew. We expressed enthusiasm and kept pace, soon reaching a low bluff overlooking the ocean. Black clouds backdropped a rising tide, and the sunrise illuminated breakers crashing against a small rocky point, a heap of boulders just south of us. Beyond, smoke plumes rose from the village of Tsooes, where several of our crew resided.

We were late. At the distant point, a small group had gathered around Sister Mother's beach'd canoe. They couldn't see us. We drew closer, discerning Madame Bulygin's pregnant profile, the Yutramaki woman, her niece, the Quileute tyee and three armed companions. Their canoes lay concealed in the boulders. Maria sat, bound hand & foot.

We approached as fast as we could without revealing our presence, but as we arrived on the scene, we heard voices raised o'er the surf. The tyee seized the niece by the wrist, pulling her to him, shielding himself.

Too far to shoot. Faint screams.

*I'm not going to read this part.*

A pistol fired.

With a curse, Timofei charged out onto the open beach, churning the cobblestones, yelling over his shoulder at Kahmooks to run to Waatch and fetch help. The malamute departed northbound at a brisk trot, back the way we'd come. I followed Timofei.

Madame Bulygin ran toward us, pursued by a bellowing, bleeding Quileute, his scalp ripped by a bullet. She stumbled, fell, scrambled on hands & knees, her bulging belly swaying. The Quileute snatched a handful of her hair, stomped on the small of her back, raised his club. She scream'd in agony.

Timofei dropped to one knee and fired, his shot hitting Madame's assailant in his chest. A pink spray burst from the man's back. He paused, swayed, then toppled forward, collapsing over his prey with a gaping exit wound between his shoulder blades. Vertebrae & pink tissue extruded.

Timofei dropped his smoking gun at my feet, snatched mine from my hands, and charged again.

The Quileute tyee, his shoulder bleeding, launched a canoe, loaded his bound & squirming prize aboard, and pushed off into green breakers. Maria remained tied up on the beach. Sister Mother sat, groggy. I loaded Timofei's musket.

The two remaining Quileutes both had muskets. One ran forward to meet the charging Timofei, then stopped, raised his gun and fired. Timofei waited to see the flint spark, then dropped, rolled, came up running, musket still in hand. I couldn't hear the Quileute's shot above the booming surf, but I saw his ball miss Timofei and come skipping merrily down the beach toward me. It shatter'd a clamshell and poof'd the sand, then pierced the raised palm of my burn-scarred hand. Blood drain'd from my head and head'd for my new wound, rushing to escape my sinful flesh.

I sat down to compose myself, to watch the intricate rigging of my hand's suddenly-exposed tendons stretching & contracting. Dizzy, I lay back to regard the heavenly expanse: brilliant morning stars and a lingering moon still spinning recklessly in an indigo sea. With my good hand I clutched at the beach, fearing that I must get a grip or surely I would come loose from the planet.

The tyee paddled hard oceanward, his canoe battling foamy breakers. His comrade, the musketeer who'd just fired, had dropped his smoking gun and stepped forward with a stout piece of driftwood to meet the oncoming Timofei, but then decided discretion was the better part of valour. He dropped the driftwood and ran, his retreat covered by his mate a stone's throw off, who drew a bead on the charging Cossack.

Timofei snatch'd up the branch and hurl'd it spinning at his fleeing quarry's heels, throwing him off his stride. The Quileute, startled, had not supposed his pursuer to be quite so close. His next step was not squarely planted, and he stumbled face-first into the sand.

Timofei leaped upon his prey with his knee in the Quileute's backbone, seized the man's chin with both hands and jerked back. Sharp audible crack.

A gunshot. Blood splash'd from Timofei's shoulder and he fell beside his twitching adversary. The Quileute musketeer who'd shot him dropped his smoking gun and charged with a club raised high, a hideous cry in his throat.

My mangled hand had gone numb, but I'd nonetheless loaded Timofei's gun with my good hand & my teeth. I realized I must rally and shoot the attacking Quileute before he killed Timofei. If I waited, or shouted a warning, it would be too late. I would have to chance hitting Timofei, who was trying to rise to his knees. The Quileute shortened his stride, cocked his club for the first stunning blow. Timofei, fumbling about, found his spent weapon, seized the barrel, swung the musket hard & low, whacking the Quileute on his knee. The Quileute shriek'd, dropped his club, clutched his knee, hopped about. Timofei stagger'd to his feet, swung the gun's butt at the Quileute's anguish'd face. Pieces of the gunlock & trigger-assembly went flying. Blood spurt'd from the Quileute's eye and he fell, trying to shield his face. Timofei stood over him, pounding until the Quileutes' hands dropped to the sand, and then kept on beating until his hands held naught but a bent & bloody gun barrel.

The tyee's canoe still bobbed out in the breakers. He had paused and sat watching, singing, serenading his bound treasure, awaiting the outcome: so far, he'd traded three comrades for a reluctant bride. Timofei ran out into the shallows, waiting for me to arrive with a musket that probably hadn't been loaded properly, what with all the distractions. The tyee decided there was no point in unnecessary risk and bade us farewell with an upraised paddle.

No matter. The shot was too far.

Nonetheless, I kept running. Blood spurt'd from my throbbing hand. No air in my lungs, heart pounding, feeling faint. Timofei stood staring at the departing canoe, tide swirling about his knees, shoulder bleeding. A wave ran up across my path and I splashed through surging sea, gun held high. Timofei reached out to me, grasping at windblown froth. Pebbles fell away beneath my treading toes. Staggering, falling, I threw the gun to Timofei with my last ounce of strength. The tides receded, carrying me seaward. Engulf'd, rolling, I grasped at shifting sand. Chill brine stung my hand. My blood was in the sea, and I heard a whale's faint song.

No time for that. I resolved to crawl higher on the beach in the lull between waves. Where was Timofei? Salt stung my eyes. There he stood. He'd caught the gun. He was aiming, drawing a bead on the distant canoe. How could the powder be dry? He had no shot.

The tyee's canoe slipped over the breaking crests, its occupant shading his eyes against the rising sun. A flock of gulls, brilliant against a wine-dark sky. Timofei, aiming, felt the wind on his cheek, followed the surf's spray, noted the squawking auklet on the updraft. Again, the tyee saluted with his paddle, a final fare-thee-well.

Timofei's musket boom'd.

The blade of the tyee's paddle dissolved into splinters.

Timofei sat in the surf, the smoking gun sizzling in his hands.

From down the beach, faint shouts. People coming.

Out in the breakers, the tyee cast the broken paddle away and bent to snatch up a spare in the bilge beneath his bride-to-be. She kicked. He staggered in the rocking canoe and snatch'd at the moist breeze, but it offered scant purchase. Man overboard.

Three Waatch men charged past us into the surf, daggers clenched in their teeth. They plunged like dolphins through the breakers, stroking hard for the canoe. Timofei & I continued to slip seaward.

Hands seized us, pulled us back. People were strung out down the beach, running, shouting. They swam out and pushed the canoe to shore and the niece was freed, distraught but apparently none the worse for wear. Her abductor, taken into custody, cast a baleful eye at Timofei.

Madame Bulygin lay moaning beside the dead Quileute, dimpled knees raised. Sister Mother was struggling, her hands between Madame Bulygin's thighs. Maria rushed to them, stripping bindings from her wrists, crying out at the sight of too much blood. Sister Mother cut the umbilical cord with a clamshell. Madame Bulygin heard her newborn daughter's first cry and held her to her breast before the last of her life flowed into the sand.

More blood flowed as two of the dead Quileutes were decapitated; the third's head, beaten by Timofei to a pulp, was not deemed suitable for display purposes. The Quileutes' bodies were cast into the surf, and the sullen captive tyee began the trek back to Neah at spearpoint, with the head of a comrade dangling from each hand. Women pressed seaweed against my wounded hand, and from the look of it I doubted that it would ever lift anything again. Other hands lifted me and carried me home.


ALDER LEAVES WERE BROWN, AND THE SKY WAS GRAY. *Delete pun or cite reference.* I'd been for a walk on a winter's day, and now I was off to the creek for a swim, my good hand clutching my blanket about me, my scabbard bouncing on cobblestones.

Rising clouds revealed Vancouver Island's mountains across the strait, flaunting new snow. The Cape People were related to the Vancouver Island natives, and canoed back & forth to visit. Yutramaki said that in the distant past a branch of the islanders had broken away from their main village and settled here on the cape, driving previous residents to the east and displacing the Quileutes from their traditional fishing grounds on the cape's ocean coast.

The cape's rounded breasts peek'd from a foggy gown. The beach wobbled, and I endeavour'd to keep my balance. My wet footprints sizzled on smooth stone, and a passionate rapture burned within my flesh, untempered by the chill. Snowflakes kissed my ravaged hand. A timid tide ran up to taste my toes, withdrew, whispering.

My toe stubbed a brick. In the spring of 1792, while the American captain Gray and the Englishman Vancouver cruised offshore, conquistadores from the Spanish garrison at Nootka on Vancouver Island sailed south across the strait to build a tiny adobe outpost down here by the creek, then abandoned it five months later, due to deteriorating relations with their hosts (improper conduct regarding the women) and a precipitous decline in the structural integrity of the fort itself (rain, high tides, mud bricks). Seventeen years later, the curious tourist would find little trace of Spanish habitation. Yutramaki owned a Sevillian tile.

Also still extant beside the creek were three Quileute skulls on poles, picked clean by ravens, and the four stakes which had restrained the captured tyee as he lay beneath the vacant gaze of his disembodied companions. On the second day of his captivity the tied-up tyee began arguing with the heads. Sand crabs plagued him, and the heads reproach'd him mercilessly for his errors, judging from his angry retorts.

After a four-day deliberation within Yutramaki's longhouse, my master's cousins came forth and draped their struggling captive over a log. A crowd gathered. Yutramaki emerged from his long-house testing the edge of the samurai sword against the moist air, and after a brief prayer-song he sever'd the Quileute's neck with a single stroke. The head rolled away, blood spurting, and as it came to rest the tyee's gaze found mine. His lips moved. Last words? A curse? Stunned, I returned his stare as the blood drained from his skull, and I wonder'd if he could still see, or think, or feel.

A pall linger'd over the village: Madame Bulygin's violent demise in the throes of premature childbirth left a restless residue. Sister Mother told her brother that the women's plan was to dangle the niece before the tyee, then pull a double-cross. While not opposed in principle to cheating Quileutes, the niece's father was incensed that his daughter had been thus endanger'd. Sister Mother was above reproach, so he demanded that Madame Bulygin's body be thrown into the ocean, as any slave's would be.

Women carried Madame Bulygin's corpse to the ebbing tide and gave her to the sea, and now 'twas whisper'd that her mournful ghost haunt'd these shores, a sad strolling spectre searching for her newborn babe, clearly visible when the light was at a certain angle. *Clarify. Just because you and I can see her doesn't mean other people can.*

The owl appeared too, but only in the dreams of influential tyees, demanding that Timofei be cast out of his master's house and exiled to a rude hut. No explanation. The village was dumbfound'd. Nobody lived alone, only those found guilty of serious crimes, miscreants who were temporarily banished from the village as punishment. Banishment was like being tossed from a canoe into the sea; to be forcibly displaced from hearth & home was the worst fate imaginable, and Timofei was a bona fide hero, a Quileute-Killer, a designation acquiring significant cachet hereabouts.

Then the owl issued yet another nocturnal decree: Timofei must be inducted forthwith into the Wolves, a secret but prestigious order of which Yutramaki was a charter member. Timofei was this year's only inductee, and the Wolves' first fishbelly. Several leading Wolves had the identical dream.

Yutramaki scheduled an initiation potlatch, sending forth delegates to the Cape People's winter villages with hidatabeys, invitations, but he otherwise avoided discussion. Speculation regarding the owl's pronouncements ran rampant. Working feverishly, Timofei began both a fast and the construction of his new domicile, a mound of driftwood & whalebone. At eventide, a dozen Wolves painted Timofei's face black like their own and dragged him off on a silent parade around the village, preceded by slaves who lit the way with torches. Timofei, clad in a scrap of blanket tied about his loins, sport'd garlands of hemlock boughs on his head, waist, arms, ankles. He gazed, dazed.

Wolves called from the forest. The human Wolves responded in kind, and a cacophony of dement'd shrieks broke the silence, the humans blowing into wooden whistles in imitation of their namesakes' mournful call. They were quite serious, but it was hard to keep from chuckling, and ridicule was taboo. Fortunately, the English are reserved by nature and I managed to remain straight-faced, but the native slave beside me failed to stifle a snicker, even with both hands.

The procession halted abruptly. The slave crouch'd, belatedly aware of his transgression, wide eyes peeking through trembling fingers. Yutramaki glanced at the slave's owner, a masked tyee, who in turn beckon'd to an attendant, who stepped forward, grasped the offending slave's lower lip, ripped it from his chin, and flung this scrap of flesh into the fire. The procession resumed, entering Yutramaki's longhouse. The maimed slave clutch'd his ravaged mouth, wailing in agony.

I offered solace: "Stiff upper lip, old sport."

NEXT DAY, AT EVENTIDE, YET ANOTHER TORCHLIT PROCESSION. Wolves in masks, some plain & undecorated, some bizarre & grotesque. Yesterday's grim mood had vanished, and the crowd of several thousand souls now sang, accompanied by rattles carved in the shapes of various birds, including Thunderbirds, but not owls. Again, their songs joined with the cries of the forest wolves. Singing whales drifted at rooftop level.

Yutramaki brought forth Timofei, who was pale, glassy-eyed, with gashes on his forearms.

"Behold my wounds, brothers," he said. "With my blood I purchase your redemption. Your sins are my sins. I take the blame for your wrongdoings. I bleed, but you are blameless."

The crew, incensed: "Torture. The Brotherhood demands revenge."

"Shhh. Quiet, or we won't get dinner."

Timofei spread his ravaged arms in acceptance of his fate: "Forgive our captors, brothers, for they know not what they do."

Yutramaki showed us old scars on his own forearms: "Those who seek to become Wolves must cut themselves with a sharp mussel shell. In this way we remember our ancestor Ha'sass, a warrior whose brothers bled him and thus took away his human scent so he could sneak into the den of the Wolf People and learn the secrets of their power."

The crew mutter'd, confused: "But if this Ha'sass has no blood, he dies. And still he would stink."

A feverish Timofei displayed his ravaged arms to the forest, crying out: "How much longer must I suffer?"

After dark, the Wolves hauled him off on another meandering march around the neighbourhood, the villagers watching from inside their homes. The mask'd Wolves were joined by Wasps, who threatened to sting onlookers with sharp bones, as well as mischievous Raccoons, who scurried about thieving. Once back inside Yutramaki's house the revelers celebrated, log drums pounded, and when the door blanket was flung back, the fire reveal'd the faces of entranced celebrants etch'd in grotesque shadows. Timofei's frenzied screaming chill'd our bones into the wee hours.

On the fourth day, the entire village gathered as darkness fell. We were joined by men wearing antlers, delegates from the all-male Deer Dancers, a group with influence equal to that of the Wolves. Women came as Eagles, Woodpeckers and Thunderbirds, but no Owls were in evidence. Another unruly procession snaked through the houses, with the Wolves again dragging the masked Timofei. Singers shook rattles.

Timofei jumped about, howling. To calm him, the Wolves attempted to snatch away his mask, but he'd have none of it. He ran off, his lopsided headpiece obstructing his vision, a pack of Wolves in pursuit.

Yutramaki explained: "Timofei has to come back and be human again, but he likes it where he is, so the Wolves will have to force him. Strong man like Timofei, it won't be easy."

A bit of chasing-about ensued, with a screaming Timofei leading his pursuers around the village for ever so long, but eventually the Wolves wrestled him to the ground. He fought, but his mask was ripped away and instantly he was passive, mesmerized.

The singing & dancing continued. We supposed that surely this wild night must be the festival's culmination, but Yutramaki's exuberant shout broke dawn's chilly stillness.

Low tide. Sandpipers picked the muck. Thousands of bleary villagers crawled from their blankets into costumes, gathering on the beach under low clouds. Even Yutramaki's infant daughter Annie attended (*Attended? I was the main attraction*), nursemaid'd by Maria, Olga, and Sister Mother, whose beaded deerskin gown graced her matronly figure. Though residual Wolf energy still filled the air, the mood was mellow, cleansed. A sense of joyous peace flowed over us, and a song rose, with log drums launching into a bouncing beat. With great flourish, Yutramaki burst onto the beach in a colourful new Wolf mask, four feet long from vicious snout to pointed ears and even more ostentatious than the previous. Despite the heavy mask he was a whirling dervish, and was soon joined by the other dancers, mostly menfolk, but some masked & costumed women too. We slaves observed from the celebration's edge. We stacked blankets and hung bladders of whale oil, gifts for the forthcoming potlatch ceremony.

Timofei, in loincloth & mask, again got out of hand and was wrestled to the ground. After the requisite struggle and forcible unmasking, he sat entranced, sweat streaking his blackened face. Around him, the ceremony gathered momentum.

'TWAS A THREE-DOG NIGHT. SHIVERING HOUNDS CRAWL'D to fireside on snake-bellies. I bade them welcome. The wise slave befriends the canine in winter, for they are bless'd with nocturnal warmth.

Wave after wave of cold wet sou'westers assault'd the cape and stormy seas pound'd cliff & shore as ocean & atmosphere joined to seek dominion o'er the Earth. Rain drain'd from the roof through whalebone gutters, but the thick cedar planks did not deny entry to frothy wind-blown spume and dripping fogbanks, and gusts rattled the heavy timbers on the roof.

The village hibernated. Songs & stories filled the darkness, but not our bellies. The dogs were at fireside, but the wolf was at the door. Hunger had followed us up the coast to the cape, and we'd become burdensome to our hosts, who prided themselves on their hospitality but nonetheless found their larders & generousity dwindling. Yutramaki's household always seemed to get by (he could pull a fish out of the sea at will), but Shubin's owner, suddenly luckless at hunting & fishing, was forced to trade a sea otter pelt for ten dried salmon. We had inflicted a serious dent on the Hoh & Quileute food supplies, and those villages now exchanged captives for Yutramaki's whale oil. Our host then retail'd those captives to other Cape tyees with the promise that a trade ship would soon arrive bearing a ransom of guns, enough to alter the balance of power hereabouts once & for all. Rumours of ship-sightings wafted like zephyrs, with similar substance. Alas, this was the winter of our discontent. *Reference or delete.*

We strived to earn our keep. The Aleuts & Kodiaks proved adequate hunters & fishermen, and even I could dig clams. Timofei, our best sharpshooter, was allowed to hunt, but when he ventured into the forest he sought only to speak with the owl, and she remained absent from trees & dreams.

Yutramaki told us of a beautiful lake a day's walk to the south but within the Cape People's territory, one that teem'd with fish & rainbows. Timofei fear'd he'd misunderstood the owl with regard to Rainbow Lake's location. He'd babbled about the bag of silver he & Kozma had hidden north of the shipwreck. A fortune, enough to buy our freedom & passage to Kauai or anywhere, and it lay within a day's walking distance. *Delete everything about silver. Don't argue. It was entrusted to my mother but it was stolen by your comrades but we got it back so it's mine and I say it's a secret so delete.*

But we were captives, and surviving the winter was our priority. The owners of Petukhov, Shubin, and Zuev stopped feeding them because they couldn't work, and this pitiful trio turned up at Yutramaki's lodge seeking refuge. They called out but received no response from within, and they knew better than to enter the longhouse without permission.

They peeked into their ataman's mossy mound: "Timofei? Are you in there? We heard you have a basket of juicy clams. Do not be shellfish." *Delete puns please thank you.*

Timofei, from within: "The clams are, slurp, gone. The Wolf meditates."

Pleading piteously, the runaway trio finally gained entry, but their owners arrived toting sealing spears, inquiring as to their whereabouts. Yutramaki emerged from the house & indicated Timofei's dwelling. The tyees probed the mound with their lances. The four Russians crawled out muttering, blinking. Spears raised, the owners threatened punishment.

Yutramaki urged restraint: "We are a kind, humane people, known far and wide for being *makah* (generous with food). We must fatten these people up before the next ship comes, or we will be stuck with them forever. I will offer yours sanctuary until you can afford to feed them. They can sleep out here with Timofei."

Abram's owner: "The owl said Timofei must sleep alone. He screams in his dreams."

Zuev's owner: "Timofei must tell these three to get back home or else."

Timofei: "Abram, Dimitrii, Savva, hear me, my brothers. We must obey our owners. Your whimpers do not fall on deaf ears. The owl hears. She feels your pain just as I do. Remember, these torments only strengthen us for the work to come."

Zuev: "'Us'? We work, you meditate. We're cold and hungry, but you get clams and a wolfskin and your own little hut."

Timofei blinked, offended: "Envy does not become you, Savva. As you know, this is the den of Timofei the Wolf. I must be alone in the darkness with my mushrooms, for only then can I see what is real."

Shubin: "We are real. We want to sleep in there with you. It is warm when we all snuggle up."

Timofei: "You have bugs. The Wolf bathes in the ocean and scours his sinful flesh with spruce needles."

Yutramaki tried to deal with the tyees: "We must put all the wood behind the arrowhead. They must be fed if they are to live until spring. I will take these three off your hands. Name your price."

The tyees, affront'd: "No. You are planning something. It was your idea to trade oil to the Quileutes. You foresee a ship coming in spring, offering guns as ransom. We know the crazy Englishman is worth twelve muskets, so the others must be even more valuable.

You want guns so you can give them to us at potlatch to make us look bad. No, we keep our ho'kwat."

Yutramaki gripped his scalp with both hands: "Keep what? They're skin and bone. What if they get sick and die? Who trades guns for skeletons?"

Shubin's owner tugged his goatee: "Hmmm. If we had new guns and fresh powder, we could go visit the Quileutes and get our oil back."

The other two dragged their feet: "If they get hungry, they can eat each other."

Yutramaki sighed, turned to Timofei: "Reminds me. Sad tidings. Your captain has, ah . . ."

Timofei, aghast: "They ate him?"

"No, perished in one piece. Well, almost. Lost another tooth. His owner, Tatoosh, is building his longhouse longer, and he needed a male slave to bury under his new corner post, to please the house spirits. Bulygin had the consumption, coughed all night, kept the whole house awake. Wasn't going to see springtime anyway."

Timofei moaned: "Owl despairs."

"The owl is pleased," Yutramaki said. "The slave that goes in the hole, the house spirits require that his heart still beats as the big corner post is dropped into place on top of him, otherwise the dwelling will be cold and unhappy. He must be alive, but not necessarily awake. Bulygin tried to climb out of the hole, so Bolotov had to stomp on his fingers while the other slaves were wrestling the post into position for the drop. The captain almost took Bolotov in with him. Left a tooth in Bolotov's ankle. Tatoosh said if one warm slave under the post guaranteed a happy household, then two might . . . Well, anyway. Quite a show, we are told."

I say: "Pity that Bulygin's taken his version of these events to his, ahem, grave. If anyone should ever ask, Tim, we might say cause of death was consumption."

A chill wind whistled in the eaves.

Timofei clutch'd his wolfskin about his shoulders: "What becomes of us?"

Yutramaki: "Your captain becomes one with his master's house."

NATURE'S REBIRTH UNFOLDED ANEW: spruces sprout'd, tidepools bloom'd, fungi flourish'd, and yellow-bellied slugs roam'd afield, their glistening slime-trails lacing the woodlands.

The spectre of famine prowl'd too. The fishing & hunting were abysmal, and no one could recall a leaner winter. The lookouts atop the cape reported that whales abound'd in the strait & ocean and sometimes float'd over the village, but none consented to appear in the dreams of the whalers.

Why? Various theories: Yutramaki's illicit affair was mentioned, as was his paternity of the baby girl resultant therefrom. The Bulygins' ungraceful deaths still troubled the villagers, and many believed that the presence of the crew itself boded ill. Throughout the villages, loyalties were tested, friendships strained. Growing resentment focus'd on Timofei the Wolf: was he prophet or fraud, saviour or imposter?

We moved again to the small whaling house on the cape's north flank. Yutramaki's crew resumed their prayers for strength & guidance, then embark'd in their canoe, vanishing over the horizon, sometimes for days, only to return with desperation haunting their faces.

We were visited by the ancient & eminent tyee Tatoosh. Fur-draped, he alight'd from his resplendent whaling canoe, his long white mane blowing in the breeze. Though Tatoosh was quite daft, he retained a stern & commanding presence, his features suggesting Asian ancestry. With none of the usual preliminary protocol he rudely confront'd Yutramaki, loudly alleging that our tyee's patronage of the *St. Nicholas* crew had jeopardized the whaling season, thus endangering tribal stability.

Tatoosh's nose bone bounced, punctuating his indignation: "We are cursed, Yutramaki. The whales are angry. They demand a sacrifice."

Yutramaki stared him down. Tatoosh departed in a huff. The debate on what should be done with us intensified over the following weeks, with a growing consensus demanding a sacrifice of supplication to the spirits who'd inflict'd this turmoil, that they might relent. Tatoosh called upon the tyees to volunteer their captives for ritual execution, that a sacrificee might be chosen from amongst us, and all but Timofei & I were dutifully offered. Yutramaki steadfastly reaffirmed our potential trade value and his intent to protect us, urging his colleagues to do likewise. They had a duty as responsible slave owners, he told them. Again, opinion shifted. Argument & indecision ensued. Our master believed this brouhaha to be temporary, but after a week of bickering Tatoosh impetuously brought the crisis to a head, announcing that he would end the impasse by offering his own slave first.

Kozma was to be sacrificed.

WORD REACHED US AT THE WHALING house, just as Yutramaki's canoe returned from another unsuccessful overnight hunt. Timofei & I scrambled aboard the whaling canoe and we embarked for Neah, our paddles blurs, a white wake curving under our prow.

A restless crowd gathered on the beach around Tatoosh, but the villagers calmed & parted at Yutramaki's approach. Perhaps disaster had been averted by our timely arrival. Kozma knelt, surrounded by Tatoosh's henchmen, hands lashed behind his back, our Samson weakened, overpowered, subdued. He strained silently at his bonds, bloody & bruised, his eyes fastened on the approaching Timofei. The ataman rushed forward, knife unsheathed, only to be stopped in his tracks by Tatoosh's spear-carriers.

Tatoosh waved his harpoon at our master: "Tell him the truth, Yutramaki."

Yutramaki shrugged helplessly. Timofei agonized as spear points poked pale splotches into his chest.

Tatoosh poked Kozma's chest: "The owl is not what she seems, Timofei. *Twin Peaks reference.* She is a false spirit. She speaks *kliminawhit*, lies. You are not her messenger. Admit that she has led you astray, or I will stick Kozma in the belly. It will take him all day to die."

Timofei wept. Tatoosh exchanged his harpoon for a henchman's club. "Here, Timofei. You kill him. Hit him with this club."

Timofei trembled. Tatoosh called to the forest: "Owl, come help Timofei. Steady his trembling hands. You are a fool, Timofei. Where is she now, when you need her?"

With a shriek, knife upraised, Timofei lunged at Tatoosh, but the tyee's henchmen knocked him to his knees. Tatoosh glared down at him. Timofei, dazed, a bloody cut over his eye, fumbled for his dropped knife, but found instead the club, and he staggered to his feet as though he might attack again.

Spears, raised. The moment slowed down. Tiny details: an owl's feather danced across the stones, tickling my toes. Black humps on the gray bay: whales watched us. Timofei, wild-eyed, babbling, pushed Tatoosh's club against my chest. I hid my hands and backed away. The club fell to the ground.

Tatoosh drew his harpoon back. Kozma, belly exposed, breathed deeply, his broad chest & shoulders rippling as though he were swimming. Tears trickled into his thick beard.

Timofei fell to his knees beside Kozma, pleading to be killed instead. His eyes rolled back and he fainted dead away as though he'd been bash'd by the club, which still lay at my feet.

Tatoosh: "Pick up the club, Englishman. Famous killer! This should be easy for you."

Tatoosh shook the club at Yutramaki: "Tell your Englishman. He hits Kozma on the head, or I stick him in the belly."

Yutramaki murmur'd in my ear: "Tatoosh wants Kozma's blood on somebody else's hands. He knows he's gone too far, but he can't back down. You must take what he offers. If you hit him on the side of his head, brains all over. Straight down, hard as you can. He won't feel it."

The club, so hard, so heavy.

Look away. This can't be happening. Gaze out upon the strait. See Waadah Island floating in the bay like a pea in a spoon, joyous whales leaping in its lee. See angelic eagles suspended, wings spread. In a moment, look again. It will all be over, a bad dream.

Yutramaki nudged me: "Do you love him that much?"

I kissed Kozma on his grimy, tear-stained cheek and grasp'd with my good hand the cheetoolth, the Death-Bringer. Tiny intricate carvings, each detail etched in old blood.

Kozma smiled at me, tears glistening: "Don't miss, poppy-puffer."

Look away for a moment.

Don't look until somebody says "*KLIPCHUCK*," deep water.

Yutramaki's canoe speeds oceanward, paddlers pumping furiously. Behind me, Yutramaki has a finger on Kozma's throat. A pulse, still. Kozma's eyes, open but vacant. Blood in the red-painted bilge. Timofei, beside me, sobbing.

The bay and then Tatoosh Island recede. The canoe is a silent spear aimed at the point where the sun's arc will intersect the horizon, paddlers & canoe joined as one.

Yutramaki nudges Timofei: "Breathe into his mouth. Press against his chest. The whales must hear his heartbeat if they are to find him in time."

Timofei sets to work. "Come back," he shouts in Kozma's face. "Come back."

After another mile, Yutramaki calls for a stop and puts his ear to our comrade's chest. We strip the rags from Kozma's thick body, lash an anchor stone to his furry chest, roll his naked bulk over the gunwale. He disappears in bubbles.

We sit on the silent expanse with not even a passing gull for company. Timofei, in shock. Yutramaki & crew, statues. The cape is a bump on the horizon, the sun a dull white ball descending seaward.

Yutramaki raises his hands. A deep rumbling vibrates, seemingly from the core of the planet. The sea around us trembles with tiny concentric circles, as though stones had been tossed into a placid pond.

A jubilant fifty-foot humpback erupts from the sea. Then another, then a dozen fly about us on wing'd tails, filling the air with cetacean celebration. The sea is a maelstrom. We are tossed about & soaked by their exultant splashings. Yutramaki sings, exuberant, harmonizing with the whales' ethereal voices. I fear our canoe will be crush'd, but we hang suspended in a strange blue atmosphere. Neither water nor air exist apart from the other, and together these elements cover us with a blue cathedral light. Whales fly, gazing down benignly.

A thund'rous boom. A shadow sweeps over us, an expanse of dark wings. Huge claws descend, barbed talons, and their curved pincers spit bolts of blinding white light. Awestruck, we can only stare as a bird-monster with fiery eyes snatches a whale from the swirling mass and flies off with its prey tightly clutched in its curved beak, great wings churning.

The whales disappear into the depths from whence they had sprung. The atmosphere distills, returning to water & air. Storms boil aloft. The ocean still vibrates, frothing. With an ear-shattering scream the bird-monster ascends with the writhing whale into black rumbling clouds lit by lightning brighter than the sun.

SUNSHINE.

A north wind beat the gray morning sky until it was bright blue. At high tide, booming wind-driven breakers ran up the bay's gentle slopes, threatening slow children and indeed our very doorsteps. Solar brilliance burned the beach, enticing us to venture forth, ripping rotten rags from our ravaged flesh, running joyously at water's edge. Stiff gusts knock'd us back on our heels. We exposed pale gaunt skin to the sun, flea-bitten, goosebump'd, alive. Blinded by the light, tears in our eyes, we embraced without knowing why. Though reserved by nature, I performed a splashy jig in tingling tidewash, amusing my mates.

Timofei watched, deep in thought. Yutramaki, elderly today, also looked on silently. The reticent Japanese quartet followed, observing our antics from a distance.

The crew, cavorting: "A beautiful day. Look at the gulls swoop."

"Imagine if we could fly like that. Hey, we could make a kite. Do you remember how?"

"We would need cloth, or paper. Our clothing is but rags."

"We have paper. Perhaps our kind friend Yutramaki will return our Vancouver map. We could use fishing line as string. If Timofei was not so sad he could help us."

"What was that, Timofei? Listen, brothers. Timofei says our kite could have wings, like a bird. What kind of bird, Timofei? An owl? Good idea. It will fly way up high. Perhaps a ship will see it."

Yutramaki raised a hand in warning: "Perhaps the owl sees it. Remember, she warns us, 'Mock me not, and don't be fashioning images of my appearance, lest I be angry. Depict me as Thunderbird, the Whale-Bringer, big and scary, with lightning bolts shooting out of my talons.' You boys take it easy."

The crew murmur'd: "No wonder we never see any owl carvings. No owls woven into the baskets or garments. Whales, wolves, Thunderbirds. No owls."

Yutramaki: "Better hope she don't find out about that token with the owl engraving you gave poor old Liuliuliuk. Messing with big medicine. Stay out of trouble."

The crew whined: "Please, tyee? Why do the whales keep Kozma? Does he ever return to us? This Thunderbird, the big flying monster, he . . ."

Yutramaki: "She. The owl is Thunderbird."

". . . she brings back the whale and with her claw she slices open the belly right here on the beach and there is your anchor-stone, but no Kozma. What has the owl done with him? Is he dead? Alive?"

Timofei gazed at an inner horizon: "Kozma lives, brothers. I feel him. Sometimes he seems so close I . . . Master, if our kite calls the owl from the forest, we will beg her to return our comrade."

Yutramaki slapped his forehead as though pain'd, a gesture Timofei interpreted as reluctant assent. He ran to the longhouse, found Vancouver's map and disappeared into his mound, clutching driftwood sticks and strips of dried bird's tendons. Days later he emerged with his creation, which he successfully launched into the northerly breeze.

A tyee observed: "Hey, Timofei, watch out for the tree."

The kite swoop'd & soar'd perilously near trees. Timofei gambol'd heedlessly, stumbling over wet stones, his eyes cast heavenward.

The crew let their ataman run: "At least, for the moment, he is happy. See how our kite swoops and soars, tugging at our heartstrings, expressing feelings that words cannot. The kite is a symbol of our longing for freedom, for a release from the drudgery of this pointless existence."

"I thought the kite was to call the owl."

"The owl forgets about us. The kite only gives me sorrow. If I could fly like the kite, I would fly away from this miserable place."

The Japanese pointed down the beach: "Kite go *sayonara*."

Alas, Timofei had stumbled, the line slipped from his grasp, and the kite departed over the treetops, southbound. Timofei slump'd in the stones, deject'd.

His mates consoled him: "Timofei, if you love your kite, you must be willing to set it free. Come, cavort with us. Dance away the sadness."

TIMOFEI WAS NOT TO BE DISSUADED FROM HIS GRIEF. After the loss of the kite, he became more distant & fearful.

Yutramaki kept him busy making things. Brow furrow'd, Timofei set to work carving rough blocks of cedar, employing wee tools he'd made from iron nails pounded on fireside stones. In a fortnight he could chip out a splendid little bowl, on which he would be complimented.

But our master already possessed a variety of carved wooden dinnerware and other household accoutrement, compared to which Timofei's roughhewn offerings seemed crude. Spirits plunging, Timofei meander'd through the forest, sometimes without his gun. Risky behaviour this, for the woods teemed with carnivores, and Quileute slave-raiders might lie in wait for berry-pickers. Worse, though he joined Yutramaki & I for nocturnal swims, the whales wouldn't come near him, the owl likewise remained absent from his dreams, and again frightening nightmares haunt'd his slumbers. In spring, when we moved back out to the whaling house, all agreed that Timofei should continue to sleep apart. He voiced no objection, and again he built a rough dome from driftwood & whalebones, caulking the gaps with mud & moss. Ominously, this new structure had window openings large enough to shoot through.

Question'd about the windows, Timofei was evasive. His eyes darted this way & that. He'd taken to calling himself The Wolf. Our questions agitated him.

"Why windows? So The Wolf can shoot at his enemies from inside his lodge, that's why. What enemies? You forget the Quileutes have sworn to kill me? Maybe the Company sends an assassin because I know too much. Sometimes I suspect that even my own followers will betray me. Yes, my foes are many, and jealous of my special purpose on this earth. They seek to suppress the owl's teachings, and that means they must kill her messenger. If they come at me from the sea, I must be ready."

He scanned the strait with narrow'd eye. He pointed.

"See? They are here."

THE BRIG APPROACHED SEDATELY, HER BILLOWING SAILS glowing in the day's last light. She caught a breeze on her starboard beam, trimmed her sails and glided into the bay on a smooth reach, the Stars & Stripes fluttering from her mizzen.

'Twas May the 9th, 1810. We had not seen a ship since we'd left our own vessel wreck'd on the beach a year and a half ago. The trade ships spurn'd this bay; the Cape Flattery natives were sharp traders and allowed little profit. This could be an Astor ship, looking for the blackguard John Williams.

We pushed off in the big canoe for Neah, watching the Yankee brig as she sound'd for an anchorage that would allow a speedy return to the strait. The bay's residents, thousands strong, gathered along their crescent curve, singing, beating log drums. Men sat on rooftops, thumping their heels on the planks. Dogs & children, frenzied. Yutramaki's slaves rushed to meet us, hauling our arriving canoe above the tide.

Yutramaki squint'd at the ship through my telescope: "Aha. Thought so. The *Lydia*, out of Boston. Master's name was Hill, last time we saw her. He paid the Nootkas a ransom for young Jewitt five years ago."

Ransom. The news rippled through the crowd. The Japanese failed to contain their ecstasy.

Yutramaki gave me the glass, remarking that the apparent captain, a bearded red-faced Yankee in a brass-button'd navy coat on the quarterdeck, didn't look like Captain Hill. I watched the *Lydia's* crewmen scramble in the rigging, furling their sails. Her bow anchor splashed.

Yutramaki pointed: "Lookee there, top of the mast. The Raven returns, in full feather. I better go hop in my suit. Better get Timofei spruced up, too."

How had the *Lydia* found & rescued our Raven?

The village, a'buzz. Yutramaki canoed for the brig, resplendent in his suit & beaver hat *avec* face paint and whalebone nose-piece. Timofei, in the bow, disguised in a ratty wolfskin and the shredded remains of the dressing gown, planned to play the fool and thereby discern whether the Americans were enemies, or if they were ready to learn about the owl. I was to remain ashore until our visitors' intentions could be discover'd, so I watched through the telescope as my master met Brass Buttons on the quarterdeck. Their conversation appeared amiable. A ship's boat piled high with water casks soon pulled away for the creek, prompting the women at the creek to return to their homes. Negotiations continued until dark. Yutramaki left Timofei aboard as a good-faith gesture.

I met my master on the beach. He poked his thumb at the *Lydia*: "The captain, name of Brown, he says to me, 'Shipwrecked Russians, hey? And four Japanese? Got any English you want to get rid of?' Told him we got an old Brit named John Williams. 'Really', he says. 'How old?'" *Good question.*

We passed a sleepless night, assembling on the beach in the morning, huddling in our blankets: Maria, Olga, Five, Pavel, Abram Petukhov, Bolotov, Kurmachev, Shubin, me, Zuev, Zypianov. We gaped at the bare-masted brig emerging from the fog like a wispy apparition, a painted backdrop on a stage. Aromas of coffee & tobacco drift'd. 'Twas not a dream, we agreed, but a real ship. Eight bells rang. Groggy sailors relieved themselves from the poop deck.

A nattily-attired Yutramaki arrived with bad news: "Shubin's owner went whaling, and we can't trade his slave without his say-so. We sent word, but . . ."

Shubin moaned, cursing his fate.

Yutramaki: "Captain Brown looks at you through his spy glass. Says he ain't in the rescue business. Wants to see Williams first. I told him, take them all or no deal, but he ain't agreed yet, so try and look healthy."

Yutramaki's crew launched his canoe and beckon'd me to jump in, even tho' I wasn't presentable. Tatter'd blanket, barefoot, beard a mess. *So not much has changed.* My journal & sword were in my master's longhouse. Soon the *Lydia* loomed above us, rocking ponderously, joints creaking, stinking of the sea. Her scruffy crew leaned over the rail, commenting rudely. They were well-armed, with musketeers on the masts. Both their fore & aft swivel cannons were ready to fire.

I climbed the cargo net and had a ship under me again. My toes caress'd the teak decking and my sea legs recalled the anchor'd ship's gentle roll, but I gazed awestruck into the maze of spars, sails, and lines above, unable to remember their names or functions.

The Raven remembered me. He scrambled down from aloft, glossy feathers all a'flutter, querying me on the fate of his comrades, jubilant at the prospect of reunion. He'd nearly lost all hope during his stay with the Chinooks, and feared he'd ne'er *(try "never")* be found, but then the *Lydia* had come to his rescue. He didn't dare to leave the ship, fearing recapture. He didn't know what had become of Filip & Yakov.

CANOES CIRCLED THE BRIG, PADDLERS CHANTING. Our owners were anxious to learn our ransom value, but balk'd at Brown's insistence that they disarm before coming aboard. Yutramaki convinced his colleagues that it was safe to do so, and the tyees complied, but with profound misgivings, inasmuch as the *Lydia's* seventeen-man crew was brandishing a variety of weapons. From the swivels, the scent of sulfur, of smoldering slow-matches. The tyees knew each cannon could wipe out a canoe's occupants with a sudden spray of grapeshot.

Finally, a brave tyee divested himself of his weaponry and climbed warily over the *Lydia's* rail, his paddlers singing courage chants. Others followed.

Brown's supercargo, the clerk responsible for the ship's trade goods, hauled bolts of cheap wool up from the hold, then kegs of gunpowder & shot. He opened a barrel filled with loose scrap iron: worn-out tools, bent nails, rusty hinges. Detritus of a distant civilization, a past life faintly remembered. The tyees mutter'd, wondering when the guns would appear. Yutramaki opened negotiations for my ransom.

Brown, astonish'd: "Twelve guns? Outrageous. Ain't him any-way. The John Williams I want is younger than me. Look at the poor old bastard: lost in a fog, seaweed in his beard. Three of these nice wool blankets, final offer."

Yutramaki: "Have a heart. Him speakum English, just like you."

I croak'd: "Read & write too, by Jove."

Brown harrumph'd: "I'm yanking my anchor. No wonder nobody puts in here. Tell ye what, chief: the blankets, plus this purdy little looking-glass thingee for your favorite squaw (*delete*). How's that?"

Yutramaki, affront'd: "Count fingers on hand. Five wife. Five blanket. Five looking-glass thingee."

Brown: "Not likely. How about I throw in this locksmith file? Act o' charity."

Bargaining continued, and after an hour of haggling my value was established: five thin blankets, five *sazhens* (about thirty-five feet) of cheap wool cloth, a locksmith's file, two steel knives, one mirror, five packets of gunpowder, and the same quantity of small shot. Not often a man finds out what he's really worth.

Trading proceeded slowly, with all parties disgruntled. Half of us were on deck, but half remained in the canoes, their owners wait-ing for an auspicious moment to commence business. Yutramaki translated, brokering variations from the list of items paid for me, smoothing the rough spots that inevitably resulted from the cap-tain's stubborn refusal to cut a better deal for my fellow captives. Alas, the tyees were dismayed at Brown's stingy offerings, and he was disgusted with us.

Our saviour wrinkled his red nose: "Speak up, Rooskies. Who's your leader? Where's your captain? Too busy to join us?"

"His troubles weigh heavily on him. The crazy one, Timofei, he commands us."

Timofei had been offering mushrooms to the ships' company, finding no takers. He tugged at Brown's sleeve: "Captain? You will free us from captivity?"

Brown: "Ain't freeing nobody until your captors get serious with the ransom demands."

The tyees protested: "All same as the Englishman."

Brown: "They ain't all the same. Big tyee worth more than slave, right? See, now, the Englishman, his family or the owners of his ship, they'll reimburse me, but the others . . ." He eyed my woebegone mates. "If they're so valuable, how come Baranov ain't come looking for them? How many we talking about, anyways? I'll take that Maria, and maybe the fat gal too, but . . ."

Maria: "Our men come with us. All eleven."

A tyee: "Eleven? What about Sobachnikov, the one who lives with the Hohs?"

We gasped, dumbfound'd: "Sobachnikov? But he . . ."

Yutramaki, palm to paint'd forehead, a habit he passed to his daughter *(And your point is?)*: "Forgot to tell you. Things slip past me like little fishies in a stream. Yes, the Hohs are fond of Sobachnikov, and he of them."

Painfully we recalled our wounded comrade's headlong departure from us a year-and-a-half ago, straight into the clutches of our pursuers. All this time we had thought him dead.

A tyee thump'd his chest: "Sobachnikov *skookum* (potent, powerful). Many papoose." *Not a Chinook term as you know.*

Yutramaki nodded: "But now a slave woman warms his blankets and bears his children, and he was born to fish, so . . ."

RANSOMING RESUMED. OUR DISAPPOINTED OWNERS, confronted with Brown's intransigent refusal to trade guns, gradually consented to ransom even Maria & Olga for basically the same goods paid for me, rather than hold out for the arrival of a future ship and possibly a better deal. Tho' they were much aggrieved at this paltry outcome, negotiations continued until the owner of Bolotov & Kurmachev came aboard with his fat brother in tow, leaving our comrades tether'd in his whaling canoe.

The tyee stubbornly folded his arms across his chest: "Two Russians, twelve guns."

"And no junk," the chubby brother said. "Has to shoot."

Brown laughed: "Give me a good sea otter pelt and I'll take them off your hands. How's that?"

The tyee spat on the deck and in high dudgeon stomped to the rail, threatening to end the bargaining. Bolotov & Kurmachev called plaintively to us from the canoe, their hopeless cries catching in their throats. Shubin still waited hopefully at water's edge, as did the four Japanese. The villagers' curiosity began to ebb, as did the tide, which turned seaward. The villagers returned to their homes.

We called to our comrades: "Courage, brothers. We do not leave without you."

Brown: "Belay that. I say when we leave, and I'd like to make a little profit if it ain't too much to ask. Losing money as 'tis. Oops, lookee there, tide's going out. Ain't rubbing my keel in the mud. Too far from home."

Yutramaki whispered to the captain. Brown nodded & consulted with the mate, who saunter'd up behind the brother and produced a long blade, pressing it against the brother's bobbing Adam's apple, drawing a thin red trickle, causing the brother to gurgle & squirm, nose-bone twitching. The tyees contemplated their deplorable lack of weaponry. Every sailor's hand held a cock'd pistol, rusty cutlass or loathsome dirk. Yutramaki looked pensive. A boatswain threw a line over the lower main yard, knotted a hangman's noose under the brother's wobbly jowls, and two sailors pulled it tight.

The brother's eyes bulged. He tippy-toed, clawing at the rope.

Brown: "Same deal for the last three."

The brother: "Gack."

A long moment passed. The bay's receding tides licked the *Lydia*'s hull, and the ship creak'd, fretful, sensing the bottom. With arrows shooting from their eyes, the tyees produced the three remaining Russians and received their allotted trade goods. Our comrades scrambled aboard, fell to their scabby knees and kissed the deck.

Brown, grumbling over his depleted trade goods, slipped the noose from the brother's neck and gave the order to weigh anchor. The tyees spat on the same deck our comrades had just kissed and departed the ship. Yutramaki, without so much as a fare-thee-well, tossed the items of my ransom down into his canoe and likewise disembarked. Canoes circled, angry occupants waving rusty locksmith's files. The crew secured weapons and scrambled aloft. Sails billow'd, and were trimmed. *Lydia* hasten'd for deeper water.

A dwindling crowd watched her go. On the beach Sister Mother held baby Annie, who was howling. *I remember that like it was yesterday.* Our faithful malamute howl'd too; he'd decided to stay. *Good dog.* The Japanese bowed, weeping, palms pressed. Out on the bay a whale danced with wing'd tail.

I hugged my companions and we wept too, remembering our struggles and our lost comrades. Zuev plunk'd a melody on his balalaika, cocking his ear to a faint fiddle tune on the breeze. Timofei, in tears, called to Kozma: come back, the ship departs.

This was our last moment together and it was only a moment ago. I threw my old bones over the rail and into the water, and I swam to Yutramaki's canoe.

*Delete murder, opium, cannibalism, and my silver. Writing about the whales and going to the other side is just inviting the crazy people to come sit on our front porch, so don't. Delete slugs, mushrooms, and what you call the "funny bits." I don't want any part of this, so remember to delete my comments if you're going to send this out, which you shouldn't.*

D AVID HOOPER HAS BEEN A WRITER and editor with Northwest magazines and newspapers. *Ho'kwat* is his first novel, and it won the Pacific Northwest Writers Association's best historical novel award. He lives on Seattle's Capitol Hill with his wife Candace Frankinburger.

www.ingramcontent.com/pod-product-compliance
Lightning Source LLC
Chambersburg PA
CBHW011513100726
47899CB00010BD/3340